A TWIN CROWNS NOVEL

KING OF BEASTS

PRAISE FOR THE TWIN CROWNS SERIES

'TWIN CROWNS cast a spell on me from the very first pages with its glittering blend of harrowing adventure, charming wit, and intricate world-building. Add in delightful romance and two unforgettable narrators, and I was thoroughly bewitched by this marvelous book! Don't miss it!'
Sarah J Maas, #1 *New York Times* bestselling author of
A Court of Thorns and Roses series

'TWIN CROWNS has all the charm of THE PRINCESS BRIDE and all the stakes of GAME OF THRONES – but Wren and Rose are in a league of their own. Addictive, swoony, tender and vivid – I loved it with all my heart.'
Kiran Millwood Hargrave, bestselling author of
The Mercies and *The Girl of Ink and Stars*

'Riotously funny, fast-paced and dripping with romance, TWIN CROWNS manages to deliver a tale as familiar and nostalgic in the way of childhood blankets and fireflies in jars, while at the same time wholly refreshing with its levity, charm and quirky tale of sisterhood rediscovered. TWIN CROWNS is so joyous that days after reading, I'm still grinning.'
Roshani Chokshi, *New York Times* bestselling author of
The Gilded Wolves and the Aru Shah series

'An absolute delight from start to finish. TWIN CROWNS is a dazzling gem of a book. Magical, clever, surprising, and pure fun from its captivating start to its spectacular finish. If you love wicked kings, sexy bandits, and sister stories that are full of heart, this is a must read.'
Stephanie Garber, *New York Times* and
Sunday Times bestselling author of *Caraval*

'Doyle and Webber give readers twin plots of daring deception, spectacular settings and two very appealing love interests . . . you'll root for both twins in this dangerous web of intrigue.'
Kendare Blake, #1 *New York Times* bestselling author of the *Three Dark Crowns* series

'Reading TWIN CROWNS left me giddy. Adventure, romance, TWO incredible protagonists, magic, sisterhood . . . I loved it.'
Laura Wood, author of *A Sky Painted Gold*

'Fresh, funny and exciting.'
Louise O'Neill, bestselling author of *The Surface Breaks*

'A gripping fantasy series for teens'
The Times – one of the 50 best Irish children's books to buy for Christmas.

'I haven't cried over a book in ages . . . I rarely laugh out loud and I'm also just bawling my eyes out!'
Amber Bayley, author of *The Haven Ten*

'Such a rollercoaster, a million out of five stars'
Ella likes Books

'One of my favourite reads of the last year'
Sam Falling Books

'A magnificent marvel of a book'
Becca, Pretty Little Memoirs

'I couldn't put it down!'
readinginwonderland.com

**BY KATHERINE WEBBER
AND CATHERINE DOYLE:**

Twin Crowns
Cursed Crowns
Burning Crowns

CATHERINE DOYLE

A TWIN CROWNS NOVEL

KING OF BEASTS

First published in Great Britain 2026 by Electric Monkey, part of Farshore
An imprint of HarperCollins*Publishers*
1 London Bridge Street, London SE1 9GF

farshore.co.uk

HarperCollins*Publishers*
Macken House, 39/40 Mayor Street Upper, Dublin 1, D01 C9W8, Ireland

Text copyright © Catherine Doyle 2026
Map illustration © Tomislav Tomic 2026
Cover illustration © Grace Zhu 2026

The moral rights of the author have been asserted

PB ISBN 978 0 00 868855 4
Waterstones Exclusive ISBN 978 0 00 880436 7

Printed and bound in the UK using 100% renewable electricity
at CPI Group (UK) Ltd

1

A CIP catalogue record for this title is available from the British Library

All rights reserved. No part of this publication may be reproduced, stored in a retrieval system, or transmitted, in any form or by any means, electronic, mechanical, photocopying, recording or otherwise, without the prior permission of the publisher and copyright owner.

Without limiting the exclusive rights of any author, contributor or the publisher of this publication, any unauthorised use of this publication to train generative artificial intelligence (AI) technologies is expressly prohibited. HarperCollins also exercise their rights under Article 4(3) of the Digital Single Market Directive 2019/790 and expressly reserve this publication from the text and data mining exception.

Stay safe online. Any website addresses listed in this book are correct at the time of going to print. However, Farshore is not responsible for content hosted by third parties. Please be aware that online content can be subject to change and websites can contain content that is unsuitable for children. We advise that all children are supervised when using the internet.

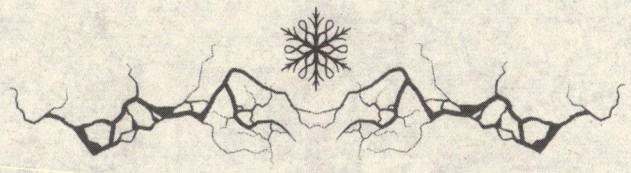

For Katie Webber,
Friend, Sister, Co-Conspirator, Queen

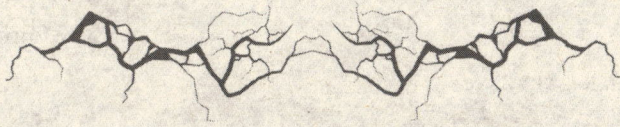

*No beast is so far gone,
that they cannot be tamed.
That they cannot be loved.*

I
Wrangler

CHAPTER 1
Alarik

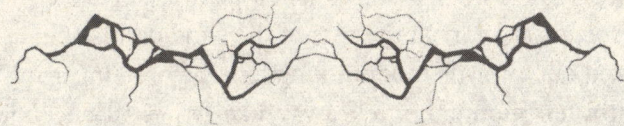

Deep in the icy heart of the kingdom of Gevra, where a towering palace of glass and stone speared up from an ancient mountainside, a young king awoke, restless from his slumber. Though the air swirled with the beginnings of a blizzard and the ground glittered with new frost, Alarik Felsing went barefoot to his balcony.

He scowled up at the night sky. The full moon was far too bright, its determined silvered shards slipping through the gap in his drapes and jostling him from sleep. *Again*. At least that's what he told himself as he stood alone at the balustrade, cursing the stars. It was better than entertaining the alternative – that those awful nightmares, blood-soaked visions of battles long past and ones yet to come, were becoming more frequent. That the king of Gevra, ruler of the fiercest kingdom on the northern continent, was anxious.

And he didn't know why.

Attuned to the shift in his mood, the king's wolves stirred from their place at the end of his bed and followed him outside. Nova, the eldest of the two and black as a starless night, paced the length of the balustrade, guarding his master. Luna, soft and silver as moonlight, came to sit by Alarik, her bushy tail settling across his feet to warm them.

Scratching the sweet spot behind Luna's ears, Alarik huffed a frustrated sigh, watching his breath cloud in the air. Though his chest was as bare as his feet, the cold didn't bother him. Winter was a constant gnawing presence here. He sought comfort in the bite of the wind on his skin as he looked out over his moonlit kingdom. Before him, a spill of frostbitten mountains fell away like waves in an endless grey ocean, reaching towards the curling woodsmoke and flickering lamplight of faraway towns, and beyond them, the meandering fjords and vast stillness of the Sunless Sea.

Gevra was beautiful in its bleakness, but it was not for the faint of heart.

Nor was its king.

A north gust blew, bringing a nighthawk with it. The bird swooped low over the mountains, catching moonlight on its wings. Nova stilled, raising his snout as if to scent it. A low growl rumbled in his throat, echoing the rumble of unease inside Alarik. As the bird drew closer, he noted the metallic glint of its feathers and realized his mistake. Its wings were the colour of steel, longer and slimmer than that of a nighthawk. Its large beak possessed the same shine and was curved at the end, as sharp and foreboding as any man-made blade.

It was not a Gevran bird at all. Rather, a silvertip, a hunting eagle from Vask, one of only two kingdoms that shared a border with Gevra. The same kingdom whose spies had been caught trekking through the Blackspire Mountains barely a week ago. A pair of plain-clothed men who claimed they had got lost on a hike, only to surrender a litany of weapons between them when searched, as well as a partially drawn map of the northern mines of Gevra.

And now this – a silvertip, hundreds of miles south of its territory, circling the palace of the king.

Frost kissed Alarik's forearms as he leaned across the balustrade, his gaze glued to the bird. It was on the hunt, scouring the snowcapped Fovarr mountains that clustered around Grinstad. It floated on a slip of wind, wings barely beating as it watched the terrain. Minutes passed, the midnight moon glowing brighter as though it was watching, too.

At a flash of movement from below, the silvertip shot down like an arrow, spearing the snow and disappearing entirely. Alarik sucked in a breath, holding it until the bird emerged with a shriek of triumph. The sound raked down the king's spine. There was a hare in the bird's talons, neck snapped, its white fur mottled with blood. Alarik watched the eagle as it came to perch high on the mountainside. In one fluid movement, it threw its head back and swallowed its prey whole.

A shudder rippled through the king. Sensing his master's discomfort, Nova's hackles rose. Even Luna, such a gentle creature, surrendered a low growl. Ordinarily, Alarik wouldn't have glanced twice at a bird feeding itself in the night, but he couldn't stomach the sight of a predator of Vask trawling his mountains, gorging on Gevran spoils.

He peeled his lips back, wishing he was as skilled with a bow as he was with his sword. He would have shot that bird out of the sky and sent its carcass back to Queen Regna as a warning.

Keep your predators out of my kingdom.

And yet, as he turned from the mountains, Alarik's unease gave way to a cool prickle of fear. He thought of the rapacious queen of Vask, steel-eyed and ever clawing too close to that northern border they shared, and had the sudden creeping sense that if he were to send her that message, it would already be too late.

This time, when he climbed back into bed, Alarik's wolves curled up on either side of him, as though they had the same disquieting feeling.

After breakfast the following morning, Alarik stalked through Grinstad Palace like an ice bear on the hunt. His bad mood swirled around him, turning the air as bitter as the three cups of coffee he had just downed. Servants lowered their gaze as he passed, some slinking into the alcoves to avoid his ire. They knew their king well enough to steer clear of him in foul humours. And in good ones. Not that there had been many of those lately.

Captain Astrid Vine, head of the royal guard and Alarik's second in command, was waiting for him at the top of the stairwell on the first floor. At six foot, Vine was almost as tall as the king himself, her body a study of hard lines and lithe muscles honed from years of training. She had warm brown skin and keen dark eyes, her cropped black hair better revealing her strong cheekbones and squared jaw. She was wearing her military uniform, a pristine frock coat of midnight blue and silver, black trousers and sturdy boots made for sparring. And winning.

She looked the king over as he stomped up the stairs, her frown pressing a dent between her slender brows. 'You look like hell.'

Alarik offered her his most fearsome scowl. Vine was one of only a handful of people he allowed to speak to him in such a manner. He might have taken her sword for that kind of comment once, but she had proven herself an invaluable soldier and strategist over the last year, and a worthy replacement for her predecessor, Captain Tor Iversen. Tor had left Grinstad over a year ago, following his heart south to the kingdom of Eana, where he had fallen in love with one of its witch queens, Wren Greenrock, a woman Alarik had once thought to seek for himself. A stirring if fleeting notion, which had swept in alongside an ancient curse that had bound Wren and Alarik together, leading them to combine their armies and fight a war against the ancient witch who had cast it.

A war that had decimated his army.

Following a punishing battle on the west coast of Eana, Queen Wren and her sister, Queen Rose, had emerged victorious, though the losses on all sides had been many. The war had cost Alarik a third of his own soldiers and as many beasts. It had cost him his second in command and prized wrangler, too. For Tor Iversen had been the only soldier at Grinstad who could train the king's beasts for battle, controlling them in their droves with little more than a whistle. That was the way of the wrangler – a rare and mercurial ability that, for centuries, had led the Gevran army to victory in one vicious battle after another.

A year on, Alarik was still rebuilding his army, intent on maintaining his reputation as the fearless king in the north, a dauntless ruler who would destroy anyone who dared to threaten his kingdom. Captain Astrid Vine, an ambitious, battle-honed soldier, who had risen through the ranks of his own surviving army, was helping him do that.

So, he let her needle him every once in a while.

'I have no need of your frank assessment today, Vine,' he said, a bite in his voice.

Her brows lifted. 'Then you are already aware of the dark circles under your eyes.'

'Take care not to miss the warning flashing inside them,' he said, pointedly. 'I have not slept well.'

She pressed her curving lips together, drawing her arms behind her back as they walked along the upper glass corridor, which provided ample views of the courtyard below. Ordinarily, Alarik looked down on the stone arena within with simmering fondness – the place where he had spent countless hours sparring with soldiers and beasts alike, first as a young boy eager to please his father, the late King Soren, and then as a young king, eager to prove himself to his soldiers. To his beasts.

This morning, the arena was a far cry from the bravery and skill that often graced it. A group of quivering soldiers were attempting to corral a snow tiger and two leopards – a mere fraction of the regiment Alarik had been replenishing all year – and yet the twelve soldiers chosen to train them were all cowering against the walls.

Not a damned wrangler among them.

'Give them time, Majesty,' said Captain Vine, as though reading his thoughts.

He curled his lip. 'The one on the end is openly weeping.'

'No, he's— Oh, *Garvin*.' She muttered a curse. 'He

promised me he was ready.'

'Let's see how ready he is when that tiger makes a toothpick of him.'

'That's not funny.'

'No,' muttered Alarik, folding his arms as he looked down at his trembling soldiers, at the beasts snapping and growling like they owned the arena. Owned the palace. 'This is far from funny.'

Vine chewed on her lip, her silence a reluctant agreement.

'I watched a Vaskan eagle hunt in my mountains last night,' said Alarik, after a moment.

Vine stiffened. 'If Regna's birds are here, her falconers cannot be far behind.'

Alarik frowned. His thoughts exactly. Word had clearly spread of the war in Eana, and the losses the king's army had sustained. 'She thinks I'm weak.'

Outside, a soldier screamed as the tiger began to circle him. He turned and scrabbled up the arena wall, losing his left boot and longsword in the process. Alarik swallowed a growl of annoyance.

'We are weak,' said Vine.

He glared sidelong at her. 'That is not what I want to hear from my war captain.'

'Our soldiers are well-trained,' Vine went on, tempering her criticism. 'But they are still fewer than they were last year. And as for the beasts . . . without regular training, the older ones have gone half wild. And the new ones are not trained at all. If we took them to war, they would likely devour as many of our own soldiers as our opposition.'

'Contain your optimism, Vine.'

The kingdom of Gevra was long known for the might of

its war beasts, just as it was for the strength and skill of its soldiers. The combination of both was why the northern kingdom hadn't lost a war in over eight hundred years. Alarik did not intend to start losing now, but he could not deny the sorry state of his army as another soldier's scream rang out. A young leopard had pounced, pinning him with a large, snowy paw. It took five flailing soldiers to beat the beast back, and not one of them seemed to realize the creature was simply playing.

Alarik pinched the bridge of his nose. 'We have to do better than this.'

Vine gripped her sword, a frown tugging at her jaw. 'I'm no wrangler, Majesty. I have tried with the beasts these past months, but it takes a certain skill. A certain type of soldier . . .' She trailed off, the rest of her sentence hanging unsaid between them.

A type of soldier they no longer had. Not since the departure of Captain Tor Iversen. Yes, what Alarik needed now – and sorely – was a true wrangler. Someone who possessed that crucial inborn connection that allowed them to read the shift in a beast's mood, to cajole and coax them, to train them. Wrangling was the closest thing to magic that existed in Gevra, but Captain Iversen's talent, while exceedingly rare, was not entirely unheard of. At least not on the small rock of an island, Carrig, where he hailed from. A blot of grey in the middle of the Sunless Sea, as cold and unforgiving as the scythe of mountains that surrounded Grinstad Palace. Perhaps even more so. And yet the king hoped that Carrig might offer them a solution to their worsening problem. 'It's time to find a wrangler, Vine.'

She stepped back from the window. 'As far as I'm aware, Tor Iversen is the only soldier capable of wrangling your beasts.'

'I don't want a soldier.' He had plenty of those. 'And anyway, Tor is long gone.' The words were crisp, final. Alarik would not drag his former captain – and more importantly his oldest friend – away from the woman he loved, and the peace he had found in her kingdom, only to return to the blood-soaked battles of his past. No, Captain Vine had missed his meaning entirely. 'Send word to Carrig,' he clarified. 'Get me one of Tor's sisters.'

Vine blinked away her surprise. 'Which one?'

A pertinent question. Alarik was aware that Tor had three sisters, he'd even met one of them – the eldest – briefly, many years ago at Grinstad, but he did not know the name of the other two. He did not especially care about their names, only that he knew they shared their brother's gift for wrangling. Outside, a mewling rasp echoed through the courtyard. Alarik turned from the sound of a soldier's answering shriek. Those infernal cowards would sooner hand his country to Regna on a silver platter than face down a bear cub.

'I don't care which sister,' he said, storming off.

CHAPTER 2
Greta

The blizzard that swept through Carrig was so fierce it ravaged the pine trees in the low hills and left behind a blanket of snow that made hunting almost impossible. The deer bolted up the mountain, scattering across the craggy terrain, while the goats migrated to the jagged peaks, finding shelter in the narrow rock caves there.

The winds that followed were brutal, but the howling cold was not enough to scare off Greta Iversen, who met every storm on Carrig the same way she faced its beasts – with quiet determination. These past few months on the island had been crueller than most, winter crushing the island in its icy grip and refusing to let go. With Papa's injury worsened by the interminable chill and Mama still recovering from the fever that had stolen her strength several months ago, Greta's family was near starving. Returning home without food was not an option. She reminded herself of that as she stalked through the cedar forest that hugged the eastern shelf of Carrig, an arrow already nocked to her bow. Her bootsteps were soft and silent, the worn collar of her woollen cloak scratching the underside of her chin.

Despite the blistering cold, Greta's eyes were quick and keen, scanning the rippling expanse of snow as she prayed for a flicker of movement. But the creaking trees offered nothing but falling pine needles. Even the birds had scattered. She huffed a frustrated sigh, unsettling the copper-streaked strands that had slipped free of her braid. 'Come on,' she muttered, moving deeper into the forest. 'Give me something. *Anything.*'

All too soon, the pale sun arced overhead, heralding the afternoon. Hours passed, with nothing to show for it but stiff fingers. Greta cursed the grumble of her stomach as she stopped in a small clearing to rest. Tucking her braid back under her cloak, she sipped from her skein of water and reached for that sliver of determination that had sent her out at dawn into the retreating blizzard.

All but defeated, she sunk to her knees. The hunt was proving fruitless, and the wind was picking up. She would have to strike soon if they were going to eat tonight. But there was nothing to catch. She wished she could find a beast to help her hunt. When the good weather held, it was easy to find a wolf to corral. A gentle hum and a few stirring words would entice the perfect hunting mate to lead her to the best spoils. Spoils that they would share at the end of a fruitful morning. But there were no beasts in the cedar forest today. With food so scarce, so too were the bears and wolves she used to wrangle with ease.

Carrig was starving.

A familiar panic stirred in her gut, reaching up through the bones of her ribcage and stealing her breath.

Oh no. Not here. Not now.

She slammed her eyes shut, measuring her exhales, just like Papa had taught her. If she panicked now, the hunt would be lost to her. She would be lost to herself, and it was far too cold to sit in the snow and let the storm in her heart ravage her. She began to hum, low and soft, trying to wrangle the frightened beast that lived inside her. The tightness in her chest loosened. She didn't dare stop. The trees rustled, a lone blackbird peering out of its faraway nest to listen in. Greta's heart lifted as she drew new breath, greedily filling her lungs. Her humming blossomed into song, the lilting words of an ancient legend soaring from her like a plea until the cloud in her head cleared and she felt like herself again.

Across the clearing, the snow rippled.

Something flickered in the side of her vision. Another animal stirring at the nearness of her song. She spun, lightning fast. A snow hare bounded from its burrow, one hop, and then another. By the third hop, it was dead, Greta's arrow flying straight and true. It pierced the hare's heart, and it flopped to the ground, a starburst of crimson marring the perfect snow around it.

'Sorry, little one.' Greta rushed to scoop up her kill, muttering a quick prayer of thanks to the creature, thin and paltry as it was. It would make for a small stew, enough to chase away starvation for another day. And with the wind picking up, it had come just in the nick of time. She cleaned the arrow and returned it to her quiver. Then she slung her bow over her shoulder and turned for home, stumbling as the tension uncoiled from her shoulders.

Greta went straight to her parents' cottage, which was nestled half a mile uphill from the one she shared with her two older sisters, Hela and Kindra. Mama was dozing on the couch in the small sitting room, with Farron, her docile snow leopard, curled up beside her. Mama's long dark hair was streaked with strands of grey that had taken root the same time as her fever, the hollows in her cheeks so deep now they gathered shadows. It had become an effort for Greta not to flinch at the sight of them, not to turn her face to the sky each morning and curse the wicked sun that brought them no heat.

As Greta eased the door shut behind her, Mama sprung up, blinking the sleep from her eyes as though she hadn't been passed out cold a moment before. Her face was as pale as the falling snow but she summoned her strength and rolled to her feet, offering a smile to her youngest daughter.

Greta returned it, trying not to linger on the spindles of her mother's arms or how she could feel the contours of her ribcage as they embraced. She kissed her cheek and handed her the hare. 'Your dinner. Sorry I'm late.'

'My little nightingale, only you could best that scourge of a blizzard,' said Mama, her stomach grumbling as she took the hare. She carried it through the wooden archway and into the narrow kitchen, where she fished out a handful of carrots from the cupboard.

Papa was sitting at the table, his broad shoulders hunched, his bad leg propped on the chair next to him as he tinkered with the handle on the broken kettle. His copper hair was shaggy, the curls dipping into his storm-grey eyes as he worked. With his trouser leg rolled up, Greta could see the full length of his artificial limb, the wooden planes of his calf stretching up to the steel joint at his knee, which had become mottled with rust these past few months.

Another problem they could not afford to fix.

Greta pressed a kiss to the top of his head then set down her bow and quiver by the back door. She frowned at the dwindling fire. 'You're almost out of firewood. I can—'

'I'm going now.' Papa set down the kettle and reached for his cane. 'I was waiting for the snow to settle.'

'It's vicious out there, Papa,' said Greta, laying a hand on his shoulder. 'Let me go—'

'I can do it,' he said in a half growl, and Greta stepped back, knowing better than to argue with him. He hobbled to the back door, pulling on his cloak and huffing from the effort, before stepping out into the snow and slamming it behind him.

Greta's mouth tightened as it rattled in its frame.

'Let him do it,' said Mama, gently. 'It's a matter of pride.'

Greta bit back her argument, gripping the chair to keep from running out and grabbing the axe from her father. She hated to wound his pride, but the idea of him traipsing through that deep, swirling snow with an unsteady, rust-bitten leg and an empty belly sent a fissure through her heart.

She turned back to her mother, who was already skinning the hare. There was barely a handful of meat on it. 'I'm sorry it's not much,' said Greta. 'I'll go higher tomorrow, take the mountain pass and—'

'Nonsense.' Her mother swished a dainty hand. 'You forget your mother is the finest cook this side of the Sunless Sea. I can easily stretch this little fellow five ways.'

'Two ways,' said Greta. 'The hare is for you and Papa.'

She frowned. 'And what about you, Kindra and Hela?'

'I caught another one,' said Greta, grabbing the peeler

and setting to work on a carrot so her mother wouldn't notice the blush staining her cheeks. Of the three Iversen girls, Greta was the most honest. Often to a fault. Especially when Hela sought an opinion on one of her woeful, homespun tunics, or Kindra opined on the handsomeness of her betrothed, Mikkel, whose drawn face bore an uncanny resemblance to their father's mule. Greta hated lying – the taste of it souring her mouth – but she had learned to do it on occasion for the greater good. 'Kindra is skinning it as we speak. She's going to make her own stew, though I doubt it will be as fragrant as yours.'

'I'm sure it will be just as delicious.'

Greta lingered a while longer, peeling the rest of the vegetables and using the last of the firewood to boil water. She reminded herself there would be more along shortly to stave off night's creeping chill, but when she finally turned to leave, refastening her cloak and fetching her bow from where she had left it by the back door, she noticed a shadow on the doorstep. She pressed her forehead to the window, her heart cracking when she saw it was her father, sitting in the cold in his winter cloak, still trying to summon the strength to go out into the woods.

'Leave him,' said Mama softly, from where she stood at the stove. 'He'll come in again.'

It was an effort to wrench herself away from the door, to swallow the cry inching up her throat. 'All right, Mama. You know best.' Even though it was Greta alone who had witnessed the accident that had mangled her father's leg, sliced through his torso and nearly killed him. It was Greta, at just seven years old, who had thrown her little body on top of his, screaming for their lives. It was Greta who had watched her father break that day in the low mountains. It was Greta who had broken along with him. She brushed her hands over the silver scars on her left cheek, before shoving the memory away and heading for the front door.

'I'll come back after dinner to see about that fire,' she called to her mother.

As the door shut behind her, Greta almost sagged with relief at the sight of her sister, Hela, stomping uphill towards her with an armful of chopped wood. She ducked her head around the teetering pile, frowning as she looked her over.

'How was the hunt?'

'Gruelling,' said Greta, hating to disappoint her sister. 'I caught a hare.'

'Good.' Hela conjured a grim smile, which for her was practically effusive. 'I chopped down an entire cedar tree this afternoon.'

'Of course you did.' Greta was seized by a familiar rush of gratefulness for her eldest sister. Hela, who watched over their family with the attentiveness of a nighthawk, who guarded them with the strength of an ice bear, even on days when her legs trembled and her stomach keened with hunger. Of course Hela had seen the dwindling firewood at their parents' cottage, and instead of pointing it out like Greta had done, had simply gone and cut down an entire tree.

Greta wished she had caught a deer for her family. She cursed the hare, cursed herself for not gathering her courage and climbing north into the mountains. Tomorrow, she would do better.

'Go and get warm, Greta,' said Hela, reading the guilt in her eyes as only a sister could. There was a softness in her voice now, a swathe of blue moving through the storm grey of her eyes. 'You did well today. You bested a blizzard.'

'A measly hare is hardly worth the praise,' mumbled Greta.

'Mama will think so when she sleeps tonight with a full belly. And Papa, too.' Hela continued past her towards the cottage. 'Go on home. I'll be back before dark.'

Greta continued downhill, the weight on her heart shifting, if only a little. These past few months had been cruel to Carrig. Cruel to the Iversen family. They had lost many of their beasts in the lead up to the war in Eana a year ago, and had spent much of the time since trying to replenish that loss, raising and training more animals to sell. But the going had been tough, and though their brother Tor sent coin home every month, the recent ferocious weather had killed off more than a few messenger birds, capsized several boats and chased most of the animals away. The fish, too. There was little to eat, and everything at the market had tripled in price. With Mama's lingering sickness and Papa's injury preventing them from steady work, it had fallen to Hela, Kindra and Greta to keep the family afloat.

Though Greta tried not to bow to the pressure, it was beginning to crush her. Panic visited her most nights, snatching her from the little sleep she got and filling her lungs with ice. Filling her head with storm clouds, until she felt as helpless as she had been that day in the clearing with Papa at seven years old. In the mornings, her soul felt as grey as the sky. Hunger was a constant companion, gnawing at her day and night, chipping away her nails and breaking the ends of her hair, until she felt like the ghost of the girl who used to run barefoot with the snow tigers through the low mountains and sing like a nightingale in the forest until the birds of Carrig swooped down to join her.

Greta was tired now. In her bones and in her heart. She was desperate for the weather to settle, for the snow to ease and new flowers to bloom. Desperate for a life that stretched beyond this endless, fruitless hunt that yielded too little and took too much from her.

When she returned to the cottage she shared with her sisters, Kindra was in the kitchen. There was a fire burning in the stove, and Lupo, the grizzled old wolf Greta had known and loved for all the eighteen years of her life, was slumbering in front of it. Aya, Hela's owl, was perched on the back of her favourite chair, peering out at the falling evening. The wrangler in Greta sensed the bird's anxiety, like a strange hum in the air.

'Good news! Mikkel just dropped off a carp as long as my arm,' Kindra called out from the kitchen, where she was making dinner.

'And they say romance is dead,' Greta called back. She didn't know much about love, but with her hunger growling like a wolf, she couldn't think of anything more achingly romantic than a big, fat, sizzling fish.

She kicked off her boots and hung up her cloak, stowing her bow and quiver before curling her arms around Lupo and pressing her face into his shaggy scruff. He turned to lick her face and the weight on her heart lifted.

She went to help her sister in the kitchen, snatching up an onion. It was only when she grabbed the chopping knife that she realized her hand was trembling. She turned from the sink, but Kindra was too quick.

'You're weak, Greta. Sit down. I'll make you a cup of

sugar tea.'

'I'm fine,' said Greta, not wanting to waste their precious store of sugar.

'You're swaying.'

'I'm *fine*, Kindra.' She did a little jig to prove it, only to lose her balance and nearly topple into Aya. The owl shrieked and Greta flushed, sinking quickly into a chair.

Kindra peered down at her, worry pinching the sides of her mouth. Beside her, Aya's golden eyes were admonishing. In Hela's absence, her owl was just as bossy.

'I'm sitting,' grumbled Greta. 'You don't have to glare at me like that.'

She didn't know which of them she was talking to, but she was glad when the owl returned her attention to the window and Kindra went off to make her tea.

Greta took the mug without protest, revelling in the sweetness of the sugar on her tongue. 'When will Mikkel be back again?'

'Not for another week, at least.' Kindra chewed on her lip, worry alighting in her eyes. 'The shoals are so far out now it takes days to reach them. He was lucky to catch that carp so close to shore.'

She paused, both of them eyeing the gleaming oily fish, and in the swelling silence, Greta knew her sister was thanking the stars for Mikkel. She thanked them, too. For the fish, and the hare, and that armful of firewood. For one more night, and the promise of tomorrow.

Hela returned home after sunset, as though she could smell the fragrant fish stew Kindra had prepared, even leaving some for Lupo, who was too old now to go hunting. The three of them sat around the kitchen table, devouring every mouthful until their bowls were empty.

Hela finished first, using the pad of her finger to mop up the juice. She sighed as she looked outside, where the howling wind was flinging fistfuls of fresh snow at the window. 'If the weather doesn't let up soon, we'll have to pawn something.'

Greta snapped her chin up. 'We've already pawned everything worth selling. Our winter stoles. My hunting daggers. Your favourite sword, Hela.'

Kindra stilled, her gaze falling on the simple silver band on her left hand and the pin-sized sapphire within. 'Not everything.'

'No.' Greta shook her head fiercely. 'Not your ring, Kindra. That's your future.'

'It's just a symbol.'

'Symbols have meaning,' said Hela, voice firm. 'We will not sell your ring.'

Kindra opened her mouth to argue, but then closed it, letting the matter settle. She did not want to give up her ring any more than they wished her to. Hela was right. It *was* an important symbol. One that whispered of a brighter future, of dancing and merriment and cake, something to live for beyond the cold snap of tomorrow.

'In the morning, I'll go up to the rock caves,' said Greta. 'I'll find a goat and—'

'What?' Hela swung her head around. 'Let it tumble with you down the mountain? You're barely bigger than a goat, Greta. You might be able to kill one, but the climb down will kill you.'

'Then we'll both go.'

'And die together?' Hela snorted. 'Do you know how

expensive coffins are these days?'

'We should write to Tor,' said Kindra. 'He has no idea how bad it's been.'

Hela was already shaking her head. 'Tor has been travelling for weeks. And even if Aya finds him, what do you expect him to do? Give up his happiness – his life in Eana – to come back here and freeze alongside us?'

'He can send more coin,' said Greta. 'He would want to—'

'We cannot live off the purse of another kingdom, Greta.' Hela scraped her hands through her hair, her slender brows knitting. 'I told him I could take care of us. I *promised* him.'

Greta read the anguish in her sister's eyes and saw the same pride there that burned inside their father. The same wound. She reached for her sister's hand. 'That was before Mama's fever. Before the blizzards and the—'

She stopped at a loud tap on the window. The fright of it drew a growl from Lupo and sent Kindra to her feet. Her chair clattered to the floor as she went to the window, where a nighthawk was peering in at them. There was a scroll tied to its foot.

Greta and Hela rose from their seats, staring at the bird with matching looks of confusion. Kindra unfurled the scroll, her brows lifting as she read the brief missive.

'What is it?' said Hela, reaching to snatch it from her.

Kindra leaped backwards. 'It's from Grinstad Palace,' she said, a giddy trill in her voice. 'The king needs a new wrangler.' She looked up, her eyes shining. 'And he is willing to pay handsomely.'

For a moment, the three Iversen sisters stared at each other in lingering disbelief. Then Kindra's lips twitched, her smile dissolving into a strange, hiccupping laugh. Hela joined in, bracing herself against the table as she howled with manic amusement. Greta gave herself over to the same hysteria, tears of relief sliding down her cheeks as she came to the same glittering understanding.

Hope had come, at last, to Carrig.

CHAPTER 3
Alarik

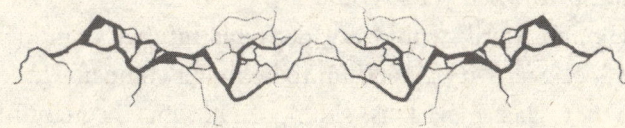

It was just after midday when Alarik Felsing arrived at his mother's private chambers in the most westerly turret of Grinstad Palace. Like a hangman dragging his feet to the gallows, he wound his way up the never-ending spiral staircase, where oil portraits of stern-faced kings and queens peered down at him in silent judgement. His bootsteps were silent on the midnight-blue carpet but his pulse was a drumbeat in his ears.

At the top of the stairwell, he stalled outside the door, sconce-light gilding his wheat-blond hair as he steeled himself for what lay on the other side. It had been months since his mother had summoned him here, since she had sought his company at all beyond the odd stilted exchange at breakfast or a passing smile in the palace hallways. The same hallways that once rang with her laughter and echoed with the notes of her beloved pianoforte.

Ever since the death of her youngest son, Prince Ansel, a year and a half ago, the dowager Queen Valeska had never quite returned to herself. Just like Alarik's father, the late King Soren, long lost to the sea, his mother was a ghost.

Alarik had tried to paint in the edges of her with invitations to the garden where they could stroll together, or to the opera where they might forget their sorrows, or even to her own music room where she would play for him, her only surviving son, but they had all been met with the same tepid response – *perhaps tomorrow*.

Tomorrow had yet to come.

Though Alarik would not deny his mother's summons now – or ever – it pained him to be in her company, to look into her glassy eyes as she looked right through him, thinking of her other son. Her better son. Ansel.

Even Anika, Alarik's fiery, sharp-tongued sister had sailed south a year ago, removing herself from the whorls of grief that surrounded the palace in pursuit of the love she had found with a witch from Eana called Celeste. Often in the midnight dark, when sleep evaded him, Alarik thought of his sister and envied her freedom to travel far beyond the bounds of Gevra. Freedom from the weight of their father's crown, and from the grief that stalked these hallowed halls in his absence.

But Alarik was the king, and the king did not get to leave. Not the country. Nor its pain.

Drawing a breath, he knocked on the door.

His mother's response came at once. 'Come in!'

Alarik blinked at the chirpiness in her voice. He stalked inside, barely registering the staggering beauty of the domed stained-glass ceiling, which was coated in a blanket of fresh snow. Aside from the library and his painting studio, his mother's reading chamber was his favourite room in the entire palace. It was warm and inviting, the walls bordered by curving walnut shelves filled to the brim with all manner of books, from dense Gevran war treatises to tales of swashbuckling adventure. Everything a young prince could possibly want. A king, too.

A glittering snowflake chandelier hung from the high ceiling, and in the middle of the room, a set of blue velvet couches were arranged around a roaring stone fireplace. On the glass coffee table between them sat a silver tray of tea and sandwiches, warm butter biscuits and coconut cream tarts. The king's favourite. And jutting out of an ice bucket on the side was a vintage bottle of frostfizz.

Alarik frowned at the bottle, suspicion grumbling deep in his bones.

A study of poise and stillness, the dowager queen was seated by the fireplace. Her flowing silver dress was the same shade as her sheath of long hair. Her skin was pale but there was colour in her cheeks today. Colour in her eyes, which were as bright and blue as his own. Beside her sat Lief, the Queen's Hand and longest-serving steward, a middle-aged man who gave the vague impression of a forest nymph from a children's fairy tale. He had smooth golden skin, a veil of long white hair and unnervingly large eyes of pine green. He was as tall and narrow as a beanpole, and always smiled with every one of his teeth.

'Good afternoon, Your Majesty,' he said, smiling now.

The grumble of suspicion inside Alarik grew.

His mother waved him over. 'Come and sit, Alarik. I hope we haven't interrupted anything important.'

'I was about to spar with a mountain lion.'

Lief burst into laughter, the sound dying in his throat when he saw that the king was deadly serious. 'Terribly sorry to keep you from . . . uh . . . that rousing activity,' he said, hastily. 'This shouldn't take long.'

Alarik lowered himself on to the opposite couch, looking between his mother and her steward. 'It's been a while since we've had tea together, Mother.' His gaze flicked once more to the bottle. 'Or indeed frostfizz . . .' In fact, Alarik could not remember the last time they had cause to celebrate anything.

Valeska knitted her hands together on her lap, sharing a conspiratorial smile with Lief. Which reminded Alarik . . . 'Lief, I don't believe you and I have *ever* had tea together.'

Lief dipped his chin. 'It is my *honour*, Your Majesty.'

'Yes, it is.' Alarik kicked his legs out and looked to his mother, brows raised. 'To what do I owe this unexpected pleasure?'

'Lief,' she hissed. 'The frostfizz.'

The steward practically leaped across the table, hands trembling as he popped the cork, sending it soaring towards the domed ceiling. He poured it into three goblets. Valeska scooped hers up, prompting the steward to do the same. She looked expectantly at Alarik.

He did not move to take his goblet. 'What are we toasting to?'

Valeska's lips curled and if Alarik didn't know her better, he might not have noticed the anxiety vibrating around the edges of her smile. 'Your upcoming wedding.'

There was a thunderous silence.

Alarik stared at his mother, waiting for the joke – terribly misjudged as it was – to land.

'Such glad tidings!' crowed Lief, before the silence strangled him. He took a loud slurp of frostfizz. 'It's been so long since Grinstad has had such a joyous—'

'Shut up,' snapped the king.

Lief nearly swallowed his own tongue.

Alarik had not broken his stare with his mother, the same frosted-blue eyes meeting across the room.

She cleared her throat, summoning a sliver of the authority she'd once wielded like a sword. 'Alarik, the time has come for you to take a bride.'

He might have laughed if she didn't sound so serious. Instead, he crooked a brow, a challenge rising in his voice. 'Has it indeed, Mother?'

Lief drained his goblet and poured another. 'So fragrant,' he said, between gulps. 'You can *really* tell it's vintage.'

Undeterred by the frigid snap of her son's mood, Valeska went on. 'We are teetering on the verge of war. Queen Regna has been watching our borders for months, coveting our ore. Our mines. Our very kingdom.' Alarik's lips twisted at the salient reminder of his own weakened position. As if it didn't already plague his every waking thought. She set her goblet down. 'What do you plan to do about it?'

He didn't miss a beat. 'I plan to butcher Regna's soldiers with my beasts, then storm the border and take her head as a trophy.' Lief quailed, shrinking back into the cushions. Alarik curled his lip as he spoke his next words. 'Or would you prefer I bend the knee to the queen and marry one of her odious daughters instead?'

'Of course not,' said Valeska, wrinkling her nose. 'I'd sooner see you wed an elk than a princess of Vask.'

'So there *is* a standard,' remarked Alarik.

'Of course there is a standard. You are a formidable prize, my son.'

He recoiled from the words.

'You must see the sense in making an alliance,' Valeska went on, an old fire inside her rekindling. 'Gevra's position on this continent is the weakest it has been in centuries. Vask's designs are just the beginning. Our enemies will soon be clamouring at our doorstep.'

Alarik flinched at her hidden meaning, whether she intended it or not. That he was as weak as his kingdom, that he was bowing under the pressure of King Soren's legacy. 'I have it in hand.' He shot to his feet and went to the window to keep from hurling the tea tray in a tantrum. He was trying to cut back on those. The last time he punched a suit of armour in a rage, it'd nearly shattered his fist. 'I am preparing for war.'

'It will take more than a new wrangler, Alarik.'

Alarik couldn't keep the bite from his voice when he turned on her. 'What *will* it take, Mother?'

'A wife with an army at her back. A kingdom of her own.'

'And a heart as pure as a lark's song!' said Lief, perking up.

Alarik turned his blistering glare on the steward, who shrunk back into his seat.

'Or just the war stuff,' Lief squeaked. 'A big, scary army with lots of stomping soldiers. In a way, that's just as romantic. Dare I say even *more* romantic than—'

'Stop talking.' Alarik's nostrils flared.

'Stopping. I've stopped.'

Valeska laid a bracing hand on Lief's knee. 'Alarik's heart is his own business.'

The king didn't give a damn about his heart. He cared about his reputation. He cared about his kingdom and its future. And his mother, wise as she had always been, even in her sorrow, knew there was a greater chance of the Fovarr Mountains splitting open than Alarik Felsing ever making a love match.

He turned back to the window, gazing out at his beloved mountains as they glistened under the pale sun. 'Who do you have in mind?' he said, if only to satisfy his curiosity.

There was a long breath of anticipation.

Lief rattled his hands against the table, using it like a drum.

Alarik rolled his eyes.

'Princess Elva of Halgard!' announced the steward.

The name frittered past Alarik like a cool wind. 'I am not familiar with Princess Elva.'

Nor do I plan to be.

Though he knew Halgard well enough. A verdant, wealthy country of rolling hills and pooling lakes, silver mountains and bustling farms, where the livestock outnumbered its people three to one, and the rivers were so clear they glittered. Halgard was his mother's home country. As a favoured third cousin of the queen there, she had been a member of court before marrying Alarik's father almost thirty years ago. While Vask hugged the north-west of Gevra, Halgard shared a smaller mountain range with Gevra to the north-east, and though it was barely half the size of Alarik's kingdom, Halgard was well-armed and twice as wealthy. It was undoubtedly the best-placed kingdom to help him stave off the threat of invasion from Vask.

The alliance made sense.

But the idea of a wedding, of an entire *marriage*, sent a shudder skittering down Alarik's spine.

'Elva is clever. Well-read and well-respected . . .' his

mother went on, listing the princess's qualities like they might make a dent in his resolve. Alarik tuned her out, watching the sky for Vaskan birds.

Before him, the mountains shifted, as though they were taking a breath.

He frowned, sure he had imagined the movement, but on closer inspection, there was a crack in the terrain that hadn't been there the day before. He stared and stared, until the earth rose once more, unsettling a snow drift and sending it sliding down the mountainside. He strained, listening for the faraway rumble of an avalanche but there was only the north wind wreathing the glass dome.

He spun on his heel. 'Is it my imagination or are the mountains breathing?'

Valeska frowned. 'Have you been listening to a single word I've said?'

Unease stirred inside Alarik. He rubbed the spot between his brows, sure the stress of the last few months was finally getting to him. Foreign birds and foreign spies, feral beasts . . . and still, his wrangler had yet to arrive. 'I think I'm losing my mind.'

'Ah, but you are gaining a most illustrious bride,' said Lief, raising another bubbling goblet. 'I, for one, cannot wait to meet Princess Elva when she arrives with her delegation.'

Alarik stared at the steward. 'What did you just say?'

'I've already written to King Nilas. The date has been set,' said Valeska, rising from her perch and coming towards her son with such light in her eyes it made a dent in Alarik's chest. 'Princess Elva is coming to Grinstad in two weeks. And when she arrives, we must welcome her with open arms.' She took his hand and squeezed it, just as she used to when Alarik was a boy, afraid of the brutal battle tapestries in the war room, and then as a young teenager, afraid of the sea that had stolen his father. 'Please, Alarik. Won't you at least try with Elva, for me?'

Alarik stared down at his mother and let all the angry, hateful things he wanted to say dissolve on his tongue. It had been long months since he had seen her face alight with such hope.

He had no intention of getting married. But nor did he wish to dash the fragile happiness that now dwelled in his mother's heart. If he could give her nothing else, he could give her this: an answer that might keep that fire inside her eyes flickering, if only for a little while longer.

So, he lied and said, 'I'll consider it.'

Her answering smile was as lovely as a sunrise. She laid her head against his shoulder and turned to face the sky. 'At long last, I have something to look forward to.'

With a weary sigh, Alarik rested his head atop his mother's and watched his mountains inhale, as though they were steeling themselves for what lay ahead. It occurred to him that perhaps he should steel himself, too.

CHAPTER 4
Greta

Greta didn't think twice about the letter from Grinstad Palace. If the king needed a wrangler, then of course she would volunteer. It was her sisters who took convincing. Though the question was not *if* one of them would go, rather, it was a matter of *which* of them would travel to the mainland and give up her life as she knew it, her freedom – frostbitten as it was – to serve the king.

It had to be Greta. Kindra had a betrothed on Carrig – and Mikkel provided a vital connection to the island's fisherfolk. And more crucially, their generosity. Not to mention she was the only one of the three of them who could cook worth a damn. And as for Hela, she was far too valuable to Mama and Papa to leave. She was their guardian, possessing an uncanny ability to anticipate their needs before they voiced them. And more importantly, she was able to meet those needs with a strength that never faltered, no matter her hunger or exhaustion.

And even besides those convincing reasons, there was a far simpler one – of the three of them, Greta was the most gifted wrangler. Better, even, than Tor. Trained by Papa since the time she could crawl, Greta could scent a snow tiger's mood across a glacier, calm a leopard with a low whistle, subdue an ice bear with an admonishing look. She could speak to a wolf's heart as though it were her own, draw a pack of them to her like moths to a flame. Train them to dance, if she wanted to. Or to howl at the sun instead of the moon. For Greta, wrangling was as natural as breathing.

That was the crux of the argument, and in the end, it was the only thing that mattered.

By the time the moon rose that night, Hela and Kindra had given in. They crowded around the kitchen table as Hela scrawled their response.

We accept the king's request. Please send a boat to Carrig at your earliest convenience.

With the letter secured to its foot, the nighthawk took off, turning east towards the Sunless Sea, and Grinstad Palace far beyond it, before disappearing into the gathering snow. Greta watched it go, her heart hitching at the sudden twist of her destiny.

When she turned to face her sisters, their faces were strained.

'All will be well,' she told them, and they pulled her in for a hug, the strands of their copper-streaked hair mingling as they held each other tight, anchored to this moment – to the beginning of goodbye.

For the next few days, Greta tried not to think about her departure. She took advantage of the break in the poor weather and hunted as far as the mountains, killing a goat big enough to feed her family for a week. And still she hiked, stalking the pine forests until she returned with a grouse for Farron and Lupo to share.

Greta hunted to keep the swill of her nerves at bay, but as the days wore on, she couldn't stop her thoughts from turning to the mainland and the foreboding mountain palace Tor used to tell her about when he came home on leave. How the beasts that lived there had a whole forest to themselves, how they trained in an ancient stone arena from noon until night, and on days off roamed the palace with their guards. A treasured few even slept in the king's bed, and yet the most fearsome beast of all, more fearsome even than Borvil the ice bear, was the king himself.

On the fifth morning that followed the arrival of the king's letter, Hela was pacing in the living room when Greta came downstairs, having packed all her worldly possessions into the rucksack on her back. The rare spate of calm weather meant the ship Grinstad Palace had sent for Greta had arrived in good time, and was already anchored in the bay, waiting for her.

Hela's eyes pooled when she beheld her sister in her travelling cloak and boots. 'What will we do around here without your song, little nightingale?'

Greta blinked back her own tears. 'You will have to sing for the beasts now.'

'And make my eardrums bleed?' said Kindra, sweeping in from the kitchen where she had been wrapping up a small loaf of sweet bread for the journey. 'You know Hela bleats like a goat.'

Hela elbowed Kindra in the ribs, their sadness dissolving into a reluctant giggle.

Greta took the loaf gratefully and folded it into her rucksack. 'Thank you, Kindra. I'll try not to eat it all in one go.'

'Do if you like,' she said, pressing a kiss to her cheek. 'Get some meat on those scrawny bones.'

'Don't worry, I plan to eat the palace into destitution. By the time I come back, I'll be able to lift an ice bear above my head.'

'That's our Greta,' said Hela, gently tugging the end of Greta's braid. Her smile wobbled. 'When I look at you, I still see the little girl who used to balk at the fisherfolk in their oversized tarps. The girl who used to yelp at her own shadow because she thought it was a monster.'

Greta laughed to hide the sting of the truth. That quivering little girl died the day Papa was attacked. Shadows didn't scare Greta now. She had known true horror and survived it. She had the scars to prove it. 'I'll be all right,' she said, hitching up her rucksack. 'There are no monsters at Grinstad Palace.'

Hela's eyes darkened. 'You have not met the king.'

Greta swallowed thickly. Hela was the only one among them who had met Alarik Felsing. It was many years ago, a fleeting encounter in the entrance hall of the palace during a visit to Tor, but the king's frostiness had still managed to unsettle Hela. Greta had heard all kinds of stories about the hardened young ruler over the years – the brutal war king who cut down his enemies like trees, tortured his traitors, scattered threats like ashes and ruled over his kingdom with an iron fist. And yet her own brother held the king in such high regard they had eventually become best friends. Perhaps meeting Alarik Felsing as a boy and growing up alongside him in King Soren's palace meant Tor knew things about him that no one else did. Greta had often wondered what those things were, but they remained a mystery to all but Tor.

Perhaps it was better that way.

'I'm not scared of the king,' she said. In fact, over these past few days she had barely thought of Alarik Felsing at all. Only of the coin she would send home to her family, and the food that would return the colour to their cheeks.

Hela pulled her into a crushing embrace. 'Go on, then,' she said, into her hair. 'Before one of us starts to blubber.'

'Iversens don't cry,' Kindra reminded her, even as she sniffed.

Greta knelt to say goodbye to Lupo, burying a rogue tear in his fur. 'Take care of these two,' she whispered, sensing the wolf's sorrow as keenly as her own. It hung like a cloud around them, making the air heavy. 'I promise I'll send home treats.'

Lupo blinked his big amber eyes in approval. She kissed him again, ruffling his fur as she stood.

When Greta opened the cottage door, she nearly crashed head first into her mother. Mama was standing on the doorstep, swaddled in a woollen blanket, her nose reddened from the cold. Papa hovered behind her in his winter cloak, leaning heavily on his cane.

'What are you doing out here? I told you I'd come up to say goodbye!' Halfway to a heart attack, Greta tugged her mother into the warmth of the cottage, then reached for her father. He remained in the snow, refusing to budge.

'He wants to walk you down to the boat,' Mama whispered, pressing a kiss to her cheek. 'I'm afraid this is as far as my strength will take me.'

And what about Papa's strength? Greta wanted to demand,

but there was no arguing with either of them.

Greta embraced her mother, leaving Hela and Kindra to take care of her, before stepping out into the crisp morning air.

Papa summoned a smile, offering his arm to her, just like he used to when she was a child going hunting in his shadow. She took it, eager to let him place some weight on her if he needed to, but he never faltered.

They walked on down the hill towards the strand, slow and careful, like they had all the time in the world. Aya flew overhead, the snowy owl watching over them as though Hela herself had willed it. Likely, she had.

For a long while they were silent, Papa's laboured breaths casting clouds between them. Greta tried not to worry about his journey home, how long it might take him to climb back up the hill, how badly his leg would hurt at the end of it.

All too soon, the bay rose to meet them, and there, bobbing among a raft of battered fishing boats, was a sleek, dark-wood vessel with bright silver sails bearing the royal crest of Gevra.

Greta's throat tightened, her arms curling around the swill of nerves in her stomach.

Papa tugged her closer, drawing her against his side, where the warmth of his body seeped into hers and settled the trembling in her bones.

'There is no beast in that palace you haven't already wrangled here on Carrig,' he said, gruffly. 'Guard your back, follow your instincts and listen with your heart. Just like I taught you.'

'I will, Papa.'

They came to a stop at the edge of the rocky strand. He gripped her shoulder, turning into her until all she could see was the storm raging in his eyes. It echoed the one in her heart. 'Remember, Greta. You're an Iversen. The song of the wild flows in your veins. A magic as old as the hills of Carrig, a gift beyond compare. Just as you are.' His voice softened, and he raised a gentle hand to trace the scars on her cheek. 'Don't let anyone in that palace give you hell, little nightingale. That goes for the soldiers *and* the beasts.'

Greta straightened her spine.

'And it goes for the king, too,' he added, with a fierceness she had not heard in many years.

A terrible lump rose in Greta's throat as she threw her arms around her father, burying her face in the crook of his shoulder. Of all the goodbyes, this one was the hardest to bear. 'I'll miss you, Papa.'

'Not as much as I'll miss you.'

'Be well,' she said, a plea in her voice.

'And you.' He pulled back, eyes shining. The storm inside them was breaking, and rain was coming. 'Be careful, Greta.'

'Always.'

'And write often.'

'I will.'

He squeezed her hand in a last goodbye, and she took off at a run before her chest cracked open and she lost the courage his words had given her. She hurried along the pier, where a pair of Gevran soldiers in pristine blue frock coats were waiting to escort her on board. Within minutes, she was on the king's boat, exchanging greetings with the captain as the crew hoisted the anchor. Greta went to the back of the ship, climbing the railings to look out on the little island that held her whole heart.

As the king's ship sailed out to the Sunless Sea where the gulls cried to welcome them, Greta waved goodbye to her father. He stood in that same spot on the strand, leaning on his cane as he watched her sail away. The wind whipped up and new snow began to fall but he didn't move, not until long after the mist came down and swallowed the island, taking him with it.

It was only then that Greta allowed herself to cry, hot tears sliding down her cheeks and falling into the sea. As the ship turned east towards the mainland, and the rising wind punched the mainsail taut as if to hurry it along, it occurred to her that this was the furthest she had ever been from Carrig. And there were hundreds of miles yet to go.

Greta slept in a cabin below deck for most of the voyage, only rising when the ship slowed to pass through the Dead Crevasse, a treacherous all-too-narrow inlet overlooked by the mainland's jagged ice cliffs. She rushed to the prow, straining to see the bustling shore, where curling smoke and flickering lights feathered the falling dark.

Soon, the cloying stench of brine gave way to the familiar scent of woodsmoke and pine. The ship docked and Greta was escorted past a teeming marketplace along the shore where a wooden wolf-sled bearing the royal crest awaited her. The sled driver was a stern-faced, red-haired soldier dressed in the blue and silver uniform she knew all too well. He offered her a flat smile as she clambered into the bench behind him, settling her rucksack beside her and unfolding one of the fur blankets that had been laid out.

They took off without preamble, the sled pulling away from the shore and thundering into the falling night, where icy hills and frost-ridden roads rose to meet them. The wolves never faltered, the moon guiding their way as they wound deeper into the countryside, where the mountains grew taller and the valleys steeper. The soldier offered little in the way of conversation and Greta welcomed the silence. It allowed her the time to breathe in that familiar scent of woodsmoke and pine while she munched on Kindra's sweet bread, allowing thoughts of home to settle her nerves.

They rode on and on into the wilderness, until a swathe of clouds swept in from the west and smothered the moon. Darkness fell, and bundled warmly under the fur blanket, Greta's lids grew heavy. She slept deeply, the world whipping past her in whorls of navy and white. She woke as the sun was rising above the staggering Fovarr Mountains, their icy peaks jutting up as if to skewer it. The wind stirred as they rode through the pass, and she sat stiffly in her seat, sensing movement in the rock. Something breathing. Something *stirring*. But she could see nothing beyond the spill of snow on jagged rock.

How strange.

Then the mountains fell away and the sensation passed, the rugged landscape parting to reveal the glittering facade of Grinstad Palace, a towering fortress of glass and stone.

The rising sun bounced off its glass towers, until Greta had to shield her eyes from the glare. Before her, a pair of huge black gates groaned open, and after a brief inspection from the tower guards, the sled passed through the entryway, the palace growing taller and more foreboding as they trundled towards it. Greta had to crane her neck to take in the full spectacle, her heart leaping into her throat as her gaze snagged on the stone balustrade protruding high above her. For there, in the glaring morning light, stood Alarik Felsing, shirtless and unkempt, wearing a scowl made for war.

For the first time since the nighthawk had come, Greta shrank back in her seat and wondered what on earth she had got herself into. Her father's voice found her through the fog of her fear. *Don't let anyone in that palace give you hell, little nightingale.*

No, she would not. Formidable as it was, the palace was a home like any other and Alarik Felsing was no more ferocious than the ice bears she had wrangled back on Carrig. She straightened her spine and swallowed her anxiety, reminding herself there was nothing to fear here.

Greta Iversen was not afraid of beasts.

Or kings.

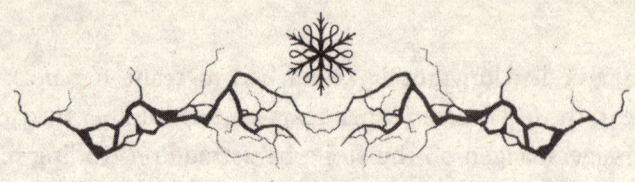

CHAPTER 5
Alarik

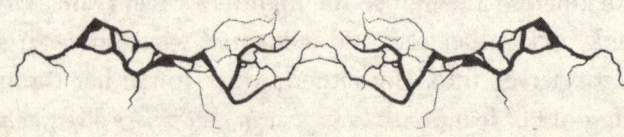

Alarik woke up in a cold sweat, sure he could hear the steel war drums of Vask pounding in the wind. He leaped out of bed, nearly tripping over Nova as he ran to the balcony, his feet bare on the snow. The sun was rising over the Fovarr Mountains, his servants and soldiers waking to face another day in Grinstad. There were no drums, just the distant howls of his beasts and the unsteady thrum of his own heartbeat.

It was only a dream. But every time he blinked, he saw Queen Regna's bloodless smile beneath the visor of her crimson helmet, her wild grey hair streaming behind her as she rode to war.

To Gevra.

Perhaps, then, it was a warning. Still scowling, the king turned from his balcony and shut the drapes behind him, welcoming the slick of darkness. He slumped on to his bed, counting his breaths until they settled.

Someone knocked at his bedchamber.

'GO AWAY!' Alarik barked, just as his steward, Johan, poked his head around the door, grey eyes wide in his round, pale face. The king huffed. 'What do you want, Johan?'

'Just your breakfast order, Majesty,' said Johan, without daring to come inside. 'What are you having?'

'Stress,' muttered Alarik, rising from the bed and stomping into the adjacent bathing chamber. 'Round up my war council and have them meet me in the war room.' He paused, before adding, 'Make sure there's a pot of coffee in there as big as your head.' Another pause. 'And also pastries.'

'Yes, Majesty.' The door eased shut and Johan disappeared, leaving Alarik to bathe and dress himself. As he liked it. He chose a pair of black trousers and boots with silver buckles, and a high-collared grey frock coat that brushed his chin. He raked his blond hair back from his face, lingering on the ink-black streak in the middle. The one that appeared the morning after his father drowned. The same day he was crowned the new ruler of Gevra.

Useless king, hissed a vicious voice in his head. He shook it off, grabbing his sword and fastening it to his hip. His fingers curled around the icy pommel as he recalled the first lesson his father ever taught him. *A good king arms himself in battle. A Gevran king arms himself everywhere he goes.* Alarik marched from his bedchamber into the brightly lit glass corridors of the east wing, where guards and beasts dipped their heads as he passed.

Johan met him again on his way to the war room, leaping into Alarik's path like a startled gazelle. 'There's been a change of plan,' he said, swatting a strip of lank brown hair away from his face. 'The war room is in use.'

Alarik glared down at his steward. 'Oh? Is there another king of Gevra I don't know about?'

Johan shook his head. 'I believe the room is being

rearranged. Or, um, dusted?'

Alarik's brows hunched, his patience so thin he could snap at any moment, throw a priceless vase from the third-floor hallway, and send Johan flying after it.

'The battle council has convened in the orangery instead,' his steward went on.

Alarik's frown sharpened. 'What in freezing hell is an orangery?'

'Uh, follow me, Majesty.' Johan turned on his boot heel. Seething with a dangerous mix of frustration and impatience, the king stalked after him.

The orangery was located in the south wing of Grinstad and was a small, unseasonably warm room made entirely of windows that looked out on the manicured lawn. The room was filled with citrus trees; lemon and lime and orange, planted in large baskets of rich, wet soil. All of them appeared to be thriving, despite the hostile climate. In the centre of the room was a low tea table surrounded by five wrought-iron chairs.

The few trusted members of Alarik's war council were already here, each of them looking as bewildered as he was to find themselves in the orangery.

Astrid Vine, captain of the king's soldiers, was inspecting one of the lemon trees, trailing her fingers along a delicate white blossom. 'I didn't know these things came with flowers,' she remarked to no one in particular.

General Vesper Hale, the king's armourer, who was in charge of weaponry, was sitting stiffly in one of the wrought-iron chairs. She had forgone her Gevran soldier's uniform for her preferred outfit of black leather, her dark hair pulled into a ponytail that was shaved on one side and fastened so tight it pulled her violet lips into a strained smile. Her light brown skin glistened in the flood of morning sunlight, her kohl-rimmed hazel eyes focused on the map in front of her.

Beside her, Elias Hansen, Alarik's spymaster and illegitimate first cousin on his father's side, was a study of leonine grace. His silver-blond hair was slicked back with oil, his sharp bone structure and smooth golden skin making him appear strangely ageless.

He was wearing a black leather tunic, matching trousers, and heavy-buckled boots. The uniform of a spy, not a soldier, but Elias was as loyal to the crown as Vine. After all, he was Alarik's own blood, not that King Soren's younger brother Steffen had ever deigned to recognize his own son. Elias had grown up in a small cottage in the foothills behind the palace, kept at arms' reach from the Felsings and their fortune, until Alarik himself offered Elias a role in court.

As a child, Elias was always fascinated by the machinations of royal life. He would often sneak on to the palace grounds at sunrise to eavesdrop on the soldiers' training sessions, skulking like a rat in the shadows of the arena. Alarik was the only one who'd ever noticed him.

He was staring into his mug of coffee now, his blue eyes depthless as though he was reading secrets within.

Captain Vine plucked a lemon off a tree and held it up in greeting. 'I didn't take you for a fruit farmer.'

'I didn't even know this room existed,' said Alarik, glancing sidelong at Johan. 'Since when do we have an orangery?'

'Since Anika demanded one,' said Johan.

Alarik huffed a long-suffering sigh. Of course this ridiculous hothouse was his sister's doing – another one of her random whims carried out with expert Gevran precision.

And the crown's coin. An orangery of citrus trees to rival those of Caro on the southern continent, and she hadn't even bothered to stick around to pick the fruit.

'I do miss your sister at our council meetings,' said Vesper, sitting back in her chair and kicking one long, leathered limb over another. 'She was something of a weapon herself. All gunpowder and temper.'

'A living, breathing cannon,' muttered Alarik, with rare fondness. He missed his sister, too. The clack of her towering heels on the marbled tiles, the shrill echo of her voice as she sashayed through the halls, barking orders at the guards like she, and not he, was the king. 'The palace is certainly a lot quieter without her.'

'Unless you count that ceaseless chorus of roaring beasts,' said Elias, who, having returned to the palace late last night, was already tiring of it. Alarik could tell by the ruinous scowl on his face and the crinkles gathering on his nose. Elias made no secret of his unease around the beasts that lived here, and they were certainly far noisier now that so many of them were untrained. 'Which reminds me, where *is* your new wrangler?' He nodded at the empty chair opposite him. 'We're not yet a complete war council.'

'You're my spymaster,' said Alarik, pointedly. 'You tell me where she is.'

'My eyes have been on the north border, as you commanded.'

'The wrangler was due to arrive this morning,' said Captain Vine, frowning at the empty chair like it might make her appear. 'I've left word with the servants to bring her up when she gets here.'

'I'm not waiting on her account,' said Alarik impatiently,

and the others grunted in agreement. It was far too hot in here already, and the heady citrus scent was giving him a headache. Anika and her whims.

At a wave of dismissal from the king, Johan dipped out of the room. Alarik chose the nearest chair and reached for a pastry, washing it down with a slug of coffee.

There. The blackness of his mood faded to a misty grey.

Captain Vine sunk into the chair opposite him, and all four of them leaned forward to pour over the map. It depicted the upper territories of Gevra, the north border sketched as an unbroken line of dark peaks that marked the Blackspire Mountains, and beyond it, the unchartered plains of Vask.

Elias placed red pins in six spots along the mountain range. 'Spies have been detained here, here and here,' he said, skewering the parchment. 'And five more in the tunnels themselves.'

'What are they after?' muttered Alarik. 'Is Regna so poor that she must scrabble in our dirt for ore?'

Elias pressed his lips together, frowning.

'Something tells me her ambitions are far grander than that,' said Vesper, uneasily.

Alarik was inclined to agree. Regna was clearly up to something. Or rather, searching for something. In *his* kingdom.

He hissed, his anger mirrored by Captain's Vine's clenched fist. The lemon inside it split open, releasing a burst of citrus.

'They will cross the border eventually. And continue south,' said Alarik, tracking a pathway from the Blackspires all the way to Grinstad Palace. 'A two-day march in fair weather.'

'Fair weather?' Elias snorted. 'Never heard of it.'

'Forget the weather. She'll be dead before she sets foot on Hunter's Pass,' said Vine, with the kind of stirring confidence that had made Alarik promote her in the first place. 'Our army will maim hers.'

'They'll have to do it with their swords and bows,' said Vesper, uneasily. 'We can't use fire lances that close to the mines. The tunnels will collapse.'

'We'll have our beasts,' said Vine, and all four of them glanced at the empty chair.

Where the hell was she?

Alarik reminded himself of the treacherous blizzards that had swarmed Gevra these past weeks, ripping through the seas and yanking trees from the ground. No doubt they had made for a choppy crossing from Carrig. Still, impatience gnawed at him.

He looked to Elias. 'Forget Regna's spies. Where are her troops?'

Elias shook his head. 'Not yet at the Blackspires.'

'Then push your scouts further north. Send them into Vask. I want to know her numbers. Her weaponry.'

Elias raised his brows. 'And if she catches them?'

'Then you're not very good at your job, Elias.' Alarik levelled him with a hard look. 'You're the best spymaster on the northern continent. Are you not?'

Elias bristled. 'On *all* continents.'

Growing up as the unclaimed bastard son of King Soren's youngest brother had made Elias hungry to prove himself at court. It was Alarik who had given him the opportunity, time and time again. Elias had not failed him yet.

'I want numbers. Positions. The full scope of her plan, as

best you can get it.' He looked to Vine. 'Start the soldiers on battle drills. From today.'

'We eat, sleep and breathe battle drills,' said Vine.

The king almost smiled. 'The first archer to bring me a dead Vaskan eagle gets a month's wages on the spot.'

Vine smirked. 'I'll hike the Fovarrs myself if the coin's that good.'

Vesper turned to the king, not wanting to be outdone. 'I'm still working on our fire lances. But the range should be three times as far as our cannons.'

Alarik noted her twitching fingers. 'You're nervous, Vesper.'

She hesitated.

He pitched forward. 'Tell me why.'

But Vesper looked to Elias, a question in her eyes.

Alarik whipped his head around, skewering his spymaster with another blistering gaze. 'Keep your secrets, Elias. But never from your king.'

'It's not a secret. It's a rumour,' said Elias, a hitch in the usual silkiness of his voice. 'Unconfirmed, but . . . concerning.' At Alarik's thunderous silence, he went on. 'A merchant sailor from the north-east came to trade with the kitchen staff last week. He told your cook, Harald, that there are rumours swirling in Vask . . . rumours that say Regna has a beast of her own.'

'We have hundreds of beasts,' said the king, dismissively.

'A dragon,' Elias amended. 'They say Regna has a dragon.'

That word – *dragon* – chased the warmth from the room.

Alarik peeled his lips back, his hand coming to the pommel of his sword like he might fell the rumour before it took flight. A *dragon* here on the northern continent. A thing of war and flame. And after all this time, when such creatures had long faded into myth and legend.

Almost at once, his thoughts turned to his mountains, to the strange rise and fall of their peaks, and the uncanny sense that something might be hiding there. Or perhaps . . . *waking*. A beast that belonged to another time entirely. A beast he used to dream about, before the nightmares came. He was reminded suddenly of a half-forgotten tale often whispered to him at bedtime when he was a boy and his father would come to tuck him into bed.

Once upon a wilder time,
When beasts soared as high as hawks,
And fire streaked across the sky . . .

No. It was not possible. There hadn't been a sighting of such a beast in two thousand years. Dragons had been extinct for so long, they dwelled now only in stories.

'This is a trick. The queen's game,' he said, darkly. 'I will not play it.'

'It's not possible,' said Vine, lending her voice to his. 'Dragons are a relic of the past.'

Even Elias himself seemed unsure. 'Well, whatever she has, people are talking . . .'

'I hope they're wrong,' muttered Vesper. 'I have nothing in my arsenal that can kill a dragon.' After all, how would a ballist, versed in fire and gunpowder, fight a creature of flame? There wasn't a beast in all of Gevra that could best such a thing.

There was an uneasy silence.

Alarik glared once more at the empty chair, fighting the urge to pick it up and smash it through the window. He dragged a breath through his nose, settling the dangerous swirl of his panic, and turned to Elias.

'Get me proof,' he said. 'Whatever she has, I want to know it.'

Elias frowned, nodding.

Alarik reached for his coffee, downed it, then poured another. They went on, all four of them tearing into the platter of pastries as they poured over war strategy until the king's head began to pound.

Vesper glanced at the clock on the wall, then cleared her throat. 'It's getting late. I've got a shipment of gunpowder coming in from—'

'Go,' said Alarik, waving her off. 'Both of you. We'll reconvene next week.'

Vesper and Elias got up and left without a breath of hesitation.

Only Captain Vine remained. She took a bite out of her lemon, then immediately spat it back out. '*Eugh*. What the hell is this evil, squishy mouth curse?'

Alarik looked up at her. 'Haven't you ever had a lemon before?'

She licked her sleeve, trying to rub the taste from her tongue. 'I have not had the distinct displeasure.'

Alarik bit back his laughter. 'It's better on the second bite.'

Vine glared at him, then slowly set the lemon down. 'Sadist.'

He surrendered the ghost of a smile. 'I forgot what an impressive judge of character you are.'

'Why would anyone want to *grow* this stuff, let alone eat it?'

'You forget my sister's a sadist, too,' remarked Alarik,

plucking his own lemon from a nearby tree and biting into it. He held Vine's gaze as he swallowed it down, rind and all.

There was a sharp knock at the door. Alarik whipped his head around expectantly only to find Lief, poking his head inside. He swallowed a groan. 'Your Majesty, pardon the interruption.' Lief glanced at Vine nervously, then back at the king, dipping his head in deference. 'But if you could please follow me, there is something urgent I must discuss with you.'

Alarik lowered his brows. 'Is it more urgent than war, Lief?'

The steward was unmoved, his face as serious as Alarik had ever seen it. 'I would wager that it is, Your Majesty.'

Despite his annoyance, Alarik was seized by a rush of worry for his mother. Why else would her steward have come to seek him out, and interrupted a war council, no less? He was on his feet in a heartbeat, at the door in the next.

'Then *move*,' he urged the steward, following him out into the hallway.

CHAPTER 6
Greta

When the sled finally came to a stop outside Grinstad Palace, Greta tossed the blanket aside and grabbed her satchel. She hopped out, her boots crunching up the frosted steps to a pair of enormous iron doors. They groaned open and she stepped over the threshold, out of the blistering cold and into the glittering mouth of the palace.

And *oh*, what splendour awaited her. The facade might have been terrifying but the inside dripped with warmth and opulence. The vast entryway was floored in exquisite white marble, threaded with veins of sea blue and mountain green, the high ceiling hung with so many crystalline chandeliers that their flickering lights cast rainbows along the pearlescent walls. Across the sprawling entryway, a grand imperial staircase led up to the first floor, before branching off into the east and west wings of the palace. Greta tipped her head back, marvelling at the rippling tapestries on the walls, depicting great battles of old, ancient Gevran kings and queens fighting valiantly alongside their mighty beasts, riding dragons and ice bears into battle.

The atrium was magnificent, the grand majesty dwarfing

Greta as she stood in a puddle of morning sunlight, trying to catch her breath. She was vaguely aware of the guards watching her from their stations, the beasts peering out of their alcoves to assess her. Greta assessed the creatures in return, counting four male snow leopards and two female mountain lions, poised but wary.

Impeccably trained, thanks to her brother.

Greta smiled just as a tall, spindly woman in a simple blue dress came sweeping into the atrium. By her wizened face, tight knot of silver hair and formal apron, Greta guessed she was the head servant here. By the way she looked Greta up and down in bold assessment, it was clear she was. 'So, you are the wrangler?' she said, thin lips twisting.

Greta nodded. 'My name is Greta Iversen.'

'You're too short,' she said, in a voice that was neither cruel nor kind. 'Too pale. Too thin.' Her gaze lingered on the scars on Greta's cheek, before sweeping over her snow-dusted cloak. 'And you're late.'

Greta rolled her shoulders back, refusing to shrink under her frankness. Growing up with Hela, she was well used to it. 'I can't change any of that,' she said. 'But I can train your beasts, if you show me where they are.'

The old woman arched a brow, and one corner of her mouth lifted. She turned on her heel, beckoning Greta to follow as she stalked down a long corridor, the determined clack of her footsteps soon swallowed by the plush blue carpet. 'First, I'll show you to your room. You can leave your things there. After, you'll meet the king. Then the beasts.'

Greta's bedchamber was located in the bowels of the palace, down a spiral stone staircase and halfway along a sconce-lit corridor. According to the head servant, who remembered to introduce herself as Nanna on their way downstairs, the other rooms there belonged to the palace guards. The chamber was a short walk from the main courtyard, and so close to the arena, Greta could hear the beasts growling and snapping at their handlers. Despite the uneasy chorus, the room itself was surprisingly cosy. A single bed adorned with furs occupied one wall, while a narrow wardrobe, a wooden desk and a mirror shared the other. There was a sheepskin rug to offset the dampness, and a small bathing chamber where she could dress and wash each morning. There were no windows, which made Greta's throat itch, but the room was well lit by two large oil lamps, and she reminded herself she was only a staircase away from fresh air.

Nanna left her to freshen up. She washed quickly, pleased to find jasmine-scented soap and an assortment of creams in her bathing chamber. She brushed out her hair and re-braided it down her back, before applying rose oil to her dry lips and some face cream to soothe the windburn on her cheeks. She changed into a sensible pair of dark grey trousers and her favourite fur-lined navy tunic. She was lacing up her boots when Nanna returned to collect her.

Greta clasped her hands to keep them from twitching as they climbed one set of stairs and then another, the palace sprawling out on either side of her in a maze of meandering halls and winding turrets until, at last, they came to a stop before a large iron door framed by two identical suits of armour. They held real swords, their pommels gleaming so brightly, Greta glimpsed her wide eyes in their reflection.

'This is the war room,' said Nanna, in a low voice. 'The king has convened his war council inside. I am not permitted to enter but he is expecting you.'

Greta blinked. A war council on her first day. Holy snow. She didn't know the first thing about war. Was the king expecting a soldier like her brother? Had there been a terrible misunderstanding? Her throat tightened, anxiety swirling inside her. She briefly considered turning on her heel and bolting for the atrium, but if she fled now, a guard would surely snatch her up and drag her back here, and besides, the very act of such cowardice would shame her family for all eternity. No, she had to open this door and face the king. She had to face this new life she had chosen for herself.

As Nanna disappeared in a swish of blue skirts, Greta smoothed the stray wisps of copper hair from her temples and raised her chin. And knocked.

No answer.

She knocked again, then said, in little more than a squeak, 'Hello?'

Nothing.

She frowned, pressing her ear to the metal to find silence on the other side. She tried the handle and it yielded, the iron door creaking open to reveal a large vault that smelled like metal and gunpowder. She stepped inside, letting the door fall shut behind her. There was no one else in here. Unless she counted the horrifying faces on the walls. Oil lamps flickered high and bright, illuminating vast paintings of war ten times more brutal than the tapestries that hung in the grand entryway. These ones didn't shy away from blood and guts, nor severed heads and prowling beasts with greedy mouths full of limbs. Everywhere Greta looked, wild-eyed Gevran soldiers slashed their enemies in two, climbing hills made from their corpses to hoist the Gevran flag.

War shone out from the four stone walls in all its unapologetic, blood-soaked glory, and she hated every inch of it. She suppressed a shudder, refocusing on the round table in the middle of the room. It was covered in maps of Gevra. There was even a three-dimensional model of the kingdom, complete with tiny soldiers hewn from stone. And there were beasts, too. Greta examined an intricate carving of a tiny ice bear rendered mid-roar, and wished her sisters were here to see it.

She rounded the table, only now noticing the suits of armour that were arranged around it, like soldiers standing to attention. There were twelve of them, and for some strange reason, they were all dressed up.

Greta trapped a gasp of laughter on the palm of her hand. The statue nearest the door was wearing a ruffled cream doublet, wrought with golden swirls. The suit next to it donned a green frock coat with a high collar and floor-length tails. On the other side, a statue sported a double-breasted blue waistcoat with so many rows of gleaming buttons, Greta didn't know where it even opened.

She turned slowly, marvelling at every single one. It was, without a doubt, the finest display of clothing she had ever seen. Just how wealthy was the king of Gevra that he would dress up his suits of armour so decadently? How *bored* must he be?

Was this how kings played with dolls? When Greta was a child, Papa used to whittle figures from cedar bark. Mama would sew tiny outfits for them, leaving Greta to play with the wooden figurines for hours at a time, enacting increasingly elaborate scenarios in her head. Did Alarik Felsing move around his giant suits of armour, snapping their grills open and shut, pretending they could talk?

Greta snorted at the image. Then another, darker thought burst the bubble of her amusement. Just how *selfish* was Alarik Felsing that he would adorn inanimate statues with such riches while his own people starved and suffered, beaten down by blizzard after blizzard? She thought of Papa sitting on that freezing back step, trying to summon the strength to stand, and felt her insides grow warm. She thought of Mama holding her stomach to keep the hunger pangs at bay, and suddenly wanted to scream.

She gripped the collar of the nearest frock coat, which was inlaid with hundreds of sparkling crystals, and imagined the faceless helmet above it was the king's scowling face. She rose to her tiptoes and rattled it, setting loose a scattering of gemstones. *You self-indulgent, self-centered wretch of a ruler*, she imagined herself saying. *How dare you—*

She froze at the sound of rising voices. A fistful of jewels flew as she ripped her hand away. Someone was coming. If they peeked inside, they would see her skulking in here alone, plucking crystals from the king's statues, like some kind of thief. She'd be sent back to Carrig on the first sled out of here. Or worse – chucked into the dungeons under the mountains! She spun on her heel, her eyes darting. There was nowhere to run. She dived behind the table, desperately scrambling for a hiding place just as the door swung open.

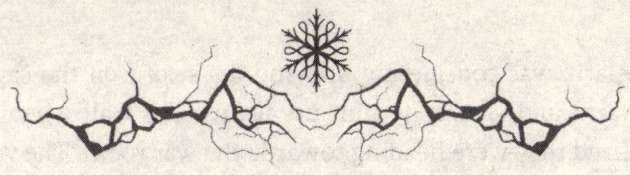

CHAPTER 7
Alarik

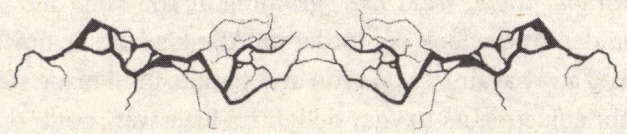

Despite being pummelled by Alarik's questions, Lief said very little as he stalked ahead of the king, leading him down one hallway after another. Captain Vine, who had followed Alarik from the orangery, fell into step with the king.

'What in freezing hell is this all about?' she muttered.

Alarik was thinking the same thing. 'I don't know,' he ground out.

'All will be revealed!' crowed the steward, who was growing chirpier by the minute. Alarik scowled at the back of his head, so mired in concern for his mother that he was still holding the bitten lemon in his fist, the rind crushed so tight, juice was spilling over his fingers.

'Where is my mother, Lief?' he demanded, for the fifth time.

'Oh, the dowager queen?' said the steward, like the idea of her whereabouts had only just occurred to him. 'Well, I expect she's reading in her chambers.'

'Then that's exactly where you should be, too,' said Captain Vine. But the steward ignored her, scurrying up another stairway.

Alarik was considering drawing his sword on the cagey steward and slamming him up against the wall when he realized they were heading towards the war room. The very same war room he had been expressly told was out of use that same morning. He slowed, his anxiety receding. In its place, suspicion grumbled.

'Almost there!' said Lief, grinning at the king over his shoulder. At the look of murder on Alarik's face, he quickly looked away again. 'I hope you don't mind, but I made some minor adjustments to your delightful little war room.'

A roar gathered in the king's chest, impatience quickly curdling into rage. So, his mother's busybody of a steward was the reason Alarik and his council had been relegated to that blasted orangery. Somehow, a palace servant had trumped the will of the king himself. His mother might be off reclining in her reading room, but he sensed her hand in this slight.

'Of course I mind,' barked Alarik, drawing his sword in the heat of his anger. 'What the hell is going on here?'

Lief yelped and scurried on, flinging himself at the iron door like it might protect him from the king's ire.

Captain Vine's hand came to Alarik's arm. 'Try not to behead him just yet. Your mother will be very displeased.'

Alarik's other hand twitched around the lemon.

'And do not throw that lemon at him,' she added. 'You're better than that.'

Alarik glanced sidelong at her. 'Am I?'

'No,' she admitted. 'But I, for one, want to see where this is going.'

The iron door groaned open and Lief bounded inside. He rounded the large table and turned to face the king, bouncing on the balls of his feet. 'Come in! Come in!' he crooned. 'Your surprise awaits!'

Alarik stepped into his war room and froze. The grip on his sword tightened as he turned on his heel, beholding the unfathomable sight of twelve towering suits of armour dressed in full royal regalia.

Captain Vine stepped in behind him, a gasp sticking in her throat.

Lief splayed his arms. 'I present the final contenders for your wedding wardrobe!'

Alarik's blood roared in his ears. His left eye twitched, but all his words – including his favourite litany of swears – left him.

Vine threw her head back, releasing a wheeze of laughter. 'This is so much better than anything I imagined.'

Alarik shot her a withering look. He had never been so horrified in his life, and he had been to war. Several times.

The steward went on, babbling through the King's thunderous silence. 'It's a fine selection, as you can see.' He reached out to caress a violet frock coat before frowning at the missing gems along the collar. 'But still very much in progress. Your mother designed these herself and personally oversaw their completion with the palace seamstresses. Of course she wouldn't dream of choosing your ceremonial coat without your . . .'

He trailed off as Alarik raised his sword. Blood still singing, the king stepped towards the first suit of armour and with a swish of his blade, knocked the helmet from its body. With a second swish, he sent the rest of it clattering to the floor, frock coat and all.

Then he looked up at Lief and said through gritted teeth,

'No.'

The steward swallowed thickly. 'You don't like the tails, then?'

Alarik swung at the next suit, which was little more than a mass of cream ruffles. It went flying, the clatter of metal reverberating around the room. '*No*,' he said again, the word coasting on a growl.

Lief cleared his throat, taking a careful step backwards. 'Perhaps I should fetch the dowager queen,' he said, glancing towards the door. 'I know she's particularly fond of this violet one.'

Alarik fired the lemon. It bounced off the coat, dislodging another fistful of gemstones, before falling to the floor with a splat.

The steward looked down at it and gasped. 'A lemon . . . a *lemon*!' He clapped a hand against his forehead like the answer to some great riddle had at last been revealed. 'Of course! You favour the colour yellow! A nice pale tone to match your hair.' He scrubbed his brow, chuckling to himself. 'How foolish of us, really, not to have prepared a single garment in—'

'*Lief*,' hissed Alarik, swinging at another suit of armour and knocking it over. 'You're not listening.' He kicked the torso away. 'I don't care about frock coats and frills.' Alarik decapitated another suit of armour, imagining it as one of Regna's soldiers. He had felled half of them already, and still he stomped, swinging and shouting. 'War is coming to Gevra, and for some incomprehensible reason, *you* thought it would be a wise idea to interrupt *my* council to drag me to this insulting parade of ruffles and silks.' He swung again, toppling a suit of armour and then kicking it across the room for good measure. 'So, unless you have something meaningful to offer me and Captain Vine about the art of Vaskan warfare, I would advise you to run very fast and very far away from me before I run out of things to behead.'

Lief was silent for a long moment, his face scrunching like he was truly reaching for something worthwhile to offer his king. 'You know, in their own way, weddings are not unlike war . . .'

'Holy snow,' muttered Captain Vine. 'What is *wrong* with this guy?'

Alarik struck again, sending another suit of armour crashing into the wall. He shoved aside chairs as he moved, stalking the trembling steward all the way around the table.

'You said this was important!' he shouted. 'You stole my war room, displaced me to a damned orangery and then interrupted my meeting for the kind of mindless frivolity even my sister would turn up her nose at.' Deep down, Alarik knew he was overreacting, but his temper had broken free of its short leash. All the stress of the last few months crowded in on him; his feral beasts, his waning army, the rising threat in the north – and worse, the rising fear that he was a weak king, a poor imitation of his father, that the weight of Soren's legacy was slowly crushing him.

Another swing, this one lobbing a helmet across the room, to where Captain Vine ducked to avoid it. 'I think you've made your point,' she said, picking it up and polishing the visor with her sleeve.

Alarik turned on Lief, eyes flashing. 'Have I?'

Lief nodded. 'On reflection, maybe this was a bad time?'

'You think?' snapped Alarik. Only three frock coats remained standing, their glimmering buttons taunting him.

He slammed his foot into one and slashed at another, making his way towards the last one standing. It was a black velvet frock coat, inlaid with gold brocade.

Alarik brought his sword down in an arc, sending the entire suit of armour careening to the ground in a crashing blow.

It yelped as it fell.

Alarik froze.

He blinked, once, twice, the mist of his rage clearing. And then he saw her, a trembling maidservant huddling behind the shattered suit of armour. She was covering her head with her hands and crouched so low in the dimness that had it not been for her scream, he might not have noticed her at all.

The helmet stopped spinning, and silence descended. Alarik stared down at the cowering maid, waiting for her to look up at him. Guilt prickled at the sight of her, but he was not typically in the business of apologizing to servants. Or anyone, for that matter.

He cleared his throat.

Slowly, she raised her head, a pale, heart-shaped face appearing in the cradle of her arms. Her skin was smooth and snow-kissed, save for three silver scars brushing her left cheek. Strange. She stared up at him, her wide eyes caught somewhere between blue and grey. They moved to his right hand, where his blade was still raised.

It occurred to Alarik that she thought he was going to kill her. He quickly sheathed the sword and stepped back. She stood up, brushing a stray copper tendril from her face. Instead of excusing herself, she pointed to the velvet frock coat that lay in ribbons between them and said in a voice that now possessed no fear at all, 'For what it's worth, that one was my favourite.'

For the second time in as many minutes, words deserted Alarik. He watched as she deftly arced around him and bent to retrieve something from the floor. It was the lemon. She frowned as she set it on the table. 'There are people starving throughout your kingdom.' She raised that dauntless gaze, revealing to him the storm of her anger. 'Next time you decide to waste food, you should remember that.'

Alarik bristled at her unrestrained insolence, this mouthy little maidservant who barely reached his collarbone, but she was already turning from him, her steps quickening as she slipped past Captain Vine and hurried from the room without looking back.

All three of them stared after her.

Too late, the king found his voice. 'Who in freezing hell was that?'

Although a part of him was already knitting it all together. Through the fog of his surprise, he had noted the shine of her copper hair and the telltale lilt of her accent, not to mention the fact that she had been waiting for him – seemingly – in his war room.

By the smirk on Vine's face, he could tell she had come to the same conclusion. 'I believe that was your new wrangler.'

An Iversen, then. And one that was sorely in need of an etiquette lesson or two. Alarik's lips twisted, his gaze falling on the crushed lemon. 'I wasn't expecting her to be so—'

'Dainty?' said Lief.

'Short?' guessed Vine.

'*Brazen*,' said Alarik, in a growl. He didn't care if she was his best friend's sister. That wayward wrangler owed him an apology. And a simpering bow. 'Get her back here.'

Vine peered out into the hallway. 'She's long gone.'

But Alarik was already moving, marching from the room like he was going into battle.

CHAPTER 8
Greta

Greta's heart thundered as she bolted down the hallway, trying to put as much space between herself and the king as possible. But no matter how fast she ran, whizzing past bewildered-looking soldiers and startled beasts, she couldn't outrun her own foolishness.

Why had she spoken to him like that? Why had she spoken *at all*?

For days, she had been preparing herself for the importance of this moment, the one upon which the fate of her family rested, and in a few short sentences, she had completely messed it up. Instead of dropping her head in deference and introducing herself properly, she had snapped at Alarik Felsing over a damned lemon.

She had *scolded* the *king of Gevra*.

Stars above. If Tor was here, he'd wilt with disappointment. If Hela found out, she would come down on Greta like a hurricane. And then there was the king himself. Alarik Felsing had been wild-tempered, and yet when the suit of armour fell, revealing her hiding place, her surprised yelp had startled him into silence.

Greta was not foolish enough to consider that silence a reprieve. She had heard too much about the king to think he wouldn't punish her for her insolence. After all, she had disrespected him in his own palace, in front of his steward *and* his war captain.

And then, to make matters worse, she had bolted from him like a frightened doe.

She was *still* bolting from him.

Greta's manners were far from impeccable, but her survival instincts were second to none. She reached the staircase and swung herself around the balustrade, nearly crashing into a maidservant. She shouted an apology over her shoulder as she took the stairs two at a time, nearly barrel-rolling to the bottom. It was not far enough from the glare of that icy gaze or the flash of those sharp canines, which, in the dim lighting of the war room, had made Alarik Felsing look more wolf than man.

And yet, in that interminable moment when she had found herself caught out by the king, she had felt the beast inside her rear up, not in deference but in defiance.

That *stupid* lemon.

It was a dangerous thing, Greta's inborn sense of unbridled honesty. Papa had warned her about it when she was a child, cautioning her to leash her words when she felt her temper rise. Between all the hunting and wrangling, Greta had never quite learned to swallow her tongue. All she could do now was run from the consequences of it.

Another staircase led her down to the atrium, where two stern-faced soldiers stood either side of the front door. She didn't dare flee. That would only make matters worse, and despite her woeful first impression, she still needed this position. Badly.

She headed away from the eye-watering grandeur and priceless tapestries. She needed to go somewhere she could blend in, a place to hide while the king worked through his anger. She would return to find him later, bend her knee and apologize profusely for speaking to him in such a bold manner. In no uncertain terms, she would pledge her support to the palace and its beasts. Hell, she would even take a vow of silence if she had to. She had come too far to return to Carrig empty-handed. She was far more afraid of letting her family down than she was of the king and his diamond-bright gaze.

She followed the sound of growls to the back of the palace where she slipped outside into the chilled morning air. The north wind kissed her cheeks and cooled the fire of her panic. She inhaled the familiar scent of snow and pine and felt her shoulders loosen.

The courtyard sprawled before her in a patchwork of granite and weathered stone. In the centre sat a grand arena hemmed in by a high wall that was gated on two sides. Greta climbed the steps to peer over the wall and noted three separate tunnels leading out of the arena into the vast cedar forest behind the palace, where she could see hundreds of holding pens.

There were three young snow tigers in the arena and twice as many soldiers. They were so frightened she could practically scent their fear as they pressed their backs against the wall, clutching their swords with both hands. The tigers seemed not to notice them at all, and were instead lazing together in a shaft of morning sunlight, licking their paws. Greta smiled, her heart lifting at the sight of the beasts who appeared to be well-kept and even-tempered.

The soldiers on the other hand . . . Captain Vine had her work cut out for her.

Greta rounded the arena until she came to a small hut, tucked away at the far edge of the courtyard. She guessed it was a resting post for soldiers.

She slipped inside, revelling in the delicious blast of heat as she pulled the door shut. The hut was small and dimly lit, populated by a handful of threadbare armchairs, a low wooden table, and a crackling fireplace. There was a soldier reading beside it. He didn't seem to be much older than her, and had a mop of curly black hair, olive skin and dark stubble. He looked up from his book, a quizzical look in his brown eyes.

'Sorry to interrupt your break,' said Greta, offering an awkward wave. She pointed to the chair opposite him. 'Do you mind if I just sit down for a bit?'

He shrugged, smiling. 'Go ahead.'

She slumped into an armchair. 'Thanks. I'm Greta by the way. The new wrangler.'

The soldier slammed his book shut, pitching towards her. 'Thank the stars,' he said, his pearly smile growing. 'I'm Aren. The falconer.'

'*Oh*.' Greta smiled back. Not quite a wrangler, but another animal lover. An ally, she hoped. She was just about to pepper Aren with a hundred questions about Grinstad when the door to the hut swung open and the king stomped inside.

Aren's eyes went wide, his mouth falling into a perfect O.

The king took one look at him and said, 'Evaporate.'

Aren moved so fast he tripped over the door frame.

Greta stood up.

'Not you,' said Alarik, slamming the door behind him and sealing them inside.

Greta's eyes darted, instinctively searching for an escape from his thunderous mood, but the only window was small and frosted shut, and the king was standing in front of the door, his broad shoulders and towering height filling the entire frame. Since it made little difference whether Greta stood or sat, she sank back down into the battered armchair.

Alarik folded his arms as he looked down at her, a muscle working in his jaw. 'So, *you* are my wrangler.'

Greta tried not to bristle at the possessiveness in his tone. She was no one's wrangler. But she had already disrespected the king once today and was not about to test her luck. So, she swallowed her annoyance and nodded. 'My name is Greta Iversen.'

Alarik frowned. 'I was expecting Hela.'

'You didn't ask for Hela.'

His grimace sharpened. 'How old are you?'

Greta blinked. She could feel the icy prickle of his gaze as he assessed her, no doubt cataloguing her diminutive height, her slight frame. He lingered over the scars on her cheek, and her face flared. She wished she had worn her hair down so she could use it as a curtain now. 'Eighteen,' she answered him, and then, feeling like she had something to prove, she jutted her chin out and added, 'I'll be nineteen a week from today.'

A corner of his mouth lifted in a sneer. 'So, you still celebrate your birthday?'

Her cheeks flared again. Damn him. She had meant to prove her maturity, but he was making her feel like a child. 'Is it that unusual to note the passage of time?' she parried, with more bite than she intended.

He cocked his head. 'Are you this bold back on Carrig?'

She frowned. 'No. Yes. I don't know.'

'And are you aware I am the king of Gevra?'

'Of course, I am,' she said, in surprise.

'I just thought there might be some confusion,' he remarked. 'Since I am not in the habit of wearing my crown.'

She sensed he was toying with her. There was no confusing Alarik Felsing. He was like a wolf, all feral grace and simmering brutality. He spoke with such authority, it was hard not to cower beneath him, and even besides the sheer command of his presence, she recognized the sweep of his pale blond hair marred by that single streak of black, and those cruel blue eyes. Then of course, there was the expensive sword and the finery of his outfit, which was worth more than everything Greta and her sisters owned.

'I know you're the king,' she said, again.

He moved closer, the floorboards creaking with each lethal step. 'Then why have you not yet bowed to me?'

Greta dropped her head. 'Majesty,' she muttered.

She could feel the heat of his gaze on the crown of her head, and when she raised it once more, it dropped to the scars on her cheek. He did not ask about them, and she was relieved. Until he opened his mouth again.

'The way you spoke to me just now in the war room was unacceptable.'

'I'm sorry,' said Greta, quietly. Though she regretted her actions, she could not bring herself to take back her words.

'I should have held my tongue.'

He snorted. 'Yes, I can see you're positively ragged with regret.'

She rearranged her face to look more contrite, chewing a little on her bottom lip. 'I didn't mean to interrupt your wedding fitting.'

His eyes flashed. 'Are you attempting a joke, Iversen?'

She shook her head. 'Definitely not.'

'That was not a wedding fitting.'

What it was, was a terrible waste of fine clothes. But this time, she kept her mouth shut. She knitted her hands, pinching at the soft space between her forefinger and thumb. *Be good. Be polite. Be quiet.*

But Greta was none of those things by nature, and in the king's icy presence, she found she wished to rebel against them even harder. Fighting the instinct, she bit down on her tongue.

'Are you frightened of me?'

She frowned again, thinking about it. 'I don't know.'

His voice darkened. 'You should be.'

'Then I am,' she said, looking up at him. She would be whatever he needed her to be. He must have read the thought on her face because he drew back then, huffing a mirthless laugh.

'You are not at all like your brother.'

Greta was not at all like anyone. And that was more the truth of it.

'I'm . . . not very good with people,' she admitted. She didn't *know* very many people beyond her family and Mikkel. She liked it that way, had always preferred the company of animals. They were simpler creatures, easily understood and easily pleased.

'I'm not *people*,' said Alarik. 'I'm a king.' A pause. '*The* king.' Another pause. '*Your* king.'

Greta nodded. Yes, of course. Yes, she understood. *Be good. Be quiet. Even if it rankles you.* It was hard not to squirm under the penetrating light of that frosted glare, but harder still to tear her own gaze from it. Hard not to speak again and say, 'I suppose I'm just . . . more of a beast person.'

'Then think of me as a beast.' She didn't need to hear the growl in the king's voice to know he meant it as a threat. She decided not to tell him she already thought of him that way. He went on. 'Out of respect for my enduring friendship with your brother and the years of loyalty he has shown to the Crown, I will forgive your impertinence this morning and refrain from flinging you into the dungeons.' He flashed his canines. 'Just this once.'

Greta closed her eyes, a whimper of relief catching in her throat. She had not forfeited her position here, after all. She had not dishonoured her family and thrown their future to the wolves.

'Thank you,' she said, opening her eyes and finding herself again snared in his gaze. Only now, she couldn't quite read it, or perhaps understand the curiosity there. The fire crackled in the silence, and she decided it was far too hot inside the little hut. She would give anything to be outside in the wind-whipped arena, sparring with beasts who did not unsettle her so easily.

Alarik looked to the window, his attention turning to the world beyond them. When he spoke again, his words were quick and low. 'You will begin your duties at once. I expect you to attend the next war council. On time and in uniform.'

'And in the orangery?'

He whipped his head towards her. 'Is this funny to you?'

'Not at all.' Greta swallowed her smile. Bad joke. Bad timing. Big mouth. She cleared her throat. 'I don't know anything about war.'

'You are a Gevran. Whether you like it or not, war is in your blood.' Greta didn't like it at all, but she could see no way around that now. 'I expect you to train my beasts to heed my commands. You will attend my war councils and learn the art of war, just as your brother did.' He took a step back, and Greta welcomed the cool whip of air that came between them. 'War is coming to Gevra, and as my wrangler, you will have a part to play in it. That part begins today. Don't let me down, Iversen.'

'I won't,' she said, raising her chin to meet his challenge. Letting down the king meant letting down her family, and she would not damn them to an endless winter of starvation. Not when she had the means to save them.

He nodded in approval. 'Captain Vine will show you around the arena. Today, you will meet the beasts. Tomorrow, you will begin training them.'

He turned to leave, and Greta stood, the words springing from her before she could stop them. 'What about the beast in the mountains?'

The king froze. She watched his shoulders tense, his hands twitching at his sides. For a long moment, he didn't say anything at all, but she could hear him breathing too quickly in the silence.

Slowly, almost cautiously, he turned to look at her, that spark of curiosity returning to his pale blue eyes. They lingered on hers for a beat too long. 'Leave the mountains for now, Iversen.'

'Very well,' she said, on a shallow breath.

He left in a rush of cold wind. Greta slumped into her chair, feeling like she had just faced a blizzard, and only narrowly survived.

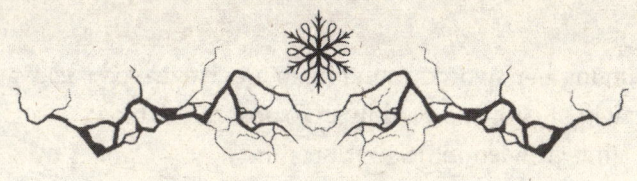

CHAPTER 9
Alarik

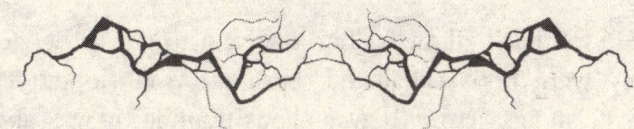

Taking advantage of the fleeting dry spell that followed another night of heavy snowfall, Alarik stood on the frosted lawn of Grinstad Palace, facing off with Captain Vine. They had been sparring all morning. The king's arm was starting to ache, and he was parched, but he could still feel the dull roar of frustration in his bloodstream and was determined to drown it out. To do something useful while he waited for Elias to return from the Blackspires with his report.

Alarik raked his sweat-slicked hair back from his face and raised his sword. 'Again,' he said.

Vine huffed a breath, raising her own weapon. 'We've been at this for three hours. How many more times do you want me to knock you on your—'

Clash!

Alarik struck, their swords meeting in a blinding strike. Vine cursed, ceding a step. Alarik advanced, dealing three more blows in quick succession. 'Careful, Vine. You're flagging.'

'You wish.' Vine pivoted to the left, and the king's next strike met thin air. He stumbled a beat and she twisted, bringing her sword around in an arc. He leaped backwards, drawing his own sword flush to absorb the blow.

Vine growled in frustration.

The king smirked. She really was flagging. He shoved and she tripped, her foot catching a wayward rock. He pounced, but she rolled over before he could pin her with his boot heel.

He fell back, allowing her a second to get to her feet. They were both exhausted, both growing sloppy. This wasn't about victory. It was about training. It was about feeling useful in these interminable moments between preparation and all-out war. It was about drowning out the rush of his own panic and those terrifyingly vivid thoughts of ash clouds rising above the Blackspire Mountains, of his beloved kingdom bowing under the heel of Queen Regna.

Alarik roared as he swung, directing his frustration at a nearby hedge. He lopped off six branches in one go.

'Way to piss off the landscapers.' Vine sheathed her blade. 'I think that's enough for today.'

With a ragged sigh, Alarik lowered his sword. Vine was right. He turned to face the lake. Across the yawning sheen of ice, he watched the reflection of the Fovarr Mountains heaving in the weak sunlight. Not heaving, *breathing*. He jerked his head up, finding the mountains before him. He swore he heard the peaks groaning as they rose and then fell a moment later. Though Vine kept telling him he was imagining the slight movement, Alarik knew he wasn't wrong. And he wasn't the only one at Grinstad who sensed the strangeness in those mountains . . .

Which reminded him.

'Tell me about the wrangler,' he said, as he approached

the lake.

'She's determined,' said Vine, drifting after him. 'She's been working day and night since she arrived last week.'

'Is she making progress?'

'The beasts are falling into line.' A note of admiration had crept into Vine's voice. 'Quicker than I expected.'

'Good,' muttered the king. He had suspected as much. The chorus of howls at Grinstad had already quietened substantially. He was no longer woken in the night by the roars of unsettled beasts or the strangled shouts of his own soldiers.

'Though our soldiers seem to be keeping a wide berth of her,' Vine added, after a beat. 'They don't seem to know what to make of her. Or whether she's worthy of their respect.'

Alarik hmm'd. 'Do you suppose it bothers her?'

Vine shrugged. 'Does it matter?'

Alarik came to a stop at the edge of the lake, peering down at his own glassy reflection. His face was pale and drawn, and his eyes were wild. Even his teeth looked sharper than usual. He recalled with some discomfort the morning he had stalked the Iversen girl into the soldiers' hut and demanded her subservience. How she had faced him with disconcerting ease, like he was no more than one of her beasts. A thing to be called to heel.

Alarik was used to being feared. Even as a scowling child, the servants fled from him. He was used to soldiers watching him from the alcoves as he passed, dipping their chins to avoid his gaze, flinching from the bite of his anger whenever he stalked through the palace halls.

Like the Gevran kings and queens who had come before him, Alarik was a weapon, honed for war. His father had raised him to be strong, not kind. To be fearless. And feared. He was a beast expected to maim and kill to protect his kingdom, a destiny Alarik had always embraced even if it sometimes frightened him. He didn't suffer betrayal or weakness, incompetence or insubordination. He rarely even suffered the company of friends. He was the king, and the king of Gevra stood alone. Not because he wanted to, especially, but because most often, people were too scared to stand anywhere near him.

Once, over a year ago, he thought he had found someone who might stand beside him. A witch with a quiet ferocity of her own. But he had been mistaken about Wren Greenrock. Or more likely, mistaken about himself. Perhaps he was destined to be a lone wolf. Lethal and vicious, always prowling at the edges of war.

And yet the wrangler had shown no fear in his presence. She had just stared at him in a way he was unused to – as though she was studying him, quietly learning the rhythm of his moods. Even now, that sensation of being studied, of being *known*, prickled under his skin. He should have been sterner with her in the hut that day, crueller. He told himself it was his loyalty to her brother, Tor, that had clouded the full might of his anger and made him afford a level of leniency he was not known for. Or perhaps it was desperation that dampened his rage and kept him from throwing her into the dungeons. For months, he had needed a wrangler, and suddenly, there she was, mouthing off in his war room.

Unbelievable.

'As far as I can tell, she keeps mostly to herself,' said Vine, into the silence. 'Although on occasion, she has lunch with the falconer. He, at least, seems to have taken a shine to her.'

Alarik wrinkled his nose. 'I don't care. So long as she stays.'

'She'll stay,' said Vine. 'She needs the coin.'

His chest tightened, a knot forming at those words. They proved his own suspicions true. He'd noticed how slight the Iversen girl was that day in the war room. There were hollows in her cheeks from what he thought must be hunger, and despite the fire of her temper, there was no colour in her cheeks. She was too pale, too small, nothing at all like the soldier her brother had been here – well-fed and well-trained, tall and hulking and thrumming with the strength of ten men. No, it was clear to Alarik now. His wrangler was not just hungry for work. She was hungry for food, for survival. And what of the rest of her family? Wasn't Tor taking care of them?

He jabbed at the ice with his sword, until a crack spiderwebbed across the lake.

'She's up to the task,' said Vine, misreading his frustration. 'She might look more like a doll than a soldier, but she'll do a good job here. She has a way with the beasts. I'm pleased with your choice.'

Alarik nodded. Yes, *that* was what mattered here – that he was pleased with his choice. That his captain was happy. Not that the wrangler was happy with hers. He would pay her handsomely for her work here, and beyond that, her home life was her own business. If the Iversens needed help, Tor would reach out to him. Or more likely, Tor would ask his own queen for subsistence. It was not Alarik's business – not any more.

He shook off the distraction as a figure came crunching across the lawn. It was Elias, the king's spymaster returned at last from the northern mountains. Alarik stalked past Vine, rushing to meet him.

'How bad is it?' he said, by way of greeting.

'That depends on your mood,' said Elias, cagily.

'Spit it out, Elias,' said Alarik.

'Regna is stationing her soldiers twenty miles from the border.'

'How many?'

'Hard to tell. The camps are large. Enough to house fifty thousand soldiers. Maybe more.'

Vine bit off a curse.

'And worse, she's dredged up a war captain from the bowels of hell itself,' Elias went on. 'There are rumours she's hired a mercenary to lead the charge. They call him the Spear. A seven-foot warrior with steel teeth and no fear. They say he runs like a tiger and fights like a blizzard. Undefeated in over twenty years of warfare.'

Alarik remained unmoved. 'Well, there's a first time for everything.'

'The Spear comes from the kingdom of Ryberg. He led Ryberg to war twice without so much as being nicked by an arrow. He kills his enemy's soldiers, then uses their bodies as shields.'

'Sounds impractical,' muttered Vine.

'I won't tell you what he does with their heads.'

'Yes, save *something* for dinner conversation,' said Alarik.

Elias glared between them. 'In Ryberg, children speak of the Spear to frighten each other at bedtime. They say he's not even human.'

'Good thing I'm not a child, then,' said Alarik, folding his arms. 'If this Spear you speak of moves against my country,

I welcome the chance to make the first nick. And the second. And the third.' He flashed his canines. 'Let's see what colour the living legend bleeds on the point of my sword.'

Elias scrubbed a hand across his face.

'Any soldier can be felled,' said Vine, taking heart in Alarik's confidence. 'And for all you've said about the Spear, I've heard nothing of dragons. Or wyverns. Which is a good sign, is it not?'

Elias hesitated.

'It seems that while Regna is still on the hunt for a winged beast of her own, she has had to make do with gliders. Light metal sheaths designed to work as wings.' Alarik didn't know whether to laugh or wince at his cousin's words, but then Elias put his arms out and mimicked a giant bird in flight, causing him to snort.

'Regna is training her soldiers *to fly?*' he said, in disbelief.

Vine chuckled. 'We'll have a battalion and she'll have a *flock*.'

Alarik barked a laugh, scattering the blackbirds along the hedges.

'Regna never could resist the allure of a little invention,' remarked Elias, conceding the barest hint of a smile.

'I, for one, prefer brute force,' said Alarik.

'With any luck, a brisk wind will take them out before they get to us. But in the meantime, I'll double our archers and speak to Vesper about the lances,' said Vine. 'Regna's soldiers will fall the second they try to fly. And our beasts can enjoy the fun of retrieving their bodies. Wings and all.'

For a moment, the wind stilled, and Alarik watched his mountains inhale.

Ignoring his unease, he again looked to his cousin. 'Anything else to report?'

'Just that I'm starving,' said Elias, with a huff. 'I've been riding all night.'

'Come,' said Alarik, turning back towards the palace. 'We'll eat in the war room.'

Alarik was reclining in the war room, with his boots kicked up on the table and his gaze on the bloody battle painting above him, when the servants arrived with lunch, which consisted of two large wooden boards of cured meats and cheeses, an entire tankard of ale, and a loaf of crusty bread so fresh it made Elias pitch forward in his seat.

The iron door had barely closed behind the servants when it whooshed open again. Another platter arrived, carried this time by Lief.

Alarik took one look at his mother's meddlesome steward and swore.

Lief waggled his fingers. 'Good afternoon, Your Majesty. Please pardon my interruption.'

Alarik's eye twitched. 'You must have a death wish, Lief.'

'Certainly not.' Lief chuckled as he set his platter down, before backing up several paces, probably in case the king decided to lunge across the table and throttle him. 'No death wish, just this array of delicious tiny cakes.' He swept his hand towards the silver platter which contained several miniature frosted cakes. 'They are a gift from Queen Valeska.'

Elias and Vine exchanged a bewildered look.

Alarik was still glaring at the steward. 'I did not ask for cake.'

'Why, that is the very nature of a gift, Your Majesty. You do not need to ask for it.' The steward shuffled uncomfortably. 'And every wedding must have a cake.'

There was a finger-snap of deadly silence. Then Alarik lunged across the table. Vine shot up, dragging him back before he could strangle the steward. 'Calm down,' she said. 'It's just cake.'

'*Wedding cake*,' hissed Alarik.

'Who cares what kind of cake it is,' said Elias, dragging the platter towards them. 'Sugar is sugar. If you ask me, we could all do with some right about now.'

'Then *you* can marry the princess that comes with it,' muttered Alarik.

He flashed a wolfish smile. 'Oh no, *Majesty*. That esteemed honour belongs to the king.'

Lief tiptoed closer. 'The dowager queen has instructed me not to leave this room until you have chosen your favourite cake . . .'

Alarik returned his glare to the steward. 'Do you wish to play the jailor?'

Lief paled. 'No, thank you.'

Vine sighed. 'Tell us about the cakes, Lief.'

He pressed his palms together gratefully, then quickly went on. 'Well, first, as you see, we have a delightful sponge with strawberry jam and fresh cream, sprinkled with a fine dusting of powdered sugar.'

Vine swiped up the tiny cake and bit into it. 'Perfect,' she said, through a stuffed mouth. 'I choose this one.'

Lief glanced uncertainly at the king, before going on.

'Next to it, we have a delicate lavender sponge with gooseberry jam, topped with rich whorls of buttercream—'

Elias devoured it in two bites. 'You won't beat this one,' he said, swallowing thickly. 'But feel free to try.'

'Traitors.' Alarik leaned back and closed his eyes, wishing he was anywhere but here. Hell, he'd take afternoon tea with the Spear over this particular brand of boredom.

'And our third cake is infused with lemon curd and—'

'No,' Alarik barked, surprising himself. He snapped his eyes open and sat forward. 'No lemon.'

Lemons made him think of his wrangler. *There are people starving throughout your kingdom. Next time you decide to waste food, you should remember that.* That undisguised ire in her eyes, then the unwelcome twist in his chest at her words, each one as precise as a blade.

Lief blinked in surprise, but perhaps feeling relieved to have the king's input at all, he complied, placing two of the little cakes to one side. Elias and Vine made quick work of them.

Alarik's head was beginning to pound. 'That's enough,' he said, wearily.

Lief frowned at the remaining cakes. 'The dowager queen really did insist that I—'

'Which one is my mother's favourite?' said Alarik, eager to bring a swift end to this ridiculous charade. 'She has curated these options, so she has clearly tried all of them already. It wouldn't surprise me if she's hiding outside the door right now, listening in. So, just tell me, Lief, which one is her favourite?'

Lief pointed to the smallest cake, a perfect, three-tiered circle. The white icing was gold dusted and decorated in delicate purple flowers. 'The dowager queen is partial to this passion fruit and white chocolate one. The fruit itself is extraordinary. It comes all the way from—'

'Fine,' said Alarik, shoving the platter away. 'I choose that one. Now, get out.'

Lief scooped up the platter. 'Very well, Your Majesty. Thank you for your speedy—'

'*Go*,' snarled the king.

Lief was halfway out the door, when the king shot up in his seat, an idea occurring to him so quickly, he didn't have time to second-guess it. 'Wait.'

The steward paused.

'Leave the cake on the table. Go find a candle. As small as your baby finger.'

Vine looked at him strangely. Elias was now too engrossed in the cheeseboard to care.

'Right away, Your Majesty.' The steward set the platter down as instructed, then scurried off without daring to question his king. Alarik waited for the door to close, then turned back to the table, ignoring the sparkling little cake and reaching instead for a curl of meat.

'Right,' he said, turning his gaze to the bloody painting above him, as though the previous interruption had never happened. 'Back to war.'

CHAPTER 10
Greta

Greta Iversen never imagined she would be spending her nineteenth birthday in Grinstad Palace. Or any birthday, for that matter. Not that she felt much like celebrating.

She had only been at the palace for a week, but the work here was grinding and ceaseless. There were over two hundred and fifty beasts to train and most of them were either half wild or entirely unused to behaving properly. Greta had been rising each morning at dawn, shovelling down a quick breakfast of porridge heaped with honey in the dining hall before grabbing a flask of hot tea and hurrying out to the courtyard to see to the beasts. She had spent the first two days introducing herself to the beasts, cautiously approaching their pens and coming to her haunches, removing her gloves and offering the back of her hand through the bars for them to sniff. To show them she was a friend and not a foe.

For the most part, the beasts had acclimatized quickly to her presence. Those that were slow to trust received extra attention and meaty lamb chews. Food; the best persuasion for beasts and men.

Despite the long hours, Greta had already picked out her favourites. She spent her mornings with the ice bears, the oldest of whom were a pair of sisters called Baldur and Nel. Tor had told Greta about them some years ago and she had been delighted to find them still in residence at the palace when she arrived, if a little battle-scarred. Baldur was missing her right ear and Nel had lost half of her teeth and all the claws on her left paw. Then there was Saga, the heavily pregnant snow leopard, who was not yet trainable but particularly sweet-natured for her kind. Greta visited her in the afternoons, often climbing into the holding pen and humming to the beast to set her at ease. Earlier that day, as though sensing that Greta was missing home, Saga had curled up on the hay beside Greta and rested her large head in Greta's lap, her snuffling breaths a warm comfort.

But it was the wolves that Greta loved the most. Tollo and Gale were favourites, a pair of greybacks with amber eyes, who reminded her of her own beloved Lupo. Only these two were younger and far more prone to mischief. Yesterday evening, she had been late to dinner having spent over an hour chasing after Tollo and wrestling a live chicken from his jaws.

She was making fine progress, training the king's beasts to heel on her command. Soon, she would train them to snap and leap, and finally, to attack. Yes, the beasts here were easy. It was the soldiers she found tough.

Every evening, as the last of the guards trickled out of the courtyard, not a single one spared even a parting glance in her direction. Greta tried to convince herself she didn't care. She hadn't come here to make friends. And yet . . . a basic modicum of respect – or even a shred of conversation here and there – might have been nice.

It seemed the soldiers at Grinstad were as icy as their king. They weren't interested in welcoming an interloper from Carrig, a girl with no discernible combat skills, who was barely taller than some of the beasts here. No doubt they thought her a poor replacement for the mighty Captain Tor Iversen. A poor wrangler, too. Not that they ever watched her training sessions long enough to see for themselves.

Of course they were wrong. But their frostiness still needled Greta. She was grateful, at least, for the kindness of Aren, who would come and visit her down by the pens whenever his schedule allowed. She had missed him today. Though not half as much as she missed her sisters.

Back on Carrig, Kindra always made Greta's favourite butter cake on her birthday, jostling her awake at the crack of dawn so the three sisters could make the most of the day together. Greta had never spent her birthday alone before.

As she returned the last of the beasts to their pens in the forest to rest, the pang in her heart grew. Sighing, she pocketed the keys to the arena in her fur-lined frock coat and turned for bed, reminding herself that she was doing important work here. Work that would feed her family and make her mother well again. She did not regret coming to Grinstad, and she did not want to go back yet, no matter how out of place she felt.

It was all right to feel lonely today. Tomorrow would be brighter.

It was late by the time Greta returned to her bedchamber, and the oil lamps were already lit. Her stomach rumbled at the lingering smell of stew. She had missed dinner, and although the soldiers' dining hall was closed for the night, Nanna had left a bowl of food on her desk. Although the curmudgeonly old maidservant would likely never admit it, still, she fretted over Greta like a reluctant mother hen. On Greta's second day at Grinstad, Nanna had insisted on altering her oversized uniform to fit her, taking up the hem of her trousers and the sleeves of her blue frock coat, even cinching the waist to keep it from swamping her.

Greta shrugged off her coat now, letting it fall to the floor with a satisfying thunk. She undid the buttons on her trousers and kicked off her boots, then sank into her chair. She devoured the stew in record time, revelling in every single mouthful of mashed potato, glazed carrot and tender lamb, all drowned in rich gravy. The food at Grinstad alone was almost worth the sacrifice of being so far from home. Despite the long days, Greta could feel herself getting stronger, the abundance of red meat and fresh vegetables doing wonders for her energy. Already, the hollows in her cheeks had faded and there was colour in her face again.

After eating, she unbraided her hair and went to wash up in the bathing chamber, scrubbing the day's dirt from her skin and washing her hair with scented soap until she no longer smelled like a beast herself. When she finished getting ready for bed, she had to fight the urge to bury herself in the warm furs and instead returned to her desk. She had promised her father she would write and had already let a week pass without so much as a single word to her family. With guilt prickling inside her, she set aside her exhaustion and fished out her journal.

For a long time, the only sound was the light scratching of her pen and the echo of a restless wolf howling at the moon. Greta smiled as she wrote, the distant chorus reminding her of Carrig. Perhaps she was not so far from home after all. She began by telling her father about the palace, describing the towering fortress of glass and stone, the mountains that moved as though they were drawing breath. Then she spoke of the beasts, the ice bears and the wolves, pregnant Saga who would give birth any day now. She mentioned the people who had been kind to her. Nanna, in her own quiet, busy way and Aren, the falconer, who, when time allowed, would make Greta a mint tea to warm her hands between training sessions.

She wrote of Astrid Vine, the king's formidable yet kind war captain, knowing her family would be interested to know about Tor's replacement. But her pen slowed when her thoughts turned to the king himself, how angry he had been that day in the hut with her, how he had loomed over her like an ice bear, nothing but frost in those pale blue eyes.

Greta did not dare mention that particular incident in her letter. For one thing, she didn't want Papa to worry about her. But more pressingly, she didn't want to be scolded for making such a terrible first impression on the most important man in Gevra. And besides, what if the king intercepted all outgoing post from Grinstad and didn't like the way she wrote about him? That would constitute a most unfortunate second impression. No, Greta would stick to the beasts and say nothing of the raging king, his rude soldiers, or the prospect of war creeping towards them like a dark mist.

She had almost finished her letter when a knock at the door made her jolt. A glance at the clock on the wall told her it was almost midnight. She rose from her chair, suddenly conscious of her nightgown as she eased the door open.

It was a night servant, a young man with pale skin and wide grey eyes. He was carrying what looked like a miniature cake, adorned with purple flowers and a single flickering candle. He held it out in offering.

'For you,' he said, clearing his throat.

Greta looked from the man's face to the candle and back again, blinking in utter confusion. If she didn't know better, she'd swear this was a birthday cake, but nobody here knew it was her birthday. She hadn't made mention of it all day. 'From whom?' she inquired, politely.

The servant looked at his boots. 'The kitchen sent it up.'

Greta stared at him a moment longer, and then sensing his discomfort, or perhaps disinterest in this particular mystery, thanked him and took the cake. He left at once, and she eased the door shut. She set the cake on her desk, marvelling at the delicate flowers and gold-dusted icing.

There was a notecard on the side of the plate.

She snatched it up to find two words, scrawled in haste.

Happy Birthday

Had her family sent it, somehow? She shook the thought off, embarrassed to have considered it. What a selfish notion. There was barely enough money back on Carrig to purchase a bale of hay, let alone the fanciest cake Greta had ever seen. The cost of delivery alone would bankrupt her family.

She sat and stared at the tiny cake, as though it might

reveal the mystery of itself if she waited long enough. The flame flickered, taunting her.

She frowned. There was no sense in wasting a perfectly good wish. It was her birthday, after all. Wherever this cake had come from, it meant that someone, somewhere, was thinking of her. The thought warmed her heart and chased the sadness from her bones.

She smiled and closed her eyes.

I wish for things to get better.

She pictured Carrig in those better days, the verdant hills bursting with flowers, the wild beasts running through the sun-dappled trees, the colourful fishing boats creaking under the weight of their hauls, and the sound of laughter mingling with birdsong in the wind.

She blew out the candle and sent her wish up to the stars, hoping for those better days. For something to truly celebrate. When she opened her eyes to a faint plume of smoke, a memory curled up with it, and she stiffened as she recalled her conversation with the king last week.

I'll be nineteen a week from today.

She had told him her birthday was approaching, and he had sneered at her.

So, you still celebrate your birthday?

She frowned at the gold-dusted cake.

No. There was *no way* it had come from Alarik Felsing. She doubted he even remembered her saying that, or cared enough to keep track of the days since. The thought alone was laughable. Why would the king of Gevra send her a cake? Why would he send *anyone* a cake? She snorted at her own absurdity. There was obviously another, simpler explanation, but right now she didn't need one. She jabbed her fork into the cake and devoured her first mouthful, groaning in pleasure.

Gold dust coated her lips as she chewed, her mouth watering as white chocolate danced on her tongue. She detected sugary buttercream and fresh sponge, and the sweet and sour tang of a fruit she had never tasted before. It was so divine she smiled through every single bite.

Happy birthday indeed, she thought, welcoming the fizz of sugar in her bloodstream as she crawled into bed. She was still smiling when she fell asleep.

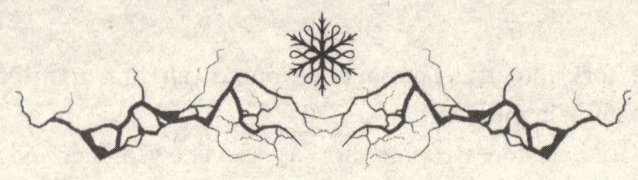

CHAPTER 11
Alarik

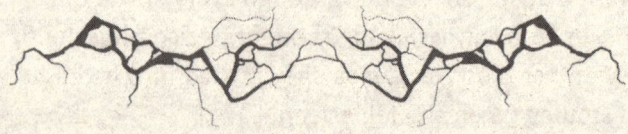

Alarik was getting dressed in his bedchamber when he heard the drums again. He stilled, sure he was imagining the thrum in the wind, just like before. Only this time, Nova was growling, and Luna had woken from sleep with her hackles raised.

The king bit off a curse as he fled his dressing room with his shirt half buttoned. The drums were getting louder, matching the thunder of his pulse. He grabbed his sword on instinct and ran to the balcony, steeling himself for the sight of Queen Regna's soldiers storming the mountains around Grinstad.

But that was not what awaited the king of Gevra as he leaped on to his balcony. The drums were real, but they were not the steel war barrels of Vask. They were made of vellum and oak. They cast a soft and steady rhythm, like a hum coming up from the earth.

Not a threat, but a greeting.

The twenty-strong troop that carried them were dressed in fitted uniforms of olive green, trimmed in silver. They wore tall helmets that obscured their faces, but Alarik knew those colours just as he knew the flag they carried. He recognized the outline of dark green mountains cresting under a full moon.

These soldiers had come from Halgard.

Understanding curdled in Alarik's gut. He looked past the procession and saw the royal carriage at the end, a large wooden coach pulled not by horses but four towering weaver elk, their jutting gold antlers glimmering in the sunlight.

He knew precisely who was sitting in that carriage. Not just a princess, but the fruits of his mother's plotting these past few weeks.

'*No,*' he muttered, squeezing his eyes shut, wishing he could blink it all away.

A knock sounded on his bedroom door and Johan burst inside, without waiting for permission.

'Your Majesty!' he huffed. 'Your presence is requested in the entrance hall. The princess of Halgard has . . .' He trailed off at the sight of Alarik standing on his balcony, wearing a look of such horror, it stopped Johan in his tracks. 'Ah . . . you've already . . . figured that out . . .'

Despite the dull roar of his panic, Alarik had the good sense to step in from his balcony before Princess Elva of Halgard peered out through the drapes in her carriage and noticed the king, half dressed and scowling at her arrival.

Back in his bedchamber, Alarik paced the floor, raking his hands through his hair.

How long had it been since he first met with his mother in her tower? When had he made her that vague promise he never intended to keep? Weeks had passed with little thought of anything but warfare, and now it was too late to stop this madness. The princess was already here. With her drums and her elk. Her expectations of marriage.

Freezing hell.

He groaned into his hands, trying to find a way to undo the machinations of his mother's grand scheme, but it had already gone too far. The Halgard delegation was inside his gates. He couldn't turn them away. Any move to reverse their course would be seen as a terrible diplomatic sleight at best, and at worst, an act of war. Alarik had enough war on his hands already.

Johan cleared his throat. 'Your Majesty,' he said, daring to step closer. 'Is there anything I can do?'

Alarik shook his head mournfully. 'Where is my mother?'

'She's in the entrance hall, preparing to welcome the princess.'

'Of course she is,' Alarik muttered. He released a long string of swear words. Then briefly considered locking his door and crawling back into bed for the rest of the week. But that was the action of a boy, not a man. Certainly not a king. No, he must make the best of this unfortunate situation. Halgard was a valuable ally, and even if he had no intention of marrying its princess, he intended to keep their loyalty.

Somehow.

'Go,' he said, waving Johan off. 'I'll be down shortly.'

Alarik finished getting dressed, choosing a pair of fitted black trousers and a plain black frock coat to mourn the death of his own free will.

Vine was waiting for him at the end of the hallway, looking impeccable in her uniform, and with her hands dug into her pockets. She frowned as she looked him over.

'Whose funeral is it?'

'Yours, if you piss me off today.'

'Did you even brush your hair?'

He glared at her.

She flashed him a smile. 'Oh, cheer up. Today might be fun.'

'For whom?' he groused, stalking past her. 'Don't you have somewhere else to be?'

'No way,' she said, matching him stride for stride. 'I wouldn't miss this for all the frostfizz in Grinstad.'

Alarik rolled his eyes but refrained from biting back. Despite his anger, he was glad not to have to face this particularly excruciating moment alone.

When he reached the top of the stairs that led down to the entrance hall, he paused to take in the bustle below. The Halgard delegation, which included a host of soldiers and courtiers, were milling about the atrium, admiring the tapestries and cautiously observing the beasts.

Alarik heard the trill of his mother's laughter wafting through the air and thought for a moment he was hallucinating. The sound was so foreign to him now, he almost didn't recognize it.

'At least one of you is enjoying this,' remarked Vine.

Alarik surrendered a sigh. Given the choice, he would always place his mother's happiness above his own. It was just a shame that her joy this morning had to come at the expense of his. There was no sign of Lief anywhere. For all he knew, the meddlesome little turd was erecting a wedding chapel somewhere.

The dowager queen was dressed in a velvet gown of midnight blue, the silver-fur sleeves catching the light as she moved to embrace Princess Elva, who stepped through the doors of the palace with such confidence it looked like she had been living there her whole life.

'Holy snow,' muttered Vine, sweeping her gaze over the foreign princess.

Alarik glanced sidelong at his captain. 'You're drooling, Vine.'

She folded her arms. 'This might be the only time in my life that I've ever felt jealous of you.'

Alarik snorted. Whatever spell had fallen over Vine had entirely evaded the king. He didn't care how beautiful the princess was, how easily she glided into his palace or how effortlessly she commanded each conversation she stepped into, greeting his servants with the same warmth she had afforded to his mother. For more than a year now, the door to Alarik's heart had been bolted shut. He intended to keep it that way. There was no princess on this continent, or any other, that could ever hope to open it.

He tucked his hands behind his back as he drifted downstairs, all the while assessing Princess Elva. She was certainly attractive, possessing the kind of beauty that reminded him of oil paintings from previous centuries. She was tall, almost as tall as he was, in fact, with thick golden hair arranged into a crown of intricate braids threaded with silver ribbon. On top, she wore a simple silver diadem.

Her gown was pale green. It tapered at the waist and had long, billowing sleeves that made her look ethereal. Her face was sun-kissed, with a strong jaw and high cheekbones to match the arch of her brows. She had bright teeth and brown eyes, the crinkles around them hinting at a merry disposition.

Princess Elva looked up from her conversation with Queen Valeska just as Alarik stepped off the stairwell, as though she had been subtly tracking his descent the entire time. They locked eyes across the bustling atrium, and a hush came over the hall, soldiers and servants drawing breath as they gazed upon this fateful moment – a meeting, not just of two future lovers, but of two kingdoms.

Alarik offered a small, practised smile as he came towards her. Princess Elva returned it, striding to meet him. She raised her hand, and he took it, barely brushing his lips against the back of it. Her gaze met his, and he startled a little. For what he saw there was not warmth or excitement, as he was expecting, but rather a strange sort of amusement, as though they had found themselves in the same game.

'You are most welcome to Grinstad, Princess Elva,' he lied, effortlessly.

She quirked a brow. 'It is a pleasure to be here among your people, King Alarik.'

He sensed a lie in her words, too, but that perfect smile never wavered.

Valeska drifted over, taking Alarik by the arm. 'My son, Alarik. Isn't he handsome, Elva?'

Alarik winced. '*Mother*.'

'I dare say I've never seen a more handsome Gevran,' said Elva, with a smirk.

Valeska looked to Alarik, eyes shining. 'And isn't Elva a beauty?'

'A rare treasure indeed,' said Alarik.

Queen Valeska beamed. 'You two must take tea together. After such a long journey, Princess Elva must be starving.'

'*Famished*,' the princess confirmed.

'I'll have Nanna take care of your retinue,' said Valeska, sweeping away.

'Come,' said Alarik, offering his arm to Elva in a bid to outrun all the eyes trained on them. She took it eagerly, and they hurried out of the atrium without so much as a backward glance.

'You should know I have no plans to fall in love with you,' Princess Elva said between sips of cinnamon and apple tea. 'And I won't be persuaded otherwise.'

Alarik's brows rose, her candour so refreshingly unexpected that he almost laughed. 'Trust me, Princess, I have no plans to seduce you.'

'Good. Because you will not succeed.'

'Consider my ego sufficiently dented.'

'You're not my type,' she amended, a touch more tactfully. 'No offence.'

Alarik stared at the princess as she reached for a sliver of salmon rolled with cream cheese and chives. They were seated across from each other in the cedar lounge in the south wing, a decadent tea room warmly lit by two fireplaces and decorated with rich furs and accents of forest green. The candles here all smelled like pine, and the draped furniture was made of pale oak.

'Now that we've got your revulsion for me out of the way, what else do I need to know about you?' said Alarik, refilling his coffee cup. 'Are you interested in this marriage?'

She swallowed her mouthful. 'Are you?'

'Not remotely,' he said, matching her candour with his

own. He sat back in his chair, kicking one leg over the other. 'Does that offend you?'

'Mortally. Consider *my* ego sufficiently dented.' Her smile curled. 'I don't care for marriage one way or another. It's the alliance my father favours.'

'And you?' said Alarik. 'What do you favour?'

She leaned forward, brown eyes wide with wonder. 'I favour adventure,' she whispered, as though telling him a secret. 'And Gevra is a great adventure. Your mountains. Your glaciers. Your beasts. Your endless snow.' She spoke with such awe, it softened Alarik's mood. At least Elva recognized the worth of his country, if not its king. 'So, I intend to stay a while and try it out. We can endure each other.'

'*Endure?*' Alarik arched a brow. 'For all you know, I might be great company.'

She canted her head. 'Is any king on the verge of war great company?'

'So, you know about that.'

'Everyone on the northern continent knows of Queen Regna's ambitions,' she said, with a snort. 'Secrecy is a foreign concept to her.'

'And you are not frightened?'

'Why would I be frightened of your war? We may lend you our soldiers, but I certainly do not plan to fight in it. If I wanted to get my head lopped off, I'd think of something more original.'

'If you like, I can have my ice bear eat you once he comes out of hibernation,' offered Alarik.

Her eyes danced. 'I cannot wait to meet your beasts.'

As though she had willed it with her excitement, the

door to the cedar lounge swung open and Captain Vine appeared in a swell of panic. 'Sorry to interrupt,' she said, eyes darting between them and lingering for a moment on the princess. 'There's been an, uh, incident out back.'

Alarik set his cup down. 'What kind of incident?'

A ragged scream rang out.

'That kind,' said Vine, grimly. 'One of the beasts has turned.'

Alarik shot to his feet. 'Where's the wrangler?'

'I have no idea.'

Alarik was already stalking to the door. 'Wait here, Princess. You'll be—'

'Right behind you,' said Elva, scurrying after him, and batting his hand away firmly when he tried to stop her. 'I'm not missing this.'

Vine raised her brows, looking impressed. Another desperate cry echoed through the palace. There was no time to argue. Alarik turned to his war captain. 'Stick with the princess. Don't let her out of your sight.'

Alarik bolted through the palace and tore out into the courtyard. Chaos had descended there, soldiers screaming as they scattered, most too frightened to even notice the king standing in their midst.

Alarik tracked the terror all the way around the back of the arena, where the stone courtyard bled into a grassy field, and beyond it, the forest where the beasts were kept. Up ahead, two soldiers were tending to another who had passed out in the dirt. Not far from them, another soldier wailed as she clutched her bloodied leg, the man beside her whimpering as he cradled his dislocated shoulder.

Alarik did not have to search long for the source of their

distress. Right on the treeline, a large snow leopard was stalking back and forth, attacking anyone who came near it. There was blood around its maw, on its underbelly and dripping from its fangs.

Alarik crept towards the beast, craning his neck for a glimpse of his wayward wrangler. *Where in freezing hell was she?* Panic stirred, tightening like a vice around his chest. His eyes darted, his blood chilling. There was no sign of the Iversen girl anywhere. Just this rabid creature, who was making mincemeat of his soldiers.

He pushed on, desperately scanning the trees.

The leopard stilled as he approached, its hackles rising.

He pointed his sword at the beast and roared, 'HEEL!'

The leopard released a rasping cry. A warning. Alarik drew a steadying breath, his father's words ringing in his head. *A king who bows to his beasts is no king at all.*

He walked on, hissing through his teeth, *'Heel.'*

The leopard began to circle him as he approached. It was then that he saw the blood trailing from its holding pen. No. *No.* He tried not to picture his wrangler's body inside it, but he couldn't unsee her glazed blue-grey eyes, that slight frame curled in on itself, pale hands turned stiff and blue.

It was his own terrible mistake. Reckless, desperate fool that he was. To throw her to his beasts without proper assessment, without training. It was her blood on his hands. Her loss gutting his chest. Tor would never forgive him. He would storm the palace and tear Alarik limb from limb, kill the thoughtless king who had carelessly thrown his sister to his beasts without bothering to check in on her for days.

Shame flooded Alarik, a tidal wave of self-hatred coming on the heels of his fear.

'HEEL!' he roared again.

The beast roared back.

The leopard was beyond training. Beyond repair. Alarik raised his sword as it sprung towards him. He struck, bringing his sword down just as another cry rang out.

'DON'T HURT HER!'

Alarik didn't see his wrangler until she was leaping in front of him. She crashed right into the leopard, throwing her arms around its neck and knocking it to the ground, just as his sword came down and skewered the dirt.

Alarik froze, his blade embedded less than a foot from his wrangler's neck. His hands trembled as he unstuck it from the earth, staring down at her like she was some kind of an apparition. Not his wrangler but a ghost who, for some incomprehensible reason, had just thrown her body between a rabid beast and the point of his sword.

He blinked, but the spectre remained. She was scrabbling now, not to get away from the beast but to cling tighter to it, crawling over its torso, through blood and fur and dirt, until she was covering it with her own body. She turned then, blinking up at Alarik through blood-streaked strands of copper hair.

At the sight of her rasping for breath below him, relief swept through Alarik like a cold breeze. A fleeting breath of calm before his anger exploded from him. 'WHAT IN FREEZING HELL ARE YOU DOING?'

She swiped her hair from her face so he could see the same rage reflected in her eyes. 'Saving this poor animal from your temper tantrum!'

Alarik's eyes widened, his blood pounding so hard, he almost raised his sword again. He leashed his temper, all too aware of his soldiers gathering at his back, feasting their eyes on the spectacle. 'Get up, Iversen,' he growled. 'Let me put this beast down.'

'*No.*' She cut her eyes at him. 'If you wish to kill Saga, you'll have to kill me first.'

Alarik jerked, like he had been struck. He stared hard at her and knew by the crack of lightning in her eyes that she was deadly serious. Not only would she die for this feral leopard, but she would also likely fight him for her. And something about that made his blood roar even louder, until the rest of the world fell away entirely – the soldiers and the blood and the trees and the wind – until it was just the king and his wrangler, locked in a seething glare that suddenly felt far more dangerous than the beast trapped between them.

CHAPTER 12
Greta

Greta did not dare take her eyes off the king. He did not take his eyes off her. They were brighter than she had ever seen them, as cold and hard as chips of ice. His fingers twitched around the hilt of his sword, like he was thinking about killing her. Killing them both.

Brutal wretch.

Her breath punched out of her, her chest rising and falling in sharp heaves. She should have known better than to leave Saga unguarded, even for a moment. She should have known better than to trust the king's useless gaggle of soldiers to actually follow her orders and keep their distance. The king was brutal, yes, but *she* was the fool here.

This was her mess. Her fault.

She raised her chin, finding strength in the flood of her adrenaline. 'Please, just listen to me,' she said, calmly. 'I will explain.'

The snow leopard let out a strangled mewl. Greta's heart ached as the thrum of Saga's anxiety brushed up against her own. She scented the acrid tang of her terror, and feared the creature might bolt any second, likely right into the king's sword. She turned her face into the leopard's fur and hummed, low and soft to settle her panic. 'It's all right,' she murmured. 'I've got you.'

The leopard snuffled, then fell still. When Greta looked back at the king he was staring at her as though he had never seen her before.

'What are you doing?' he said, in a low voice.

'Wrangling,' said Greta, keeping her voice soft. 'She's frightened.'

'Imagine how my soldiers feel.'

'That's not my job.'

His nostrils flared. 'What did you just say?'

She swallowed, thickly. 'I'm here to take care of your beasts. Not your soldiers.'

'You're here to *tame* my beasts,' he barked. 'Not set them on my soldiers.'

Greta's eyes flashed, her words coming fast and sharp. 'Your soldiers set themselves on her!'

'Enough,' he hissed. 'Get up, Iversen. I won't ask you again.'

Greta quailed as the heat of his anger rolled against her. His jaw clenched the same moment as his fist, the sword rising over her. She had pushed him too far, protected one beast only to corner another. If she wasn't careful, he really would strike her. And she did not wish to die here in the dirt. She would not let her temper destroy the fate of her family.

'I will get up, Your Majesty,' she said, a plea in her voice. 'But when I do, please let me return Saga to her pen.'

'You are in no position to bargain with me, wrangler.' He flicked his sword, gesturing at her to hurry up. 'That beast will be meeting the swift point of this blade before she can do any more damage.'

Panic flared inside Greta. Sensing the shift in her mood, the leopard released a rasping cry.

'There's been a terrible misunderstanding.' Greta sat up, still using her body as a shield.

'Of what sort?' sneered the king. 'Did your pet mistake my soldiers for a sack of feed?'

'Of course not,' she snapped, bristling at his tone. So much for leashing her temper. 'Saga was protecting her family when those dead-brained oafs you call soldiers barrelled into her pen.' The king's eyes widened at her words. Greta ploughed on. 'Saga gave birth to cubs this morning. I had to step away briefly, but I left orders that she was not to be disturbed. Her pen should not have been opened.' She clenched her fists, digging her nails into her palms. 'Your soldiers didn't care to listen to those orders. They chose not to listen to me. They thought they knew better, so they stormed into her pen anyway and decided to prod at her cubs for their own amusement.'

Alarik frowned, his gaze flitting over his shoulder to where a group of soldiers were hovering by the treeline, nervously watching their exchange.

'Perhaps they did not know,' he muttered.

'Or perhaps they did not care,' said Greta, pointedly. And that was the truth of the matter. She might have garnered the respect of Grinstad's beasts, but many of its soldiers still looked down on her. More than once, she had overheard them talking about her in the hut. They thought her too weak and too small, too easily startled. She saw how they stared too long at her scars and knew they passed judgement about her skills as a wrangler because of them.

To most of the king's soldiers, she was just a lowly farmgirl, flung too far from home. A poor addition to their courtyard and a shoddy replacement for her brother. No, Greta was nothing at all like the brave and fearless Tor Iversen. A man of beast and war.

She brushed it all off. Other people's opinions never mattered to her. It was the beasts she had come for, the beasts she cared for, but today, the soldiers' lack of respect for her position had caused unnecessary carnage and she would not let Saga pay for it.

'If your soldiers possessed even half the sense of a common moth, they would know a mother will always attack to defend her cubs. *Especially* right after giving birth.'

He cast his eyes at her. 'You should have told them as much.'

'What makes you think I didn't?' she replied. 'It's not my fault they don't listen to me. I only hope they listen to *someone* around here. Otherwise, there's no hope for them on whatever battlefield you find yourself next.'

The king curled his lip. 'You certainly have a lot of thoughts in your head, Iversen.'

'Someone around here should,' she said, before she could stop herself. It was too late now. She might as well go down swinging.

Alarik glowered at her words, but Greta was beyond caring. She could hear the distant squall of Saga's cubs and knew the leopard was seconds from bolting.

She leaped to her feet and rolled her shoulders back. Undaunted. Unyielding. 'I'm taking Saga back to her cubs. You are welcome to join me.'

Before the king could formulate a retort – or worse, swing his sword – she spun on her heel and gave a low whistle. Saga sprung to her feet and ran for her pen, Greta jogging a few steps behind the leopard to guard her back. Without the shield of her adrenaline, her panic returned with a vengeance.

You foolish girl, scolded the voice in her head. *You've disrespected the king and squandered your future, all over the fate of a snow leopard.*

Greta shook off the words, but more came in their place, taunting her. The king would never forgive her for such impertinence. She had yelled at him, threatened him, faced his sword and all but mocked him in front of his soldiers. She curled her fists, blinking back her tears.

Don't let them see you cry. Don't let them see you break.

There came the telltale crunch of footsteps behind her. She didn't dare look back to see if the king was following, but she prayed it was he and not one of his soldiers come to drag her off to the dungeons. More than that, she wanted Alarik Felsing to see what she had fought for just now. She wanted him to look upon Saga's litter and understand the kind of joy that sparked at the other side of warfare. Not death, but life. Two perfect cubs, like matching tufts of mewling snow. Both blind and helpless, crying out for their mama.

Saga darted inside her pen, snuffling as she returned to her cubs. Greta felt the creature's relief like a breath of cool wind as she lingered by the gate, watching them.

'So, you are not a liar, at least,' said a voice close to her ear. 'Just a brat.'

Alarik Felsing stood behind her, peering over her shoulder

into the pen.

Greta stiffened at his sudden nearness. 'I'm not a brat.'

'An impudent terror, then.'

She turned to glare at him, her hair brushing the underside of his chin. 'These are your precious beasts. If they live, they will ultimately serve you, like the rest of us. Surely even *you* would not enjoy striking down a new mother and leaving her newborn cubs to die?'

He dipped his chin to return her glare, suddenly so close they were sharing the same breath. 'What makes you think I *enjoy* striking down anyone?'

'Everything I've ever heard about you,' she said, before thinking.

'Do you talk about me often, Iversen?'

'Hardly ever, in fact.'

'Then you don't know me,' he said, curtly. '*Or* what I enjoy. So, you may refrain from guessing.'

'Fine,' she said, conceding the point. She looked away, suddenly all too aware of his body half curled around hers, how his breath ruffled her hair. 'The sight of those cubs might not tug at your heartstrings, but you must admit it would be a terrible waste of resources to harm their mother. They would die without her. Someday, one of them might save your life in battle.'

'You have made your case, wrangler.' Greta could have sworn she detected a hint of amusement in the king's voice. 'Your little leopard will live to maim another day.'

She turned around, pressing her back against the fence. 'That's not funny.'

As if only just realizing how close they were standing, the king cleared his throat and stepped away from her. He frowned as his gaze dropped to her filthy coat and trousers. 'You are covered in blood.'

Greta had hardly even noticed. 'Well. I apologize for my distasteful appearance.'

His frown sharpened. 'Are you injured?'

'Me? No. This is not my blood.'

He blew out a breath, taking another step back. A slow blink, and whatever thought had scrunched his brows was gone. At last, he sheathed his sword. 'Tell me exactly what went on here today, so I can ensure it does not happen again. Where were you when that leopard attacked my soldiers?'

Greta winced at the memory, scrubbing her hands through her hair. 'There was a third cub in the litter. A female. It wasn't . . . she didn't make it.' She gestured at the blood in the pen, the blood on herself, trying to push away the sadness that came with it. How she had wept to find it dead in the corner of the pen, still in its birth sac. 'I . . . took the body away. To bury it.'

The king blinked. 'You buried it?'

Greta nodded, her cheeks heating. She knew it was absurd. What kind of wrangler buried its war beasts? 'I wasn't gone long,' she said. 'I found a shovel in the hut, then a patch of wet earth in the forest. I was quick. When I heard the shouts, I came running . . .' She wrinkled her nose. 'I should have bolted the pen and taken the key. I shouldn't have trusted them to . . .' She trailed off. 'Never mind.'

'I will mind,' said Alarik, pointedly. 'Tell me.'

'It's just that . . .' Greta didn't know what loosened her tongue, whether it was the lingering edge of her sadness or the genuine concern rippling in the king's eyes, the muscle that tightened in his jaw as he waited for her to go on. 'Sometimes when I speak, it would be helpful for them to *listen* to me and not laugh at what I say or dismiss it outright. Every beast comes with its own risks and any order I give is for the safety of your soldiers . . .' She frowned, her voice turning rueful. 'I know I'm not one of them.' She looked at her boots, hating the heat that stained her cheeks. 'I don't pretend that I am.'

'I don't need another soldier,' said Alarik. 'You are far more valuable to me.'

She looked up at him. 'But I'm not my brother.'

He snorted. 'Oh, I'm well aware of that. What does it matter?'

'I think it matters to *them*,' she admitted, and then immediately regretted it when his eyes darkened. What was she doing, singing like a canary for the king? What good would come of any of this? She had caused enough trouble already. The other soldiers would only hate her more now. 'I'm just . . . I'm just trying to do my duty here, Your Majesty. I'm not trying to get anyone—'

He raised a hand. 'I understand. Consider the matter escalated.'

'No! I didn't mean to escalate anything!' said Greta, desperately. 'I was only trying to explain—'

'The complete lack of respect you've been shown by the soldiers who are supposed to work alongside you?' he said, raising his brows.

'Please don't tell them I said that!'

'Very well,' he said, mildly. 'I'll say Saga filed the report.'

Greta groaned, wishing she could take back every part of

this terrible morning and do it all over again. 'Please, just let me handle it. If I'm to earn the respect of your soldiers, I have to fight for it myself. And I intend to.'

Yes, she would simply come up with a plan to scare them into line. She would show them the measure of her worth before they cast her aside for good.

'You may do as you like. Just as I will.'

She raked her hands through her hair, tugging at the strands.

The grass crunched as he moved closer. Slowly, and with surprising gentleness, he took her wrists in his hands and tugged them away from her hair, until all her focus fell on him, standing right there in front of her. 'Look at me, Iversen.' And she did, raising her chin to find herself snared in the light of those searing blue eyes. 'It's very simple. I do not suffer insubordination in my ranks, and neither will my wrangler. Not while we are on the verge of war.'

Greta stared at her wrists in his hands and felt a curious flutter in her chest. 'I'm sorry for yelling at you back there.'

'Good. Anything else?'

'And for threatening your life.'

'Technically, you threatened your own life.'

She grimaced. 'I should not have done that.'

'Correct.'

She frowned. 'My adrenaline got the better of me. When I get fired up, it's hard to think straight . . . it's hard to . . .'

'Bite your tongue?'

'Something like that,' she mumbled.

'That kind of bravery is useful in war . . . but lethal at court. Perhaps you should have been a soldier, after all,' he said, smiling faintly as he let her go. Greta raked her hands through her hair to dampen the urge to reach for him again. What on earth was wrong with her today? 'Though who's to say you wouldn't turn on your own commander if they looked at you the wrong way?'

She jerked her chin up. 'I know how to follow orders.'

'I look forward to the day when you begin.'

She ignored the barb. 'So, I'm not dismissed, then?'

He scrubbed a hand across his jaw. 'It seems to me that dismissing you from your post would be *a terrible waste of resources*. As you like to point out.'

She nodded, daring a relieved smile.

'Although, I will say, of all the creatures in this palace, I think you might be the wildest,' he went on, his brow furrowing. 'The question is, who do I find to wrangle *you*?'

Greta blinked, seized by a sudden rush of heat.

'Oh, my giddy stars, are those *newborn cubs*?' cried a new voice, jolting them from their conversation. Greta turned to find two figures coming towards them. Alarik stepped away from her, his hands clasping behind his back.

'Indeed they are,' he called out. 'Less than a day old.'

Greta recognized one of the figures as Captain Vine. The other was a tall, beautiful woman Greta had never seen before. She wore a delicate tiara on a crown of her own golden braids and a dress so fine, Greta curled her arms around herself on instinct, afraid the blood on her own clothes might somehow rub off on it. But the woman seemed not to care at all. She pressed herself against the gate to get a closer look at the leopards. 'It was a mama, all along!' She glanced over her shoulder, teeth gleaming. 'Thank goodness you didn't behead that poor beast, Alarik. The guilt would have eaten you alive.'

'I'm sure,' he muttered.

'You can sleep soundly tonight, thanks to your wrangler,' she said, smiling at Greta.

Greta was compelled to smile back, so effortlessly charming was the woman before her. Though she could tell by the lilt of her accent that she was not from here.

'I've read all about your kind, you know. Your innate skill with beasts. How you can read them. Bond with them. It sounds like a kind of magic.'

'I've always thought of it that way,' said Greta, a little sheepishly. She didn't usually waste much thought on her own appearance, but it was hard in that moment not to feel like a mussed-up swamp rat next to such a towering beauty. 'My name is Greta.'

'Hello, Greta.' The woman reached for her bloodstained hand, seeming not to mind at all, and shaking it. 'I'm Princess Elva of Halgard. King Alarik's betrothed.'

Greta stiffened without meaning to. 'Oh.' Her stomach twisted and, for a fleeting moment, she felt a little sick. Before she could help it, she glanced at the king. Perhaps it was her imagination, but she thought he looked a little sick, too.

'Let's not bore Iversen with such tedium,' he said, dismissively. 'You should return to the palace before your tea gets cold, Elva.' He nodded to Greta as he stepped away, gesturing at the others to follow. 'Tend to your beasts, wrangler. Captain Vine and I will see to the soldiers.'

With that, he turned and stalked back to the palace. Greta loosed a breath as she watched him go, a smile flickering on her lips. It was not his parting words that pleased her, rather the startling realization that perhaps she had found an ally in Grinstad after all.

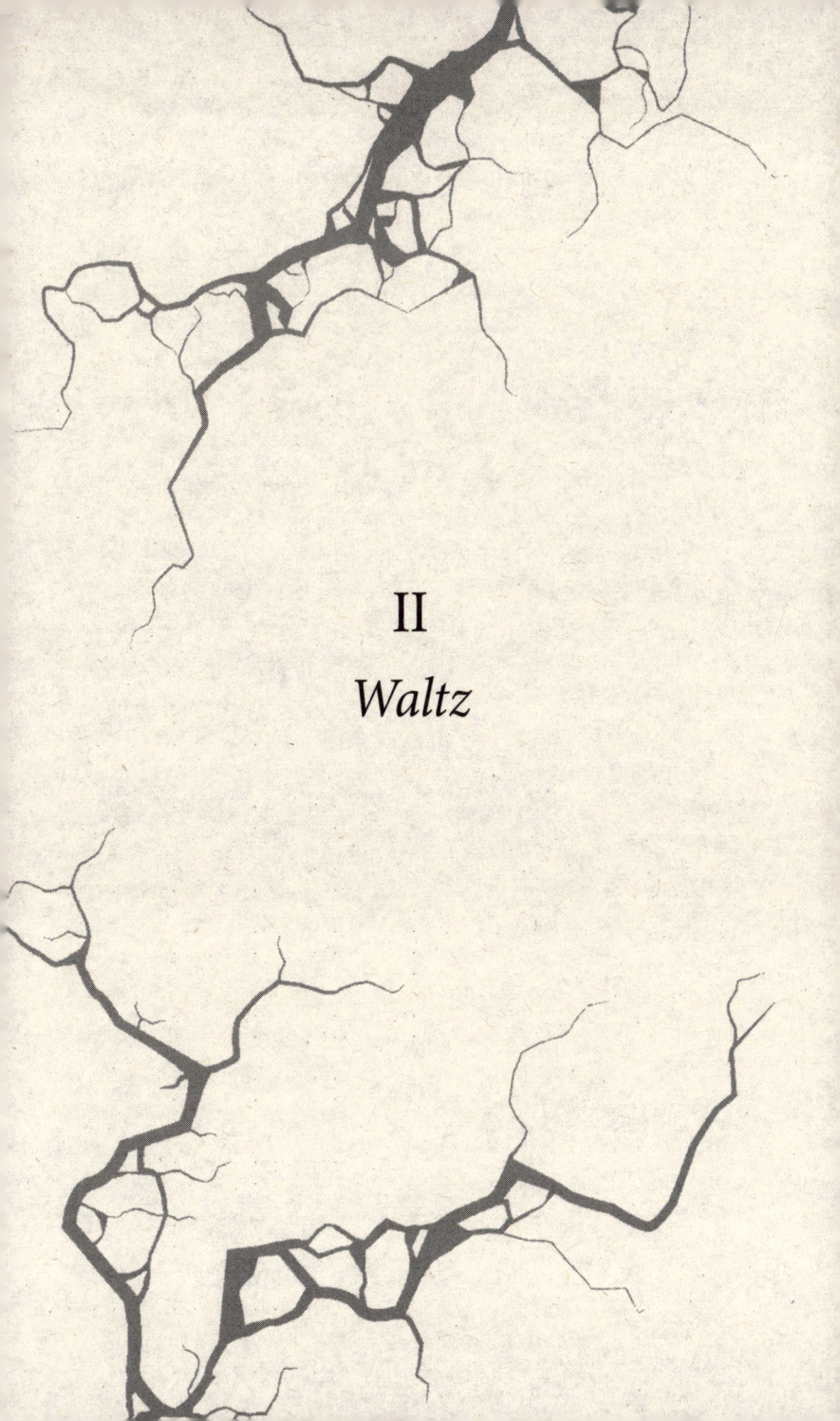

II
Waltz

CHAPTER 13
Alarik

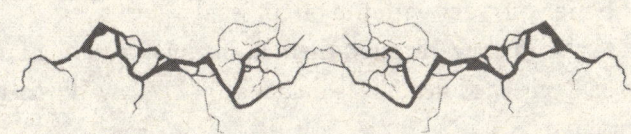

Alarik was sitting alone in the furthest corner of the palace library, pouring over a stack of papers, when the soft patter of slippers announced the arrival of his mother. He slumped down in his wing-backed armchair, sliding so close to the roaring fireplace that the heat licked his boots.

'I can see you,' came the dowager queen's voice. She moved through the passage of towering bookshelves and came to perch on the arm of his chair. 'What on earth are you doing back here?'

She cast a wary glance over the papers as he shuffled them into a pile. He had been scowling at them for almost an hour, slipping away after breakfast to privately digest the information he had garnered from one of the Vaskan spies Elias had carted back to the palace. The rest of Regna's ill-trained scouts were still shivering in the dungeons, awaiting their own interrogations, which Alarik intended to personally oversee once his breakfast had settled. The stack of papers carried reports of the gathering Vaskan army, as well as rudimentary sketches of the gliders Regna had commissioned for her experimental aerial legion.

Alarik looked up at his mother. 'If you must know, I'm hiding. Every time I enter my war room, your creeping little toad finds me there and saddles me with another inane decision.' He surrendered a long-suffering sigh. 'Yesterday, he had me choose between *seven* identical types of parchment for wedding invitations.'

'I hope you went with the birch,' said Valeska.

'I let Nova chew through them at his leisure, while Luna chased your meddlesome sidekick all the way down the front lawn.'

Now, it was her turn to sigh. '*Alarik*. Do not set your beasts on my steward.'

'Do not set your steward on me.' He rubbed the spot between his brows, and she clucked her tongue at the bruising along his knuckles.

'Where did those come from?'

'You know I like to be hands-on with my interrogations,' he said, waving off her concern. In fact, the interrogations had been good for him these past few days. Alarik had been quite enjoying working off his frustration on the spitting, cursing faces of his enemies.

'At least use your sword, Alarik. You're not a barbarian.'

He hummed to himself. Just how thin was the line between brute and barbarian anyway? He had spilled enough blood, cut down enough enemies, to be considered both. But it was not the brutality of his methods that bothered his mother – she was a queen of Gevra after all – rather it was his willingness to get his hands dirty, to scuff his own knuckles, instead of drawing his sword and issuing a deeper, cleaner punishment. But Alarik liked his way better. It was more personal, more rewarding. He revelled in the crunch of his enemy's nose under his fist, blood foaming in their teeth. In this eerie calm before the gathering war, every strike made him feel useful. It made him feel like his father.

'What is it that you need, Mother?' he said, when she continued to linger.

'I'm here about Elva. The princess is bored stiff, Alarik. Most days, I see her drifting through the palace like an unmoored vessel.'

He leaned back, propping his leg across his knee. 'What a luxury,' he remarked. 'What I wouldn't give to be *bored*.'

His mother loomed over him, firelight gilding the silky veil of her hair. 'Elva has been here for two weeks, and you've only taken tea with her twice.' She wrinkled her nose, and for a moment she looked so like Anika that Alarik's heart panged for his younger sister. '*Once*, if you don't count the day that snow leopard turned.'

Alarik bristled at the memory. But when he cast his mind back to that dread-filled morning, it was not Princess Elva he thought of. Not her grand arrival to a chorus of drumbeats, nor their meeting in the entrance hall or even the conversation they had enjoyed over tea shortly thereafter.

No, that was the day that Alarik had seen the Iversen girl for the treasure she truly was. A wrangler who not only fought for his beasts but cared for them. Trained them and tended to them, sang to soothe them, and even went out of her way to bury their dead . . .

She was willing to go to war for them. And they would go to war for her, too. Which meant they would go to war for him. As long as his wrangler was kept safe. And crucially – alive.

'Alarik?' His mother gently flicked his nose, and he looked up, blinking away the fleeting memory of those snowy cubs, and the woman who guarded them with the ferocity of a leopard. 'Are you listening to me? Go and entertain your bride before she changes her mind about you and goes home.' She left a meaningful pause. 'Taking the promise of her army with her.'

He scrubbed his hands across his face, wishing he could wipe away the entirety of his mother's plan, which seemed to be spiralling further from his control with each passing day. She spoke again, quietening the storm of defiance inside him. 'This might not be what you want right now, but this alliance is what your kingdom needs. It's what your father would want.'

Alarik slumped in his chair. 'Fine,' he said, with a scowl.

'I wish you wouldn't do that to your face. You're so handsome when you smile.'

'I'm surprised you remember,' he muttered.

She leaned forward, covering his hand with her own. 'You will find cause to smile again, son. We both will.'

I'll smile when I mount Queen Regna's head on a pike, he thought, viciously.

His mother rose and swept from the library, her pale blue gown trailing along the marble floor behind her. Alarik watched her go. Then, with great reluctance, he dragged himself from his hard-fought solitude and went in search of his future bride.

By the time he found Princess Elva tinkling on the pianoforte in the music room, a blizzard had kicked up. The snow was coming down with a vengeance, frosting the spires of Grinstad Palace and blanketing the lawns again. It was too cold for a walk.

Alarik paused in the doorway, half thinking about slinking away when Elva stopped playing. 'Do you know how many people would kill to have an audience with me back in Halgard?' Her words floated over her shoulder. 'And yet the surly king of Gevra takes breakfast in his bedchamber, dinner in his war room and disappears into his own dungeons every other day to avoid me.'

Alarik stepped into the room. 'I'm not avoiding you.' *Any more.*

'Liar.' She spun on the stool, casting her eyes on him. She was dressed in a velvet dress of pine green, her pale hair spun into a long, thick braid that traced the length of her spine. No jewels, no diadem, just that menacing pout. 'What are you so afraid of, now that all our cards are on the table? That we might actually end up becoming friends?'

Alarik frowned. 'I'm afraid that you'll seek things from me that I cannot give you,' he said, with stark honesty. 'And the truth is, Elva, I have nothing to offer.'

There was nothing left inside him. Only war and regret, and grief for the people who had left him over the years – his brother, his father, his sister, his best friend. His heart was a hole through which the people he loved fell, down into death and oblivion. He could not afford to tuck anyone else inside it.

'Don't be so dramatic,' said Elva, coming to her feet. 'There must be a personality buried somewhere underneath all that angst.'

He shot her a scathing look.

She returned it. 'You are a terrible host.'

'Agreed,' he said, slumping against the door frame.

'Now what?'

'Try to be a marginally better one, and I won't write to my father and declare this beautiful country of yours an utter lost cause.'

'Are you blackmailing me?' he said, with a snort.

She shrugged. 'Call it what you want. Just get me out of this room. I've played this damned pianoforte so much my wrists are cramping.'

'I was coming down here to invite you on a walk, but it seems the weather has other ideas.'

She glared out of the window. 'It's been positively hateful these past few days.'

He gave her a flat smile. 'Welcome to Gevra, princess.'

'I want to see the beasts,' she said, folding her arms. 'Surely there are some kept indoors that I can play with?'

He stared at her. 'I don't keep a nursery, Elva.'

'Perhaps you should, because I am dangerously close to throwing a tantrum.'

'Fine. Come with me,' he said, as an idea occurred to him. Something that would appease both his mother and the princess, without wrenching too much time from his day. 'I know somewhere we can walk. And if you're lucky, you'll see some beasts, too.'

Her face lit up as she strode to meet him and with the kind of ease he usually felt only with his sister Anika, Elva tucked her arm through the crook of his elbow and fell into step beside him.

It was a short walk to the glass corridor on the upper floor of the palace. Vine was already there, looking out over the courtyard with her hands tucked behind her back. When she spotted Alarik and Elva coming towards her, she broke into a grin. Alarik did not, for one moment, think his war captain's delight had anything to do with his unexpected arrival. Rather, the beautiful princess on his arm and the full-mouthed smile she was returning.

'Finally, a friendly face around here,' said Elva, skipping over to Vine. 'Where have *you* been hiding all week?'

'Shouldn't you be out in that blizzard, training our soldiers?' said Alarik, by way of greeting.

'We've been training since sunrise,' said Vine, indicating the mud stains on her boots and trousers. 'The soldiers are on lunch, and I'm waiting for the feeling to return to my nose.'

'While spying on my wrangler?' he said, turning to the snow-spattered window and straining to see the arena below, where he knew his beasts would be training, hard as ever, even despite the weather. 'Are you afraid her regiment is better behaved than yours?'

Vine didn't rise to the bait, instead offering him a sly smile. 'Don't act like you don't come up here to spy on her, too. Servants talk, you know.'

Alarik looked away, sharply. It wasn't as if he spent his days lurking up here. He only came this way every now and then to keep an eye on his wrangler – to make sure she was safe. Hell, she was his best friend's little sister. He owed it to Tor to watch over her. It was as simple as that . . . And so what if he liked to watch her train his beasts? That's what he was paying her for.

'Oh dear,' muttered Elva. 'I think you've touched a nerve, Captain Vine.'

They pealed into laughter.

Alarik huffed as he looked between them. 'I think I'll

leave you two to your mindless giggling and do some real work.' He cracked his knuckles, thinking of those Vaskan spies in the dungeons.

'You'll miss out,' said Vine, idly turning back to the window. 'Your wrangler is down there dancing with your wolves.'

Alarik was only mildly embarrassed by how quickly he returned to the window. He pressed his palms against the pane, his breath fogging the glass as he squinted to find her. She was standing in the middle of the arena, the hood of her frock coat pulled up to stave off the gathering blizzard. The fur lining made a silver halo around her face, and even despite the snow, he could see her smile from here. Her mouth was open mid-laughter, and he found himself straining to hear it over the howling wind.

Twenty wolves arced around her, hanging on her every breath. They rose to their hind legs at the click of her teeth and danced – no, *pranced*, like the prized ponies of Caro. She clapped her hands and they returned to all fours, before springing back up again and repeating the shuffle. Up and down they went, left and then right, hopping on their hind legs while the wrangler twirled and clapped, creating her own rhythm.

'What on earth is she doing?' murmured Elva, her nose snubbed against the glass. 'It looks like she's holding royal court out there.'

'Perhaps she's training them for your official welcome ball,' said Vine.

Elva crowed with laughter. 'Or maybe she's as bored as I've been around here and has decided to make up her own fun.'

'No,' said Alarik, more to himself than to the others. 'Whatever this is, there is a method to it.' His gaze roamed along the courtyard as he tried to unpick the mystery of what she was up to. He made note of the soldiers crowding around the arena, peering over the outer wall to look down on the spectacle. They were captivated by the wrangler and her wolves, glued to the way she darted across that arena, a slip of a thing dancing between beasts that were three times her size. More soldiers came, pouring out from the dining hall and the hut, to see what all the commotion was about.

Most of them were laughing.

As though oblivious to their sneers, Iversen kept moving, twirling her way among the wolves until she stopped abruptly. Her hand shot up and the wolves froze. She moved her wrist – barely a half turn. The wolves crouched in a circle, their sharp teeth bared. Gone was the merriment of a moment ago. Now, they looked like the beasts they truly were, poised to lunge.

Another flick of her wrist and they turned around, showing their backs to her. The circle widened as they prowled towards the outer wall.

The soldiers stationed there stopped laughing.

Alarik smirked.

The wrangler whistled through her teeth.

The wolves leaped – higher than he had ever seen them jump before. The largest of them reached the lip of the wall, its claws gleaming as it swiped at their gawking audience.

The soldiers yelped, drawing back in fright.

Another sharp whistle and the wolves retreated, circling the wrangler once more.

The wrangler tucked her hands behind her back, waiting

for her audience to gather their courage.

The wolves sat in utter stillness.

Slowly, cautiously, the soldiers crept back to the wall. More arrived, growing bolder as they crowded the periphery. Soon, the arena was fuller than Alarik had ever seen it.

Iversen gave a subtle nod. At the other end of the arena, three stuffed mannequins were dropped into the pit. The one in the middle was dressed in the colours of Gevra – a midnight-blue frock coat, trimmed in silver. The other two wore the colours of Vask – crimson and gold.

Iversen stomped her foot, her cry soaring on the wind. 'ATTACK!'

The wolves thundered across the arena, setting upon the mannequins with a viciousness that made Alarik's heart leap.

'Look!' said Elva, gleefully. 'They're not even touching the middle one!'

'And they're ripping the others limb from limb,' said Vine, with a huff of laughter. 'Clever beasts.'

Clever wrangler.

Down below, the soldiers watched on in awe. Some whooped and hollered at the spectacle, while others clapped their hands in triumph. In a matter of moments, the Vaskan mannequins were utterly dismembered, their uniforms strewn across the arena in tattered red ribbons.

At a sharp whistle from the wrangler, the wolves returned to her. The largest of them carried the head of a mannequin in his maw. He dropped it at her feet. She leaned down to scratch under the wolf's chin. He preened, arching his back like a spoilt pup.

'They *adore* her,' said Elva, in a quiet, awestruck voice.

'Who? The soldiers or the beasts?' said Vine, and Alarik had to stop himself from saying, *both, obviously*. By wrangling the wolves, Iversen was wrangling the soldiers that feared them. Not simply telling them there was nothing to fear, but *showing* them. Using her own body as a demonstration, as a promise that they were safe with these beasts. They were safe with her.

This was not some frivolous spectacle. It was a show of skill and control. A demonstration of power. And more than that, it was an invitation to the king's soldiers to trust the beasts that would soon be their allies again, to stow their fears and hold fast to their courage.

Alarik almost smiled. Just when he thought it couldn't get any more brilliant, his wrangler stepped backwards and sketched an elaborate curtsy, as though she were a princess departing at last from the dance floor. When the wolves bowed their mighty heads to mirror her gesture, the king burst into laughter.

Elva turned to stare at him in surprise.

Vine stepped back from the window. 'So, that's what your real laugh sounds like. I'm not sure I've ever heard it.'

Alarik stiffened, quickly strangling the sound. 'That was a cough, Vine.'

She arched a brow, but before she could issue a retort, Elva whirled on them. 'Damn this snow, I want to pet a wolf!'

She squared her chin, silently daring the king to forbid her.

He only shrugged. If he couldn't trust his wrangler after that demonstration, then he never would. He looked to Vine. 'Take the princess down to the arena. I'm sure your soldiers can spare you for another hour.'

'Join us?' said Elva, tugging at his arm.

'I'd hate to make Nova and Luna jealous,' he said, dryly. 'You two go ahead. I'll watch.'

They scurried off in a fit of excitement, leaving Alarik alone in the corridor. He returned to the window, tracking his wrangler as she marched up and down, effortlessly spooling every wonderstruck soldier and dutiful beast around her little finger.

As Alarik stood transfixed at the window, watching his wrangler for far longer than he would ever dare to admit, he couldn't help but think she had spooled a part of him, too.

CHAPTER 14
Greta

It was mid-morning at Grinstad, and Greta was standing in the grand atrium, waiting on the king. She had been here for almost an hour already, and there was still no sign of him. She regretted rushing in from the courtyard now, panting so hard she had to bend double by the banister just to catch her breath. But when the maidservant had come outside to relay the king's message – *tell my wrangler to meet me in the atrium at noon* – Greta had bolted inside like a skittish deer, afraid to be late, unwilling to give Alarik Felsing any reason to question her respect for him.

But now she found herself questioning the king's respect for her. Not to mention his beasts' training. She could have worked through an entire defensive manoeuvre with the ice bears during the time she had been standing here. It didn't help that the guards were all staring at her, and when asked politely, had offered no clue as to where the king was.

To make matters worse, her head ached. Her slumber last night had been disturbed by dreams of a creature trapped in ancient rock. Keening . . . *calling* to her. She woke, thinking of the mountains beyond the palace. Sometimes, if she concentrated hard enough, listening over the howl of the wind, she swore she could sense the thrum of an anxious heart there. Of a beast suffering just beyond her reach.

It left her feeling unsettled.

Greta slumped on to the stairwell and chewed her bottom lip, waiting . . . *scowling*. When a servant darted by, she leaped from the bottom step and grabbed his arm. 'Wait!'

He spun around, wide-eyed, and she recognized him as the same servant who had brought her that divine miniature cake on the night of her birthday. 'I'm looking for the king,' she said, urgently. 'I believe he's looking for me, too. Do you know where he is?'

The young man frowned. 'He's in the dungeons.'

'Please take me to him,' said Greta, relieved to have a point of direction. 'I can't sit here for another minute.'

The servant hesitated. 'His Majesty doesn't like to be disturbed . . .'

'That makes two of us,' she said, with a huff of impatience. 'But *he's* the one that summoned me from a training session, and I do need to be getting back, so if you could . . .' She rolled her hands in the general direction of the dungeons, which she knew were located somewhere underground. '*Please.*'

At her imploring look, the servant gave in with a sigh, turning back the way he had come. Greta followed him across the atrium, and down a long corridor that ended in a large metal door. There was a steep stone staircase on the other side. Down, down, down they went, the air chilling as the steps grew rough and uneven. Despite the warmth of her frock coat, her breath hung like clouds in the air, and she had to pull her hood up to keep from shivering.

The world got colder and deeper until the stairs flattened out and the dungeons unfurled in a series of burrowing tunnels filled with small dark cells. The servant's footsteps quickened, his blue tunic and leather trousers doing little to stave off the chill. Greta felt bad for insisting he bring her to the king, but it was clear Alarik Felsing had forgotten about their meeting, and she was not about to waste an entire day up in that atrium waiting for him to remember her.

She kept her gaze forward as she walked, avoiding the prisoners that spat and cursed at her from their cells. She hated the sight of those thick iron bars and all those bitter, wasted lives behind them. At the end of the passage, they came to a narrow wooden door. Grunting echoed from within, followed by a string of guttural swears so foul they made her cheeks redden.

The servant knocked. Steeled himself and knocked again. After a long moment, the door flew open to reveal the king of Gevra, looking violently furious. His pale hair was unkempt, and his eyes were wild. His white shirtsleeves were rolled up to his elbows, while the rest of the garment was spattered with blood.

'What do you want, Johan?' he barked. 'I told you never to disturb—' He stopped abruptly, his gaze falling on Greta, who had shrunk back from the doorway and was hovering uncertainly behind the servant. He cleared his throat, working to lower his voice. 'Why have you brought her down here?'

Johan swallowed thickly, and Greta was overcome by a wave of guilt. She had not intended to unwittingly nudge him – or herself – into the storm of the king's temper.

She stepped forward. 'I made him take me down here,'

she said, noting with increasing discomfort the flecks of blood on his cheek. The bruises on his hand. 'I heard you wanted to see me in the atrium . . . but you never came.'

She was embarrassed by the quiver in her voice, as though the king of Gevra had stood her up for some kind of date.

There was another string of curses from inside the chamber, and then the sound of a fist connecting with bone.

Greta quailed at the *crack*!

Alarik ignored it. 'I said to meet me at noon.'

'It's past noon.'

He frowned, sweeping a rogue lock of hair from his face and smudging a drop of blood on his forehead. Greta's eyes darted, searching for the source of it. 'The time got away from me.'

She nodded slowly. That much was obvious. 'What are you doing in there?'

'Conversing.'

She frowned. 'That's not what it sounds like.'

'I have a very *particular* conversation style.' He offered the ghost of a smile as someone behind him swore in a heavy accent. Vask, thought Greta. Or perhaps Ryberg. 'Go back upstairs, Iversen. I'll come find you when I'm done.'

Ordinarily, Greta would have been rankled by his complete lack of apology for wasting her time, but she was distracted by all that blood. 'Are you all right?' she said, quietly.

He blinked. 'What?'

She dared a step closer, until she had to tilt her chin up to look at him. 'There's blood . . .' she said, tracing her finger over the streak on his collar. 'You have blood on you.'

He peered down at her through a veil of dark lashes, an odd quirk to his mouth. 'I often have blood on me,' he said, just as quietly. 'It is very rarely my own.'

'Oh. I see.' She was struck by a surge of embarrassment. She took a step backwards, her arms coming around herself. How painfully naive she must seem to him, thinking the king of Gevra was somehow injured in his own palace, that he might need her concern. She felt foolish for even offering it, but that slight smirk remained, and at the very least, her question seemed not to have bothered him.

His gaze slid over her, narrowing on Johan. 'Don't bring her down here again. I know she's bossy as hell, but as my personal steward, you should know better.'

'Of course, Your Majesty. My mistake.' Johan dipped his chin. 'I'm sorry.'

Alarik closed the door with a determined thud, without looking at Greta again. She slumped against the wall, relieved to have navigated the encounter without another scolding. Though she couldn't say the same for poor Johan.

'Sorry,' she said, sheepishly.

He sighed. 'I'm used to it.' He turned back towards the palace. 'He's usually angry with me about something. It's been like that ever since his younger brother died. The war in Eana only made it worse. Sometimes, he blames the poor weather on me, too.'

Greta fell into step with him, feeling a pang of sympathy for Alarik Felsing. She had heard of the loss of Prince Ansel over a year ago – like the rest of the kingdom, the people of Carrig had sent lanterns up to the sky to mourn him – but she had never stopped to wonder how deeply that unexpected loss had affected the king. She wondered if the raw anger he so often wore might be cloaking something deeper and far more painful. 'Are you really the king's personal steward?'

Johan nodded, somewhat glumly.

'I thought you worked for the kitchens . . .' she said, remembering the night he had brought her that tiny birthday cake, and wondering now if it truly had been the king all along who had sent it. But *no*. It was an absurd thought . . . that a man who wore the blood of his enemies with such casual indifference, and whose scowl alone could frighten off a mountain lion, would ever do such a thing. And yet she couldn't help but ask . . .

'Do you remember the night you brought me that cake, Johan?'

He nodded, distantly.

'Where did it come from?'

'The kitchens,' he said.

'Yes, but from whom?' she clarified. 'Who wrote the note?'

He took a long time to answer. 'I don't know,' he said, and though she didn't know Johan very well, she sensed the lie in his words, read the caginess in his darting eyes.

A smile curled her lips as they returned to the stairwell.

Later that afternoon, Greta was in the arena, working on recall with a pack of unruly wolves, when the king came to find her. She didn't notice him at first because she was busy scolding Tollo, who had rolled on to his back and was playing dead in the middle of her lesson.

'Get up, you shameless drama king!' She whistled through her teeth, and the other beasts stood to attention. She had made progress with them at least. 'This isn't funny, Tollo.'

Tollo kept his eyes shut, but snuffled as if to say, *treats please*.

'He has the right idea, if you ask me.' Alarik's voice floated across the arena. She startled at the sight of him striding towards her, dressed impeccably in a fitted blue frock coat, dark trousers and high black boots. His hair was perfectly coiffed, and there was no sign of the blood she had seen on him earlier. 'I could do with a nap, too.'

Greta dragged her hands through her hair. She hated the king seeing her like this, nagging a wolf, instead of wrangling it. 'He's learning, I swear. He's just angling for lamb strips.'

'Clever beast,' remarked the king, who had not so much as batted an eyelid at the other animals in the arena. He was as comfortable with them at his back as he was with them at his front, which meant he either truly trusted the animals, or he truly trusted her.

'We're making fine progress,' Greta felt compelled to say. 'Despite this hiccup, there's been considerable improvements across—'

'Relax, Iversen. I know you're good at your job. I've been watching you.'

She flushed, a violent heat stealing across her cheeks. Why did that make her so nervous?

He went on, 'You can train my beasts however you see fit, so long as you make them chew up my enemies when it counts.'

Her stomach twisted at the hint of war. It was absurd to

admit, but even though she was training a regiment of the Gevran army, she didn't like to think about battles or bloodshed, or pain or death or—

'Can you finish up here? We have somewhere else to be.'

'Don't you ever say please?' The words flew out of her mouth before she could catch them.

He stared at her for a long moment. 'Never.'

Her brows lifted. 'Even a king should have manners.'

'Why would I need manners when I have a perfectly good sword?'

It was an effort not to roll her eyes. 'Well, at the risk of being skewered, may I ask where I am expected to be?'

'We're going on a trip.'

'To where?' she said, cautiously.

'The grazing fields beyond the mountains,' he said, looking south as though he could see them through the sprawl of the palace. 'I'm going to introduce you to an entirely new kind of beast.'

Greta couldn't help the smile that broke across her face. 'In that case, I'll meet you out front shortly!'

She quickly returned the beasts to their pens, where she fed and watered them, before returning to the palace, giddiness making her bounce on the balls of her feet. She couldn't tell if it was the promise of a mysterious new beast or the fact that she was going on a trip with the king himself that filled her stomach with butterflies, but when she spied the royal sled through the atrium window, her heart flipped in her chest.

She bounded outside and, in her excitement, nearly crashed head first into Princess Elva, who was standing on the front steps, wearing a magnificent silver fur cloak and matching hat. Impossibly, she looked even more beautiful than the last time Greta had seen her.

'Greta! There you are!' she said, flashing her perfectly dazzling smile. 'I'm so pleased you can join us on our outing!'

Greta's smile faltered, her heart sinking into her shoes. 'Me, too,' she said, a beat too late.

'But then, I suppose it's not like you have a choice,' said the princess, misreading her disappointment. 'Alarik can be quite a tyrant. I hope he didn't tear you away from anything important.'

Greta shook her head slowly, suddenly dreading the thought of accompanying Alarik and his betrothed on a romantic jaunt through the mountains. A quick glance around the front courtyard revealed the sled driver, who was harnessing his wolves, and Captain Vine, who, mercifully, was also wearing her travelling cloak.

Greta blew out a breath. She was not to be a third wheel, after all.

'Be warned, he's in a foul mood today,' said Princess Elva, as the king came stalking across the courtyard. 'I did warn him that's what happens when you spend the morning beating your enemy's spies into a bloody pulp.'

Greta followed the chatty princess down to the sled, suddenly conscious of every scuff on her boots, the stray wisps of hair that had come undone from her braid and the million stubborn wolf hairs that now decorated her frock coat.

I am a wrangler, she reminded herself.

I am the *wrangler.*

She didn't need to look beautiful. Or be remotely charming.

That was not why the king had invited her.

The royal sled was large and sleek, comprised of two leather benches that faced one another. Greta clambered up first, settling herself on the far end of the first bench. Next came Captain Vine, who seated herself on the opposite bench. Then the princess, who chose the spot beside Vine, picking up one of the fur blankets and unfurling it.

'Well, this is cosy,' she said, as she draped the blanket over her lap and Vine's. Perhaps it was Greta's imagination, but she could have sworn the captain blushed.

The king was the last to climb into the sled, and to Greta's surprise – and traitorous flicker of delight – he passed over the empty space beside his betrothed and sat beside her instead.

She bit back her smile as he splayed his arm along the headrest behind her.

'Onwards,' he called to the sled driver.

The wolves set off at a steady pace, pulling the sled behind them.

'WAIT FOR ME!' A strangled voice rang out, and Greta looked over her shoulder to see the same frightfully tall man she had glimpsed in the war room on the day of her arrival. He was tearing across the front lawn after the sled, his brown satchel swinging through the air behind him.

'Go!' Alarik pounded on the side of the sled. *'Faster!'*

But they were already slowing, and before the driver could heed the king's order, the spindly man caught up with them. He grasped on to the edge of the sled and flung himself inside, his satchel opening in a mess of twigs and loose flowers as he landed in a heap at the king's feet. With those gangly limbs and wide, unblinking eyes, he looked like a fawn on ice.

'You forgot me, Your Majesty!' he said, scrabbling to his knees.

Alarik rolled his eyes. 'I didn't forget you, Lief. I was *escaping* you.'

Lief gathered up his sticks and flowers and shoved them back into his satchel. 'I heard you're going to the grazing fields,' he said, lunging to sit beside Alarik. The king shot out his arm, shooing him to the other bench. 'That's an hour's ride from here. Perfect time to go over more wedding details!' He smiled far too widely, glancing between the princess and the king, both of whom looked distinctly uninterested in his proposition. 'Is it not?'

'No,' said Alarik flatly, before turning his entire body towards Greta, and looking at her like she was suddenly the most fascinating creature he had ever seen. The sudden intensity in his gaze made her squirm a little in her seat. 'I will be speaking to my wrangler.'

'For how long?' said Lief, crestfallen.

'Eons,' said Alarik, without tearing his gaze from Greta. He idly toyed with the edge of her hood, the move so casually intimate, her throat dried out. 'My wrangler and I have *lots* to catch up on. Don't we, Iversen?'

She summoned a smile, playing along. 'Enough to fill at least two sled rides.'

To her surprise, the king smiled back and for a fleeting moment, the warmth in his gaze didn't feel like a ruse at all.

CHAPTER 15
Alarik

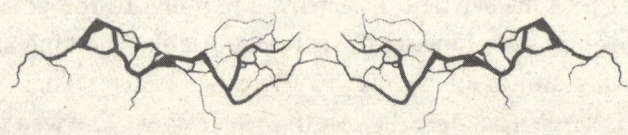

The wrangler was expertly playing along with his diversion, reeling off all the training exercises she had been working on with his beasts. Alarik found himself leaning closer, drawn to the spark in her blue-grey eyes and the way her full mouth moved, fast and smiling, as she spoke.

Tor had been an exemplary wrangler – and a formidable soldier – but in all the time he had spent at Grinstad, he had never spoken about the beasts with such fondness. It was infectious – her unbridled enthusiasm – and what had begun as a ploy to ignore Lief soon became a conversation that Alarik wanted to pour himself into, just to hear her speak.

Across from him, Captain Vine and Princess Elva were engrossed in their own conversation about Halgard, leaving Lief to harrumph loudly as he shuffled through his satchel.

'It's elk, isn't it?' said the wrangler, in a conspiratorial whisper. 'Weaver elk from Halgard. That's what's in the grazing fields.'

'I wanted it to be a surprise,' mused the king, but now that he could see the way her face lit up, he was glad she had figured it out.

She bounced in her seat, straining to see beyond the cresting mountains. 'I've always wanted to see a weaver in the flesh. My father says they can run faster than a leopard on the hunt.'

'And can skewer an armoured soldier with the point of their antler,' said Alarik, with the same gleaming enthusiasm. 'The mere tips of their horns are so poisonous a single prick can prove deadly.'

Her face fell, and he regretted his casual bloodlust, a thing that came naturally to him, but that he could see made her uncomfortable. These past few weeks, he had come to realize that while his wrangler loved his beasts, she did not care for his wars.

'*Ahem.*' Lief pitched forward in his seat, waving a limp bouquet of flowers back and forth. 'I don't mean to interrupt—'

'Yes, you do,' said Alarik, flatly.

'But now seems like an ideal time to discuss centrepieces,' he went on, valiantly undeterred.

Alarik frowned. 'I don't even know what a centrepiece is.'

Lief made a cry of alarm, startling Captain Vine and Princess Elva from their conversation.

'A centrepiece is a *statement*, Your Majesty. A specially curated decoration around which your wedding guests congregate, a thing that echoes the beauty and grand majesty of your wedding. Your very union!' He shoved the flowers forward. A petal tickled the underside of Alarik's chin. 'I was thinking orchids. Classic, timeless. *Or*, if you want to add a little flair, I suggest midnight lilies would work rather nicely.'

Alarik batted the flowers away, decapitating half of them. 'How about we use the skulls of our enemies instead?'

Beside him, the wrangler stifled a horrified gasp.

Captain Vine sighed. 'Why are you like this?'

'What, Gevran?' Alarik retorted.

'Just say candles.'

'Or antlers?' suggested Princess Elva. 'Our weavers shed theirs twice a year.'

'*Poison-tipped antlers?* I'm afraid the dowager queen would have a conniption,' said Lief. 'You might as well fetch a witch to curse the entire union.'

'Now there's an idea.' And it certainly wouldn't be the first time Alarik had been cursed, though thankfully he had managed to free himself from that particularly unfortunate bind. He exchanged an amused glance with the princess. Without a shred of true love between them – or the intention to kindle it – wasn't their union already cursed?

Elva turned to the wrangler. 'What do you think, Greta? Skulls or antlers?'

Greta shifted in her seat, a frown tugging at the sides of her mouth. 'I don't know,' she said, with a little shrug. 'This isn't really my area.'

'Do you have a betrothed back on Carrig?' said Elva.

The king stilled, staring hard at his wrangler.

She shook her head, chewing on her lower lip.

A dangerous heat curled in Alarik's stomach.

'What? Not even a lover?' Elva pressed.

That heat grew to lick his ribcage. A nobler king and a better man would have ended the conversation right there, told Elva his wrangler's home life was none of her business and that these questions were clearly making her uncomfortable, but Alarik was not a good man, he was a Gevran, prone to brutality and possession, so he said nothing, clamping his lips together and letting the silence swell until she filled it with her answer.

Because he wanted to know it.

'There aren't many, um, options . . . for me . . . on Carrig,' she said, muddling through her awkwardness. 'Unless you count the fishermen, I suppose.'

Alarik decided he hated the fishermen of Carrig. Then scolded himself for the thought. It was protectiveness, that was all. Wariness borne of his responsibility to Tor, his best friend and brother in arms.

'My sister, Kindra, is betrothed to a fisherman,' she added, as an afterthought.

'Ooh. Is he handsome?' said Elva, greedy for more.

The wrangler wrinkled her nose, neatly skipping over the truth, which was plainly that he was not. 'Mikkel is a good man,' she said, diplomatically. 'He's kind and dutiful. And he does his best to keep us fed—' She stopped abruptly. Her cheeks heated and she looked away, to where the mountains spilled out on either side of them, the glassy road narrowing as it led them through the pass.

'Why does he need to keep you fed?' said Alarik, quietly.

She turned back to him. 'That came out wrong. I didn't mean it that way.'

'How did you mean it?'

'Just . . . that he's good to us,' she said, a dent forming between her brows. 'He brings us fish.'

'Do you need fish?'

'No.' She shook her head, her throat bobbing. What a

poor liar.

Alarik's frown deepened. He willed her to look at him. She would not. 'Iversen.'

'No,' she said again. Another lie. *Why* was she lying to him? 'Not fish.'

'Enough about fish,' said Elva, flopping back against her seat. 'Back to love!'

'Back to centerpieces!' said Lief.

'No. *Love*,' said the princess firmly. 'Do you plan to marry, Greta?'

'These are . . . difficult questions,' she said, her cheeks turning an absurdly alluring shade of pink. *Stop that*. Alarik pinched the back of his hand until it stung. 'Can't you ask me about beasts instead?'

'Well, you can't very well marry a beast,' said Elva, with a crowing laugh. 'Perhaps you might find yourself a nice soldier here at Grinstad . . .'

Alarik shot her a blistering look. 'Iversen came here to work.'

'Sure, during the day,' she said, smirking. He knew she was teasing him – testing that possessive streak – and it made him want to growl at her. Which meant he was failing. Ugh. 'But the nights here are so *long*, Alarik. And *cold*. I would know.'

The wrangler looked up, confusion pinching her mouth as she glanced between them, no doubt piecing together where the king preferred to spend his nights – alone, in his own bedchamber.

'Oh, I know! What about *dried* flowers?' said Lief. 'That has a sense of the macabre about it, and will still manage to keep your mother happy . . .'

And just like that, they were back to mindless tedium.

The mountains crowded in on them, the air warming as the world got smaller, closer. Nestled in the narrow pass, Alarik's skin prickled with a familiar awareness. He looked past Lief, watching the craggy rock face rise and fall.

Instinctively, he whirled around, looking to his wrangler. Her eyes were closed, her mouth downturned in concentration. She gasped, soft and low, her eyes flying open to meet his.

The others were talking among themselves, oblivious to the thread of awareness that went taut between the king and his wrangler.

'Can you feel it?' he said, in a whisper.

She nodded slowly. 'There's something in the mountains.'

He tried not to hint at the fear coiling in his gut, but the last creature his soldiers excavated from these mountains was a terrifying undead witch who had nearly razed his palace to the ground and then started a war that decimated his army. He did not like to imagine there was something else hiding in there. Something even more dangerous.

'I believe so,' he said, uneasily.

'It feels wild and . . . ancient,' she whispered. A pause then, her breath quickening as the sled picked up speed, trundling towards the end of the pass. 'I think it's *frightened*.' She closed her eyes again, the breeze toying with the loose strands of her hair. 'I can feel its heartbeat rattling.'

'Perhaps it's angry,' said Alarik, darkly. After all, it was trapped. And despite his growing awareness of it, he had done nothing to free it. Rather, he feared the very thought.

She opened her eyes, curiosity shining there. 'What do you think it is?'

He had a theory, not that he had ever dared to voice it aloud for fear Vine would think him mad. And yet there was something about the wrangler that made him want to confide in her. In this matter, she was his closest ally. A confidante who could sense the same strangeness – and more – in his mountains.

He leaned in, keeping his voice low. 'When I was a boy, my father used to tell me bedtime stories about a snow-swept land, full of dragons.'

Her eyes went wider still. 'A Gevra of long ago,' she said, smiling a little. 'My father used to tell me the same stories. I was so enchanted by them I would try so very hard not to fall asleep.'

Alarik smiled to find themselves on common ground. Whispers of the same bedtime stories, of the fathers who sat at their bedside and regaled them. Magical, half-forgotten tales of the northern continent before the last great thawing of the ice thousands of years ago. A time when dragons filled the skies, painting the clouds with their fire.

He went on. 'There was one story in particular that my father favoured. Or perhaps it was the one I always begged to hear. It was the story of the Last Dragon. It belonged to the king of Vask, a covetous, war-hungry man who went to battle against Gevra only to fall in love with its queen.'

'I can't think of a less romantic setting,' muttered Iversen.

Alarik huffed a laugh. 'Are you sure you're Gevran?'

She gently swatted him. 'Keep going.'

'The Vaskan king tried everything to woo the Gevran queen. He called off his troops. Ceded the Blackspires to her. Even promised a peace treaty for a hundred years. But the queen remained unmoved. Growing desperate and still hopelessly enamoured by her, the king of Vask gifted her his last dragon.'

The wrangler beamed. 'And she fell in love?'

'With the dragon, certainly,' said Alarik, chuckling at her surprise. 'Not with the old fool who gave it up! I can only imagine Vask is still smarting about that. I hope it haunts Regna every time she falls asleep.'

'So, the queen kept it?'

'Of course,' said Alarik. 'She and the dragon bonded at once. Not just friends, but allies. They shared a soul-connection, borne of power and royalty. The queen rode the dragon into every battle for the next sixty years and won every single time. Until the night Vask sent its mercenaries into our kingdom.' An all too familiar story. He suppressed a shudder. 'By then, the old king was dead, but his people had not forgotten his foolishness. His son intended to reclaim his father's dragon and restore Vask to its former glory. But first, he had to break the bond between queen and dragon.'

The wrangler gasped. 'He killed the dragon?'

'He killed the queen.' The wrangler paled. 'In her own bedchamber, as she slept. An easier target, I expect.' Alarik's lip curled. 'Vaskan cowardice at its finest.'

'This is quite an unsettling bedtime story,' she murmured.

'It gets better,' he assured her. 'When the dragon felt the severing of their bond, it incinerated the snivelling Vaskan prince where he stood. And his mercenaries for good measure.'

She stared at him blankly.

'That was the happy bit,' supplied Alarik.

She remained unconvinced. 'What became of the dragon?'

Alarik drew a breath. This was the part he was afraid of. Would she laugh at him, or think him foolish? 'My father used to say it retreated deep into the mountains. Cowed by grief and pain, it grew angry and restless, and so the soldiers at Grinstad had no choice but to keep it there. Trapped.' He swallowed. 'Eventually it fell into a slumber, sleeping deep and undetected as the ice crept over it and froze its thundering heart.'

There was a long, interminable silence. She pressed her lips together, taking in the weight of his words.

'It's just a theory,' Alarik felt compelled to say. 'Over a year ago, there was a great quake here at Grinstad. We pulled an ancient witch from one of the mountains. She had been slumbering there for a thousand years. I can't help but wonder what else might have awoken during the avalanches that followed. When the deep ice began to melt . . .'

Frowning now, Greta looked past him, towards those unknowable snow-swept mountains. 'I don't know what a dragon *feels* like.' She rubbed the space above her heart. 'I've never . . . well, I have no experience . . .'

'You don't believe me mad for thinking it?' he said.

She looked at him again, sincerity in that stormy gaze. 'No,' she said, quietly. 'And that's the trouble.'

Well, indeed.

'If there is a dragon in those mountains, I'm afraid it's very much awake. It's trapped.'

'Good,' he said. 'I don't relish the thought of being eaten while we're on the verge of war.'

'Do you think Regna knows about it?' she asked.

Another thought that kept him up at night. Did the

queen of Vask have a spymaster skilled enough to rival his own? 'I don't know. Though I can't imagine she'd have the courage to do anything about it if she did.'

The wrangler returned her gaze to the mountains. 'Is there a way to get inside?'

'Only the old mining tunnels.'

'I could go in. Try and find it. Perhaps even try and wrangle—'

'*No.*' The word was sharp and fast, and utterly final. 'No.'

Had she lost her senses entirely, or was this some misguided attempt to impress him?

He cleared his throat, reaching for his composure. 'It's too dangerous.'

He would not risk it. He would not risk his kingdom. Not while there was war to consider. They had enough enemies to worry about, without adding a raging dragon to proceedings.

And even if the beast could be wrangled, she was Tor's little sister. He wouldn't send her into those cruel, cursed mountains to chase a thing they knew nothing about. Better to keep it trapped. It was safer that way, smarter. 'Put it out of your mind for now. Devote your efforts to my beasts. The ones we can use against Regna.'

She swallowed, fighting the words she no doubt wanted to say, quelling that indomitable spirit that made her reckless in the face of her king. And yet a part of Alarik enjoyed it – how obvious that struggle was, how it made her squirm in frustration. She opened her mouth. Closed it. Opened it again—

'Don't ruin a perfectly good day by arguing with me, Iversen.'

'I could help it,' she said, anyway. 'Maybe it could even help you—'

'If you want to be helpful, turn your thoughts to today's task.' Something they could control, not some unnamed, hidden creature that might devour her. His eyes flicked to those silver scars on her left cheek, curiosity mingling with unease. 'The matter is closed.'

She turned away, tugging her hood up to hide her face, and he regretted his obviousness just now, and worse, that she might think he was judging her.

'Pardon my intrusion,' Lief piped up, reminding Alarik of his very existence. 'But I couldn't help but shamelessly eavesdrop on some of your conversation. Without overstepping—'

'You are already lunging,' interjected Alarik.

'I would just like to say that if there is a dragon hiding out around here somewhere, I would very much like you to keep it out of sight for the wedding. For one thing it would completely ruin the ambiance.'

'And it would probably eat all our guests,' Elva chimed in.

Lief let out a cry of alarm.

Captain Vine frowned. 'What's all this about a dragon?'

'Nothing,' said Alarik, smoothly. 'It was just an old bedtime story.' He glanced pointedly at his wrangler.

She forced a laugh. 'Nothing to get worked up over.'

'And you should thank your lucky stars, Lief,' added Alarik. 'Because if there was a dragon around here somewhere, I'd make sure you and these hideous flower arrangements were its first meal.'

Lief quailed.

For a brief moment, there was blessed silence.

Then the conversation turned again, the steward boldly launching into an out-of-tune bridal march as the pass widened and the mountains fell away, taking their hidden beast with them. The sled emerged into a sprawl of frosted fields. They stretched on and on, spilling into a glorious patchwork of skeleton trees and silvered grass. And there, grazing just up ahead, were hundreds of magnificent weaver elks, a mere fraction of the beasts King Nilas had promised as a wedding gift to Alarik and Elva.

'Holy snow!' The wrangler hopped to her feet, propping her leg on the bench to steady herself. The sled jerked at a dip in the road, and she yelped, losing her balance. Alarik lunged to steady her and for one thundering heartbeat, she stood flush against his chest, his arm tight around her middle, cradling her body in the heat of his own. He heard the soft pitch of her surprise as she searched for breath, smelled the jasmine in her hair and on her skin, felt the supple curve of her hips as they swayed against him. A groan gathered in his throat.

She pulled away, slumping on to the bench and gripping the edge to steady herself. 'Pardon me,' she said, not quite looking at him.

'That's all right,' he said, not quite looking at her.

And then, all at once, they had arrived, the sled coming to a stop at the first frost-kissed meadow.

'Tell us, Greta,' said Princess Elva, as they disembarked the sled. 'Have you ever wrangled a weaver elk before?'

'Not yet,' said the wrangler, rolling her shoulders back. 'But I'm certainly up for the challenge.'

The weaver elk were huge – each as tall as a fully-grown ice bear, and larger even than the wild moose that roamed the untamed reaches of Gevra. Their bronze coats were short and shiny, save for the coarse woollen shag that clung to their necks, lending the impression of a heavy winter scarf. Their gold-tipped antlers protruded in menacing points, each tip as sharp as a blade and filled with the strongest poison known to man. But more impressive than their natural weaponry was the speed with which they charged, moving so fast and deftly through the towering oak forests of Halgard that they had earned the name *weavers*.

'I want to see them run,' said Alarik, as they slowed to observe one grazing nearby.

Elva snorted. 'I'm afraid our elk are wilfully stubborn. You'll have to make it worth their while.'

'Shall I pat that one on the rump?' suggested Vine.

'Only if you want to lose your hand,' said Elva.

'Let's give them something to chase.' Alarik looked over his shoulder, to where Lief looked up from his corner of the sled, eyes wide. 'I have someone in mind.'

'Just don't touch the tips of their antlers,' warned Elva. 'And keep your gloves on at all times.'

'Gladly,' mused Alarik, imagining all the damage they could do in war.

His wrangler, meanwhile, was a world away, assessing the creature before them in contemplative silence. She circled the elk, chewing on her bottom lip. He hated when she did that, finding it unreasonably distracting. He was still watching her from the corner of his eye when she dipped her chin, her shoulders stiffening as she came to some internal decision.

He drifted towards her. 'Don't do anything reckless.'

She smiled at him, shrugging lightly.. 'I'm a wrangler, Your Majesty. You might as well tell the snow not to fall.' She took a handful of steps, then paused to look back at him. Concern flickered across her face. 'Don't come any closer. This will be dangerous.'

His brows raised. 'I'm the king of Gevra, Iversen. You might as well tell the wind not to howl.'

She rewarded him with a laugh, the music of it making clouds between them. He wanted to snatch them from the air and stow them in his pocket.

Get a hold of yourself, Alarik.

He stood back as she approached the elk, giving her space to work. She was slow and careful with the creature, coming at it from the front in small, measured steps. To his horror, she removed her gloves and offered the back of her hand. He had to remind himself that she was an expert in this field, one of the finest wranglers in Gevra . . . and yet he stiffened when the creature bent down to snuffle at her pale skin, its large brown eyes wary as she laid her hand on its muzzle.

'Your gloves,' he said, unable to help himself. 'Those antlers are full of poison.'

'I know,' she said, without turning around.

To the weaver elk, she murmured soft and low, stroking it all the while.

Alarik couldn't hear what she said to the beast, only the melodic hum of her words, but he caught the moment the elk's demeanor shifted. The tension leaked from its wide, rigid shoulders and it dipped its mighty head, drawing level with hers.

She rounded the beast, keeping her strokes soft and soothing. She moved those small, practised hands through the tuft of its mane, her fingers rising to trace the root of its left antler. Alarik clamped his lips shut, trusting her to keep herself safe, but he couldn't help the sharp twist in his stomach as he watched her work.

Mercifully, the elk didn't buck. It merely closed its eyes, content at her nearness.

She was soft – so very soft – with the creature in a way that made Alarik's chest ache. It made him wonder how she might use her hands on him, alone in the dark, in a place where the only beast was the one that growled in his chest. His eyes glazed, his thoughts tumbling out of the meadow and into faraway, forbidden territory, his blood heating as he imagined the warmth of her fingers in his hair, those soft, breathy words brushing the shell of his ear.

He blinked himself back to propriety at the sound of a determined grunt. The wrangler leaped from the ground in one swift movement and climbed the mighty elk like a tree. She curled her fingers in its woolly mane and hoisted herself higher, until she was straddling the sprawl of its bronzed back.

There was no hint of fear on her face. Only determination, a telltale spark of triumph setting her eyes aglow.

And yet Alarik couldn't help the swill of his own nerves. 'What in freezing hell are you doing, Iversen?'

She smiled down at him, the wind tussling with her long copper hair, and though she wore no crown or beads or finery, she looked just like a queen, a ruler of something wild and deep and ancient, the soul of the earth made into flesh and bone and beauty.

The sight of her punched through him, scouring a hole in his soul. He wanted to fill it with her.

Snap out of it, you reckless fool.
Tor will take your head from your body.
And King Nilas will burn the rest of it.

'You wanted to see the elks run,' she said, oblivious to the war raging inside him. 'So, watch!'

Alarik had no choice but to watch because she was already rising to her haunches, her hands fisted in the wool of the elk's mane, her thighs clenching just behind its shoulders, as if to say, *go, go, go.*

The elk set off at a canter, its strides growing faster, harder. The earth trembled beneath its hooves, divots of frosted dirt kicked up in its wake. The beast was entirely hers, the wildness in their souls tangling so effortlessly it looked like the wrangler had been riding it her entire life. Like this day – this moment – was nothing but sport for her.

She rode faster still, the wind racing to catch her, and Alarik watched with unblinking eyes, praying she wouldn't fall, and knowing, of course, that she would not. Soon, she was little more than a blur in the distance, a thread of laughter on the wind, a view he itched to return to his easel to paint.

Captain Vine and Princess Elva fell out of their conversation, wordlessly drifting to where the king stood watching her. And even Lief, who seemed to have no interest in anything beyond prayer rites and frock coats and centrepieces stood up in the sled to watch her go.

Just when Alarik thought his view of the wrangler couldn't get any more arresting, she threw her head back and released a shout he had heard a thousand times before.

It was a call to arms, a cry of war, the sound so stirring he absently gripped the pommel of his sword.

There came a rattling thunder, but the sky held its rain. It was the earth that trembled as the rest of the elk broke into a run, charging headlong through the fields as though to chase their wrangler all the way to the horizon.

Alarik's heart raced as he watched them spill out in a sea of bronze and gold, imagining all the soldiers they could trample on a battlefield of his making. It was even easier to imagine how this gentle, soft-eyed wrangler, who sang to her beasts and flinched at the mere sight of blood, might end up turning the tide of war – of history – in his favour.

Vine's breath hitched at the sight of the stampede, the word slipping from her on a sigh. '*Magnificent.*'

'Yes,' murmured Alarik. 'Yes, she is.'

CHAPTER 16
Greta

Greta replayed her trip to the grazing fields for days afterwards. It felt like a dream now, how the elk had responded so readily to her call, charging with her like wild things across the snow-kissed earth.

It reminded her of the first stag she ever wrangled on Carrig, back when she was no taller than a cedar sapling. She still remembered the way her father had lulled the towering creature into submission with only the lilt of his song. The stag had bent its head to the earth, its antlers gleaming in the falling light, and Greta had laid her small, trembling hand upon its muzzle, picking up the thread of her father's song and letting her spirit sing to the beast before her. It had watched her, doe-eyed and cautious, as Papa lifted her on to its back, careful – so very careful – and then all at once, she was astride the regal creature, riding headlong through the forest, as though all the trees and lakes and craggy hills were a kingdom of her own making.

The weaver elk was a stranger sort of beast, but its spirit had called to hers in much the same way, that same fire rearing to life in her chest the moment she mounted it. The rest – the riding and the wrangling – had been as simple as breathing.

The king had been pleased – so pleased he was grinning when she returned to him, the devastating beauty of his smile softening his chiselled jaw and making him appear even more handsome, though she tried not to notice. He had jumped at her offer to join her atop the elk, and they had spent an entirely marvellous afternoon whooping and laughing as they charged through the grazing fields together. And on the way back, he had spoken only to her, ignoring his beautiful bride-to-be as though Greta – and not the effervescent Princess Elva – was the most arresting person in that sled. As though his thoughts were as far from his impending wedding as she was from Carrig, and he cared only for the same beasts that she did and the thrill of how they ran when they were truly free.

She knew it was dangerous to dwell on those moments and how important they had made her feel, but the searing sunlight of the king's undivided attention had kindled a new warmth in her chest that she simply could not ignore.

Even so, she refused to let the memory distract her from her work. Thanks to long, tireless hours in the courtyard, most of the beasts had been successfully wrangled, trained to heel and strike on her command. Now, it was time to teach them their most important task: the protection of the king of Gevra at all times, and all costs.

It was this next, crucial stage of training that came to occupy Greta's mind, sending her away from the courtyard early one morning in search of the king himself. As she wandered through the palace, she came upon a flurry of activity, the servants milling to and fro with vases of fresh flowers, glittering ice sculptures and armfuls of pillar candles. She watched them go, dread unfurling in her stomach as she realized what was approaching, as fast and thundering as a weaver elk: the king's wedding.

A cloud of melancholy settled over her, snatching the smile from her face. Shame nipped at her heels as she wandered down hallway after hallway in search of the king, wishing now she didn't have to face him at all. Of course, it shouldn't matter if Alarik Felsing was getting married. What did it have to do with her? The king's heart was entirely his business, and beyond that, the alliance made sense, especially under the looming threat of war.

Still, she couldn't help picturing the wedding. She tortured herself with images of Princess Elva gliding up the petal-strewn aisle in a trailing ivory gown, adorned with jewels and flowers and—

Stop it, Greta.

You're a wrangler, not some lovelorn fool.

She was here to work, not daydream. She was a commoner, not a princess.

But Tor was a commoner when he won the heart of Queen Wren.

Greta nearly slapped the thought out of her head. She was half raving. It was the exhaustion, she knew, her tired mind reaching for absurd notions. She had spent too many long days and cold nights in the courtyard, running herself ragged. She had run her mind ragged, too, and now it was toying with her, filling her with opinions and *emotions* she had no business feeling.

The sight of Johan scurrying towards her, carrying an elaborate centrepiece of branches and pine cones, jolted her from her spiral. She leaped into his path, almost causing him to trip.

'Hi!' she said, catching a tumbling pine cone and returning it to its perch. 'Have you seen the king? I need to speak to him about the beasts.'

Johan glared at her over a gilded holly branch. 'He's in the sparring room.'

'Great.' She blew out a breath. 'And . . . where is that?'

He sighed. 'Follow me. I'll show you on my way to the ballroom.'

They soon came to the sparring room, which was nestled in the east wing of the palace. The chamber was grand enough to be a formal drawing room, the corniced ceilings and filigreed wallpaper suggesting it perhaps had been one once, but all the furniture had since been cleared away, save for a stately fireplace and a rack of sparring swords that occupied one wall. A leather viewing bench spanned the other.

Johan didn't announce her, and as he scurried off with his teetering centrepiece, she guessed he didn't want to risk the king's ire again after what had happened in the dungeons. She knocked as she eased the door open, then froze on the threshold, momentarily struck speechless.

The king was sparring with another man who, in the blur of movement, looked just like his double. They circled one other, light-footed and quick, their swords clashing high and then low. Greta marvelled at the grace with which they parried, twisting and lunging as though it wasn't a fight at all, but a dance. The other man, who appeared to be older than the king though not by much, wore his longer, silvered hair scraped back into a leather tie. They were both dressed casually in loose white shirts and fitted leather trousers, their boots gleaming in the morning sunlight. They were the same height and possessed the same lithe build, the king's gaze an icier shade than his opponent's, though both were keen and sharp.

Greta watched them, mesmerized by every measured clash and unmeasured curse that slipped through their gritted teeth.

It was the king's opponent who spotted her first. A quick glance, his brows lifting. He leaped backwards, out of the king's reach, and pointed his sword towards the ceiling. A pause in play.

'Well, well,' he said between breaths, as he took in the sight of her dawdling, slack-jawed in the doorway. She felt his gaze move over her like a trickle of ice-water, from the scuffed collar of her blue coat to the wayward strands that had slipped free of her braid, and finally, those three pale scars on her left cheek. 'It seems you have a visitor, Your Majesty.'

'If you're trying to distract me, Elias, it's not going to work,' said Alarik, keeping his stance low, his sword engaged.

But Elias's eyes remained on Greta. 'You're new,' he said to her.

'Well, sort of,' she said, thinking it might be a good idea to speak at some point.

At the sound of her voice, Alarik whirled. He cast his sword aside, raking the sweat-slick hair from his face and said, 'Iversen.'

Elias grinned. 'Tor's sister.'

'Among many other things,' she said, eager to claim her

own identity, and climb out of the box he had so neatly placed her in. 'My name is Greta.'

'He already knows that,' said Alarik, reaching for a cloth to wipe his face and the back of his neck. It was an effort for her to tear her gaze from the golden sheen of his skin and the way the charcoal streak in his hair flopped across his eyes. He raked it back again. 'Elias is my spymaster.'

Greta raised her brows. 'You must know a great many things, then.'

'Almost everything, wrangler,' he said, with a silky laugh. 'Or should I say, elk tamer?'

'I make a mean cup of tea, too. You can add that to your notes.'

Alarik laughed, setting the ember in Greta's chest aglow.

Elias smirked like he could see it. 'Have you come to spar with us, Iversen?' he said, swirling the point of his sword at her. 'Are you as good as your brother? If so, I insist—'

'My wrangler abhors violence,' said Alarik. 'Raise that sword to her, and I'll take the hand that wields it.'

Elias quirked a silvered brow, but said no more, trudging over to the bench to stretch out his legs.

'Is something wrong?' said Alarik, facing her now. She felt his gaze drift over her like a warm breeze, and knew he was searching for scrapes, marks, new injuries.

'It's the beasts. I need something for the next stage of their training.' She edged into the room. 'They have to learn your scent, so they'll know who to protect in battle. The older ones might remember it, but I'd rather not bet on it. And the younger ones don't know you well at all. An item of your clothing should do it. Or a pillowcase. Something that smells like you.'

Her skin prickled at her own words. Or perhaps it was the sharpened point of his attention, so like the blade he had just discarded. Why was the king looking at her like she had made an indecent proposal? Why did it feel like she *had* just made one?

He cocked his head. 'So, you want my shirt?'

'I— No. Not right— *Oh*.' He pulled off his shirt in one fluid movement, revealing the corded muscles of his arms and the glistening planes of his chest.

Greta gasped, her hand shooting up to cover her eyes. But the devastating image was burned into her mind: the king standing before her, half naked and smirking, as if he were her lover. Her cheeks burned at the thought, the same heat spiralling deep in her core.

Oh no.

'Iversen?'

'Yes?' she said, still shielded.

'Are you all right?'

'I am somewhat uncomfortable.'

I am a living flame, Your Majesty.

Press your lips against me and put me out.

Greta crushed her nails into her palm in a desperate attempt to regain control of herself.

The floorboards creaked and then he was before her, the broadness of him casting her in shadow. His hand came to her wrist, his fingers gently circling it. He tugged her self-made blindfold from her eyes with a low chuckle. 'Am I so hideous that you can't even bear to look at me now?'

'Of course not,' she said, far too swiftly. 'It's the opposite.'

His brows lifted, his gaze taking on a strange new intensity. She realized too late that he had been teasing her, and she had shown her hand, revealing her embarrassing crush. She took a step back, clearing her throat. 'I didn't mean to make you undress, Your Majesty.'

He wasn't blinking.

Why wasn't he blinking?

'That was not what I meant,' she went on. 'Or my intention.'

He offered her a wan smile. 'I apologize for my indecency but I'm nothing if not efficient.' He held his shirt out. 'You may take this with you. Use it however you like.'

'Thank you.'

She clutched the shirt to her chest, her lids growing heavy at the heady scent of him, a mix of woodsmoke and pine, like the first flush of winter.

He was still staring at her, and she had the absurd fear that he could hear the sudden rattle of her heart. 'If you want me for your training exercises, you need only ask,' he said, quietly. 'It's no trouble.'

She stalled in the doorway, half thinking about taking him up on his offer just so she could see more of him, so they could continue to share in that simmering passion for all things wild and unfettered, to talk more about the beast in the mountain, but then a scurrying servant carrying a vase of lilies bumbled past her. And she remembered—

'I'll leave you to your wedding preparations, Your Majesty,' she said, vaguely gesturing towards the stately ballroom. 'I'm sure I'll manage.'

He surprised her with a snort. 'This unseemly chaos has nothing to do with my wedding, Iversen. It's for tonight's welcome ball.'

'*Oh*.' She slammed her teeth into her bottom lip to keep

from smiling in relief. 'My mistake.'

He frowned. 'Hasn't anyone mentioned the ball to you?'

'I don't see why they would.' She shrugged, as she stepped back into the corridor. 'I hope it all goes well, Your Majesty.'

'You'll see for yourself.' He braced his hands on the door frame as he leaned out after her. 'I expect you to be there.'

And then he was gone. Greta stood alone in the hallway, the stir of her relief quickly turning to panic. The king was insisting she attend his ball.

And she did not have a single dress to her name.

CHAPTER 17
Alarik

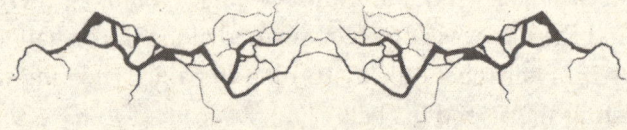

Alarik stood in the heart of the ballroom of Grinstad Palace, wearing an ivory frock coat and a menacing scowl. Beside him, stood the dowager queen Valeska in a trailing lavender gown and a diamond-encrusted tiara. Alarik was already regretting choosing his father's crown for the occasion. The gilded branches were digging into his scalp and making his head pound.

Or perhaps that was the welcome ball itself, the importance of tonight weighing heavily on his shoulders. The first members of the Halgard delegation had already arrived in regalia that proudly displayed the exorbitant wealth of their kingdom. The princess's court had dressed in an array of magnificent gowns. Autumnal hues of amber and gold and sage and ochre, their ringleted hair adorned with vines of fresh flowers. Their guards were dressed no less finely, in fitted olive-green frock coats emblazoned with the silvered crest of Halgard and carrying ceremonial swords with ornate pommels and long, narrow blades.

They mingled gladly with the Gevran nobility, who had come in traditional outfits of leather and fur and velvet, and were clustering around the edges of the room, sampling canapes from gold-leaf platters. There were all sorts of delicacies on offer, including mini sausages rolled in a fluffy pastry crust, cheese tartlets drizzled in honey, sage and anchovy fritters, and pork belly slathered in chilli and marmalade. Grand ice sculptures of howling wolves marked each serving table, spouting frostfizz into tiers of goblets.

There were pillar candles everywhere and even more hanging from the ceiling, casting a romantic glow about the ballroom, which was expertly complemented by countless vases of midnight lilies. Unlike the previous balls at Grinstad, the king's beasts were not on display tonight. For one thing, Alarik didn't want to distract them from their training, and for another, he thought it wise not to frighten off the entire Halgard delegation so soon upon arrival.

Word of tonight's ball would soon reach King Nilas, and if proceedings did not go smoothly, he might decide to rescind his offer of assistance in the oncoming war. Only Borvil, Alarik's beloved ice bear, had been brought inside for the occasion. Still sleepy from hibernation, he was snoozing contentedly on the dais beside the king's throne.

Alarik sighed as more revellers poured into the ballroom. He was already weary from small talk, his cheeks strained from forced smiling. A servant darted past with a tray of wine glasses and his fingers twitched to take one.

His mother's hand came to his arm. 'Not until the welcoming is done.'

'It's one glass.' *Then maybe six more*.

'You must be the picture of elegance and refinement tonight.'

He glared sidelong at her. She was smiling serenely,

waggling her fingers at one of her many cousins, a bearded giant with a thick tangle of hair.

'Our guests are still arriving. Try not to frighten them off with that hideous grimace, Alarik. Once the music begins, you can revel and dance all you like with your beloved.'

Alarik blew a wayward strand out of his eye. He didn't want to revel and dance. He wanted to down three glasses of frostfizz, a fistful of canapes and take his bad mood out into the cold night air where he could be as far away from his simpering court as possible.

'I hate pleasantries.'

'You have made that more than clear, son.'

'And people,' he added, churlishly.

'Not *all* people,' she said, tossing another smile at an approaching guest.

No, he supposed not. Alarik didn't hate his mother or his sister, who he missed desperately tonight. If Anika were here, she'd commandeer the entire evening and do all this hideous diplomatic chit-chat for him. Alarik hadn't hated his father either – he had worshipped him every day until he drowned. And every day since. He had adored Ansel, his idealistic younger brother who had been the best thing about his family, until he died. And Alarik didn't hate Captain Vine or his cousin, Elias. He actively sought out their company, in fact, enjoying their verbal sparring just as much as the physical.

And his wrangler – he liked her, too.

He frowned. Why was he thinking about his wrangler?

Because you are always thinking about her.

The clarity of the thought made Alarik bristle. He shook it off, making himself think of Elva instead. He could see her there, across the room. She was flitting from guest to guest, like a butterfly alighting on flowers, shaking hands and kissing cheeks wherever she went. She wasn't even a princess of Gevra, and she was doing a better job than he was, standing stiffly in his aching crown, offering tight smiles and curt words to everyone.

'Elva will make a wonderful wife,' said Queen Valeska. 'She is artful in her ways, a true poised and practised princess.'

Alarik hummed unhappily. He didn't want practised and poised. He wanted wild and untamed, snow-kissed and windswept. He wanted— No.

Don't do that.

Don't even think it.

He snatched a goblet from a passing servant and downed it in one go. The frostfizz rushed through him, cooling his blood. He set it on the tray, fighting the urge to reach for another. Not yet. It would be a long night, and the music hadn't even started.

Pace yourself.

Alarik plastered on a kingly smile and welcomed a hundred more guests, shaking clammy hands and learning names he quickly forgot.

Tonight's welcome ball marked a crucial step in his alliance with Halgard, but the thought of his actual wedding day curdled inside him like spoiled milk. How had it come to this already? How much further would it go? At night, he lay awake, staring at the stars through his window, wondering at the true cost of this alliance. He could admit at least that a strategic marriage was the right decision for his kingdom. It was a far more appealing solution than calling for aid, not that he hadn't considered sending word across the Sunless Sea to the witch queens of Eana.

But even if Wren and Rose agreed to help him, Alarik could not keep their magic here forever, nor use it to sustain his own borders. And it was magic that had weakened Gevra in the first place. Magic had killed his brother and thousands of his soldiers and beasts.

No, magic was not the answer. It was not *his* answer.

And neither was begging. If Alarik wanted aid, he would have to offer something in return, even if that something was himself.

The stern words of his father, King Soren, rang in his head: *a ruler who cannot defend their own territory does not deserve it*. The only way to defend Gevra was with an army of Halgard's finest soldiers marching alongside his own, and enough weaver elk to trample a battalion of Queen Regna's crimson-armoured warriors.

Marrying Princess Elva wasn't just a wise decision, it was the *only* decision.

And yet . . . and *yet*.

Alarik couldn't bring himself to welcome the sacrifice of it.

'Enough niceties,' he huffed, after enduring yet another limp, sweaty handshake, this time from a duke of Halgard. The ballroom was heaving now, the frostfizz flowing freely. It was time to begin the night, if only so it might end quicker. He clicked his fingers, bidding the musicians to play.

The quiet rattle of drums gave way to a soaring Gevran waltz. Alarik spied Captain Vine lingering by the chocolate fountain. She was in her uniform and chatting animatedly to Vesper Hale, who had come dressed in an obscenely tight black leather gown with a slit that would make even Anika blush. By the way her hands were moving, mimicking an explosion, he guessed she was talking about fire lances.

Finally, a little entertainment.

He took an eager step towards the fountain just as his mother said quietly, 'They played this waltz at my wedding to your father. It was our first dance.' He turned to look at her, and the warm smile she had been wearing was gone, replaced by a haunted look he knew all too well. She stared through him, her eyes glazing. 'It's been so very long now. Years have passed, and yet my heart still aches for him. Sometimes, if I close my eyes, I swear I can feel the shadow of his arms around me. I can hear his laughter on the wind.'

Alarik swallowed thickly. Grief was a thundercloud in his chest, and he was afraid if he opened his mouth all that darkness would pour out of him and make her pain worse. He couldn't think of anything to say anyway, and the longer he failed to fill the silence, the more she retreated into herself, curling her arms around her body as though the melody was wounding her.

He briefly considered drawing his sword on the musicians and smashing every one of their instruments, but then he thought of his brother, Ansel, and wondered what he might do. Some gentler instinct stirred inside him, and Alarik found himself reaching out to his mother. 'Shall we dance?'

She blinked in surprise. 'I'm not sure I remember how,' she said, slowly.

'You will,' he said. 'And even if you don't, I am a master of the waltz. Everyone will be looking at me anyway.'

He took her hand in his, her other rising to rest on his shoulder, and before she could recede into the tide of her grief, he swept her on to the dance floor, away from the long shadow of their past and the sadness that dwelled there.

They danced like starlings in spring, gliding and spinning in the flickering candlelight, until the other revellers fell out of their conversations to watch them, and then to join them.

'This is wonderful!' said Valeska, laughing as they whirled. 'I had forgotten the joy of waltzing!'

Alarik's gaze darted, scanning the sea of faces around them before coming to rest on the doorway.

Why hadn't she come?

Had he not made his wishes clear to her this morning? Or had his demand irked her, prodding at that willfulness she seemed unable to contain. Maybe she was staying away to teach him a lesson in manners. Or maybe he had spooked her by taking off his shirt in front of her. Then, pressing it into her hands, marring those perfect, slender fingers with his sweat. Could she tell in that moment that he had been imagining them not in his sparring room but upstairs in his bedroom, and that he was not the only one baring himself?

Had he frightened her with the unexpected rush of his desire?

Damn it, where *was* she?

'She's over there by the window,' said his mother, too easily reading the anxiety in his gaze. 'See?'

Alarik glanced over to where Princess Elva was standing in a puddle of laughter, a gaggle of Gevran noblewomen hanging on her every word.

'Yes, I see her,' he said, returning his gaze to the door.

'Then who are you looking for?' There was a frown in his mother's words.

'No one,' he lied, twirling her again. And again. And

again. It was not enough to spin away her curiosity.

She watched him closely now, as though she was trying to read the lines on his brow. 'Let me tell you a secret,' she said, after a moment. Her smile turned small and sad, and she dropped her voice, in case someone else might overhear. 'Even despite these long years of loss, a part of me still hopes that, even now, fate will undo its cruelty to our family and by some divine miracle, your father will come striding through that doorway, open his arms and sweep me up.'

Alarik grimaced at the words.

She went on. 'I can't help but notice that you are looking at that door the same way I am.'

He shook his head. He held no such delusions. Nor did he relish the thought of his father's drowned and bloated ghost barrelling into his welcome ball and scattering everyone in an unholy panic, but he kept his voice kind, and said, 'You mean, with hope?'

'No,' she said, softly. 'With longing.'

He opened his mouth and closed it again. He spun her away, but her words lingered long after they changed partners, the music turning jaunty and light as the clock ticked ever closer to midnight.

And all the while, Alarik watched that door, willing her to come to him.

CHAPTER 18
Greta

Greta was just stepping out of her bedchamber when she ran into Nanna. It was late evening, and everyone in the palace was at the king's welcome ball, dancing and drinking and rubbing shoulders with the noblefolk of Halgard. She yelped in surprise when the head servant came bustling around the corner.

Nanna took one look at her and frowned. 'Where are you going?'

'Uh, to the ball?' She had been pacing in her room for an hour already, trying to summon the courage to go up there and honour the king's invitation. But the admonishing look on Nanna's face was enough to snatch all that hard-fought courage away.

'You're wearing *that*?' she said, aghast.

Greta looked down at her blue frock coat and black trousers. It wasn't the most exciting outfit, but most of the senior palace guards, and Captain Vine herself, had opted to attend in their uniform. She had overheard them talking about it at lunch. And anyway, Greta didn't have another option. She had, at least, washed and braided her hair into an intricate coronet atop her head and applied some pink rouging to her cheeks and lips. 'This is all I have.'

'Your boots are scuffed.'

'Only the toes.'

Nanna sighed, her gaze lingering on the missing button of her left sleeve. 'Our beasts are in better shape than this.'

'Well, if they are, it's thanks to me,' Greta felt compelled to point out. 'And what does it matter if my boots are scuffed? I'm just a wrangler.'

It's not like the king will care.

Or even notice me.

Nanna's brows scrunched. 'You are *the* prized wrangler of Grinstad,' she said, clucking her tongue. 'You are important, and as such, people *will* be looking at you. And your scuffed boots.' She wrinkled her nose. 'No. This will not do.'

'But I—'

'Go back to your bedchamber,' she said, shooing her away. 'I'll return shortly.'

She scuttled off. Duly chastened, Greta slinked back into her bedroom and waited for the head servant to come back. Nanna kept her word, returning in short order with an armful of dresses.

'One of these should work,' she said, laying them on the bed. Greta's breath caught as she stared at the gowns, which were made from velvet and fur, each one rendered in a different jewel tone. There were five in total, all as beautiful as the next. 'You're shorter than she was but if we're quick, I can take up the hem.'

'Shorter than who was?' said Greta, with a prickle of unease.

'Ansel's bride.' Nanna sighed, her brown eyes softening.

'Before he died, Prince Ansel was engaged to Queen Rose of Eana. The dowager queen had her measurements sent over ahead of the wedding and arranged a wardrobe of Gevran gowns for her honeymoon . . .' She trailed off. 'But it was not to be.'

Greta's heart clenched as she recalled how poor Prince Ansel had been murdered on his wedding day. She knew all too well of the pain and regret that had come after. Her own brother had been assigned to guard the prince, but when the sword flew, Tor had leaped in front of Queen Wren instead, protecting his beloved on instinct. Ansel had died, grasping at the blade in his chest.

And Alarik Felsing had watched it all, powerless to save his little brother.

'So, the dresses have never been worn,' she said, quietly.

'Not these ones,' said Nanna. 'Though your brother's beloved Queen Wren did . . . visit us . . . for a time last year. She was a hopelessly clumsy creature with little regard for grace and elegance.' Greta couldn't help but smirk. Her brother had clearly made a fine choice. 'Thankfully, I saved my favourite dresses from being destroyed.'

Greta hummed as she looked over them, trailing her fingers along the delicate embroidery. Nanna was far less reverent about the whole affair, tugging off her frock coat and urging her to undress, so they could get to work.

After trying on every gown – and enduring countless unnecessary critiques from Nanna – Greta settled on a sweeping dress of midnight blue. It had a boned corset tied with silk ribbons and the entire bodice was brocaded with delicate silver snowflakes. The skirts tumbled to the floor in gossamer waves that swayed with every step, making it feel as though she was moving through the snowy night sky.

Nanna insisted on taking the hem up by three inches in case she fell flat on her face, but she was nimble with a needle and thread, making quick work of the task. Greta used the time to stuff the pair of silver slippers Nanna had brought down with handkerchiefs, until they fit snugly on her feet. Nanna helped her dress, then, tightly lacing the corset until Greta could feel every single one of her suffering ribs.

'Why are you scowling?' said Nanna, twirling her by the shoulders. 'You look like a princess.'

But I am not a princess.

I am a wrangler.

I belong to the wild.

And yet . . . when she caught a glimpse of herself in the mirror, Greta's breath hitched. She did not often feel beautiful. Not in the craggy forests of Carrig, wearing furs that were too big for her, worn boots and threadbare clothing. No one ever looked twice at her – except to linger over her scars – and Greta had never minded. She did not want to be looked at, to be noticed and judged.

But tonight . . . tonight, her eyes were bright and shining, and her smile was full. For the first time in her life, she felt truly beautiful, and it was a strangely empowering feeling. She was still smiling at herself in the mirror, swishing her skirts to and fro and wishing her sisters were here to see her, when Nanna produced a vine of midnight lilies. She threaded them through her braided hair, making a crown of flowers.

Greta's heart swelled.

Perhaps I can be a princess, just for tonight.

Nanna stood back, grinning as she beheld her. 'You might be hideously late, but at least you look the part.'

'Thank you, Nanna,' said Greta.

'Go on, then,' she said, nudging her out into the hallway. 'Forget your beasts for tonight and find a nice soldier to dance with.'

Greta followed the swell of music up through the palace and into the east wing, her slippers feather-soft on the carpet. She had never felt so graceful, gliding like a swan on still water, and yet when she reached the doorway to the grand ballroom, she paused.

The ballroom was dripping with opulence and teeming with so many finely dressed nobles, she felt dwarfed by it all, like a child playing dress-up in their mother's closet. Her fingers dug into the door frame as she scanned the room, looking for a friendly face.

As if tugged by an invisible string, her gaze fell on the king. Or perhaps it was the way he waltzed that drew her attention to him. With a flicker of surprise, she noticed that he danced the same way he fought – with effortless skill and leonine grace. Tonight, dressed in a resplendent ivory frock coat and with his hair swept back beneath a crown of golden branches, he looked more striking than ever, like a stag standing guard over his forest.

The king was dancing with Princess Elva, who looked breathtaking in a high-necked amber gown, with her hair arranged in artful ringlets. One hand held her tiered skirts as he spun her, round and round. She moved like a spinning top, her gown glowing under the flickering lights. They were as perfect as a painting, and though the sight of them together stirred an aching sadness inside her, Greta couldn't tear her gaze away. She could have watched them all night.

She could have watched him forever.

As though she had reached out and prodded him with the sheer force of her longing, the king lifted his chin up, his icy gaze finding hers from all the way across the room. It pinned her to the door frame, then roved slowly, taking in her crown of flowers, the pale column of her throat, the curve of her waist and then, the dramatic spill of her skirts.

Greta stood frozen, letting him devour the sight of her.

Something glowed in his eyes and his mouth twitched into a frown. Her throat tightened at his disapproval. She had clearly chosen the wrong dress, fussed too much on her hair. The flowers had been a mistake. Perhaps he had expected her to come in her uniform, just as Captain Vine had.

Greta flinched. She had been a fool to listen to Nanna, to let the servant primp and preen her into some poor impression of a princess. She was a wrangler and she belonged in the arena with the beasts. By the way the king was glaring at her, he was plainly thinking the same thing. Her cheeks burned with embarrassment.

She was relieved when the music arched, and Elva returned to the king's arms, laughing as she spun him away.

Greta was about to turn around and flee when Aren's voice floated through the milling crowd. 'Greta! Over here!' He was standing by a serving table, waving a goblet back and forth. He had forgone his uniform tonight in favour of a simple green frock coat trimmed in pewter fur, his usual mop of dark curls tamed into artful waves.

Aren's smile was so bright and kind, Greta couldn't bring herself to run from it. She unstuck herself from the door frame and drifted towards him.

'Thank you,' she said, taking the goblet and sipping from it. The frostfizz zipped through her, replacing her simmering dread with a welcome, giddy warmth. 'I was just about to flee.'

'You did have the look of a frightened doe about you,' he said, with a chuckle. 'Which is funny, seeing as you've faced far worse challenges than *this* in the arena.'

'Depends on what you consider a challenge,' murmured Greta, stealing another glance at the king. He was glaring at her again.

She quickly looked away.

'You look nice,' said Aren, a little ineptly. 'Better than nice, really. Beautiful. Very beautiful.'

She smiled into her goblet. 'Nanna made a project of me tonight.'

He nodded knowingly. 'She caught me in the hallway and made me return to my room to shine my boots.'

'That sounds about right,' she said, feeling better already. And perhaps a little bold. Aren looked particularly handsome tonight, and he was gazing at her in a way she hadn't noticed before. His brown eyes glimmered with hope. Would it be so wrong to entertain it? After all, their friendship these past few weeks had cheered her on many dark, lonely nights. Could it be something more? Something safe . . . a diversion from other more traitorous desires. 'Do you dance, Aren?'

'I wish I did,' he said, sheepishly. 'I'm afraid I have two left feet.'

Greta wasn't much better but the frostfizz was making her giddy and the music was so achingly beautiful, she wanted to crawl into its heart. 'What if I let you stand on my toes?' she said, teasing.

'That depends . . . Is it bad luck to squish the king's wrangler right in front of him?'

'I doubt he'd even notice,' said Greta, though the back of her neck prickled, and she had the unnerving sensation that he was still watching her. 'Why don't we revisit the subject after another glass or two of frostfizz?'

'A fine idea,' he said, clinking his goblet against hers.

They lingered at the edge of the dance floor, chatting and laughing as they sampled the mouthwatering food, ranking each dish by its deliciousness, and finding only winners. Other soldiers drifted over to join them, the conversation turning playful as the frostfizz took hold. It made for a welcome change from Greta's first week at Grinstad, when the soldiers would hardly look at her. But as time passed, and she was able to prove her skill with the beasts, she began to feel accepted. Like one of them.

Brynn, a stocky red-haired guard with a howling laugh, grabbed a bowl of sugared cranberries and whipped up a game, tossing a berry several feet in the air before catching it in her mouth. The others joined in, tossing cranberries to each other with great delight.

Greta plucked one from the bowl and threw it to Aren. He caught it on the first go, grinning as he swallowed it down.

'Good toss, Iversen!' said Brynn, with a wink. 'I wonder what you could do with a throwing axe.'

'Keep wondering!' said Greta, secretly pleased to have proven her worth, even if it was just a silly game.

Aren took a step back. Greta tossed another berry, giggling as it hit his forehead. He jerked his head to the side and rolled it expertly into his mouth.

The soldiers crowed with laughter.

'Your turn!' Aren grabbed a berry and lined up his shot. Feeling confident, Greta stepped back until she teetered on the edge of the dance floor.

Aren tossed the cranberry with impeccable aim, and she leaped, catching it between her teeth. She grinned around it, then used her tongue to curl it into her mouth, enjoying the burst of sugared tartness.

The others erupted in applause, but Aren stilled, his face falling.

'What is it?' Greta came towards him. 'Why do you look like you've seen a ghost?'

He swallowed thickly. 'It's the king . . . He's glaring at me. Murderously.'

'He's not glaring at you, Aren,' said Brynn, looking between them. 'He's glaring at *her*.' She grimaced at Greta. 'I think you're in trouble, Iversen.'

Greta turned to find herself snared again in the brightness of that devasting glare. The king was standing on the far side of the ballroom now. Captain Vine was beside him, muttering urgently in his ear, but Alarik made no sign that he was listening to her.

His attention was entirely on Greta.

Brynn was right. That look meant trouble. And when Alarik Felsing stepped away from his war captain and stalked single-mindedly towards her, she had the unnerving sense that that trouble was about to get a whole lot worse.

CHAPTER 19
Alarik

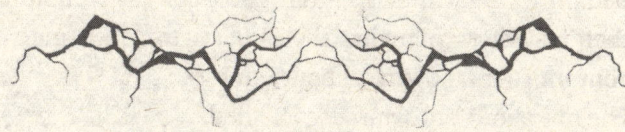

Alarik was seriously considering stabbing his falconer. Just a light stabbing. More of a warning than a fatal wound. He had been thinking about it ever since his wrangler stepped into the ballroom and stole all the air in his lungs. She had arrived hideously late, looking like some wild-born princess, sprung from the snow-capped forests of Gevra, with her hair crowned in flowers and that magnificent midnight-blue dress hugging every inch of her curves.

A bolt of longing had gone through him at the sight of her, and he had scowled at his own weakness.

While Alarik's attentions had hopelessly splintered, Elva hadn't so much as faltered in his arms, so poised and practised was the princess on the dance floor. She was a worthy waltz partner for the king, but he couldn't keep his mind from wandering. It was all he could do to spin her, again and again, away from the sight of his wrangler and the terrible things she was doing to his heartrate. But his gaze betrayed him, returning to find Iversen at the end of every perfectly executed twirl. He couldn't look away from her in that dress – in that crown of flowers – and yet every glimpse of her laughing with that damned falconer was torture.

'Why do you look like you're about to go to war?' said Captain Vine, joining the king at the edge of the dance floor. She gestured at his hand resting threateningly on the pommel of his sword.

'Remind me,' said Alarik, in a low, menacing voice. 'How important to the war effort *is* our falconer?'

Vine frowned, following the king's gaze. 'Tell me your current murder face is not about our wrangler.'

'It's not about our wrangler,' he lied.

'Then why are you staring at her?'

'I want to dance with her.'

Captain Vine sighed. '*That* is a very poor idea.'

'What are you, my mother?' Alarik snorted. 'What do you care who I dance with?'

'I don't especially care about your dance partner. What I *do* care about is all those poisonous elk King Nilas has promised us, not to mention the extra battalion he's dedicating to our cause. So, if you're itching to dance with someone, then please, for the love of Grinstad, dance with *your bride-to-be.*'

Alarik rubbed the spot between his brows. His captain was making perfect sense, of course. Elva was his betrothed, not to mention the very reason for this ball. But he had danced five waltzes with her already. What harm would it do to dance with one of his own for a change? The Halgard delegation were fascinated by his beasts, and Iversen was their leader, the very person who would lead them into war. If Alarik invited her to join him for one dance – just enough to take her in his arms and let those skirts spin around them – then it would only be to satisfy his guests' curiosity.

'You're over-reacting, Vine. She's my wrangler. My guests will want to see her.'

'Tor was your wrangler for years. Did you ever dance with *him* at a ball?'

'Don't be pedantic. Tor is a terrible dancer.'

'And you've sure as hell never danced with *me*.'

Alarik turned to his war captain. 'Would it make you feel better if I asked you to dance?'

Vine recoiled. 'Don't you dare. You know I get motion sickness.'

His attention wandered back to his wrangler at the precise moment that infuriating, mooning falconer decided to toss a berry into her mouth. She caught it with zeal, laughing in triumph.

And then Alarik was walking – no, *marching* – right through the next waltz, parting the dance floor in rivers of skirts and frock coats.

Iversen met his gaze as he bore down on her, that dainty chin raised like she was steeling herself for a blizzard. Everything else fell away, the lilt of music and the roughened guffaw of soldiers, the chattering guests and the heady smell of wine, until there was only the storm of her eyes and the cautious tilt of her head.

She stepped towards him, like she was approaching a wild beast.

Is that what he looked like to her? Some kind of rabid creature in need of taming? Or was that spark in her eyes borne of something beyond caution? Was it the thrill of a challenge?

If he was in his right mind, Alarik would have walked right past her, reached for a morsel of fresh air instead of this beautiful woman draped in the colours of Gevra – a woman who was not his bride-to-be – but it was too late for second thoughts, and anyway, Alarik never had been adept at impulse control. Gevran, to the bone.

It was only a dance. A fleeting moment of having her in his arms and then he would let her go. Of course, he would let her go.

She didn't belong to him.

And he was engaged.

She was his wrangler.

His best friend's sister.

And – he was suddenly before her.

'Your Majesty,' she said, evenly, uncowed. 'Why are you scowling? Are you angry?'

He blinked. 'No.' *Just mildly tortured.* 'I'm . . . hungry.'

He fought his flinch. Why had he said that? What was wrong with him?

She frowned. 'Hungry?'

'For sugared cranberries,' he added. 'I noticed you were tossing some about just now.'

'Oh.' Her cheeks erupted. 'You *are* angry,' she said, covering her face with her hands. He hated how she did that – hid herself from him whenever she was overwhelmed. It was then that he liked to look upon her the most. 'And after I scolded you about that silly lemon in your war room! Now here I am, tossing fruit about in your ballroom as part of some merry little game. It's so careless.'

Alarik swallowed his groan. In a bid to recover his own embarrassment, he had said the wrong thing entirely.

'I should know better, I know, but I was just so nervous when I arrived and it seemed like a bit of fun,' she went on, in a rush. 'A helpful distraction from all this intimidating grandeur, not to mention all the beautiful people, and I suppose I wasn't thinking—'

'Iversen.' Alarik took her hands and nudged them away from her face. 'Stop spiralling and dance with me.'

She stared at her hands in his. 'W-what?'

'Do you know how to waltz?'

'Well, yes . . . I . . .' Her breath hitched as he stroked her knuckles with the pad of his thumb. Once, and then again because he couldn't help it. 'Well . . . I've only ever danced with my sisters.'

'I will endeavour to match their grace,' he said, leading her on to the dance floor and ignoring all the curious sets of eyes that turned on them.

'There was nothing graceful about Hela's technique,' she said, smiling a little. 'She accidentally broke my toe. Twice.'

'So, the bar is low.' He swept her into his arms. 'I promise I will be gentle.'

She looked up at him, her eyes softened by curiosity, as if she was wondering whether that was even possible for a brute like him.

Yes, he wanted to tell her. *Let me show you.*

As the music stirred into another soaring waltz, he placed his hand on her waist, suddenly conscious of how his fingers brushed against the delicate boning of her corset. He exhaled through his nose, trying to ignore the flare of heat that rippled up his spine. She raised her arm, her left hand coming to his shoulder, so feather-light, he could hardly feel it.

'I won't break, Iversen,' he said, quietly.

'Nor will I,' she said.

He pulled her flush against him, his right hand finding hers and dwarfing it. He squeezed a little and she squeezed back, a smile breaking across her face that was more lovely than a snow-kissed dawn. The music arced and he led their waltz, pleased to find that she was not only competent, but *good*. Graceful and nimble and smiling all the while, like there was nowhere else in the world she would rather be. She closed her eyes, her chest swelling as she breathed in the music.

'Well, wrangler,' he said, dipping his head to whisper in her ear. 'Tell me honestly, am I better than my wolves?'

She rewarded him with a tinkling laugh. 'You certainly look better in a frock coat,' she teased, as he spun her. 'Unfortunately, they tend to bunch around a wolf's tail.'

'And you must admit, my footwork is far superior.'

'Perhaps. But you're unnervingly quiet. You haven't howled once.'

'That would really give the Halgard nobles something to talk about.' A laugh sprung from Alarik at the very thought.

She broke into a grin. 'Much better,' she said, approvingly.

'Are you saying I laugh like a wolf?'

'I'm not saying anything, Your Majesty.' Her eyes twinkled as she spun away from him. 'Only dancing.'

'Now, I'm wracked with insecurity. I'll never laugh again.'

'You should count yourself lucky,' she said, returning to his arms. 'My sister's betrothed laughs like a woodpecker.'

Alarik laughed again, and this time she joined in, the music of it following them across the dance floor. The waltz was far from over and he already wanted more. He wanted this waltz and the next one, and three more after that, but he was conscious of his mother's disapproving face at the edge of the ballroom, not to mention the whispers that followed them across the dance floor. He would have to release his wrangler once the music changed, and no doubt watch her return to that giddy-faced falconer and his bowl of sugared cranberries.

He shook off his annoyance, resolving to make the most of this last minute together. But when he looked down at his wrangler, she was fixated on something above his head. She quailed, her face slackening with horror.

Alarik stilled. 'What is it?'

'Some kind of winged beast,' she said, stepping out of his embrace. 'I've never— *Oh.*'

Alarik saw it then, not inside the ballroom, but through the windows. A pair of huge crimson wings soaring over the mountains. And behind it, another, and another. There appeared to be a flock of them, but as they drew closer, Alarik saw they were not birds at all, but gliders. Soldiers.

Soldiers from—

'CAPTAIN VINE!' he roared, just as an almighty crack rang out. Just over the mountains, the sky burst into flames. The earth trembled at their feet, and an ice sculpture crashed to the floor. The ballroom erupted into screams.

Captain Vine barrelled towards the king. 'GRINSTAD IS UNDER ATTACK!'

Over the rising din of panic, Alarik heard his wrangler's voice. 'It's the elk! They've gone for the elk!'

Alarm gutted Alarik as those distant flames rose to lick the sky, spitting up plumes of black smoke.

'RIDE OUT!' he yelled. 'TO THE GRAZING FIELDS!'

Captain Vine rushed past him, barking orders, while the dowager queen leaped into action, trying to calm the startled guests. The king's soldiers assembled with remarkable speed, but the beasts were still in their pens and the horses in their stables. They had to move *now*.

He spun on his heel, trying to think.

Focus, Alarik.

What would his father do?

He would go at once, and fast, before those cowardly gliders fled.

'The bear!' cried Iversen, pointing to where Borvil was now standing by the king's throne, jostled awake by all the commotion. 'He's swifter than any horse!'

'Yes, of course!' Alarik gripped her shoulders. 'I'll ride out ahead. Go to the forest and check on the beasts,' he said, but his wrangler was already turning from him, picking up her skirts and bolting for the door.

Alarik whistled through his teeth, calling Borvil from his perch. The bear lumbered towards him, parting the guests in a fresh sea of screams. Elva alone remained. She waded towards him and grabbed his arm before he could mount the beast.

'You can't ride out there alone! Wait for your soldiers!'

Alarik shook her off. 'Go to your bedchamber,' he said, urgently. 'Stay there until we return.'

He leaped on to Borvil's back without another word, seating himself with ease. Alarik and Borvil had grown up together, after all. He had ridden the mighty ice bear down these hallways more times than he could count, and then later through bloody war after bloody war.

Riding from the ballroom was no great hardship, but the swell of frightened revellers was slowing them down. At a command from his master, the bear let out a thundering roar, clearing a pathway before them. Alarik rode right down it, out the door and into the hall, and onwards still, towards the atrium, where a pair of startled guards flung open the front door and let the king and his bear loose into the night.

They raced across the front lawn and through the black gates, the night air whipping Alarik's face as he rose to his haunches and urged Borvil on, faster and harder, towards those distant flames. He loosened his collar as he rode, ripping the buttons and rolling the sleeves of his frock coat until he felt as unrestrained as the bear beneath him.

Minutes slipped by but he didn't feel them. War raged in his veins, heating his blood and narrowing his thoughts until he could see nothing but those greedy flames licking the sky. He cleared the mountain pass in record time, noting the new fissures crawling up the rock.

Not now.

There would be time to worry about that later.

When he finally reached the grazing fields, most of the elk were dead. There was smoke everywhere, all those finebred, noble beasts burnt to bone and ash.

Alarik tipped his head back and released a roar of anger. Borvil rose to join him. Alarik fisted his hands in his fur, directing the ice bear towards the edge of the field, where he spied the jutting crimson tip of a downed glider.

Borvil charged towards it, weaving through the fires with the skill of a beast who had seen many wars. When they were almost upon it, the bear slowed to let his master slide from his back. Alarik drew his sword as he approached the glider. He kicked the winged apparatus away, but the soldier was already dead, having collided too hard with the packed dirt. He wore the infamous crimson armour of Vask, the breastplate stamped with the queen's golden fist.

Alarik bit off a curse, then stalked to another upended glider, which had crash-landed in the next field. He found the same sorry scene there. He went to the next glider, and then the next, hissing and swearing as he kicked the metal wings from their crimson corpses.

The flames died out, the helpless groans of dying beasts replaced by the approaching thunder of hooves. As the first of his soldiers made it to the grazing fields, Alarik came to the final glider. He flung the metal contraption aside with a roar of frustration. A pair of wide hazel eyes stared up at him from the dirt. He glared down at the face. It was young and pale and streaked in blood. Alive. But the soldier was dying, a feeble hand pressed against the gaping wound in his neck.

Alarik pressed the point of his sword there. '*How many?*' he growled. 'How many of you are there?'

The soldier grimaced, the blood in his teeth the same shade as his armour. 'Queen Regna sends her regards,' he spat. 'To you and to Halgard.'

Alarik grabbed him by the scruff of his neck, yanking him up until they were forehead to forehead. 'If you want a swift death, tell me the number,' he hissed. 'Or I swear on my crown I'll use the last minutes of your sorry life to show you the true measure of Gevran brutality.'

Fear flashed across the man's face, and with the last ebb of his strength, he said, 'Ten. We are ten.'

Alarik snapped his chin up, counting the downed gliders. Five.

There were only five in the grazing fields.

The soldier laughed, his breath coming out in bubbles of blood. Alarik drove his sword into his heart, extinguishing the sound. He whirled then, dread prickling in his cheeks as he searched the fields, looking for those other five gliders . . .

Captain Vine was leading her soldiers through the fray, kicking out the flames and collecting the broken gliders, while Vesper hiked up her leather dress to retrieve the spent fire lances.

'VINE!' yelled Alarik. 'How many gliders do you—'

There was a sudden, earth-trembling boom. It was far, much too far from where he stood. And followed, almost at once, by a bloodcurdling chorus. Not screams this time, but roars. Ragged, terrified howls cut through the night.

Alarik whipped his head around, looking towards the palace and the forest beyond, and saw that the sky there had turned amber and gold.

And he knew, with such unbridled horror it nearly brought him to his knees, that his beloved beasts were burning.

CHAPTER 20
Greta

As the ballroom descended into chaos, Greta picked up her skirts and fled. The grazing fields were burning, and the palace beasts could smell it. They were yowling in terror, as anxious and frightened as the noblefolk inside. Her heart ached to comfort them, her slippered feet barely touching the floor as she ran.

Only moments ago, she had been waltzing with the king of Gevra, secretly pretending she was a princess. When the music began, she had practically melted into his embrace, her skin tingling at the brush of his warm breath along the shell of her ear. It was a perfect, fleeting deception. Now, the first stirrings of war had come to Grinstad. Queen Regna had launched a surprise attack, sending armed gliders over the mountains to rain down fire on the king's weaver elk.

And now they were suffering, trapped and burning in fields not far from the palace. The cruelty of it pricked tears in Greta's eyes as she hurried towards the forest, wading through the thickening snow and swirling mud, drawn to the keening distress of her animals. She went first to the ice bears at the back of the woods. She could sense their anxiety like a hum in the air, her own chest tightening in response. She sang as she neared them, reaching for a lullaby her father had taught her when she was a girl.

Greta's chattering teeth added an unexpected staccato to the melody, but after a few moments, she felt the bears quieten. Her chest loosened. She went from pen to pen, slipping inside to soothe the animals. She combed her fingers through their fur, softly singing them to sleep. She tried not to let her thoughts wander back to the king. It was hard to believe the warrior riding bareback into all those spitting flames was the same man who had held her tenderly on the dance floor, whispering and laughing as though they were the only two people in the world.

It was a kindness, she knew. Alarik Felsing had seen her upset and sought to distract her. Perhaps out of some misplaced loyalty to her brother, or to stop his prized wrangler from blubbering in front of his guests. Whatever his reasons, Greta had found peace in his arms and joy in the unrestrained howl of his laughter.

She was smiling as she slipped out of the last pen, leaving Baldur and Nel snuggled up together. Her crown of braids had come undone, and her sodden skirts gathered dirt as she made her way up to the wolves. They were still wide awake. She spotted Tollo and Gale sitting at the front of their pen, growling at the sky.

'It's all right,' she murmured, but the wolves' eyes were wide and glowing. Tollo's hackles rose, and Greta felt the spike of his fear like a shot of ice in her blood.

She turned just as a slew of gliders emerged from a low-hanging cloud and soared right over the treetops, towards the king's beasts.

Towards her.

She opened her mouth to scream, but the sound was lost to a thundering crack.

The world erupted in firelight. The trees hissed as they burned and the beasts roared as one at the gathering smoke. The gliders disappeared somewhere in the trees, but Greta's eyes were on the flames racing menacingly towards the pens. Her head throbbed with one single, pounding thought: *save the beasts!*

As guards flooded the courtyard behind her, she picked up her skirts and ran, into the raging heart of that terrible inferno.

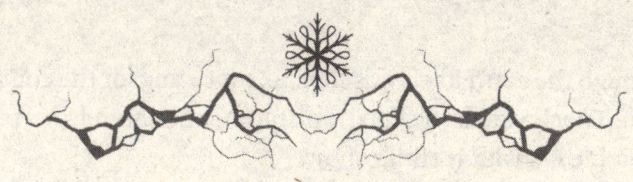

CHAPTER 21
Alarik

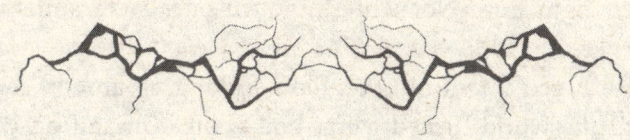

Alarik rode so fast the wind dislodged his crown. He ripped it off, clenching it in his fist. His breath sawed out of him, joining with Borvil's heaves. In the distance, smoke curled around the spires of Grinstad Palace, like greedy serpents. The sky above was amber, painted by the same flames that were devouring his beasts.

What the hell was taking his guards so long? The fires should be out by now.

Unless . . .

Unless they were worse than he could see from here. He fisted his hands in Borvil's fur, urging the bear faster. He cursed himself for leaving the palace in the first place, for letting adrenaline get the better of him. He should have sent Captain Vine while he stayed behind, preparing for the rest of Regna's assault. A smarter king would not have acted so rashly.

His father would have known better.

Alairk should have known better.

He cleared the mountain pass, the ice bear never tiring despite the strain of both journeys. The rock groaned, as though the earth itself was flexing, preparing for the coming war. Cracks spiderwebbed up the mountain and the peak trembled, shaking off its snow.

The creature was wide awake somewhere deep in the rock face. Unsettled. Angry. Alarik shoved the thought from his mind. He couldn't afford to think about the unknowable beast right now. Not while his own ones were suffering. *Burning*.

He urged Borvil on, the snow kicking up around them until the world turned gauzy and white. On and on they rode, until at last the palace gates groaned open. Soldiers rushed across the front lawn to meet their king, and he roared at them to turn around, to run towards the frightened howls at the back of the palace and all that choking smoke. Alarik arced around the side, galloping right into the plumes.

He tugged up his collar to cover his mouth as they made for the courtyard, which was heaving with soldiers. There were beasts there, too, wolves and bears and mountain lions, tigers and snow leopards and foxes, all pacing and growling as they were corralled into the arena.

Alarik leaped off Borvil and raced across the courtyard, keeping one eye on the forest. Most of the flames had been put out but the trees in the back quarter were burnt to cinders, and at least half of the pens were destroyed. Guards yelled back and forth as they drove sleds through the woods, carting huge buckets of snow to douse the last of the fires. The servants hung back, filling troughs for the beasts to drink from.

Smoke stung Alarik's eyes and clung to his clothes as he made his way into the arena, trying to count the beasts there. At least a hundred, he guessed, and there were plenty more milling around outside, struck by panic and confusion.

Alarik grabbed the nearest guard, yanking her towards him. 'How many beasts did we lose?'

She blinked in alarm. 'Your M-m-majesty,' she stammered. 'Eight. Only eight, so far.'

Eight. A paltry number compared to the massacre of elks. But a sour loss, nonetheless.

His brow furrowed. 'But half of the pens are destroyed.'

'The wrangler got most of them out.'

'Oh.' Alarik's shoulders relaxed, his breath leaving him in a short sigh. He turned, scanning the figures moving around him. 'Where is she?'

'I don't know, Your Majesty. I only saw her run down to the pens. Then all the beasts came rushing out. They were roaring, trying to get away from the flames . . . I never saw her come back.'

Alarik froze. A terrible chill went through him as he pictured his wrangler running headlong into the fire. He thought of his dead beasts and wondered if she was among them, if she had gone too far in her haste to rescue them. He closed his eyes and cursed. He could imagine her all too clearly, running recklessly into the belly of Regna's inferno.

That damned wildling.

He released the guard and left the arena without another word. Soldiers and beasts parted as he marched across the courtyard, his eyes aching as he squinted through the smoke.

He grabbed soldier after soldier, the same question growling through his teeth. 'Where is my wrangler?'

No one had seen her, not since the fires started. Dread

gathered in his chest, shoving him onwards, towards the forest. A tall man bounded into his path – and it took Alarik a moment to recognize his spymaster. He grabbed his shoulders, pulling him close. 'Give me good news, Elias.'

'We have a survivor.' Elias flashed a wolfish smile. 'The rest of the gliders are impaled on the trees in the forest, but Vine picked up one by the mountain face. He was trying to break into the old mining tunnels. Bumbling fool must have lost his way.'

Dread pounded in Alarik's heart.

Regna knows about the beast.

Or at the very least, the queen of Vask suspected something was awake inside his mountains.

Something that could quite possibly burn him to ash in the blink of an eye.

Did she mean to free it? To use it against him?

'Don't worry, he's still squirming,' said Elias, misreading the horror on Alarik's face. 'I'll make him sing.'

Alarik snapped back into himself.

Forget the beast. Find your wrangler.

He shoved his crown at his cousin. 'Put this somewhere safe. Then find Vine and drag that glider down to the dungeons. You can begin the interrogation.'

'Aren't you coming?' said Elias, clutching the gilded crown to his chest in confusion.

Alarik was already stalking past him. 'Later.'

Once he reached the treeline, the commotion faded. The call of his soldiers and the whimpering howls of his beasts were swept away by the wind. The smoke was thinning, enough that Alarik could make out the skeleton trees at the back of the forest and the charred pens beyond.

He whipped his head around as he walked, taking in the destruction. Hatred burned deep in his bones, for Regna and her gliders and her cloying avarice. Their war would come, and she would suffer dearly. He would see to it himself, slowly and painstakingly, until his blade turned red with her blood.

But revenge would have to wait. His wrangler was missing, and every step into his blackened forest made his chest tighten. There was no sign of her in the trees or down by the burnt pens. Unless she had gotten trapped inside one, hemmed in by a ring of flames . . .

The thought made him break into a run. For too long, there was only the gasp of his own panicked breaths and the thunder of his heartbeat in his ears, but as the rest of the smoke cleared and the wind quietened, he became aware of another sound. Not a cry or a howl, but a lullaby.

It was faint and lilting, and as lovely as birdsong.

Alarik chased it, his heart climbing into his throat as it got closer, louder. He was halfway through the forest, following the melody like a stream of sunlight, when he spotted his wrangler. She was sitting inside Saga's pen, with the snow leopard stretched lazily across her ankles and her two young cubs curled up in her lap. She was singing to them, and when Alarik realized the lullaby was hers – and that she was *alive* – he nearly fell to his knees in relief.

He gripped the wooden slats as he stood by the pen, watching her. She was sitting in a pool of fractured moonlight, smiling as she sang. Her gown was ripped and covered in mud, and one of her silver slippers had come off. The snow leopard was chewing on it happily.

There were smudges of ash on the wrangler's cheeks and

her copper hair had fallen from its crown of braids. She was ruffled and snow-mussed and singing like a nightingale, more beautiful in this mucky pen than she had been in that ballroom when Alarik couldn't take his eyes off her.

He wasn't just relieved at the sight of her. He was mesmerized.

Saga chirruped, noticing him, and the wrangler looked up, gasping as she fell out of her song.

CHAPTER 22
Greta

Greta froze under the icy spotlight of the king's gaze. How long had he been standing there, listening to her sing? And why did he look like he had been run through with a sword? The agony on his face was so startling that she dropped her gaze, silently fretting as she scanned him for injuries. There was no blood, only ash, marring his ivory frock coat. Two of the buttons had snapped off, and the collar was ripped. His pristine hair was unkempt, falling in messy strands across his forehead.

'Don't stop,' he said, a rasp in his voice.

Greta's heart galloped. Was he asking her to sing for him? She couldn't think of anything more nerve-wracking than serenading the king of Gevra in the ashes of a forest fire. Her voice was scratchy from the smoke, and she could barely hold a note thanks to the chattering in her teeth.

She shook her head. 'It was only a lullaby,' she said, running her hand over the cubs on her lap. 'The little ones were frightened. I was trying to soothe them.'

He nodded slowly. 'I thought you were dead.'

She blinked in surprise. 'Oh.' Was that why he had looked

so pained just now? Was he afraid the fires had gotten to her, or was he aggrieved at the prospect of having to find another wrangler?

'Well . . . I'm not.'

He gave a dry chuckle. 'So I have deduced.'

She glanced down at herself, wincing at her ruined dress. 'Although I am a bit dirty.' A severe understatement. She had completely destroyed her gown, and Saga had made quick work of her slipper, both articles of clothing that had been generously loaned to her by the palace. 'I'm sorry about the dress.'

He threaded his arms through the slats, watching her in that unnerving way of his. 'If it's any consolation, I think it looks better this way.'

She bit back her smile. 'I was about to say the same thing about that lovely frock coat of yours.'

He snorted, dusting ash off one of his sleeves. 'Now, it really brings out my blackened soul.'

Greta didn't know whether to laugh or not. She had witnessed enough of the king's quick temper and uncompromising brutality to fear him, but ever since coming to Grinstad, she had found his kindness most surprising of all. It wasn't the warm and effusive kindness of her sisters, but a quieter sort, dealt in careful smiles and bracing words. She found it in their shared enthusiasm for his beasts, and in his fierce protectiveness of her as his wrangler. It was the king's unseen kindness that made her feel safe here, like she was not quite as far from home as she once thought.

He opened his mouth to say something else, then paused at a faraway chorus of shouts. Soldiers were trawling through the forest to assess the damage now that the last of the fires had gone out.

The king grimaced. 'I think you have the right idea, Iversen.'

'What idea is that?'

'Hiding.' He unlatched the gate and slipped inside the pen. He sank to the ground beside her, pulling one leg up to his chest and anchoring it there with his arm. With the other, he reached out to absently stroke Saga's back. The leopard snuffled in appreciation.

'See?' he said, his teeth winking in the moonlit dark. 'We're best friends again.'

'It's a shame you don't have a lamb strip in your pocket. Then you'd have her for life.'

'I'd like to tell you I'm above bribery, but it's actually the cornerstone of my reign.'

She laughed and he joined in. She lost herself in the music of it.

'Fickle creatures, beasts,' she said, ruffling the cubs on her lap. 'Would you like to hold one?'

'No.'

'Too late.' She plopped one in his lap. 'You can name him if you like.'

He frowned at the cub, even as he held it with a gentleness that surprised her. 'My father always warned me not to name the beasts,' he said, as he combed his fingers through its fur. 'It makes it harder when they die in war.'

'I think it's hard either way,' said Greta, tickling the cub's chin. 'At least with a name, they can be remembered. It's a matter of honour, I think.'

He turned to face her. 'I never thought of it like that.'

'Well, you're not a wrangler.'

'Just a vicious king.'

She smirked at the cub in his arms. 'Not so vicious now.'

He arched a brow. 'Stop trying to humanize me, Iversen.'

'I won't tell a soul,' she whispered.

'In that case . . .' He sighed, lifting the cub, and inspecting him at great length. 'How about Slasher?'

She pulled a face. '*Slasher?*'

'Well, *Skull-crusher* is too long. It doesn't quite roll off the tongue the same way.'

'Skull-crusher is even worse!' she cried. 'It's so *violent*.'

He levelled her with a hard look. 'What is it that you think we do here?'

'We are not naming him Slasher,' she said, sternly. 'I refuse to call him that.'

'Fine.' He scrubbed a hand across his jaw. 'How about Hatchet?'

'Give me back the cub.'

'No.' He curled his body around the creature, burying his jaw in its scruff. She reached for the cub, and he lightly swatted her away, sending a delicious jolt up her arm. 'I am the king.'

'Well, I'm the wrangler, and I get final say.'

When he didn't budge, she pretended to snatch at him, and this time, he caught her hand. His grip was warm and tight, and she felt it thrumming in every part of her.

'You are very bossy,' he said.

'Thank you.'

She knew it wasn't a compliment, but he was still holding her hand and staring at her just a little too long. He blinked, as if remembering himself, and let her hand fall.

He gestured to the cub on her lap. 'What have you named that one? Enlighten me as to your creative genius.'

Greta beamed. 'Boo.'

'*Boo?*' He nearly choked on the name. 'Why?'

'Because he's *bootiful*,' she said, earning an elaborate eye-roll. 'Oh, come on, he's adorable!'

'He won't always be adorable.'

'*All* beasts are adorable in their own way,' said Greta, in a tone that dared him to argue with her.

'You're very strange,' he relented.

'Thank you.'

That one felt like a compliment.

He hummed as he returned his attention to the cub. 'Dash,' he said, after a moment of intense consideration. 'Will that do?'

Greta turned the name over. 'Is it because he's dashing?'

'Just like his king.'

She snorted but gave no argument. He was right. Even in his filthy frock coat, with messy hair and scuffed boots, he was the most handsome man she had ever laid eyes on. She preferred him here in the dirt with a beast on his lap than in that opulent ballroom with all the noblefolk of Halgard eating out of his palm. There was something unrestrained about Alarik Felsing out here, something that felt truer than all the pomp and glamour that came with his title. 'All right,' she said. 'Dash, it is.'

'Very well.'

He fell silent then, a furrow appearing between his brows. Greta got the sense that he was working up to something. She could feel his stress, taut as a bowstring between them, and she wondered if it had been there all along, simmering underneath their conversation.

'The weaver elk are dead.'

She sucked in a breath, feeling like she had been punched in the gut. She clutched Boo tighter, her words coming in a squeak. 'All of them?'

The king nodded, his gaze locked on the distant moon. 'Regna's gliders found their mark.'

'I'm sorry,' she whispered, placing a hand on her chest to soothe the ache there. 'Those poor creatures.'

He kept his gaze on the sky. 'If it's any consolation, they didn't suffer.'

She could tell it was a lie. He was trying to shield her from the gruesome reality of it, and perhaps, by looking at the moon, he was shielding himself from the horror on her face. She sat up straighter, trying to get a hold of herself.

This is war, Greta. And war is ugly.

It will only get worse.

'My beasts would have met the same gruesome fate if it hadn't been for you,' he went on. 'Thank you.'

'Of course,' she said, quietly.

'You're brave, Iversen.'

'It's what anyone would have done.'

'No, it's not,' he said, at last turning to face her. His eyes glittered, the blue inside threaded with silver. 'It's what *you* did. You alone.'

Her cheeks warmed at the hardness of his praise, as though he was daring her to refute it.

'Have you always been like this?' he pressed.

'What, easily embarrassed?'

'Fearless,' he said. And then once more. 'Utterly fearless.'

She almost laughed, but it was an honest question, and

how was he to know the quivering little girl she had once been? The one she still sometimes felt like when she was alone at night in the cold, cloying dark?

'No,' she said, truthfully. Her mind flitted back to that day in the low forest with her father, when his blood had painted the snow crimson and she thought she was going to lose him forever. For years afterwards, she had endured the most awful nightmares and debilitating panic attacks. Even now, whenever she felt overwhelmed, she had to catch her breath and centre her mind before it ran away from her. 'I was very scared, for a very long time.'

'Why?' he said, quietly.

'My father was attacked when I was seven. It was the most terrified I've ever been. I don't think that terror ever fully wore off.' Her hand went instinctively to the scars on her cheek. She tugged her hair free to cover it.

He leaned over and brushed it back, his fingers leaving a trail of heat along her skin. 'What happened?' he said, as though he hadn't just lit every one of her nerve endings on fire, as though he wasn't gazing at those three silver scars like they were a mark of honour.

Greta swallowed twice to steady her voice. 'Papa and I were out hunting for deer. It was late winter, and the snowfall on the island had been so heavy for so long, we were half starved. Hela and Tor were older, so they went out together. Kindra hated to hunt, preferring to stay home and tend to the animals with Mama. Papa usually went out alone, but I was so eager to go that day. So eager to help him. I loved the wildness of Carrig even then, the howl of its blizzards and its tall, creaking mountains, the cold snaps in the morning that cloud your breath and snatch the feeling from your nose.'

She smiled, picturing the pale pink sky above their little cabin, the sun fighting its way over the mountains with what little heat it had. When she glanced at the king, he was smiling too, as though the memory was theirs to share.

'We were in the cedar wood, stalking a doe,' she went on. 'Papa had been singing for hours, casting lullabies deep into the forest. When we spotted the creature, it felt like we had struck gold. I was shaking with so much excitement I almost gave us away. But we weren't the only ones tracking the deer. As we closed in, a snow leopard leaped from the trees. It was half starved, like we were.' When she closed her eyes, she could still see its emaciated body, the ridges of its ribcage and the sunken hollows of its eyes. She could still hear the desperate sawing of its breath.

'Papa shot the leopard. Then he shot the doe.'

She pressed her lips together to keep them from wobbling. She hated how the guilt still prickled at her.

'He had to kill the leopard,' said Alarik, with such devastating simplicity, she almost wept. 'You were starving.'

She dropped her head and looked at Boo. 'That's what Papa said. I know he was right. But I cried anyway.'

'That's your wrangler's heart,' he said, softly.

She smiled, ruefully. 'Troublesome little thing.'

'No,' he murmured. 'No, I don't think so.'

'The snow leopards on Carrig mate for life. I've always loved that about them. When they fight, they fight together and when they hunt, they hunt in pairs . . . Papa was so addled by hunger that he didn't think to look for the leopard's mate that day. By the time we spotted her, she was already leaping at him. It ripped his leg apart. Tore out half his stomach.'

Greta said the words quickly, hoping the panic would pass, too, but she began to tremble. Wordlessly, he inched closer, until his leg brushed against her skirts. She closed her eyes, letting the pine and smoke on his skin settle the desperate rattle of her heart.

'It all happened in a flash. I didn't know what to do. Papa was going to die, right there in the clearing. So, I leaped between them and covered his body with my own.'

Alarik tensed against her, but held his silence, willing her to go on.

'The leopard took a swipe at me, and I knew she was going to kill me, too. Kill us both.'

He turned ever so slightly, his breath feathering the scars on her cheek. 'What did you do?'

'I sang.' She closed her eyes. 'I closed my eyes and sang, just like my father taught me. And it worked. The leopard drew back. After a while, I felt her leave. I'd willed her to, with every desperate note. And when I couldn't see her any more, I hauled my father up from the forest floor, slung his arm around my shoulder and dragged him home. The trek back was just as vicious as the leopard. It nearly killed us both.'

But it hadn't killed them. It had bonded them forever, the memory of that day so harrowing, they couldn't speak of it for months. For weeks, Greta didn't speak at all.

'You saved your father's life. Without even thinking about it.'

'He would have done it for me.'

Alarik pulled back to look at her, his gaze lingering on her scars. Pride simmered there, and another softer emotion she could not seem to place. For the first time in her life, she didn't feel ashamed of the marks on her cheek. She was glad of them, of what they told of her story and the depth of her loyalty. 'Brave to the core, Iversen. I should have hired you at seven years old.'

That drew a laugh from her, the heaviness of her tale dissipating as easily as smoke. Another kindness from her king.

'I suppose I shouldn't be surprised by your courage,' he went on. 'You have never once baulked from me.'

She cocked her head. 'Do you want me to?'

'Just once, for show. I have a reputation to uphold, you know.' He was teasing her, and it made her feel giddy. 'You must know that everyone baulks at me. Even when I'm not here.'

'That's because they're afraid of the beast that lives inside you,' she said, before she could stop herself. 'I've known beasts all my life. I feel at home around them.'

'So, you think I'm a beast,' he said, wryly.

'No!' She stiffened in horror. 'I only meant that . . .' She frowned, trying to dig herself out of the hole she'd just flung herself into. 'Well, I think there's a beast inside all of us. But we spend so much of our lives shoving our beast down, hiding it away, ignoring it. We so often pretend that we're not scared or sad or *hungry* for something vital beyond what we already have . . . and your beast, well . . . your beast is wide awake.'

'That explains my feral charm,' he remarked.

'Perhaps,' she allowed. 'I think it commands and scares people in equal measure. They don't know how to feel about a king who acts exactly how he feels and takes what he wants. You are a man who listens to his beast.'

He was silent for a while, chewing on her words, and then, picking at a thread on his trousers that was very close to where her leg brushed against his, he asked, 'What is my beast hungry for?'

'I don't know,' she said, watching his fingers with rapt attention. 'Only you can answer that.'

He nodded slowly, and she wondered if deep down, he already knew the answer. His fingers moved to the edge of her gown. He worried a thread there, pulling it loose, just to toy with it. 'What does your beast hunger for, Iversen?'

Her blood heated at his question, at the nearness of his touch, hovering above all those silk tiers. She imagined a hundred different things she would have said if she was bolder, how she would have threaded her fingers through his if he was not the king and she was not a wrangler from Carrig.

She swallowed down all that reckless need and offered the plainest truth. 'Food,' she said, simply. 'For as long as I can remember, my beast has hungered for food.'

The king stilled, his hand on her skirts.

'When you wake up hungry every morning and go to bed clutching your empty belly at night, every single desire beyond food is a luxury you can't afford,' she went on. 'Now that I'm here in your palace, and I'm fed and warm each night, I hunger to feed my family. To see them through this winter, and all the ones that will come after.'

When she glanced at him again, all traces of humour were gone from his face. 'Carrig is starving?'

'Not just Carrig,' said Greta, knowing the blizzards that ravaged her little island had swept in from the east, and had been just as harsh on other villages. The fisherfolk had said as much. There were thousands of other families across the frosted plains of this kingdom, straining to survive. 'Gevra has always been a warring nation, ruled by fearless kings and queens who go to battle without hesitation, again and again, for the good of their people.' She hesitated, wondering if she should go on, but he was watching her intently, and it was too late to go back now. 'But there is more than one way for a country to suffer, Your Majesty. Starvation is a war of its own. It's not quick and bloody. It's slow and aching, corrosive in a way that eats you from the inside out.'

The king was so still, he looked like a statue. She held his gaze, watching the truth settle like a shadow behind it.

'So, that's why you came here,' he said, quietly. 'My wrangler who does not care for war.'

'I'm grateful for the opportunity, Your Majesty,' she said, quickly.

'Call me Alarik,' he said, with a bristle of irritation. 'At least when we're alone.'

Greta's heart hitched, but he seemed not to notice the weight of his words – that he was affording her a level of intimacy he shared with only a handful of others.

He was agitated now, distracted and restless. He set Dash back in her lap, his hands brushing against her bodice as he drew back. Her breath caught as he rolled to his feet, adjusting the collar of his ruined frock coat.

'Thank you for your bravery tonight, Iversen,' he said, still nursing a frown as he peered down at her. 'And your words. All of them.'

'You can call me Greta,' she said, suddenly burning to hear him say her given name just once, even if it was in frustration.

But he shook his head. 'Then I might forget you're Tor's sister.'

Now it was Greta's turn to frown. 'Why do you need to remember that?'

He stared at her for a long moment, the ice in his eyes melting. 'I just do.'

Then he left, and she felt the loss of him like a cold, sweeping wind.

CHAPTER 23
Alarik

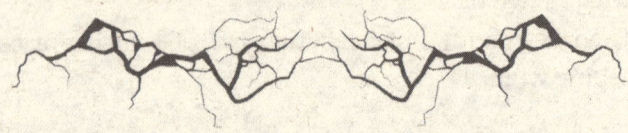

Alarik walked six paces, then stopped. What was he doing, leaving her half frozen in that pen with one shoe and a ruined dress? It was freezing out, though he hadn't noticed the chill himself until he'd rolled to his feet and left the warmth of their little bubble. He had stayed far longer than he'd intended to, and it still didn't feel like long enough. He could have sat in that mucky pen all night, trading his candour for her own, listening to tales of her childhood on Carrig, and the fierceness with which she loved her little island.

His wrangler loved her home the same way he loved his – with uncompromising devotion. She lived for snowfall and cedar trees, for craggy hills and keening winds, for dark mornings and crackling fires, for beasts in all their forms, and in all people. Every morning, she rose to the challenge of this unforgiving land and embraced it with open arms. She was everything that was beautiful about Gevra. Her song gave voice to the ancient soul of this kingdom, and if fate was fair, it would have ripped the crown from Alarik's head and placed it on hers the moment she was born.

Greta Iversen was perfect.

No wonder his beasts were so taken with her. She had a way of speaking to the heart of him, of peering right through his careful veneer and seeing the man, not the king. Not the reputation. And yet she didn't go easy on him either. Some of the things she had told him tonight had made him uncomfortable. His insides had twisted with guilt when she spoke of her family's hunger, of the starvation that plagued his towns and villages. His people were suffering, and he had been so focused on Vask he hadn't even noticed.

Had his father been careless, too? For all the time he shadowed him as a boy, Alarik couldn't recall ever hearing the great King Soren enquiring about grain stores across the country, about fishing hauls and calving seasons. Was war the only thing his father ever thought about?

Was war the only thing the Felsings were good for?

Alarik closed his eyes, losing himself in memories of beasts and bloodshed, of dead soldiers and burning pyres, of breakfasts scarfed over sprawling maps and heated strategy meetings that ran so late he often fell asleep in his father's chair. Even during times of peace, war was never far from Soren's mind. Sometimes it felt like it occupied a place at the dinner table, stalked the hallways at night and crawled into bed beside the king.

But there was more to Gevra than war. In the space of one conversation, Alarik felt like the blinkers had been ripped from his eyes. If his people were suffering, then it was his duty to help them. Just as it was his duty to keep his wrangler warm.

He shook off his frock coat and turned back to the pen, only to still at the lilt of that lovely voice.

*'Deep in the trees, where the red berries grow,
Lives a leopard who prowls on a bed of fresh snow,
Restless, he waits for the cold winds of fate,
To show him a path that will lead to his mate.'*

She was singing again. Not for him, no, she thought he was long gone. She was singing for his beasts, and the lullaby was so soft and stirring, he pressed his forehead against the slats and closed his eyes to listen.

*'High in the hills, where the black roses bloom,
Lies a leopard who nurses a heart full of gloom.
But an old breeze is stirring and tugging her east,
Where a mate there cries out to the soul of her beast.'*

When the lullaby changed, turning low and sad, he thought of his brother and his father, lost to this world. He welcomed the ache in his heart, the nearness of his grief reminding him that he was more than a brutal king of beasts. He was a brother and a son. A man, who could see beyond the bloodshed of war. A king who could fight for his people and take care of them, too.

Let that be his life's work.

Let that be his legacy.

Alarik stood in the blistering cold until he lost feeling in his fingers. When his face went numb and his teeth were chattering violently, he tore himself away from the wrangler's song. Not wanting to disturb her or let her know he had been listening, he laid his frock coat at the entrance to the pen for her to find and turned for the palace.

The night's chaos had passed. The displaced beasts were

slumbering in the arena under the watchful eyes of his soldiers, while the others had returned to their pens for the night. The fires were out and the smoke was gone, the sky pinpricked with thousands of glittering stars.

Alarik was stalking through the grand atrium when Elias found him. He came up from the west wing, his rolled shirtsleeves revealing the blood spattered along his forearms. When he spotted the king, the worry on his face turned to relief.

'Where have you been?' he called out. 'Your beloved bride-to-be has been looking for you. She's drunk in the cedar lounge with the noblewomen of Halgard. They're playing pass the hat with your father's crown.'

'Good for her.' At least Elva had found her own diversion from the horrors of the night. 'I'll speak to her in the morning.'

'Where have you been?' Elias repeated.

'I got held up.' It was no business of his cousin's where he'd been. 'How was your session with Regna's glider?'

'He sang like a nightingale.'

Alarik smiled, thinking of his wrangler. 'Anything to report?'

'More rumblings of Regna's invasion plans. We're still pinning down timing and positions. Vesper's examining the fire lances. They were a lot more powerful than we expected.'

'And what of the mountains?' said Alarik.

Elias canted his head. 'What about the mountains?'

'Never mind,' said Alarik, quickly waving his question away. So, there had been no talk of the beast or its ancient prison, then. Perhaps he was being paranoid.

Elias frowned, looking him over. 'Where is your frock coat?'

Alarik glanced down at himself. 'It must have fallen off.'

'You're acting very strangely.'

'Smoke inhalation,' he said, mildly. 'Tell me, cousin, how many scouts do we have?'

'A hundred or so. Most are up in the Blackspires, but a handful have pushed north into Vask.'

'Assemble another team. I have a new task for you.'

Elias's brows rose. 'Please don't tell me it's another war.'

'Not quite,' he said, with a snort. 'I want you to send scouts across Gevra, to glean the conditions of every single town. Their grain and meat stores, their livestock, and the fishing hauls in the villages along the coast. I want to know what food there is to eat, how much of it is in reserve, and how many people are going hungry.'

There was a long beat of silence.

Elias narrowed his gaze. 'Why?'

'Do I pay you to ask questions?'

'I'm trying to work out the angle . . .'

'The angle is *aid*, Elias,' snapped Alarik. 'I want to send them aid.'

'Oh. Right.' Elias scrubbed a hand across his jaw. 'That's probably a good idea.'

In fact, it was an obvious idea, and Alarik hated himself for never once considering it. It was one thing to be cruel in war, but another to be unfeeling at home . . . or worse, oblivious.

'There's more than one way for a country to suffer,' he said, repeating the wrangler's words with growling conviction. 'I won't have my kingdom invaded, but neither will I have my people starve. This winter has been crueller than most.'

Elias nodded, slowly digesting his words. 'I like this version of you,' he said after a beat. 'You should inhale smoke more often.'

Alarik glared at him.

He backed away. 'I'll gather some scouts and report back with my findings.'

Alarik headed for the stairwell, his footsteps heavy with exhaustion. 'I'll deal with the glider in the morning.'

'As you like . . .' said Elias, that note of confusion still in his voice. 'Sleep well, cousin.'

Alarik yawned as he climbed the stairs. With the echo of his wrangler's song still glowing in his chest, he would indeed sleep well. Comforted by the knowledge that she was warm and safe in his palace, in his coat, in his thoughts.

Even if those thoughts were a secret. Now, and always.

CHAPTER 24
Greta

Greta woke before dawn with a dull ache in her chest. She sat up, trying to make sense of the discomfort, but she couldn't remember her dreams. A week had passed since Queen Regna's assault on the king's beasts, the long night of unrest followed by days of calculated preparation. War was rising to meet them. The beasts were training as hard as the soldiers. Greta spent her days guiding them into different formations, running through defence postures and attack drills, while trying not to dwell on what it was all for: battle and bloodshed.

And, for many, death.

Too disturbed to go back to sleep, she washed and dressed, trying to ignore the anxiety thrumming in her heart. She skipped breakfast and went straight to the courtyard, where most of the beasts were still slumbering, save for Tollo and Gale who were tussling over a rope. Greta walked through the forest, listening for whimpers, and inspecting the pens for any signs of unease.

Something was wrong. The ache in her chest was not her own. Somewhere nearby, a beast was suffering. She slumped on to a tree stump and closed her eyes, listening with her heart, like Papa had taught her.

Where are you, wild one?

And why are you upset?

'You missed breakfast.' Greta snapped her eyes open to find Aren standing over her. He held out a blueberry oat muffin wrapped in a napkin. 'I swiped this for you.'

She shook off her frustration at being interrupted and returned the falconer's smile. 'Thanks, Aren. I came out early to check on the beasts.'

He nodded in understanding. 'Queen Regna's attack has had us all on edge. But you shouldn't skip breakfast. How can you take care of the beasts if you forget to take care of yourself?'

'You sound like my sister,' she teased, opening the napkin and taking a bite of the muffin. It was still warm, and so delicious she groaned.

'I'll take that as a compliment,' he said, rolling back on his heels.

'How are the birds?' she asked, between bites. 'Are they giving you any trouble?'

It occurred to her that she might be picking up on the discomfort of a nighthawk or a falcon.

He shook his head. 'Nothing beyond a little anxiety,' he said, looking towards the mews. 'I'm just about to fly them.'

'Let me know if you need any help.'

'Eat your breakfast, Greta,' he chided. 'That will help me.'

She waved him off and he sauntered away, his hands dug into his pockets as he fixed his gaze on the trees, listening to the chirping dawn birds.

Greta polished off her muffin, and decided to go for a walk to see if it might help untangle the pain in her chest. She left the forest, waving to the morning guards as she arced around the grand palace, exploring the sprawling grounds as the sun rose over the Fovarr Mountains. As she strolled, Greta's mind drifted back to Carrig. She wondered what her sisters were doing right now, and if the blizzards there were still ravaging their forests and chasing their fish away.

It wasn't long before she reached the front lawn. It was a quiet, silvered morning, and mist draped like a veil over the mountains. Greta searched for their peaks in the fog. The wind whipped up, carrying a distant groan, and her anxiety sharpened into a painful spike.

She surged forward without meaning to, her steps quickening as she moved away from the palace. The mountains were calling to her. Or rather, the beast within. She felt its panic in her throat, the hum of its fear rattling under her feet. How could she go on ignoring it while it was suffering like this? Perhaps she could find a way to soothe it, to call out to it with a song, to let the creature know it was not alone here.

The guards scowled down at her from their watchtowers.

'Where is your sled?' said a stern-faced woman in a tall, fur hat.

'What is your business?' asked a red-faced man with greying teeth.

'I'm the king's wrangler.' Greta gestured at her uniform, which matched their own. 'I need to see about a beast in the mountain.'

They exchanged a wary look.

'Unless you want it to come out and eat you,' she added, with a bland smile.

'As you were,' grunted the first.

'Move along,' added the second.

The gates groaned open, and Greta bolted through them before she could second-guess herself. She shouldn't be alone out here, but she couldn't ignore her wrangler's heart. It had never once failed her.

She tipped her head back, cowed by the towering grey mountains. They seemed to go on forever, like frothing waves. She trailed her fingers along the mountainside until she came, at last, to a crevice in the rock. It seemed the rubble had recently been moved away, creating a narrow opening. It must be one of the old mining tunnels the king spoke of. She slipped inside, following the stony path. Darkness enveloped her, the air turning damp and stagnant. She clung to the wall as she wound her way into the mountain, the slow shuffle of her footsteps echoing around her.

Shrouded in blackness, she closed her eyes, listening for the beast. There was a low keening, coming from somewhere deep in the mountain. She shuffled towards it.

It's all right, wild one. I'm coming.

Before long, the path forked, the wall falling away and leaving her grasping at nothing. She tried to swallow her fear, but panic thickened her throat. This time, it was her own. In the dark, reality crept in. She shouldn't have come here by herself. Without light and rope. Without supplies and a weapon. What could she do for the frightened beast without the tools to help it? Without a flame to show herself? If she did manage to free it, the king would never forgive her for going against his orders. She'd be sent back to Carrig on the first sled out of Grinstad.

She scrunched her fists, cursing her recklessness. She should go back and talk to Alarik. But as she twisted in the dark, her hands grasping at nothing, she realized she had lost her bearings. She didn't know the way out.

Her heart galloped, her breath punching out of her. The beast moaned, and a faint smell of burning filled the tunnel. Smoke stung her eyes and she winced, hating her own helplessness.

Calm down, Greta.

Breathe.

She startled at a faraway flash of amber, and then the sound of hurried footsteps coming towards her. She yelped as she was shoved backwards, the rock biting into her shoulder blades as a blazing torch appeared before her. A face flickered behind it, pale and seething.

Greta blinked furiously, trying to adjust to the sudden flare of light. Her assailant was much taller than her, with broad shoulders and strong arms. One pinned her to the wall, while the other brandished the flame high enough to illuminate sharp canines and a familiar sweep of blonde hair.

'Your M-majesty,' Greta stammered, in surprise.

'Close.' The voice was lower, softer. 'Try again.'

Greta shoved him away, heaving as she took in the rest of him. Dark blue eyes and slender brows, his sleek hair silver rather than gold. 'You're his spymaster. Elias.'

'And you're his wrangler,' said Elias, with a delayed huff of recognition. 'What are you doing all the way down here?'

'Uh . . . exploring?' said Greta, awkwardly.

He eyed her carefully. 'I think you're keeping something

from me, Iversen.'

It occurred to her that his presence here was just as strange as her own. 'What are you doing here, Elias?'

He blinked, taken aback by her question. Or perhaps it was her accusatory tone which likely struck him as hypocritical. 'I'm keeping a wary eye on these tunnels . . . Seeing what kind of secrets there are to be found down here. Or indeed people.' He gave her a meaningful look. 'Does the king know you're here?'

He had her on the backfoot again. 'Not exactly.'

He smirked at her through the flame. 'Oh dear.'

She folded her arms. 'There's a beast in these mountains. I wanted to see if I could help it.'

His eyebrows lifted. 'So, the rumours are indeed true.'

Couldn't he hear it keening, even now? Didn't he sense its mighty presence in these ancient tunnels?

'Is it truly a dragon?' he said, voice hitching.

'I don't know,' she said. 'We won't know until we find it.'

And free it.

Though Alarik would never allow it.

'I need to speak to the king.'

'Leave the matter to me,' said Elias, quickly. 'I am, after all, his most trusted cousin and spymaster, while you are . . . well, an attendant to the king's animals. It's not quite your place, is it?' His smile curled. 'In fact, you should scurry back to the arena. I don't need to remind you that we're about to go to war. You have your own beasts to worry about.'

She winced at his words. He was right, of course. She had been gone for over an hour, and she was supposed to start working on battle formations with Captain Vine today. Not that she was particularly looking forward to it.

'Please don't mention this to the king.'

'I'll deal with it. You get back to your post,' said Elias. But when she turned into the darkness and stubbed her nose on a rock, he lunged, taking her by the elbow. 'On second thoughts, I'll walk you back myself. If anything happened to you in here, Alarik would behead *me*. And what a terrible waste of handsomeness that would be.'

Greta worked the beasts all morning and through lunch, grabbing a sandwich to eat on the go. In the fields behind the palace, she joined a stressed-looking Captain Vine, who had an uncanny ability for barking orders that made everyone in a half-mile radius stand to attention. Together, they paired off the animals with different groups of soldiers, working through several key attack and defence formations.

They went through the motions again and again, until everyone, on two legs and four, was run ragged with exhaustion. When the dinner bell rang out, Greta could have wept with relief. In the dining hall, she sat with Aren, who looked on admiringly as she scarfed down two bowls of lamb stew and half a loaf of brown bread.

When she returned to her bedchamber, there was a letter waiting on her desk. She expected it to be from her father, who had already written to her twice at Grinstad, but was pleasantly surprised when she recognized her sister's messy scrawl.

She ripped the letter open and sank on to the bed to read it.

Dearest Greta,

Forgive me for not writing sooner, but I was waiting for something cheering to say. This past month hasn't been the same without you. Kindra and I miss your singing in the mornings, although you will be glad to learn that your beloved Lupo has invented a particularly ear-splitting howl to fill the quiet you've left behind. The weather remains a horror. It's no kinder to us now than when you left, but Mikkel has kept us fed with fresh mackerel and Mama's chickens have begun to lay eggs again, though not as often as we would like.

Your gift arrived this morning on the postmaster's ship. When Papa opened the package from Grinstad, his tongue fell out of his mouth. Even Mama squealed like a stuck pig, and we all fell about laughing. Of course, we knew your work at the palace would be well compensated, but it's been long years since we've seen such a grand sum! You must know this is enough coin for three barrels of potatoes, a month's worth of lamb's meat, a new coat for Mama and a bolt of silk for Kindra's wedding dress. She hasn't stopped grinning all day! I had forgotten how beautiful she is when she smiles. I hope you're keeping some wages aside for yourself, little nightingale. You must be working so hard for the king. I imagine the days are long and lonely there, and you are missing us as sorely as we are missing you. When the weather clears in the spring, I promise I'll come to see you, even if I have to steal a boat and a sled and a pack of wolves to do it. You know I always keep my word.

For now, write to us of your beasts, and the king, if you have managed to make his acquaintance. Is he truly as beastly as they say? Or has Tor been right to defend him all these years? There must be gossip in between all that hard work and hopefully a handsome soldier or two to distract you. As your eldest sister, I demand to know everything. Don't make me send Aya to spy on you!

Love always,
Hela x

Greta read the letter twice, trying to make sense of her sister's words. What coin was she referring to? Greta's first official wage was not due for another two days. She'd spent the last four weeks anxiously waiting to send coin home, but here was Hela, telling her it had already arrived. And in great excess, by the sound of it.

Her fingers trembled as she set the letter down, her gaze snagging on those telltale words: *when Papa opened the package from Grinstad...*

If the coin had come from Grinstad and she had not been the one to send it, then who else would have been so bold? Who else knew how her family had been suffering?

Greta closed her eyes at the sudden sting of her tears.

Alarik Felsing was the only person at the palace with such knowledge, not to mention the means and the authority to do something about it. But *why* would he do something about it?

Why were the needs of the Iversens suddenly so important to the king of Gevra?

Had he done it for her? Or was it his loyalty to Tor that had moved his hand? And why on earth hadn't he mentioned it to her? They had seen each other every day since the ball, often walking together in the mornings as they looked over the beasts, or sharing a flask of tea late in the evenings, whenever he caught her closing up for the night. He had a knack for coming upon her at exactly the right time, though she knew in her heart she would never refuse his company, even if he offered it in the midst of a snowstorm.

Didn't he think she would find out about the aid package? Didn't he care?

She leaped to her feet. She had to speak to him about it or she wouldn't sleep a wink. She shoved the letter into her pocket and hurried from her room, making her way to the upper floors of the palace. It was not yet midnight, but by his own admission, the king was a night owl. He had confided in her only two mornings ago that he was struggling to sleep, often spending his nights alone in the library, pouring over war plans. It was there that Greta went, hoping to catch him before Nanna marched her back to her room.

She took the stairs two at a time, playing Hela's letter over and over in her mind. Even from across the country, she could feel the fizz of her sister's happiness at what that coin had afforded them – not just food, but dignity. And for

Greta – peace of mind. Alarik Felsing had sated the beast inside her, allowing it to hunger for something else. Something more.

She bounced on the balls of her feet, practically skipping towards the library, which she had already visited twice this week, borrowing books on battle strategy and wound care. As she drew nearer, she heard the king's voice through the cracked door.

She pushed it open, then froze on the threshold. The library was dark, but the crackling fireplace cast him in its amber glow. He was sitting on the armrest of Princess Elva's chair, his head downturned towards her. She was smiling up at him, the firelight adding a golden sheen to her striking beauty as she hung on his every word. He said something, soft and low, and she threw her head back in laughter, revealing every one of her pearly teeth. He swept a hand through his hair and she scrunched up her face, playfully swatting him in the chest.

Despair fissured through Greta. She stumbled backwards. Out of the room, and away from the door, back down the hallway and the stairs. Away from the king and his bride-to-be, from their beautiful little bubble and their achingly perfect romance.

Down, down, down she went, into the underbelly of the palace, where she sat alone in her bedchamber, trying not to cry.

You are a wrangler, not a princess, she scolded herself, as she shrugged off her frock coat and boots.

A kindness is a kindness. Not a declaration of affection.

She unwound her braid and dragged a brush through her hair, scowling at herself in the mirror. Hating the grey of her eyes and the freckles on her nose, the windburn on her face and the scars on her cheek.

You are not here for love, Greta Iversen.

You are here for war.

Feeling wretched with regret and embarrassment, she crawled under the duvet and curled into a ball, whimpering like a wounded creature. When she slept, she dreamed of Carrig, wishing she had never left.

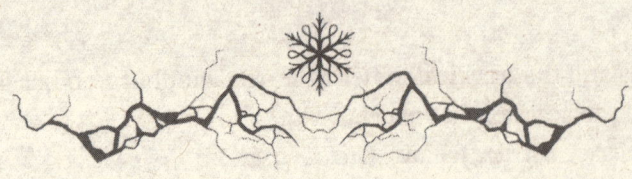

CHAPTER 25
Alarik

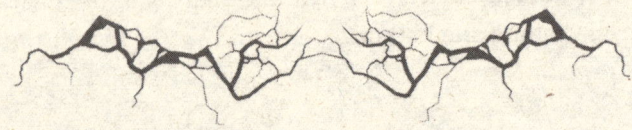

'Be honest with me,' said Princess Elva, as she peered over the frozen lake at Grinstad Palace. 'How many hours a day do you spend out here gazing at your reflection?'

Alarik snorted. 'Why would I use the lake when I have fifty-seven perfectly good mirrors in my bedchamber?'

She arched a brow. 'Well, I wouldn't know . . .'

'Are you propositioning me, Princess?'

'You *wish*.' She jostled him in the shoulder, and he smirked, enjoying the camaraderie that had blossomed between them these past few weeks. They had grown closer since Queen Regna's attack on their beasts. Princess Elva had taken the destruction of her weaver elk as a personal attack, and after sending word home to her father, King Nilas had been able to procure a further six hundred elk and three times as many soldiers, ready for war. They were due to arrive in Gevra any day now.

The wedding, of course, would come after, though they did their best not to speak of it in their daily meetings. Alarik knew it could be worse. Marriage was hardly a death sentence. Elva was clever and funny and kind. So what if he didn't love her? And so what if she didn't love him? She could tolerate him well enough, and she could have her freedom. To do whatever she liked, to love whoever she chose. A royal marriage was first and foremost an alliance, and it was the alliance that Gevra needed right now. It was as simple as that.

Alarik had risen early that morning, meaning to walk alone among the elderberry trees, and despite his ruffle of frustration at finding the princess already outside, he was glad now of her company. It distracted him from the relentless hum of his own thoughts.

'Do you have a copper?' Elva pouted, as she searched the pockets of her ivory fur coat. 'I want to make a wish in the fountain.'

'It's my fountain. The wishes are free.' He nudged her towards it. 'Although the water is frozen so it might take a while to come true.'

'I'm not known for my patience,' she sighed.

Alarik jammed his foot into the ice, making it crack. 'Patience is overrated.'

Elva perched on the lip of the fountain, watching him. The morning sun gilded the bright strands of her hair and made her brown eyes shine. It occurred to Alarik, not for the first time, that she really was a beauty. She had the kind of face kings and queens went to war over, and yet when he looked at her, he found himself yearning for a different, wilder kind of beauty, for wind-nipped cheeks and blue-grey eyes, for flyaway strands of copper hair, for muddy clothes and scuffed boots and—

'What are you thinking about?' said Elva. 'Your eyes have gone all misty.'

'War,' said Alarik, stepping back from the fountain and digging his hands into the pockets of his long grey coat.

'You old romantic, you.'

If only she knew. He hadn't seen half enough of his wrangler lately. Or at least, she hadn't seen much of him. If he didn't know better, he'd swear she was avoiding him, spending her mornings in the mews with that bloody falconer instead of meeting him at the edge of the forest with a smile and a muffin to share. She was locking up far later than usual, too. Not that that deterred Alarik. He still walked the forest most nights just to hear her sing, and lingered by Saga's cage in the mornings, watching over Boo and Dash with a kind of parental pride that vaguely unnerved him.

'It's a shame we can't wish for Lief to blow away.' Elva's groan jostled him from his thoughts. 'Look over there. He's coming right at us, like a busy little tornado.'

Alarik swore as he glanced over his shoulder. 'If this fountain wasn't frozen, I'd drown myself in it.'

'Go on without me,' said Elva, leaping to her feet. 'There's no need for both of us to suffer over napkin choices. I'll distract him.'

Alarik tossed her a grateful smile as he darted around the fountain, making for the elderberry trees on the other side of the lake. He could hear Lief calling after him and knew how ridiculous he looked – the fearsome king of Gevra running away from his mother's steward like a frightened rabbit. But it was either this or threatening Lief at swordpoint, and he didn't want to upset his mother on today of all days.

Safely hidden among the trees, Alarik slumped on to a

stone bench to catch his breath and think a little of his father. King Soren was rarely far from his mind, but today, on the anniversary of his death, he was closer than ever.

Here, among his father's beloved elderberries, Alarik looked towards the statue he had erected in his honour. It was a life-size rendering of King Soren, carved in pristine white stone and set on a base of driftwood – the last remnants of the royal warship that had gone down during a violent sea storm eight years ago, leaving no survivors. The plaque read:

In memory of King Soren,
Fierce as a wolf,
Strong as an ox,
Wise as an owl.

Alarik looked up at his father's marbled likeness and felt the nearness of his loss like a punch in the gut. He wondered what Soren would make of him now; if he would be angry at Alarik for fighting in a foreign war that had decimated his troops. Would he blame him for Ansel's death? And for Anika's reluctance to return home? Would he look upon him with pride or shame? Alarik was so lost in his worries he didn't hear the crunch of footsteps behind him or the quiet huff of laughter as a snowball came soaring through the trees.

When it whacked him in the side of the head, he jerked his chin, his eyes snapping open. His hand flew to his sword hilt as he leaped to his feet, but when he spotted his wrangler retreating through the trees, his anger turned to surprise.

She was laughing so hard she had to stop to catch her breath. She bent double, bracing her hand against a tree trunk. Big mistake. He grabbed a fistful of snow and bolted through the trees, coming down on her like a blizzard. When she looked over her shoulder, the snowball was already flying. It hit her in the face, and she staggered backwards, losing her balance.

She fell in a heap, releasing a strangled cry. 'I surrender!'

'Gevrans don't surrender.' He smirked as he stood over her, readying another fistful of snow. 'I really should make you eat this one.'

She stared up at him with round, innocent eyes. 'It wasn't even me. It was Borvil!'

'Iversen.' He came to his knees, pinning her hips between his legs. 'Do you think I fell down in the last snowstorm?'

She trapped her laughter on her hand, but it streamed from her eyes, and the sight was so lovely, Alarik had to chew the smile from his mouth.

She raised her hands. 'All right,' she conceded. 'But blame Elva. I passed her by the fountain, and she said you needed cheering up.'

'So, you decided to attack me?'

She wriggled underneath him, the heat of her body rolling against his hips. 'Isn't war your love language?'

War and *this*. Her.

Shit.

He stifled a groan.

'And anyway, that was a warm greeting by Gevran standards,' she added.

'What a good little Gevran you are, Iversen,' he said, straining to keep his voice even. 'Shouldn't you be training my beasts?'

She hesitated, guilt flickering in her eyes. 'I wanted to check on the one in the mountain . . .'

He frowned. 'I don't want you going into those mountains.'

'But the beast—'

'Is buried so deep, we can't get to it anyway,' he said. 'And those old mining tunnels below ground are unsafe. Not to mention far too narrow for my soldiers.'

'Elias seemed to do all right.'

Alarik frowned. 'What are you talking about?'

Her eyes went wide.

'Iversen?' he pressed. 'Have you been sneaking around with my spymaster?'

Why did that thought bother him so acutely?

Of course, he knew why.

She shook her head. 'No. I . . . I'm just . . . I'm worried about the creature. It's in distress.'

'Forget about the creature,' said Alarik, sterner now. In truth, these past few weeks, it was becoming harder to shove aside his own curiosity about the beast. There was a part of him that longed to discover its identity, to see if the dragon from his father's bedtime stories might be real. But with war prowling ever closer, it was not a risk he was willing to take. He would sooner face down Regna and all her troops than a temperamental, fire-breathing dragon hell-bent on revenge. No matter the wrangler's confidence in being able to subdue it.

It was not worth the gamble.

She glared up at him. 'It's *frightened*.'

'Not as frightened as you'll be when that tunnel caves in on you. And that's if it doesn't eat you first.' He grimaced at the thought.

She squirmed between his legs, trying to get free. Heat roared through him at the unexpected friction. He slammed the snowball into his own face to cool himself down.

'What are you doing?' she cried, grabbing his wrist. 'You'll hurt yourself!'

Alarik was already hurting himself. Being this close to her – no, *on top of her* – was like leaping into a bonfire.

'Now, we're even.' He rolled back to his feet and helped her up. 'Sorry for hitting you in the face.'

She shrugged, dusting herself off. 'I'm the one who started it. Your bride-to-be is far too persuasive.'

'One of her many talents.'

'I'm sure,' she said, looking away.

'I enjoyed it,' he said, sensing the strange shift in her mood. 'It cheered me up.'

She canted her head, gazing at him in confusion. 'Do you really need cheering up, Your Majesty?'

'Alarik,' he corrected her.

She swallowed. 'Why do you need cheering up, Alarik?'

He hesitated, not wishing to make her feel awkward but wanting to answer her earnestly. Because she had asked for it, and the truth was, there was very little he wouldn't give her. 'Today is the anniversary of my father's death.'

Horror dawned across her face, her eyes growing so wide he could see his reflection in them. 'Oh no.' She covered her face. 'I'm so sorry. How thoughtless of me . . .' She whimpered into her hands. 'I can't believe I just threw a snowball at your head.'

'And *right* in front of my father's statue.' He clucked his tongue. 'Talk about dishonour.'

'No!' she cried. 'I am a terrible person.'

Alarik couldn't contain his laughter. 'Calm down, Iversen. It's not like you stabbed me.'

'I'd stab myself right now if I could,' she muttered into her hands. She peeked at him through her fingers. 'I'm going to run away now. Please may I run away?'

'No, you may not.'

She groaned. 'I can't believe I did that.'

'You really are *so* unruly.' The more she fretted, the harder Alarik laughed. This little interlude had done wonders to brighten his mood. He hadn't realized just how badly he had been missing her company; her smile, her wit, her gentle recklessness. 'What am I going to do with you?'

'Please don't send me away!'

'You're the one trying to flee!'

He took her hands and gently tugged them away from her face, repeating a gesture that had become all too familiar between them. Whenever she tried to hide herself from him, he yearned to look at her even more, to feast on whatever emotion was brewing the storm in her eyes. But when he uncovered her face this time, she was crying.

His gut twisted, and before he could stop himself, he was cradling her face and swiping the tears from her cheeks. 'Why are you crying, wildling?'

'Because I'm an awful person!'

'Well, you're certainly dramatic.' He chuckled, softly. 'I don't think I've ever seen your eyes so blue.'

She sniffed. 'They only go blue when I cry.'

Another twist in his gut. 'Then I prefer the storm.'

Give me back the storm.

He wanted her smiling. Or scowling. Or singing. Or

bossing him about. Or talking about his beasts with the kind of enthusiasm that made her words trip and her cheeks flush. He couldn't stand the sight of her crying.

'Listen, Iversen. I need your help,' he said, in a low, urgent voice.

She stilled, blinking up at him.

'It requires the utmost stealth.'

'What do you need?' Her tears forgotten, she squared her shoulders.

Alarik bit back his smile. 'I intend to launch a covert assault on my mother's steward.'

She gasped in horror. A marginal improvement on devastation, but not quite what he was going for.

'Relax, I'm not going to murder him. This is a brand-new coat. Do you know how hard it is to get bloodstains out?' He knelt to gather another fistful of snow. 'I just want to lightly pummel him. Now that I know how good your throwing arm is, I insist you help me. Unless you want to spend the rest of your morning helping me pour over napkin swatches.'

'I'd rather eat an elderberry tree.' She blew out a breath, grinning as she knelt beside him, making two snowballs of her own and carefully shoving them into her pockets. 'This is the kind of war I can get behind.'

'I'll make a soldier of you yet.'

'Don't hold your breath.' She winked as she slipped a ball into his pocket. The storm had returned to her eyes. It nearly made him throw caution to the wind and kiss her right there beneath the elderberry trees. But he knew if he got a taste of her lips, he would never stop seeking them, and the spiral of his need would consume him, destroying his friendship with Tor, his alliance with Halgard, and most importantly of all, the bond he had found with his wrangler. A bond that nourished a most vital part of his soul.

After all, how could she ever love a war-hungry brute like him?

Armed to the teeth with snowballs, they stalked out of the orchard and made for the fountain, where Lief was still boring the life out of Elva.

'Ready?' said Alarik, taking aim.

His wrangler was already running, her laughter flying out behind her as the first snowball flew. Alarik bolted after her, both of them tearing across the lawn like a pair of naughty children, leaving all thoughts of war and grief behind them.

CHAPTER 26
Greta

Greta was outside in the arena, working the ice bears in their newly fitted battle armour when Aren arrived, carrying two mugs of fragrant hot chocolate. The falconer was wearing a woolly hat and scarf over his uniform, and his nose was nipped pink.

'Pardon the interruption,' he called, in his usual chirpy voice. 'It's freezing out this morning. I figured you might need something to warm you up.'

Greta almost sagged with relief. 'You read my mind.' Despite her fur-lined leather gloves and warm frock coat, she was beginning to lose feeling in her fingers, and it had been some time since she had felt her toes at all. 'I swear winters on Carrig are never as bad as this.'

After issuing a quick command to the bears to relax their defensive postures, she skipped over to Aren, gratefully taking one of the mugs. She cupped her hands around it, sighing as the steam warmed her nose. The chocolate was thick and fragrant, and heaped with so many melting marshmallows, it was streaked with white.

'I swear you've given me three times more marshmallows

today,' she said, comparing their mugs.

'Figured you could use the extra sugar,' he said, with a wink. 'It's armour day after all. I know how difficult the fittings can make the beasts.'

Difficult was an understatement. When the armourers arrived at sunrise, the beasts were already pacing, like they sensed something was afoot. Despite the sleek design and relative lightness of the plated armour, no wild thing liked being dressed in *anything*, even if it was for their own good.

'You're lucky the birds fly free,' said Greta. 'We just about got through the wolves. I swear Tollo tried to take the armourer's hand off.'

'And the snow leopards?' said Aren, stifling a chuckle.

'Remarkably well-behaved, in comparison. But we've only fitted half of them. And I haven't done their drills yet. It's going to be a long day.'

An hour before noon and it was *already* a long day.

'Then I'll bring you as many of these as you need,' he said, gently clinking his mug against hers.

Greta took her first languid sip. He did the same. His eyes were bright and burnished, drinking her in over the rim of his mug. She felt a curious heat gather in her cheeks, a sense that this moment might mean more to him than it did to her.

A stray black curl peeked out from under his hat. A part of her wanted to reach out and tuck it away. The part that said Aren could be good for her. The part that told her she should forget about the king and the traitorous flicker that ignited in her chest whenever he was near. And yet, despite the fact that Aren was handsome and thoughtful and good company, her heartbeat remained steady in her chest.

He laughed at her as she lowered her mug.

'What?' she said, feeling a flurry of self-consciousness.

'You've got a marshmallow moustache.' Before she could scrub the offending moustache off her face, he reached out, lightly smudging it away with his thumb. 'There,' he said, his eyes softening. 'Better.'

Greta blushed, taking a small step backwards. He dropped his hand. 'Thanks,' she said, with an awkward huff. 'The bears would never take me seriously again.'

'I think they're far more distracted by those terrifying-looking spiked helmets they're wearing,' he said, gesturing past her. 'Why do you suppose the king insists on them?'

'Because the king can do whatever he likes,' said an all-too familiar voice.

Greta spun around, nearly spilling hot chocolate all over herself. Alarik was standing a few feet away with his arms folded across his chest. His bright eyes narrowed as he looked between them, and by the diamond hardness of his gaze, Greta got the impression that he had just witnessed her embarrassing moustache incident.

And he was not happy about it.

'Unlike the king's falconer, who should be working right now,' he added, pointedly.

Aren paled. 'I was just taking a break.'

'And now it's over,' said Alarik. 'If you're done pawing at my wrangler, she has work to do, too. Work that does not involve *you*.'

Greta winced. The king truly was in a foul mood today.

'Yes, Your Majesty. Of course. I'll just . . . I'll go now.' Dipping his chin, Aren threw an apologetic glance at Greta before absconding from the arena with the swiftness of a hawk.

Greta sipped her drink as she watched him go. 'Was that really necessary?'

'Yes.'

'He's terrified of you.'

'Good.' Alarik stuck his hand out expectantly. 'Let me have a taste of that.'

She handed him her mug, surprised as he took a sip of his own. Grimacing, he handed it back to her. 'Ugh. Way too sweet.'

'All the more for me,' she said, clutching it to her chest.

He frowned at the mug like it had personally offended him.

Greta made a point of taking another languid sip. He watched her, his throat working as he swallowed.

This time, she made sure to wipe her mouth. His eyes lowered, watching that, too.

'I suppose you've come to check on the beasts,' she said, feeling the sudden urge to look away from him. To give herself a moment to breathe. 'The armour is well-fitted, as you can see. Minimal restrictions in movement. I was just about to run through some attack manouevres if you'd like to join me.'

'With pleasure,' he said, mood brightening.

Greta sipped her drink to hide her smile. She was well aware that the other soldiers found the king's presence at their training sessions unnerving, but the truth was she liked Alarik's company in the arena. And outside of it. She was glad of it now, even if he had chased poor Aren away.

They wandered over to where the ice bears were assembled, looking all the more fearsome in their plated armour and spiked silver helmets.

Alarik wandered up to Baldur and Nel to inspect the fit. 'Impressive work,' he remarked, as he circled them. 'I'll send Borvil down later after his nap. See that the armourers take special care with him.'

Greta laughed before she could help it.

He crooked a brow at her over his shoulder. 'Do I amuse you, Iversen?'

More often than he probably meant to.

'That bear is spoilt rotten. If I didn't know better, I'd say you're a soft touch.'

He offered a fleeting smile. 'Depends on the creature.'

'And what about people?' she said, before she could help it.

He paused, canting his head. The silence swelled. She gulped her hot chocolate, desperately thinking of something else to say.

'Only on rare occasions,' he said, still looking at her.

Feeling flustered, Greta went to place her empty mug on a nearby wall. When she returned to the bears, she launched straight into their drills, ensuring they could still stretch and lunge with ease.

Alarik remained at her side throughout, offering his own commands. The ones they had been practising for weeks now. Greta was pleased to see the ice bears responding efficiently, easily submitting to the will of their true master.

'They'll make a fine regiment,' Alarik remarked, once the bears had been thoroughly put through their paces. 'Good job, Iversen.'

Greta summoned a smile, even as her stomach twisted. Sometimes, she could forget in the thrill of wrangling that the end goal was war.

It would always be war.

'What is that?' said Alarik, watching her more closely than she'd realized. 'The shadow that's just come over your face? Should I be more effusive with my praise? I admit compliments are not my strong suit.'

She shook her head, embarrassed at her own reaction. What kind of Gevran feared the drums of war? 'I was just thinking about all that's yet to come.' She looked back at the ice bears. Those beautiful, majestic beasts all poised and ready to fight upon her command. Ready to die.

Voice quietening, Greta asked, 'Will it be soon?'

He turned back to her. 'You needn't worry about the war, Iversen. When the time comes, we will ride into battle together.' His voice took on a new intensity, his eyes blazing with the promise of victory. 'You will not have to face the steel blades of Vask alone.'

Greta quailed. How could she tell him it was not herself she feared for, but his beasts? These soft-hearted creatures who had filled her heart with such gladness these past months, these animals she had grown to love as dearly as her own beloved Lupo back on Carrig.

These creatures who were the king's own weapons.

Made to maim and kill.

Expected to die.

'Iversen.' His fingers on her wrist jolted her back to him. He looked uncomfortable now, his voice taking on an edge of concern. 'Your eyes are turning blue.'

She blinked back her tears. 'Sorry.'

'I won't let anything happen to you on the battlefield,' he repeated. 'And don't forget, you are Tor's sister. You've been training your entire life.' At her quizzical look, he added,

'You *can* fight, can't you? You have been trained?'

'Uh.' She stalled, wondering how best to proceed with this next unsettling truth.

His eyes darkened. 'Iversen. Don't lie to your king.'

She blew out a breath. 'I'm afraid things in that department are a little . . . dire.'

'What do you mean?' he said, aghast. 'You own a sword, don't you?'

She shook her head. 'Honestly, I don't even know how to hold a sword properly. I never really had a taste for it.' She rolled her hand. 'Fighting and bloodshed . . . and all that stuff.'

His jaw slackened. 'You're not serious.'

'I'm as serious as Borvil's bad breath,' she said, solemnly.

He bit off a curse, dragging his hands along his face. 'We're going to have to change that,' he muttered, more to himself than to her. 'Fast.'

CHAPTER 27
Alarik

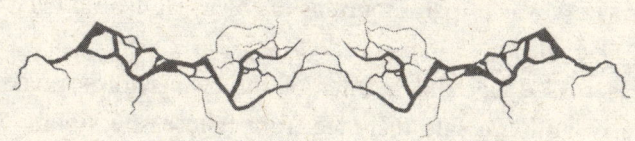

Alarik stood by the frozen lake on the front lawn, listening to the frantic footsteps of his wrangler. 'I got your message!' she called out, as she approached. 'What's the emergency?'

He turned to greet her, raising both of the swords in his hands. 'It's time for your training session.'

She skidded to a stop, nearly tripping over her own feet. 'What?'

Alarik frowned. 'We'll start with your balance.'

The wrangler raked her copper-streaked hair back from her face. It fell in loose tendrils down her back today, free of the usual tight braid that kept it out of her eyes. His message must have reached her while she still getting dressed for the day. It was obscenely early after all, but Alarik had risen before the sun, finding himself unable to sleep. And once awake, his mind became full of thoughts of her. And more pressingly, the bleak admission she had made to him yesterday morning in the arena. That she did not in fact own a sword. Or indeed know how to hold one.

Unimaginable.

'What?' she said again. '*Now?*'

'When else but now?' said Alarik, evenly. 'You'd hardly prefer your instruction in the middle of battle?'

She gaped at him. 'And *you're* my tutor?'

He flashed his teeth. 'Lucky you.' He hadn't even considered assigning one of his soldiers to the task. It was far too important. She was *his* wrangler. His responsibility. Her safety was as paramount as his own. He would trust no one else with it.

He tossed her the smaller of the two swords, making sure it landed a safe distance from where she stood. 'We should get started. Time is very much of the essence.'

According to Elias's network of spies, Regna and her army were already on the march. Soon, they would reach the Blackspires in the north, and war would be upon them. Anxiety churned in his stomach at the ever salient reminder. He became impatient, pointing towards where her sword had landed.

It was a sleek, slimmer blade than his own, forged from lightweight steel, and with a leather-wrapped hilt for ease of training. Years ago, Alarik had gifted it to Ansel for his sixteenth birthday, hoping it would inspire him to spar. But Ansel had shown little interest in the blade. He was, after all, another pure heart who spurned the idea of battle in favour of peace. Shortly after, he had ceded it to Anika who deemed the sword too flimsy for her tastes and stowed it away in favour of her throwing axes.

It seemed a good fit for his wrangler.

'Come on, Iversen. Where's that fighting spirit of yours?'

'Hang on,' she huffed, hastily tying up her hair. Alarik watched in rapt interest as she twisted it into an elaborate knot, tucking the stray hairs back from her face until he could see the storm of worry in her eyes.

'It's all right,' he said, feeling an uncharacteristic need to soothe her. 'I'm not going to hurt you.'

'But what if I hurt you?'

Alarik barked a laugh. 'I think I'll survive.'

Scowling now, she crouched to pick up her sword. And dipped a little to the right. 'It's heavy.'

It was, in fact, the lightest sword in the entire palace.

He kept this to himself.

'Walk around with it,' he said, palming his own sword. 'Shift your weight from foot to foot, like this. Lift it high and low. You'll get used to it.'

The wrangler did as she was told, her fingers flexing around the hilt as she tried to acclimatise to its weight. All the while, she stared warily at the gleaming blade, as though it were a snake that might strike at any moment.

Alarik bit back his smile. 'Any better?'

She looked up at him again. 'A bit.'

'Great.'

It was going to be a long day.

'Let's start with your battle stance.' Stowing his own sword, he moved around her. She inhaled sharply when he rested his hands on her shoulders. His grip was just light enough to feel her tremble. Or perhaps it was his own hands, betraying him.

He wasn't nervous. Of course not. The king of Gevra didn't *get* nervous.

He just . . . didn't know how to be this close to her without closing his eyes and breathing her in.

He resisted the urge, even though she was facing the other way . . . even as the scent of her – wildflowers and jasmine – tickled his nose.

Focus, you simpering fool.

He cleared his throat. 'Feet shoulder-width apart.'

She widened her stance.

'Now turn slightly, until your dominant foot is facing forward.' He moved with her. 'Good. Keep your back straight.' She stiffened under his touch. 'Crouch, a little. Yes, just like that. Raise your sword.'

She raised her sword.

Freezing hell.

Her grip was terrible.

'Your wrist is shaking.'

'It's *heavy*,' she protested.

'I watched you carry a fully-grown wolf like a sack of grain last week,' he said, pointedly.

She tossed a scowl over her shoulder. 'He was in pain. He'd hurt his paw.'

Alarik rolled his eyes. 'Well, imagine someone is about to hurt *you*. On a giant battlefield filled with blood and gore and the dying screams of—'

'I get it.'

'Hold still.' He stepped in close, until her back was flush against his chest and the crown of her head brushed the underside of his chin.

Briefly, his eyes shuttered closed.

She swayed against him, and for an absurd moment, he thought about putting his arm around her waist to steady her.

'Your grip,' he said, clearing his throat again. 'It needs work. The main component of your fist should hold the hilt tightly. Close to the blade. Like this.' *Stars help him*, he moved his hand on top of hers, inching her grip forward, pressing her fingers tight around the hilt.

Dangerous.

So very dangerous.

She swallowed thickly. 'Like this?'

'Very good, Iversen.'

Iversen.

She was an Iversen.

Tor's sister.

Don't forget.

'But your thumb and your forefinger should be lighter. For ease of movement.' He stroked her thumb, easing the tension there. 'Good.'

Step away from the wrangler.

He ignored the warning bells in his head. This was training, nothing more. A vital exercise for a vital component of his war effort.

'Tense your grip for defence,' he said, straining to stay focused. 'Draw your sword up and close to your body.' The one he could feel pressed against him, warm and supple and— 'Loosen your grip when you mean to strike. Lunge and swing, straight and true.'

She drew her sword up close, until the hilt pressed against her chest.

'Like this?' she whispered.

Not at all.

'Almost.'

Get away from her.

'Let's parry. I'll show you,' he said, reluctantly dragging himself away from the warmth of her body. He arced around her, drawing his own sword.

She squared her stance, crouching low.

Without lunging, he lightly tapped his blade against hers.

She wobbled, stumbling backwards.

He stifled a sigh.

'Wait. I wasn't ready.' She hurried forward, resuming her stance.

He tapped her again.

Dire.

And again.

Woeful.

And again.

Even worse than last time.

And once more.

This time, she nearly dropped the sword entirely.

He scrubbed his jaw, looking her over.

She bit her lip. 'I told you I was bad at this.'

'New plan,' he decided. 'Keep both hands on the hilt at all times. If someone charges at you, screech like a falcon and swing like hell.'

She did as he advised, the blade whistling as she swung it back and forth with complete and utter abandon.

Alarik backed up several steps.

'Like this?' she said, screaming madly as she spun around in a circle. 'Do I look just reckless enough to be intimidating?'

Laughter burst out of him. He had to drop his own sword and bend over just to catch his breath. 'At least your mind is as sharp as your blade,' he said, still chuckling.

Across the grass, she was laughing, too, tears streaming from her eyes. They were blue again. Bright and beautiful as sapphires. He was half a heartbeat from telling her so, when a furious boom shook the world.

The earth trembled.

Inside the palace, screams rang out.

Roars and howls filled the morning air.

Iversen's wide-eyed gaze shifted to something just over his shoulder. 'The mountains!' she gasped. 'They're breaking apart!'

Alarik spun on his heel, as ice and rubble rained down from the sky.

His heart clenched when he saw it: a brand-new crack ran down the centre of his beloved mountains, as though some almighty being had reached down from the sky to cleave them in two.

'There were explosives in the tunnels,' said Vine, the moment she burst into the atrium to offer her full report. Having just returned from the mountains, where the soldiers had been working through the debris all morning, she had run straight into Alarik.

He had been pacing back and forth, waiting for her.

'Regna,' he said, through his teeth.

There was no other explanation.

Vine nodded. 'I suspect they were planted some time ago.'

Alarik went to the window, looking out at his beloved mountains. And the crack that now split them in two. Somehow, Regna had heard about the beast – heard the rumours that something wild and ancient had awoken here. Something angry.

She was trying to free it.

Mercifully, her attempt at unleashing all hell on Grinstad had failed. The creature that snarled beneath the rock was still trapped there, though Alarik's mountains looked all the worse for it.

'Who detonated the explosives?' he said, turning back to Vine. 'Did you find any bodies?'

Vine shook her head, her dark brows pinched. 'Not a trace.'

More concerning still.

They stewed in silence, until Vine said, 'What's our next move?'

Alarik didn't hesitate. 'War.'

Her eyes darkened. 'It's about time.'

'Prepare the soldiers,' he said, stepping back from the window. 'We depart in two days' time.'

The following morning, Alarik woke early and went straight to his war room to look over his final battle plans.

He was still half asleep when he stepped inside, and so, for the briefest moment, he thought he was hallucinating the figure waiting for him at the head of the table.

Clad in a high-collared black velvet gown and with her crimson hair glimmering like fresh blood, Anika Felsing reclined in the king's chair, wearing a smile made for war. 'Hello, brother.'

'Anika?' Alarik blinked, to make sure he was awake. 'I thought you were in Eana.'

'What can I say? I was craving a little war.' She flashed her teeth. 'You hardly thought I'd let you have all the fun without me?'

Alarik returned his sister's wolfish grin, his heart soaring at the sudden realness of her, here in his war room. Home, at last. 'Your timing is impeccable,' he said, striding towards her. 'Queen Regna will be quaking in her helmet.'

'Good,' she said, rising to embrace him. 'That bitch's skull is mine.'

'Welcome home, Anika,' he said, with a dark chuckle. 'You have been missed.'

III
War

CHAPTER 28
Greta

The Blackspires were like a mouth on the horizon, an endless row of jagged teeth taking a bite out of the sky. Greta couldn't tear her gaze from them as she sat bundled in the back of her sled. They were travelling so fast the wind nipped her cheeks and stole the feeling from her nose, but she had graver matters to worry about.

They had been riding north for two days. The king's spymaster, Elias, had gone on ahead to act as a scout, while the king himself rode at the head of his army alongside his sister, Princess Anika, who had returned from the southern isles just in time for war. They were followed closely by Captain Vine and the First Regiment – seasoned soldiers that had fought more wars than years Greta had been alive. Next were the regiment of beasts and war birds, overseen by the king's wrangler and falconer, who rode together in the same sled. Greta was glad of Aren's company, though secretly, she wished she was back at Grinstad, singing lullabies to Saga and her cubs, and tossing snowballs with Princess Elva.

Coward, she scolded herself whenever the thought

crossed her mind.

She owed it to her brother to be brave. She owed it to her family, and her king, too.

The Second Regiment carted the fire lances and cannons under the command of General Vesper Hale, while the third and final troop guarded the rear, the soldiers there riding mainly on stags and horseback. All together they made for an impressive procession, thousands of soldiers and beasts marching ceaselessly across the vast frozen tundra of northern Gevra.

At night, Greta slept fitfully in the sled, her face turned to Aren's as they curled up across the narrow benches, whispering to each other of half-forgotten tales from their childhoods to keep their mind off what was to come.

But war lurked along the horizon, and soon it would sweep its greedy fist across the Blackspires, scattering soldiers and beasts alike. It was a knot in Greta's chest, tightening with each passing hour. She feared for her beloved animals just as fiercely as she feared for her fellow soldiers, but most of all – though she dared not utter it aloud – she feared for the life of her king, for the wild-hearted man who was so much more than his brutal reputation. As the spill of those black mountains loomed ever closer, she found herself hoping that that fearsome reputation would help Alarik in his quest for victory, inspiring fear into the heart of the ruthless queen who sought to rip open his mountains and topple him from his throne.

When they were several miles south of the Blackspires, they stopped at the Valewood, a pale birch forest that hugged the banks of a glassy lake. Here, they were instructed to change into their battle armour, drink their fill of water and eat what little food their nervous stomachs could handle. After a quick lunch of bread and cured meat, Greta and Aren washed up and went to check on the animals. Clanging awkwardly in her unwieldy silver battle armour and with her helmet cradled in the crook of her arm, Greta wandered among her beasts.

Overhead, the morning sun climbed up the seam of the sky. The snow had held off for two nights, and despite the chill in the wind, there were no clouds lying in wait, threatening to thwart them. It might have been a beautiful day if they weren't marching into battle.

Greta lingered awhile with the ice bears, seeking out Baldur and Nel, the sisters having seen more battle than most of the soldiers in their midst. They were sitting at the far edge of the lake, their heads bent together like they were sharing a secret. As she approached, Greta sensed the steady thrum of their heartbeats beating in perfect harmony.

'At least you're not frightened,' she said, sitting between them on the frosted grass. 'I wish I could say the same for myself.'

They blinked their big brown eyes at her, and Greta felt the sudden well of their empathy. She wished she could curl up across their laps, but she couldn't afford to look frightened or weak in front of the other soldiers. There were thousands of them clustered around the lake, and yet she could pick out the king at once. He was standing all the way across the water, dressed head to toe in shining black armour. Even from here, she could sense he was calm, steel-eyed, ready for the horrors to come. He cradled his helmet in one hand, the other gripping the pommel of his sword as he spoke with Captain Vine and Princess Anika, both of whom had yet to change into their armour.

Greta swallowed back the fear in her throat, but it rose again, thick as an apple.

Nel snuffled, laying a large paw on her knee to comfort her.

But Greta couldn't shake the storm in her heart. She was so frightened about what was coming. She hated that her last conversation with Alarik had been about battle tactics and beast formations rather than, well . . . something *real*. She had never thanked him for what he had done for her family, hadn't told him how precious his friendship had become to her, how walking with him in the forest or sharing a muffin in the courtyard was always the best part of her day.

What if she never got that chance?

He jerked his chin up, casting his gaze across the lake as though he could sense the tornado of her worries. But— *No*. What an absurd thought. He wasn't looking for her. He was assessing his beasts, making sure they were fed and watered, ready to fight. Of course, that was it. The king of Gevra was marching into war. Why would he spare a thought for her? Why did her foolish heart wish him to?

Greta tore her gaze away from him.

Baldur gave her a piteous look.

She sighed. 'I know. I'm pathetic.'

The bears stiffened at a sudden rustling from the forest. All along the lake, the king's beasts snarled. When Elias emerged from the trees on the back of his stag, followed by a stern-faced Halgardian soldier riding a weaver elk, Greta leaped to her feet and raised her hand.

The command was implicit. *Be still.*

A hush fell over the disquieted beasts as an entire battalion of Halgardian soldiers spilled from the Valewood, riding in full armour on elk-back. Greta's chest loosened as King Nilas's promised army gathered along the treeline, adding a sizable regiment to their own.

There was enough elk here to raze a thousand soldiers to the ground, to flatten the Blackspires themselves with the force of their stampede. There might even be enough to command the tide of this war. A flicker of hope took root inside Greta.

Alarik went to greet the Halgardian captain, his sister striding confidently at his side, Captain Vine on the other. Both armies spread out around the great lake, the elk dipping their mighty heads to drink their fill, while Greta called her beasts away from the water to give them room.

Time moved all too quickly after that, the armies blending seamlessly as they set off for the black mountains. For a long while, the only sounds were the trundling of sleds, the impatient huff of the elk and the faint clanging of armour as soldier and beast journeyed on, and on, towards the Blackspires.

It was late afternoon when Greta sat bolt upright, a sharp twist of fear in her gut. Something was wrong. The beasts had stilled behind her, their hackles raised. She sprung up in the sled, searching for the source of unease. Far ahead, the king pulled Borvil to a halt and rose to his haunches.

At a nighthawk's cry, they all looked up, spotting a flock of crimson soldiers gliding low over the Blackspires. There was a series of loud cracks, and before the king could loose a warning shout, flames poured down on them.

The beasts scattered in panic, causing several weaver elk to buck their riders. Twenty thousand shields went up, creating a canopy of metal just in the nick of time. Soldiers along the edges dropped and rolled along the frozen ground, desperately trying to put out the flames on their bodies. Many collapsed in the snow, face down, the fire having scoured too deep. Several wolves succumbed to the attack, the last of them dying with a helpless whimper that cleaved Greta's chest in two. She grasped the side of the sled to keep from falling to her knees, every inch of her now trembling violently.

'ARCHERS,' bellowed Captain Vine, and a slew of arrows flew right at the gliders.

'FIRE LANCES!' yelled General Hale, and more flames soared, this time towards the sky.

The gliders fell to earth, one by one. The king's soldiers were already moving, ready to finish them off. One glider fell atop a weaver elk, skewered by a poison-sharp antler. Two more were devoured by ice bears upon landing and the rest met their deaths at the end of Gevran swords.

Greta's stomach lurched as she watched it all from her sled, Aren's hand finding hers in the horror. And then it was over. A paltry skirmish that had cost far too much.

'So wasteful,' she murmured, returning her fearful gaze to the skies, where their nighthawks were circling. In the hollow silence, they all looked up, waiting for the next onslaught of gliders.

Aren's hand tightened around hers. 'That wasn't an attack,' he said, as the air began to thrum with the steel-drummed rhythm of war. 'It was a distraction.'

When Greta jerked her chin down, she saw Hunter's Pass

was thronged with soldiers wearing the crimson armour of Vask. They were charging headlong at the king, the wind pounding with their war song, their swords raised and gleaming. More of Regna's soldiers poured in from the east and west foothills, moving like red-bellied insects across the dark mountains, claiming the border in an unbroken line of crimson and steel.

Overhead, the skies heaved with more gliders, and fire fell like snow, felling beasts and soldiers where they stood. Greta froze inside the sled, her head spinning at the sudden chaos of war. It had come upon them like a blizzard, far closer and much sooner than she was expecting.

She wasn't ready.

How could she ever be ready for something like this?

Everywhere she looked, the king's soldiers were hoisting their shields and drawing their swords, tripping over themselves as they fell into hasty formation. The flames had sent the elk into panic, rearing and grunting as their riders grappled for control. Beasts whined and roared, desperately seeking direction.

'Greta!' Aren was shaking her. 'Look at me! Focus!'

She blinked, her eyes streaming at the onslaught of gunpowder and smoke. The ground was full of snow and the sky was full of fire, and soldiers were screaming. They were *dying*. The clash and clamour of battle raged with such sudden, pounding fury, she had to concentrate on Aren's lips just to hear what he was saying.

'Your helmet!' When she didn't move, he yanked it from her hands and jammed it over her head. She could smell metal and blood now, his voice echoing in the tinny surrounds. 'You have to go to the beasts! You have to command them! Your king needs you!'

Your king needs you.

Greta careened back into herself with a violent jolt. She shook off her horror and shoved away her fear. Her beasts were frightened. The flames were startling them, *hurting* them, and they were hopelessly out of formation. She had to corral them, to show them where to go, and who to fight.

She had to defend the king.

Alarik. She had to help Alarik.

Where the hell was Alarik?

She climbed on to the bench, straining to see through the fire and smoke. The entire First Regiment had descended into combat, the armies clashing violently as they fought for control of the foothills. Panic clawed at Greta's throat as she searched for a man in black armour. He was there, right on the front line, the blade of his sword gleaming red as he brought it down, over and over again. He roared in tandem with Borvil as they ripped through a line of soldiers, the king slashing viciously at anyone in his path as they pushed hard and fast towards Hunter's Pass. Desperate to reclaim the path Regna had dared to seize.

There was no sign of the Vaskan queen on the front line. *Rotten coward*, thought Greta, as she returned her gaze to Alarik, a king riding and fighting for his country. He was not alone at the helm of his army. Princess Anika was guarding his back. She was easily discernible now by her glittering pearlescent armour and the sheath of blood-red hair tumbling out of her helmet. She was riding a Gevran stag, wielding a pair of battle axes that were at least half her size. She brandished them with the ease of a lumberjack, spraying a sea of blood wherever she went.

The Felsings were as loyal and ferocious as each other. Beautiful and brutal. Gevran to the bone. The sight of them defending their kingdom without a breath of fear or hesitation made Greta's heart pound like a war drum.

A new strength rippled through her. The king and the princess of Gevra were giving every inch of themselves to this battle – to this land – without a second thought for themselves. She owed it to them to do the same, to seize every drop of courage in her heart and rise to this new challenge.

For today, for her king, Greta could be a beast, too.

She leaped from the sled, her breath hissing out of her as she ran towards the animals, yelling her first command.

They surrounded her, fearless and growling for blood. Greta took heart in their bravery as she went to work, corralling the wolves, snow leopards and tigers into an urgent attack formation, while ordering the bears into a vicious wall of defence.

As more of Regna's forces spilled out from the pass and pierced the east flank of the First Regiment, Greta mounted a running wolf and thundered into the mouth of battle, her command pouring from her like a war cry. 'CHARGE!'

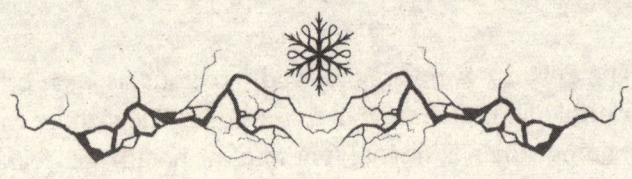

CHAPTER 29
Alarik

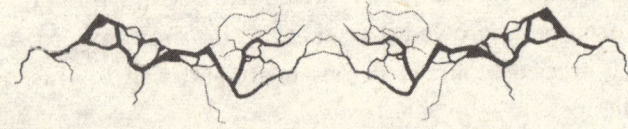

There was a rhythm to war, the thwack of blade meeting bone, then the gurgled gasp of a dying foe. Alarik found the flow with such ease, he felt like he had never left the battlefield. As Regna's troops bore down on him from every direction, he felt no fear. Only purpose. He gave himself over to war, revelling in the familiar rush of his adrenaline. He rode it right into the heart of battle, where he slashed his way through every crimson-armoured soldier who dared raise their sword to him. Blood sprayed all around him, a fountain of red painting Borvil's once-gleaming silver armour. It covered Alarik, too, but left no stain. His armour was as black as the mountains before him.

The mountains Queen Regna had dared to take for her own.

Strike by strike, and inch by inch, he railed against her troops, roaring like a rabid beast. Red-breasted soldiers swarmed him, some even managing to nick him, but Anika was there in a heartbeat, bringing her axes down in crushing blow after crushing blow.

She knew the rhythm, too.

Together, they were unstoppable.

'You still remember how to fight!' yelled Alarik, as he charged a pair of Vaskan soldiers, skewering both on his sword.

'I never stopped!' crowed Anika, easily dispatching two more. 'Did you forget how good I was?'

'How could I, after you shattered my ankle when we were teenagers?' he said, laughing.

'That'll teach you to push me into a lake!'

As they fought, Alarik kept one eye on Hunter's Pass, expecting Regna to come barrelling through it, but there was no sign of the cowardly queen. Only the soldiers she had sent to die for her.

Despite the onslaught from the skies, the king's army was slowly gaining ground, the weaver elk and their riders guarding the west flank and helping to push Regna's forces back towards the mountains and through the main pass. To the east, his wrangler rode at the head of his beasts, her silver armour glittering in the afternoon sun. Alarik would have known her anywhere – that determined tilt of her chin, the ease with which she rode on wolf-back. Her voice arced above the fray, orders flying like arrows as the beasts struck in perfect formations, making rag dolls of Regna's troops.

Alarik burned with pride. His wrangler was a force of nature, as brave as her brother and twice as fierce. Here, in the bloodied heat of battle, she had become a fighter. A soldier. A leader. Together with his beasts, she was a living, breathing work of art.

Behind Alarik, Captain Vine led the ground assault while Hale fired the lances and cannons, knocking gliders out of the sky with the help of the falconer and his birds. They made a formidable team, all of them. After hours of fighting ceaselessly, they managed to regain the frozen flats and clear the foothills.

They continued to push north, Alarik's blood singing with the beginnings of victory as they sealed off Hunter's Pass. Regna's forces were dwindling, but he was careful not to let his guard down. Not while the cunning queen refused to show her face, or play the fullness of her hand.

His instincts soon proved true.

As they ventured up through the foothills, the mountain bled fresh troops, two thousand more of Regna's soldiers pouring out of the old mining tunnels and appearing like spectres before them.

And there among them, towering in height and clad in spiked gold armour, with her long white hair streaming behind her, was Queen Regna. Vask, made flesh. Gleaming and lethal, and baying for blood.

Let her try and take it from him.

Regna raised her spear as she charged, a war cry bursting from her like a terrible aria.

Alarik bellowed a warning as the Vaskan spears flew. But the ambush had caught them off guard, and Regna's soldiers were fast. His front line fell with horrifying quickness, Borvil rearing backwards at the last second to the menacing point of Regna's own spear. It whistled past Alarik's ear and struck Anika's stag, right between the antlers.

She shrieked, tumbling from the dead beast, and only narrowly avoiding a second flying spear. She tripped over another soldier's corpse, scrabbling to find a mount as Regna's ambush closed in on them. Alarik was about to yank his sister up on to Borvil's back when a snow tiger charged from the east, sent no doubt by his eagle-eyed wrangler. Anika ran for it.

Alarik roared at his army, hastily remaking the front line as more crimson soldiers poured from a tunnel up ahead. Their gold helmets set them apart from the others Alarik had felled, but his gaze was fixed on Regna.

Take her head, and end the battle.

She is within your reach.

She pushed closer, likely harbouring the same thought. Fearless now that she had the advantage. And she had chosen the best of her soldiers to guard her. Alarik could tell at once they were skilled, brutal fighters, forgoing their shields for maces and spears.

He refused to be cowed.

'Good of you to show up at last!' he yelled, across the tide of battle. 'I'm sure your dead soldiers would thank you if they still had their heads.'

Regna cut down three of his soldiers on her way to get to him. 'You can tell them I won when you join them in the afterlife.'

Closing the last gap between them, Alarik ended six of her warriors in six calculated strikes, before sliding from Borvil's back. The rest of the war arced around them as they met in the heart of the Blackspires.

Somewhere over his shoulder, Anika's voice rang out. 'Take her head, brother! I could do with a new ornament.'

Regna made a noise of utter disgust. 'This is what happens when you send children to war.'

'Your sword hand is trembling,' taunted Alarik.

'Only in anticipation!' she said, swinging hard.

Their blades met in a singing clash. 'This won't be a clean

death,' he said, dealing another. 'I intend to gut you like you gutted my mountains.'

She growled, pushing her blade against his. 'I hear you have something that belongs to my people. We intend to take it back.'

'I don't know what you're talking about,' he said, coolly.

She snorted. 'Do not lie to me, dragon thief.'

Again, she swung. Alarik leaped backwards, letting the anger of her own momentum knock her off balance. He darted close then, pushing her back three steps.

'Didn't anyone ever tell you not to believe in fairy tales, Regna?'

'Didn't your father ever warn you, beast king? Vask has eyes *everywhere*. Even in that glittering eyesore of a palace of yours.' She struck out, seizing his fleeting surprise. He stumbled backwards, before quickly righting himself. 'I will have what's mine. By blade or by fate's design.'

They fought on, trading insults and blows, until the rest of the world fell away.

When Alarik looked up again, his front line had been decimated once more. Borvil prowled at his back, while Anika had fallen behind in the clash. Captain Vine was pushing more soldiers into the foothills but the corpses there were slowing their ascent and the rock was too loose for the weaver elk. Hale's fire lances were still trained on the sky.

Falling back, Alarik wiped the blood from his hands and regripped the pommel of his sword. For the first time that day, fear nipped at the edges of his heart. His soldiers were falling too quickly. His ranks were depleting, most of them still stuck down on the frozen tundra. Regna and her sea of steel was holding firm, and for a terrifying moment, Alarik felt entirely alone in this battle.

Was this to be his last stand? Was he doomed to fall here on the black soil, with Regna's sword in his chest?

Borvil's strength was lagging, the ice bear picking up on the thread of his anxiety. Alarik was losing control of himself. He was losing control of this war. Victory was slipping like silt through his fingers . . .

Regna grinned through the grill of her helmet, like she could sense it.

'HOLD THE LINE!' His wrangler's cry ripped through him like an inferno. He stiffened, like a wolf called to attention. The earth rumbled, and he glanced over his shoulder to find his beasts stampeding up the mountain, tearing their way through Regna's regiment of gold helmets with a viciousness that made his blood pump faster.

They swarmed Alarik in their droves, filling out a new front line that cast dread in the eyes of their enemies. Trembling at the sight, Regna staggered backwards, quickly widening the space between them. The remaining gold helmets rushed to guard her, while others turned back towards the tunnels.

Cowards.

Alarik's lips curled. Bolstered by the courage of his beasts, he shoved away his fear and fought on, slashing and roaring as he lopped off those gold helmets and sent them tumbling down the mountain. Ever moving towards Regna as she scrabbled up the slope, making for the summit.

In his mind, he heard his father's voice.

Don't think, just strike. And strike again.

Until her army falls at your front,

Or your army falls at your back.
Strike until your final breath leaves you.
And even then, strike once more.

'There's no honour in retreat!' Alarik yelled after the Vaskan queen. 'One way or another, I'll have your head!'

Anika soon returned to his side. Though he couldn't see his sister, he could hear her grunts on the wind, caught the spray of blood every time her axe found its mark. He matched her stroke for stroke, ignoring the blows that landed on his arms and legs, the blades that dented his breastplate and bruised his ribs.

He barely blinked as he fought his way up the slope, keeping his eyes on the ribbons of Regna's white hair. After a while, the sky cleared, the nighthawks circling low as they scoured the mountaintops. Alarik shouted orders over his shoulder, calling for General Hale to use the remaining fire lances on the mining tunnels. They were sealed off in short order, ten concentrated blasts setting loose a shower of rock and rubble that stemmed the flow of Regna's soldiers.

As evening fell, the war turned in their favour. Regna had reached the summit, but her strength was spent. There was barely fifty feet between them now, and only a handful of weary soldiers. Light work for a king in the full tilt of his own adrenaline.

He could get to her.

He would get to her.

And end this war, once and for all.

Then the wind changed. Regna smiled and looked to the east. He followed the line of her sight, to where a lone, crimson-breasted soldier was coming over the mountaintop. A beast of a man, with hulking shoulders and legs like tree trunks. He had forgone his helmet, revealing a broad pale face framed by a black mane and roughened beard. He had a crooked nose and wide dark eyes that seemed to take in everything as he stood out on a jutting rock, his steel-tipped spear glimmering in the waning light.

There wasn't a hint of blood on it.

He was scouring the battlefield like he was looking for someone in particular. When he turned his head, Alarik noted the thin band of black ink around his thick neck. The mark of a Ryberg warrior.

So, this was the mercenary Elias had warned Alarik about. The terrifying Spear of Ryberg, who Queen Regna had brought to battle too late to help her cause.

Alarik snorted. Not only was the Spear not fighting, he wasn't even attempting to defend Regna, who could use all the help she could get now that Alarik was mere yards from killing her.

He pressed on.

But as Alarik cut down another slew of weary Vaskan soldiers, it occurred to him that Regna was no fool. She was a master strategist. His attention splintered, and fleetingly, he wondered if he should pick off the warrior first. Fell whatever plan he had concocted with the queen.

No.

Focus.

Victory was within reach.

Mounting Borvil, Alarik urged the bear further up the mountain, towards the queen.

She wasn't looking at Alarik now. She was looking past him, towards the east flank where the rest of his beasts were fighting. Through the grill of her helmet, her smile grew, slow and cruel, revealing a glint of her famous steel teeth.

Dread trickled down Alarik's spine. What the hell was she smiling at?

Another glance to the east revealed that the Spear was on the hunt. He yanked a curved horn from his hip as he barrelled down the mountain, away from the queen of Vask. Away from Alarik. He brought it to his lips, releasing an awful high-pitched note that sent the nighthawks spiralling away from the mountain. Soldiers fell out of battle to slam their hands over their ears, while the beasts keened, scrambling away from the ear-splitting noise.

Alarik's eyes went wide, as he took in the scene unfolding before him. The animals were bolting back down the mountain, leaving his wrangler alone on the rocky slope.

Weaponless, and without a mount.

Regna's prized warrior was thundering towards her.

On the slope above him, the queen of Vask was laughing. More soldiers were gathering at her back. They must have been hiding on the other side of the summit. She was never truly at Alarik's mercy. No, she had made a distraction of herself, luring him away from the bulk of his army. From his wrangler. 'If I can't have my dragon, then I'll take someone just as valuable from you!'

Horror sluiced through Alarik.

The Spear wasn't here to kill the king of Gevra.

He was here to capture his wrangler.

CHAPTER 30
Greta

The Gevran army was teetering on the cusp of victory when a terrible shriek rang out, pounding them like a wave. The animals bolted for the flatlands, leaving Greta alone on the mountainside. She whirled, calling for them to stay and finish the battle, but her orders were lost to that torturous blare. Her head was throbbing, her knees trembling beneath her. She couldn't think, couldn't focus.

She scrunched her fists, fighting for control of her senses. The horn petered out, leaving its taunting echo inside her helmet. She ripped it off and cast it aside, gasping a steadying breath. The cold wind whipped her face, and the clash of sword fighting filtered back in. Instinctively, she whipped her head around, searching for the king.

Up the mountain, Queen Regna was retreating into the fray of more Vaskan soldiers. Alarik was still on his feet, flanked now by his sister and Captain Vine who were fighting their way up the slope. Relief rushed through Greta, until she noticed his sword was slack at his side. He wasn't fighting alongside his soldiers. He was frozen in horror, staring in her direction.

A gasp filled Greta's throat as she spotted a terrifying figure – no, a *giant* – charging towards her. He wore no helmet, his bearded face bared to the elements, his long dark hair riding the wind. He raised his spear, the silver tip as menacing as the glint in his eyes. She had seen that same look before countless times, but never on the face of a man. This creature was going to strike her. Maim her, *kill* her.

He was a hunter, and she was his prey.

Greta screamed for her beasts – for *anyone* – to come back for her, but the strange horn at his hip had done its work. Even the birds had fled.

She turned on her heel and ran, barrelling down the mountain so fast, she tripped over a jutting rock. Her ankle twisted underneath her, and pain shot up her leg. She scrabbled to her feet and pushed on, gritting through the discomfort.

Momentum shoved her down the mountain, but the beasts were so very far from her now, and the giant's footsteps were pounding harder, closer. Tears streamed down her face as she ran, the world blurring out of focus.

She knew she wasn't going to make it. Without a beast, she wasn't fast enough or strong enough. But she refused to give up, even as she heard the slow heave of his breath behind her, the determined crunch of his footsteps like a cruel countdown to her death.

She risked a glance over her shoulder to find those violent eyes barely a stone's throw away. She drew her sword, bringing it up against her chest. Bracing for the strike of his spear.

He growled as he leaped at her. She was slammed into the earth, the sword flung aside as her face collided with the cold, hard rock. She tried to raise her dizzying head, but he shoved it back down, fisting his hand in her hair.

'*Stay*,' he grunted.

Like hell she would. Greta bucked against him, screaming into the dirt as she thrashed and twisted. He flipped her over, his hand coming to her throat as he pinned her. It was like being crushed by a boulder, her breath leaving her in a painful wheeze.

'Queen Regna wants her new wrangler in one piece.' He pressed his forehead against hers, his spittle landing on her cheeks. 'So, *behave*.'

The beast inside Greta reared up. She spat in his face. 'Get off me!'

'Unruly little wolf.' He bared a mouthful of steel teeth. 'She never said you had to be awake.'

Before Greta could react, he smashed his forehead into hers. She reeled backwards, pain spiderwebbing up the back of her skull. Stars wheeled in the sides of her vision, the world growing dark, until there was only the tip of his spear at her throat, and the distant cry of her name on the wind.

Then, there was blackness.

And after that – nothing.

CHAPTER 31
Alarik

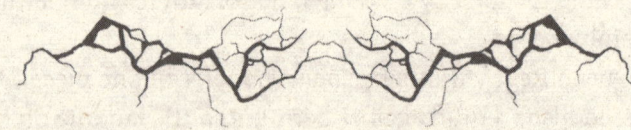

The wrangler's scream tore through Alarik, calling to the beast in his heart. It reared up in answer, all sense of duty narrowing to one single, pounding thought: *save her*.

Leaving Regna to Captain Vine and Anika, Alarik surrendered his vengeance and charged across the mountainside. The world whipped past in whorls of black and white and crimson. Rogue soldiers leaped into his path only to be cut down with a swift and bloody vengeance. Rage was a frenzy inside him, hurling him across the rocky slope. He slashed and roared, blood spraying like rain as he fought his way through every foolish warrior who dared stand between him and his wrangler.

He was a beast out for blood, a snow leopard running for his mate, and there wasn't a force strong enough to stop him. He was halfway to his wrangler when the Spear pounced, flattening her under the slab of his body.

Alarik's heart lurched.

'GRETA!' He roared her name, so she would know he was coming for her. Let the Spear hear it, too. This coin-hungry brute's seconds were numbered.

Alarik swore as the mercenary rolled her over, bringing his forehead to hers.

I will cut you limb from limb, he thought viciously. *I will bleed you dry and feed your corpse to my beasts.*

The wrangler lurched, spitting into the Spear's face. Alarik would have smiled if he wasn't so terrified for her. She was like a doll beneath him, bloodied and bruised, and still fighting with every breath.

He yelled again, her name a promise on the wind. 'GRETA!'

I'm coming, wildling.

Keep fighting.

The Spear slammed his head into hers and she slumped to the ground, limp. Rage spiralled through Alarik. He had never known anger like it, the heat of it fully unleashing the beast inside him. He leaped through the air and landed on the giant, knocking him sideways.

They rolled over each other, fighting for dominance. The Spear swung, slamming his fist into Alarik's jaw. He weathered the blow, but it cost him precious seconds. The mercenary leaped to his feet, rounding on him with his spear. Alarik surged forward, tackling him at the waist. He drove him back against a jutting rock and they fell together.

Alarik slammed the hilt of his sword into the brute's temple. The mercenary took it without flinching, jamming the blunt end of his spear into Alarik's spine. Who bowed upwards, cursing through the pain.

They returned to their feet, brandishing their weapons. They clashed again and again. The Spear was stronger, but Alarik was quicker and *burning* with a fury that felt ancient and powerful. He beat the mercenary back, back, back, keeping his body between the warrior and his wrangler. Making a shield of his rage.

'I'm going to bring you to your knees,' Alarik spat. 'And then I'll take your head as a trophy.'

'Save your empty threats,' grunted the Spear, his steel teeth gleaming. 'I don't care about your battle. I'm only here for the wrangler.'

Alarik's nostrils flared. '*My* wrangler.'

The Spear scoffed. Alarik came at him like a blizzard. He slashed twin wounds down his thighs, skewered his left arm and the side of his thick neck, making him bleed for every drop he had stolen from his Greta, for every bruise that now bloomed across her perfect face. He drove him down to his knees, kicked away his spear, until the mercenary was exhausted and weaponless, and soaked in ribbons of his own blood.

Alarik pressed the point of his sword against his throat. 'Ready to die, Spear?'

He spat out a glob of blood. 'Possessive beast.'

'*Correct*,' Alarik snarled.

The Spear glared at him. 'Regna was right. You fight dirty. Like a wolf.'

'I fight for a cause, and you fight for coin,' sneered Alarik. '*That* is why you're on your fucking knees.'

The Spear made a noise of derision. 'What cause?' he said, swaying now.

Her.

'Victory.' As a roaring chorus filled the air, Alarik gave a feral smile. He stepped back as his wolves closed in around him and left the infamous Spear of Ryberg at their mercy.

He returned to his wrangler. She was still lying in the

same place. He brushed her hair away, examining the lacerations on her chin and forehead. If the Spear wasn't already screaming his last, he might have indulged his yawning rage and finished the job himself.

But then he'd have to leave her. Her eyes were closed, the storm inside lost to him. He laid his palm against her throat, searching for the thrum of her pulse. Time stretched into a torturous eternity, and then – *there*. A pulse. It was faint, but it was there. Relief swept through Alarik, dousing the fire of his anger, as he lifted her from the mountainside and curled her into his arms. The ice bears, Baldur and Nel, flanked him, silently guarding their wrangler as he carried her down the mountain.

Leaving Captain Vine and the rest of his soldiers to deal with Regna and her stragglers, Alarik fixed his eyes on the distant sleds, making his way back to the frozen flats. The battle was all but won, but there was no triumph in his heart. Only sorrow for the soldiers he had lost, and concern for the woman in his arms.

'Stay with me, Greta,' he murmured into her hair. 'It's over now. We're going home.'

CHAPTER 32
Greta

The darkness was speaking to Greta. It whispered her name and stroked her hair, gently coaxing her back to life. But she was so comfortable here in the in-between, far from the clamour of battle and the metallic tang of blood. Away from the dying howls of beasts and the horror of corpses rolling down the mountainside. She remembered the war in fleeting bursts, the shrieking echo of that terrible horn pushing into the blackness of her mind. Then there was the giant with violent eyes and steel teeth, and the hard slap of earth rising to meet her.

She groaned, trying to shove it all away.

That voice came again, soft against the shell of her ear. 'It's all right, wildling. I've got you.'

Strong arms cradled her against a warm chest. She turned her face into it, inhaling a lungful of woodsmoke and pine. The scent drew a languid sigh from her, lulling her back to sleep. To peace.

'That's it, Greta. Rest a while.'

Sometime later, she stirred at a howl of wind. The world was rattling, her body jerking. Dimly, she was aware that she was in a sled, riding fast and hard across the frozen earth. Cold wind lashed her face while snowflakes gathered in her hair. Her teeth began to chatter, and those strong arms shifted, covering her with a fur blanket.

The world dropped away again, taking the blizzard with it. But her protector remained, holding her tightly like he was afraid the wind might sweep her away.

Who *was* he? The answer floated at the edge of her mind, like a snowflake. She was too tired to catch it. Too tired to think at all . . .

Greta gave herself back to the darkness, only stirring to drink from the waterskin that was pressed to her lips every so often. As the hours wore on, she began to hear voices, ones she recognized but couldn't place, and beyond them, the familiar keening of her beasts.

Home, she told herself.

I am going home.

But in the rippling dark, she couldn't remember where home was.

After an eternity in the windswept wilderness, the cold died away, and a luxurious warmth settled over Greta. As a rogue slant of dawn light danced across her face, she blinked herself awake, trying to clear the fog from her mind. A high, corniced ceiling blurred in and out of focus, making her frown. Where was she?

Far from the Blackspires, and the sled that had whisked her away from there. The heavy silence told her she was no longer near the other soldiers, or her beloved beasts.

Although she sensed one nearby. Watching her.

She rolled her head around. She was lying on a pillow cased in silk. There were blankets tucked up to her chin, each one lined in fur and piled so high, she couldn't see over them.

This was not her bedroom.

Something stirred at the foot of her bed. The soft padding of paws announced the arrival of a sleek silver wolf, who curled up next to her.

'Hello, darling,' she murmured. She tried to place the beautiful creature. She hadn't trained her before, but she recognized those large golden eyes. They were wise and gentle, the relaxed hum of her spirit setting her at ease. 'Have you been looking after me?'

'I'd call it more of a joint effort.' Greta stared at the wolf, her mind so addled she wondered if it really was talking to her. But *no*, she knew that voice . . .

'Alarik?' she croaked, uncertainly.

'Over here, wrangler.'

Swiftly tumbling back to her senses, Greta shoved the blankets away and sat up to find herself in the fanciest room she'd ever seen.

'This isn't my bed.'

'I know.' The king of Gevra was standing, arms folded, at the foot of it. 'It's mine.'

Greta let out a strangled cry of alarm as the world shifted into sharp, searing focus. She looked down at herself, expecting to see her scuffed uniform and stained battle armour, but she was instead wearing a pale blue nightgown finer than everything she owned, and a pair of socks that felt like warm, woolly clouds.

She looked up at the king in dawning horror. He was dressed casually in low-slung trousers and a plain black vest. His hair was damp, and his feet were bare, as though he had just finished bathing. There was a fresh cut along his jaw, and a nasty bruise marring his left cheek.

'Nanna dressed you,' he said, before she spiralled into panic. 'You were in bad shape.' He cleared his throat. 'I combed through your hair in the sled. And I cleaned your face up.' His lips twisted, his pale eyes darkening. 'There was so much blood. I couldn't stand to leave you like that.'

Greta frowned, trying to piece together the last few days, but she couldn't recall anything beyond the cold, howling wind, and her strong-armed protector holding her close. Did that mean . . . ?

'I rode back in your sled?'

'Yes.'

Holy snow.

'Just the two of us?'

He nodded. 'Do you remember what happened on the mountain?'

She flinched at the memory. 'Yes,' she whispered. 'I heard you call my name. You came for me.' Again, he nodded. 'You saved my life.'

He gave a half-smile. 'Your beloved wolves helped.'

Her heart swelled. 'You mean *your* wolves,' she said, softly.

'Our wolves,' he said, softer still.

Greta clutched at the swirling heat in her belly. If he didn't stop talking to her like this, low and gentle as a lover, she was going to burst into flames.

'And now I'm in your bed,' she said, trying to puzzle out the rest.

'I'm afraid Luna insisted.' He gestured towards the wolf. 'She said it was the best place to put you.'

Greta chewed on her smile. 'Did she indeed?'

He dipped his chin. 'She's *very* bossy.'

'Then you two must get along famously,' said Greta, scratching behind the wolf's ears, before pressing a kiss to her snout. 'You really are a beauty.'

She could feel the king's eyes on her. 'She didn't trust anyone else to watch over you,' he said, quietly.

The tenderness in his words sent a bolt of longing through her. She couldn't bring herself to look at him. So, she poured all her devotion and relief into his wolf, furiously blinking her tears away. 'Thank you for watching over me,' she said, in a cracked whisper. 'Thank you for saving my life.'

He rounded the bed, his presence enveloping her like a warm breeze as he perched at her side. 'I could no more cede my wrangler to Queen Regna than I could my kingdom.'

She sniffled as she turned towards him, resisting the urge to skim her fingers across the bruises on his face. 'The battle, Alarik . . .' She was almost too afraid to ask. 'Did we win?'

'Well, I'm not dead, so that should be a clue.' His face remained grave. 'But our losses . . . there were many. Hundreds.' He bit back a curse. 'And twice as many injured. It was a bloodbath.'

One they had barely survived.

'I'm sorry,' she whispered. It ached in her, the swell of such a loss. She thought of all those families mired in grief. And hundreds more soldiers now battling towards recovery. Then there were the stricken beasts to mourn. More pain. More loss. 'They were so brave, your soldiers. Your beasts. The way they fought. How they rallied, even when they had barely any strength left. I've never seen anything like it.'

He nodded, distantly, the ghost of a smile flitting across his face. 'Gevran, to the bone.'

There was a hint of pride in his voice, but the sadness there was greater, deeper.

She dropped her gaze to his ruined hands. 'I'm sorry,' she said again.

'It could have been worse.' He was looking at her now. She could feel his quiet conviction like a ripple of heat between them. 'So much worse.'

'Is it over?' she dared to ask.

'Regna and her forces have retreated. For now.' His voice hardened. 'It won't be over until she meets the point of my sword.' At her grimace, he leaned in, his voice low. 'I'd be a lot more *creative* with the wording of that threat, but I know violent talk of vengeful bloody murder makes you uncomfortable.'

A weak laugh bubbled out of her, causing pain to spiderweb through her skull. She winced.

He frowned as he looked her over. 'How do you feel, Greta?'

She blinked in surprise. 'You called me Greta.'

He canted his head. 'Do you like that?'

A lot more than she should have. It felt closer, intimate somehow.

She nodded.

'Then drink this, Greta.' He grabbed a glass of water from the bedside locker and handed it to her. 'My physician says you're dehydrated.'

Her fingers trembled as she took the glass. He blanketed them with his own, steadying her hand as she drank. She watched him over the rim, neither one of them looking away.

She finished the water, feeling marginally better already. He set the glass aside and returned his attention to her injuries, gently cupping her jaw to move it side to side, grimacing at the patchwork of bruises he no doubt saw there.

'Is it really that bad?' she asked.

'What I wouldn't give to kill him all over again,' he muttered. 'Nice and slow and brutal.'

'Please don't ruin the moment.'

He arched a brow. 'What moment?'

'You. Being caring.'

'I care very much for you, Greta,' he murmured, his hand rising to stroke the scars on her cheek. 'Can't you feel it?'

She swallowed hard. There was so much she wanted to say to him, but she was afraid if she opened her mouth, every wayward, wanton feeling would come tumbling out, and she would scare him away. Ruin the moment and worse, destroy the bond they had come to share, a thing so rare and precious and lovely, she treasured it above everything else.

But it was killing her, this growing whirlpool of need. Desire overwhelmed her, and gripped in its heavy fog, she turned her face into the warmth of his palm and pressed a kiss there.

He stilled. 'What was that for?'

'Just a thank you,' she whispered against his skin. 'Thank you, Alarik.'

Her heart lurched as his hand slipped from her cheek, finding hers. He raised it to his lips, his gaze burning as he returned her kiss, brushing his lips against her knuckles. 'You're welcome, Greta.'

Her throat tightened, painfully. She was all too aware of every aching thud of her heart. She wanted to rip it out of her chest and give it to him. She turned away before she did something even more reckless, her gaze finding the book on his bedside table. It was a collection of poems about love and war.

'You read poetry?' she said, with some surprise.

'Only when I want to bore myself to sleep.' A smile ghosted across his lips. 'My brother Ansel loved poetry. He used to say that it nurtured the heart.'

'Does it?'

'I don't know,' he said, in a conspiratorial whisper. 'I think mine has to thaw first.'

'Will you read some to me?' The words flew from her lips before she could stop them.

He slanted his head. 'Does your heart need soothing, wildling?'

'I don't know,' she lied. 'But my aching head could do with some tender words.'

He reached for the book, and she saw then that it was well-thumbed. 'All right,' he said, swinging his legs on to the bed, where they brushed against hers. 'Your wish is my command.'

Greta lay back, his arm coming around her as she rested her head against his shoulder. She closed her eyes and smiled as the king read poem after poem to her, with the kind of skill and reverence that told her he knew every single one of them by heart.

RAP, RAP, RAP!

Hours later, they jumped apart at a knock on the door.

Alarik stifled a curse as he rolled to his feet. 'What is it?' he barked.

Johan ducked his head around the door. 'Pardon the interruption, Your Majesty. Uh, Lief is looking for you. There's a problem with the string quartet. It seems Nova has chewed through one of the—'

'Musicians?' said Alarik, hopefully.

'Uh, cellos,' said Johan. 'Now the others are refusing to practise the wedding march.'

Alarik groaned, slamming the book shut. 'I'll be right down.'

Greta winced, weathering the cold, hard slap of reality. The spell between them had shattered. The truth was as searing as the sunlight slipping through the drapes. She was a wrangler, and he was the king of Gevra. He was promised to a beautiful princess with a kingdom and Greta belonged to the wild. Nothing in the Blackspires had changed that. Nothing ever could.

Alarik set the book back on his bedside table, and she pulled the blankets up to her chin, wishing she could disappear entirely.

'Stay here and rest,' he said. 'I'll be back soon.'

She nodded, closing her eyes until he left. Once the patter of his footsteps had faded, she threw off the covers, stumbled out of bed and bolted from the king's bedroom. One flight of stairs followed another, and another, as she spiralled down, down, down into the underbelly of the palace.

Back to reality, and back to her bedroom.

Back to her place.

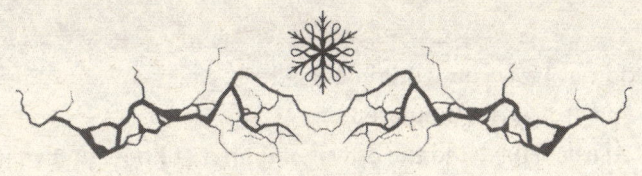

CHAPTER 33
Alarik

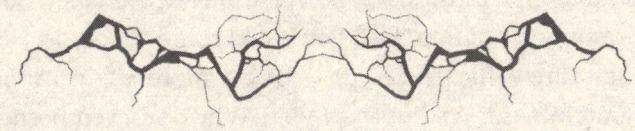

Alarik was arguing with a hysterical Lief when his mother swept into the ballroom. Sunlight gilded her yellow gown and cast pinwheels across her slippers as her steps echoed in the cavernous room. It was a far cry from the grand majesty it had beheld at the welcome ball. The room lay empty now, a blank canvas that Lief would bring to life in the days to come. It would soon be a ballroom fit for a royal wedding. A glittering monstrosity for hundreds of noblefolk to feast on.

Whether Alarik liked it or not.

'What on earth is going on?' demanded the dowager queen. 'I can hear you yelling from the west wing.'

Alarik folded his arms. 'Nothing. It's all in hand.'

'It is not in hand!' cried Lief, rushing to the queen like a shameless tattletale. 'The king's wolf chewed up Herbert's prized cello and then made off with my best neckerchief!'

Queen Valeska released a long-suffering sigh.

'It's sabotage!' said the steward. 'He has sent his beasts to sabotage my vision!'

Alarik rolled his eyes. 'If I wanted to sabotage this

wedding, Lief, you would be dead.'

The steward whimpered.

'*Alarik*,' chasisted the dowager queen. 'I know you've just returned from battle, but Grinstad is a civilized place. Please do try to be less murderous while you're here.'

'I'm *trying*,' he said, through his teeth. 'I've already offered to replace the cello *and* the gaudy neckerchief. But if you want my opinion, Lief, you could stand to lose it.'

Lief threw his hands up. 'That's more of it! Abuse! Ungratefulness! And now slander! Why do I even bother?' He stomped off towards the door, muttering a slew of swear words. Alarik had never liked him more. 'You can deal with His Majesty's foul humour. I've had enough.'

Alarik watched him go. 'You should lend him to the local theatre. He'd make a killing.'

'What is this really about?' said Valeska, wearily.

He arched a brow. 'You mean other than my complete and utter aversion to this marriage?'

'Please keep your voice down,' she hissed. 'Princess Elva might hear you.'

'Elva has gone ice skating with Captain Vine,' said Alarik, in a bored voice. He had spied them that morning from his balcony, talking and laughing as they donned their skates at the edge of the lake. The recent battle was already a distant thought to Vine. Or perhaps his captain had sought out the princess to take her mind off it. They hadn't lost exactly. But they hadn't won either.

Everything remained uncomfortably . . . unfinished.

In any case, Alarik hadn't so much as flinched when he watched them bend their heads together, Elva turning to plant a stolen kiss on Vine's cheek. Let them skate. Let them flirt. Let them fall madly in love for all he cared.

'Trust me, she's no more in love with me than I am with her.'

'Time will take care of that,' said his mother, with infuriating simplicity. 'For now, your alliance is what matters.'

Frustration burned in the pit of Alarik's stomach. He went to the window to look out at the whirling snow, trying not to think of the wrangler in his bed. There was no measure of time that would install the princess of Halgard into his heart. Not when it was already filled with someone else.

Another matter that remained frustratingly unfinished.

Not that they had even *begun*.

'You lost half of King Nilas's elk at the Blackspires.' His mother's voice drifted after him. 'Almost a third of his soldiers. And your own.'

'I know that,' he said, tersely.

'Queen Regna will strike again, Alarik. It's only a matter of time.'

'I *know*,' he growled.

But *where*? And *when*?

Not for the first time that day, he thought of the beast trapped in his mountain. A true dragon, if the old rumours held true. Was Regna goading him to free it? Or did she truly want it for himself? Did she really believe it could be tamed?

With the right wrangler, perhaps.

Which would explain her sudden interest in Greta Iversen.

'You need this alliance,' said his mother.

It remained the unavoidable truth. A thorn in his heart that pricked deeper every day. He closed his eyes, imagining a future with Elva. But when he tried to conjure the princess in her lovely gowns and sparkling tiaras, his traitorous thoughts returned to Greta. Soft and beautiful and singing to his beasts. Strong and wild and roaring into battle. Pale and bruised and bleeding in his arms.

Safe and sleeping in his bed.

A hand came to his arm, jolting him from the vision. 'Alarik. Is there something else going on?'

He turned to his mother, suddenly desperate to lay his struggle at her feet. To unload the burden of his own heart, if just for a moment. But he stilled at the look on her face. It was pale and drawn, worry deepening the lines around her eyes.

She looked tired. Fearful. Old.

Long ago, Alarik had made a promise to the memory of his father that he would keep his mother safe, that he would strive, every day, to make her happy. He had failed, year after year, to keep that promise. He was still failing.

'I know you do not wish to marry Elva,' she went on. 'In truth, I always believed it was Ansel who would make the perfect alliance for this kingdom. Leaving you to live as you like, with your freedom and your beasts.' Her smile was edged with sadness. 'The day he sailed to marry his bride in Eana, I stood at my balcony and wept. What kind of mother is too afraid of the sea to attend her own son's wedding?'

'The kind that lost her husband to the ocean,' said Alarik. 'No one blamed you for not being there.'

Alarik was glad of it now, that her crippling fear of the crossing had kept her from getting on his ship. That she did not have to sit in that pew and witness the sword skewering Ansel's heart, see the rivers of blood that flowed from his chest, painting his ivory doublet crimson.

She closed her eyes, a sigh sweeping out of her. 'I still wonder if I could have saved him.'

'No.' The word was swift and final. 'There was nothing you could have done.'

Another failure that was his to bear.

'You know, I love you and your sister very much,' she murmured, turning her gaze to the window, looking past the bounds of Grinstad into another time. 'But you are both so mercurial, married to the rogue winds of battle and adventure in a way your brother was not. You and Anika are my very heart, but Ansel was my hope for the future. For family and company, and the laughter of grandchildren filling these cold, empty halls. I placed all my hopes in that boy, and when he died . . .' She trailed off, a silent tear trickling down her cheek.

Alarik fisted his hands, rage and sadness thrashing inside him. It all felt so unfair, that he was here, and Ansel was not, that he had bowed so quickly under the weight of his legacy. If he couldn't protect his kingdom from invasion, or his own family from pain, then what good was he as a king? As a man?

She turned from the window. 'Now, there is hope again,' she said, her lips flickering. 'Hope for something beautiful, beyond battle and bloodshed. Beyond loss.'

Alarik laid his head against the window, his breath fogging the glass. For his mother, his marriage to Princess Elva was about more than an alliance. He could see it plainly now, her desire to reclaim the warmth that once lit these halls, the love and laughter that echoed here. For the first time in years, she was looking to the future, not the past.

But how could he tell her that the mere thought of that future filled him with dread? Not for what he might gain in the end, but for who he would have to give up to get there.

When he stepped back from the window, she was gone. He was alone in the ballroom, dreading the moment in five days' time, when he would have to step inside it again. Not as king, but as a groom.

When Alarik returned to his bedchamber, Greta was no longer there. Like a fool, he went to his bed and checked under the pile of blankets to look for her. Luna watched him from her spot on her pillow, judgement glowing in her golden eyes.

You really messed this up, he imagined her saying.

'I know,' he muttered. 'I'm messing everything up.'

'Your wrangler left a while ago.' He turned at the sound of his sister's voice. Anika was standing in the doorway in a long white coat and matching fur hat, with her crimson hair styled in twin braids. Despite the toll of battle, there wasn't a scratch on her. In fact, she looked revitalized, better now than when she had first arrived home last week. 'Johan said she bolted like a deer.'

Alarik ground his teeth. 'She's supposed to be resting.'

'She can rest in her own bed.' Anika stepped into the room and shut the door. 'You are betrothed to someone else.'

'Elva doesn't care,' said Alarik, curtly. In fact, it was Elva who ran to meet them upon their return from battle two days ago, fetching the palace physician and an armful of extra blankets to help warm Greta up.

Anika tossed his words aside. 'You can't have them both.'

'Get out of my room, Anika.'

'No.'

He glared at her.

She glared right back.

'Grow up, Alarik,' she snapped. 'We are at war. Don't doom your kingdom over some foolish fling with your wrangler.'

'You have no idea what you're talking about,' he said, working to keep his anger at bay. 'And I would caution you not to annoy me today. I'm feeling particularly vicious.'

'Go eat a cello, then.'

Alarik opened his mouth to snap back, but at the defiant look in her eyes, the fight inside him sputtered out. He wasn't angry at his sister. He was angry because she was telling him the truth. He slumped on to the bed, raking his hands through his hair. 'I don't know what to do, Anika.'

Her voice softened at his distress, the mattress creaking as she sat down beside him. 'Yes, you do.' She tapped his chest. 'War before desire, brother. Kingdom before heart.'

His stomach twisted. 'I don't want to let her go.'

'She's already gone, Alarik,' she said, gently.

I want to chase her. He almost leaped from the bed, caught in the primal rush of his need. In that moment he wasn't a king or a son or a groom. He felt like a snow leopard, desperate to find his mate.

Anika must have sensed the shift in his energy because she leaped to her feet and made a wall of her body.

'Leave her be,' she warned.

He jerked his chin up. 'Or what?'

'Or I'll send word to Tor Iversen. And then you really will be sorry.'

He snorted at the threat but didn't rise to it. Deep down, he knew his sister was right. It wasn't fair to chase Greta. No matter his feelings, he had nothing to offer her.

And the truth was, she deserved better.

CHAPTER 34
Greta

Greta hid in her room for three days, applying tinctures to the wounds on her face and picking at the meals Nanna brought her. She wrote home to Carrig, yearning for news of her beloved island, and missing her family more fiercely than ever. She sent word to them of the Battle of the Blackspires, skimming over the gory details and devastating losses, and focusing instead on what she had learned, on how she could improve the beasts' concentration in the face of unchartered pitches, like the horn the Spear had used to spook them at a crucial moment in battle.

Greta didn't want her family to worry about her. She wanted them to be warm and well-fed, and proud of her. So, she kept her fear to herself, even as it gnawed at the edges of her heart. She knew Queen Regna would not go down without a fight.

Greta had to go back to work. To tend to her injured beasts and better prepare them for the next battle, when death would come again to Gevra. War was a terrible, soul-rending cycle, but at least it distracted her from the painful cleaving in her own chest. It helped her forget how the king had held her in his sled, murmuring to her in the darkness, or how the phantom brush of his lips still lingered on her knuckles.

Greta had to forget, because if she didn't forget, she would break.

And she refused to break.

She could weather the sting of her unrequited feelings, shove away her longing and focus on her tasks. She had faced far worse, and survived. She could face this, too.

On the fourth morning of her self-exile, she rose at dawn. Now that her headaches were subsiding and her energy was returning, it was starting to feel like the walls were closing in on her. She was growing restless, which was a good sign. She washed and changed into her newly mended uniform, and braided her hair away from her face, examining herself in the mirror. The purple bruises along her jaw were fading to yellow and the swelling in her right eye had finally abated.

After a quick breakfast, she practically skipped out to the courtyard, revelling in the rush of cool wind on her face and the familiar rumble of her beasts rising to face the day. There were fewer now than there had been last week. She knew the losses were many, but she resolved not to grieve in front of the animals. For now, she would take on their pain and offer them comfort in return.

She made for the wolves first, relief flooding her at the sight of Tollo and Gale tussling in their pen. She grabbed the bacon strips she had swiped from the dining hall and tossed them to the wolves just as a soldier stomped into her path.

'What are you doing out here, Iversen?' said Captain Vine, dispensing with their usual greeting. 'You're supposed to be resting.'

'I was resting. Now, I'm better.' She tried to arc around Vine, but the soldier caught her arm, tugging her back.

'You don't look better.'

'I don't care how I look,' said Greta, with as much politeness as she could summon, but her patience was ragged, and she didn't care for the disapproval on the captain's face. 'I have work to do.'

'You're not cleared for that.'

Greta narrowed her eyes. 'Cleared by *whom*?'

'By the king.'

'Why does the king have to clear me for work?'

'Because he is *the king*.' Vine gave a short huff. 'Just . . . don't piss him off.' She lowered her voice. 'He's been insufferable lately.'

'That's not my problem.'

'It's everyone's problem.' Vine turned her around, gently nudging her back the way she had come. 'Return to your bedchamber and rest.'

Greta stiffened but didn't fight the captain. She was not about to get into an altercation. But nor did she have any intention of going back to her room.

'Where is the king right now?' she demanded.

'Sparring or breaking something, I expect.'

'Good,' said Greta, charging ahead.

She felt like sparring, too. It was one thing to steal her heart, without remorse, but it was another to steal her beasts. Without them, she had nothing. She *was* nothing.

She stormed into the palace, her chest heaving as she made her way through the atrium, down the hall and into the east wing. The door to the sparring room was shut, but she could hear voices within.

She shoved the door open and stomped inside. 'Clear me!' she demanded.

Alarik, who was in the middle of sparring with his cousin, paused mid-strike.

'What?' he said, spinning to face her.

Elias disarmed him in one swift move, but the king barely noticed, letting his sword clatter to the floor.

'Haven't you ever heard of knocking, Iversen?' drawled Elias.

Greta ignored him, keeping her gaze and her rage on Alarik.

'*Clear me,*' she said, again. 'I want to go back to work.'

Alarik narrowed his eyes, looking her over. 'You're not ready.'

'That's not for you to decide!' she snapped.

'Yes, it is!' he snapped back.

Elias whistled. 'Did that blow to your face rearrange your personality, Iversen?'

Alarik whipped his head around. 'Get the hell out.'

Elias raised his brows. 'It was a joke—'

'Leave us!' he barked, sending his spymaster slinking from the room.

Greta slammed the door after him then stood with her back against it. Her throat tightened, her anger twisting into something deep and painful as the king pinned her with that piercing blue gaze. His breath punched out of him, his hands curling and uncurling at his sides.

She opened her mouth, then closed it again.

Why had she come here? Why was she angry? And why did she suddenly feel like bursting into tears?

He took a step towards her, his voice softening. 'What's wrong, wildling?'

'You.' She closed her eyes, desperately fighting back tears. '*You* are what's wrong.'

Silence yawned. The room narrowed as he drew closer, tugged by that invisible string in her chest. His scent washed over her, the heady mix of woodsmoke and pine making her dizzy. 'You're angry at me,' he said, with quiet bewilderment. 'Tell me why.'

'I don't know why,' she said, in a cracked whisper. Her emotions were swirling like a blizzard. Too fast. Too many at once. She reached for a snowflake – something that had hurt her. 'You left me alone.'

'You ran from my bedroom, Greta.'

'You never checked on me.'

'I was giving you space.'

I don't want space from you.

She clamped the words on her tongue. She couldn't say that. What good would it do?

'What else?' he pressed, catching her tear with the pad of his thumb. She opened her eyes. He was standing right in front of her, and gazing at her with such tenderness it made her knees weak. Why had she come here, only to torture herself?

'What else?' he said, softer now.

She reached for a different snowflake – another point of pain. 'You won't clear me for work.'

'You're not well enough for work.'

'How do you know?' she challenged.

His gaze darkened. 'You nearly *died* on that mountain, Greta. I'm the one who carried you home. I'm the one who stayed awake in that sled listening to you breathe every minute of every hour of every day trying to make sure your heart didn't give out.' The strain of that worry still tugged at his jaw. 'So, when I tell you to take a week off, then take it.'

She folded her arms. 'And do what?'

'I don't care,' he said, mirroring her stance. 'Sleep, eat, read, dance, skate.'

'I don't want to do those things!' she burst out.

He braced his hand on the door frame, leaning into her. 'What *do* you want, Greta?'

A dangerous question. Forbidden answers crowded on her tongue.

He watched her lips, silently daring her to voice them.

She reached for another snowflake. Not anger, but curiosity. 'Did you send aid to my family?'

'Yes,' he said, at once.

'Why?'

'You know why.'

'Tell me anyway,' she said.

He dragged his gaze back to hers. 'I sent aid to your family so you wouldn't have to worry about them. I don't want your beast to hunger for food any more. I want it to hunger for other things.'

She snorted, the rueful words slipping out before she could stop them. 'Well, now it does.'

And it's torture.

His eyes flashed. 'What does it hunger for?'

She chewed on her bottom lip.

'Tell me what your beast wants, Greta.'

She shook her head. No, no, she could not.

He leaned closer, his breath feathering her cheek. 'Then

show me,' he said, a rasp in his voice. '*Please.*'

Please.

The word was her undoing. Suddenly, it was too much – this raging heat between them, that ravenous look in his eyes. She was molten with desire, so addled with lust, she couldn't stop herself even if she wanted to. She lifted her chin, closing the sliver of space between them.

Slowly, so very slowly, she brushed her lips against his. 'This,' she breathed, against his mouth. 'This is what I want.'

'*Yes,*' he groaned, sliding his hand into her hair. 'You can have it.' His body trembled against hers, and Greta sensed the force of his need like a hurricane inside him. And yet his kiss was soft and searching. An answer to her own, and a question.

A plea for more.

He didn't want to frighten her off. Greta had never been kissed before, had barely ever *thought* about being kissed, but in this moment, with this man, she had never felt so wildly alive, so close to the beast in her soul. It wanted *more*. *She* wanted more.

She wound her fingers in his collar, rising to her tiptoes until his body sank into hers, sealing every inch of space between them. She trailed her lips along his jaw, and he shuddered, still straining to taste her without devouring her.

She smiled, nudging her nose against his. 'I won't break.'

'Yes, but *I* might.' He kissed one corner of her mouth, and then the other. She opened for him, and his tongue swept in. She met him stroke for stroke, matching his hunger with her own. The beast inside her reared up, and she nipped at his bottom lip. He chuckled. 'Do you want to play, wildling?'

She nipped him again. 'Show me how.'

'With pleasure,' he rumbled.

She moaned as he deepened the kiss, parting the seam of her lips with his tongue and seizing her mouth. All thoughts spun away from Greta until there was only the thunder of his heart beating against hers, and the ragged gasps of her pleasure as he worshipped her with his tongue.

Time dissolved into nothing as she gave herself to the punishing perfection of his kiss, melting into the king's embrace like she belonged there. There was a rightness to it, the taste of him setting her soul alight, the sound of his rasping breaths echoing her own.

Her knees began to tremble, buckling under the weight of this stolen moment – this blissful joining – that felt both primal and tender, impossible and inevitable. Sensing her need as if it were his own, he hooked a strong arm around her waist, spinning her away from the door and walking her back towards the bench. He pulled her down on to his lap, and she straddled his hips, neither one of them breaking the kiss as he slid his hands up her back, moulding her body to his own. The heat between them became an inferno, every press of their lips no longer a playful exploration but a searing demand.

A desperate, burning claiming.

Greta could have stayed in his lap all day, drinking down his desire and still aching for more, if only the door hadn't swung open when it did.

She was too lost in him to hear the footsteps behind her.

He was too lost in her to see the sword sliding from its sheath.

Then a familiar voice erupted, with a cold and rattling fury. 'Get your fucking hands off my sister!'

Greta froze, her eyes flying open an inch from Alarik's. She desperately hoped she had imagined her brother's voice, but the king's face went slack with horror. Before either of them could react, Tor grabbed her hood and yanked her off Alarik's lap.

She stumbled backwards, falling against her brother's chest. She felt it heaving with anger as his sword came around her, the tip of it now pointed at the king's chin.

'Go wait outside, Greta,' said Tor, in a low, dangerous voice. 'I'm about to murder the king of Gevra.'

CHAPTER 35
Alarik

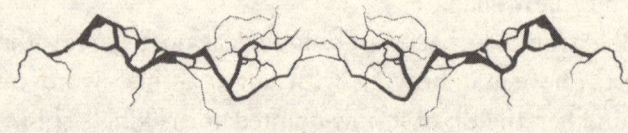

Alarik's morning had unravelled spectacularly. One minute, he was kissing Greta, greedily devouring her moans and letting his worries dissolve on her tongue, and the next, he was staring into the seething face of her brother.

His best friend wanted to kill him.

And a small, furious part of Alarik wanted to kill Tor. If only for the interruption.

Greta stood frozen in front of her brother. Her lips were swollen and her cheeks were stained pink, her chest heaving as she searched for breath. Alarik had to fight the urge to pull her back into his arms. 'You should step outside,' he said, in a measured voice, as though there wasn't a sword pointed at his chin. 'Tor and I need to speak.'

'I don't want to speak to you,' said Tor, in a voice that was all gravel. 'I want to fight you.'

Greta tried to push his arm down. 'Don't be such a brute!'

Alarik carefully rolled to his feet, keeping a wary eye on that blade as he made a wide arc around Tor.

Tor turned on his heel, following his every move. 'Pick up your sword,' he challenged. 'I won't fight you empty-handed.'

'I'd rather we didn't fight at all,' said Alarik.

'You should have thought about that before you shoved your tongue down my sister's throat. I should gut you right now for taking advantage of her.'

'That's not what happened!' said Greta, slamming her fist into his shoulder.

Tor didn't flinch.

She hit him again, then tugged at the collar of his grey travelling cloak, trying to tear his murderous gaze from Alarik. 'What are you even doing here?' she demanded. 'You haven't been back to Carrig in months.'

He glanced at her. 'I've just been to Carrig. Imagine my surprise when I returned to our island to find my youngest sister missing. Gone to work as a wrangler for the brutal king she used to fear, to train his beasts for wars that she doesn't believe in. *Freezing hell*, Greta, you can't even pluck a chicken without crying!'

'What was I supposed to do?' she said, her own voice rising. 'Let our family starve because you went away and forgot about us!'

'I never forgot about you,' he protested. 'You should have written to me.'

'You should have written to us!'

'So, this is my punishment?' he said, hurt and anger mingling in his voice. 'To have to see my peaceful, loving sister go to *war*? To watch you risk your life *over and over* for causes you can't even stomach. And worse, to survive by the skin of your teeth only to come home and play the king's pet?'

Greta jerked, as though he had slapped her.

Rage ripped through Alarik. 'Don't you dare talk to her like that.'

Tor turned back to him. 'Stay out of this.'

'I'm not a child,' Greta fumed. 'I can make my own choices.'

'Clearly, you can't.'

Alarik picked up his sword. 'You are entitled to your anger, Tor. But you can take it out on me.'

'With pleasure,' he said, turning to lunge at him.

'Stop it! Both of you!' Greta's cries were lost to the clash of their swords. Alarik felt the strength of Tor's fury in his first strike, the blade vibrating against his own. He shoved back, meeting him blow for blow as they circled each other, like beasts in an arena.

'I don't know what pisses me off more,' said Tor, swinging underhand. 'That you took my sister to war or into your bed.'

Alarik parried with three sharp strikes, pushing into the space between them. 'Don't tell me how to run my kingdom, Iversen.'

'Have your kingdom,' said Tor, tossing his sword aside and grabbing his collar. 'Leave my sister out of it.'

'Too late,' snarled Alarik.

Tor punched him squarely in the face.

'Tor!' shrieked Greta. 'Have you lost your mind?'

There was a sudden roaring in Alarik's ears. He staggered backwards, blinking through the pain. Blood poured from his nose and striped his chin, but he stayed his blade, refusing to give in to the tide of his anger. He cast his sword away, wiping his mouth with his sleeve.

'That was your free shot,' he hissed. 'Next time, I'll take your hand.'

'Not before I take yours, Felsing.' Tor was rolling up his sleeves, ready to charge the king and get himself thrown in the dungeons. If Alarik struck back, it would become an all-out brawl, and his best friend would pay for it in blood.

Greta would never forgive him. He would never forgive himself.

When Tor lunged for him, Alarik jumped out of his path.

'That's enough!' Greta leaped into the space between them, brandishing a sword that was almost the same size as her. It was heavy and unwieldy in her hands, a rusted relic she must have grabbed from the wall of weapons. She spun on her heel, teetering under the weight of the blade as she clutched it with both hands, wildly swinging it back and forth. Just like he had taught her. 'Stop hurting each other right now!'

'Put that thing down, Greta!' Tor reeled backwards, panic flashing in his eyes. 'You'll hurt yourself.'

The same panic gripped Alarik. He took a careful step towards her. 'We'll stop,' he said, calmly. 'We're stopping. See?'

She spun on him, her chest heaving. 'I can't *stand* it, Alarik,' she said, distress rippling across her face. 'When you hurt each other, you hurt *me*.'

'I understand,' he said, taking another step, Tor's glare burning into him. 'Please give me the sword.'

She gripped it tighter. 'Promise me you won't hurt him.'

'I promise,' he said, at once.

She spun on her brother. 'You have to promise, too.'

'I promise,' he said, with a huff. 'Just put the sword down.'

She turned back to Alarik. 'I *hate* this.'

'I know, wildling.' He reached for the sword, and she let him take it. He tossed it behind him, then took her hand, gently pulling her into his chest. He didn't care that Tor was watching, only that she was stricken, and he was the cause of it. 'Let me talk to him alone, all right?' he murmured. 'He's confused and angry, and I owe him that much. We can be reasonable.'

Her lips twisted as she weighed his words.

'Go on,' said Tor, with a sigh. 'I'll come find you after.'

'Fine,' she said, at last stepping away. Her voice hardened as she raised her finger in warning. 'But if either one of you moves to strike the other, I will send Baldur and Nel in here to devour you. I *mean* it.'

Alarik bit back a smile. 'Fair.'

Tor dipped his chin. 'Fine.'

Satisfied with their agreement, Greta stomped out of the room, slamming the door behind her.

They stared after her, both gathering the strands of their composure.

Tor broke the silence. 'What the hell are you playing at, Alarik?'

Alarik didn't know where to begin. He could only offer his best friend the unbridled truth, in the hope it would go some way to explaining the hellscape in which they now found themselves. 'A few months ago, Elias reported the first stirrings of a Vaskan invasion to me. I needed a wrangler to get my beasts in line. So, I wrote to your sisters. Greta chose to come.'

Tor nodded. He already knew this part. He had been home to Carrig, after all. But he didn't know the rest. 'My beasts adore her. She trains them with formidable skill and focus, and yet cares for them with softness and grace. She feels their needs as if they were her own, and she meets them without hesitation. They would do anything for her.'

Alarik couldn't help the tenderness in his voice. It must be obvious to Tor that he shared in his beasts' devotion to their wrangler, that he himself would do anything to make her happy.

But his friend's face was like stone. 'That's her way,' he said, stiffly. 'The wild has called to Greta since she was a child. She has always known how to respond to it. How to embrace it.'

'If it wasn't for your sister, I would have ceded the Blackspires to Queen Regna.'

Tor's brows lifted, pride flitting across his face. 'So, she is a good wrangler.'

'My best.' Alarik smirked. 'No offence.'

Tor snorted. 'Is that why you grossly overpay her?'

'I pay her what her work is worth.'

'Sure you do.' He rolled his eyes, the ire in them fading. 'I know what wranglers earn, Alarik. I saw what you did for my family. What you gave them when I was away and unaware of their suffering.'

Alarik said nothing. He didn't consider it a kindness, but his duty. He had done the same for countless families across Gevra since his talk with Greta that night of the welcome ball. He would continue to do it, for as long as he was king.

'Your sister opened my eyes to another kind of war,' he explained. 'To struggle and starvation, and the toll of an unforgiving winter. I don't want any of my people to suffer, Tor. Least of all your family. I sent aid to them, and to all on Carrig.'

Tor nodded slowly, taking in his words. 'So, you value her advice.'

'Greatly.'

'And her skills as a wrangler?'

Alarik nodded. Hadn't he said as much?

'And you know that she's my younger sister. The jewel of my family.'

Alarik stared at him. 'Obviously.'

Tor curled his lip. 'Then *why* did you decide to make her your pet?'

Alarik flinched. 'She's not my *pet*,' he said, slumping on to the bench, burdened by the gathering weight of one essential truth, which he had been trying so very hard to ignore. 'She's a living, breathing dream.' He rubbed the spot between his brows. 'She's *my* wildest dream.'

Silence, then.

Alarik felt his friend's shock like a whip of cold wind.

'You're in love with her,' said Tor, surprise rippling in his voice.

Alarik's shoulders slumped. There it was, as plain as could be. He was desperately, hopelessly in love with Greta Iversen. His prized wrangler. His best friend's sister.

'Freezing hell,' muttered Tor.

Again, Alarik nodded. It *was* a kind of hell, being engaged to Princess Elva, and being in love with Greta Iversen. Wanting her so badly, it kept him awake at night. 'Believe me, it's far worse for me than it is for you.'

The bench creaked as his friend sat down beside him. 'Does she know?'

'I don't know,' said Alarik. 'Sometimes I think I wear it so obviously I might as well be screaming it from the mountaintops.'

'Please don't.'

Alarik managed a half-smile. 'I'm doing my best.'

'You're betrothed to another.'

'You do not have to remind me.'

Tor was about to say something else when the door flew open. A howling blast of wind knocked them clean off the bench and sent them sprawling on to the floor.

Then a voice rang out. 'Stop fighting, you brutes! I demand peace!'

When Alarik looked up, Wren Greenrock, the witch queen of Eana, was standing in the doorway, her emerald-green travelling cloak rippling behind her.

She dropped her hand, curbing her tempest magic, and the wind died out. She took in the scene before her with a frown. 'Oh. My mistake. I thought you two would be senselessly brawling in here. And preferably shirtless.'

Tor got to his feet. 'I really wish you'd stop using your tempest magic so indiscriminately,' he said with a sigh, for what Alarik guessed must be the hundredth time. 'Gevrans hate magic.'

Wren smiled wickedly. 'But you know I like to make an entrance.'

He chuckled, his mood softening as he went to her. 'Well, you have succeeded, my love.'

'You should go after your sister. She's run off with your wolf, and by the way, Elske was making moon eyes at her, I'm not sure you'll get her back.'

Wren and Tor stared at each other for a moment, something unspoken passing between them. 'All right,' he relented, bending to kiss her. 'See if you can talk some sense into him while I'm gone.'

Wren offered a meddlesome smirk. 'You know I love a challenge.'

Tor marched out of the room, leaving Alarik alone with the witch queen he had once pined after. Ever since the Battle of Eana, Wren had become a dear friend to him, even if he would never give her the satisfaction of openly admitting it.

'Talk about awkward timing,' she said, skipping over to embrace him. It was quick and friendly, making a welcome change from Tor's greeting, which had likely fractured Alarik's nose. 'We probably should have announced our arrival.'

'I doubt it would have changed anything,' Alarik admitted. The minute Greta had brushed her lips against his, he had become putty in her hands. A slave to his own dizzying desire. He would have kissed her even if the palace was falling down around them. 'Did you speak to her just now?'

'She fled too quickly. But I know a ravished woman when I see one.'

Alarik offered no denial. 'At least you're not trying to smash my face in.'

'Well, I do know what it's like to be wrangled by an Iversen,' she said, with a wink. 'Resistance is futile.'

He chuckled, and she joined in, their laughter shattering the lingering tension in the room.

Alarik felt himself relax. 'It's good to see you, Greenrock.'

'You too, Felsing. Even if you do look a bit worse for wear.'

He went to the window and perched on the sill. 'It's been an eventful few months.'

'I could tell by your mountains.' She sat down beside him, kicking her legs out. Her boots were scuffed from travelling, her leathers damp from the falling snow. It had curled the dark strands that slipped free of her silver-streaked braid and brought a pinkness to her cheeks. Wren Greenrock didn't quite look like a queen – not like her sister, Queen Rose, who was ever the picture of poise and elegance – but even so, there was something undeniably regal about Wren, an innate ancient power that simmered in her veins. A sense that she belonged exactly where she had ended up – on a throne beside her sister, and with her beloved Tor at her side.

'You could have told me you were going to war,' she said, her expression sobering. 'You have a strong ally to the south. Witches, Alarik. Twin queens who are both fierce and *very* beautiful.'

He gave her a half-smile. 'As much as I revere the impressive and frankly *horrifying* reaches of your magic, Gevra has to be able to stand on its own two feet. If I can't fend off the threat of invasion from a neighbouring country without the magic of another kingdom, then what future does Gevra truly have? You and your witches cannot stand at my borders forever, Wren.'

'That does sound rather boring,' she said, pouting. 'As much as I like to make snow angels.'

'And that's to say nothing of frostbite,' he added.

'I understand your reasons,' she said, after a moment. 'But the offer stands. If you call on Eana for aid, Eana will come.'

'I know that, Wren. I've always known that.'

'You're just too stubborn for your own good.'

He hummed in agreement. Perhaps there was that, too.

'Do you love her?' she said, into the falling silence.

He nodded. 'Desperately.'

'How do you know?'

He arched a brow. 'Do you think me incapable of it?'

'Well, you're not exactly an emotional creature.'

He snorted. Then laid his head against the window, considering her question. 'Before Greta, the last person – the *only* person – I've ever felt any sort of feelings for was you.'

'Well, you are only human.'

He chuckled. It was no longer an uncomfortable truth, but a strange memory. A brief period of time when Alarik's feelings had become tangled with an ancient curse, causing a close bond between them that had stirred up unexpected emotions for him.

'That feels like a lifetime ago now,' he murmured, and she nodded in agreement.

'Back then, I always wanted to best you,' he went on. 'To say the smarter thing, the funnier joke. I wanted to be brave and invulnerable. Someone who impressed you.' He paused, trying to give voice to the feelings he had for his wrangler, and the bonfire she had made of his heart. 'But with Greta . . . I want to be utterly myself. Not funny or clever or fearless, but honest. I want her to know every part of me, just as I want to know every part of her.'

He smiled at how easily the words came, freed at last from the tip of his tongue. 'Every day, I marvel at her empathy and humanity, her boundless love for the challenge of life. I want to learn from her, to be the kind of man that deserves her friendship.' But it was bigger than that, still, this kind of love. 'She makes me proud to be a Gevran, Wren. She makes me want to serve this kingdom with utter devotion, so that people like her can inherit it.'

Wren stared at him like she had never seen him before. 'That was *very* mushy. Ansel would be proud.'

He huffed a laugh. 'And Tor would probably drown me.'

'No way,' she said, shaking her head. 'After a declaration like that, Tor would walk you down the aisle himself.'

Alarik's face fell. There could be no aisle, no wedding, no forever with Greta. No matter how badly he yearned for it, he was promised to another bride. Another kingdom, whose soldiers had already fallen in his battle. By the pitying look on his friend's face, he knew she had heard about Princess Elva, and the impossibility of his situation.

'Are you going to tell Greta how you feel?'

He shook his head. 'What can I offer her?'

What was his heart worth, without his hand? Without his crown?

'I once looked at Tor and thought the same thing,' she confessed. 'I used to lie awake at night, torturing myself with that question.'

But this was a different dilemma. Alarik's kingdom was weak, and he was at war. If he listened to his heart, he would doom his kingdom to ruin. And yet, if he put his kingdom first, he would doom himself.

Wren rolled to her feet, laying a bracing hand on his shoulder. 'There's always a loser in war, Alarik. You just have to figure out what war you're fighting, and what you're willing to sacrifice.'

'That's not helpful,' he grumbled.

'I'm not here to be helpful,' she said, flashing a smile. 'I'm here to eat your food and drink your frostfizz.'

CHAPTER 36
Greta

Greta left the sparring room so fast she felt like a human tornado. She stormed through the palace, her emotions so tangled she couldn't tell relief from panic. She was satisfied at least that her brother was not going to maim the king of Gevra. That Alarik was not going to have Tor thrown in the dungeons.

But as for how their conversation would go . . . she had never seen that kind of anger on her brother's face before. It was a miracle Alarik hadn't been knocked unconscious by his punch, a miracle that Tor had survived the aftermath. And yet, despite it all, Greta couldn't bring herself to regret her kiss with Alarik. It glowed like an ember in her chest, that moment of pure and utter bliss, his lips like a spell that had made time cease to exist.

At least it had been Tor and not Hela who caught them like that. Tor might have punched Alarik, but Hela would have run him through with a sword. Twice.

In the atrium, Greta nearly toppled over Elske, her brother's beloved white wolf. She came to her knees, burying her face in the tufty white fur and letting the slow thrum of Elske's heartbeat settle her own.

'Hello, darling,' she said, scratching the sweet spot behind her ear. 'I've missed you.'

Elske blinked her big blue eyes, her tail wagging in greeting.

'Do you want to come and meet my friends?' Greta was suddenly desperate to be out in the howling wilderness. She made for the courtyard, Elske padding companionably along beside her.

She was deep in the forest with Elske, Tollo and Gale, watching the wolves frolicking about in the fresh snow, when her brother found her. Tor whistled through his teeth, and all four of them turned to look at him striding through the trees with his hands slung into his pockets.

'Please don't summon me like a wolf,' said Greta, folding her arms.

'You're the one who turned around.'

She stuck her tongue out at him – something she hadn't done since she was a child. 'Despite your beastliness earlier, I'm pleased to see you're still alive.'

'Believe me, if I could go back, I would have knocked on that door. Loudly. A hundred times.' He dipped his chin in apology. 'I'm sorry for lashing out like that. I was just being protective.'

'*Over*protective.'

'You're my little sister, Greta. And *Alarik* is . . .' He rolled his hand, searching for the right word. 'A challenge. At the best of times.'

'I'm not a child any more.' She prodded his chest. 'I'm a grown woman.'

'I know that.' He opened his arms, his face softening. 'It's good to see you, nightingale.'

Greta melted at her nickname and threw her arms around her brother, her eyes prickling at his nearness. It had been so long since she had seen him. 'I've missed you so much, Tor.'

'I've missed you too. I'm sorry I've been away. I should have come home sooner. I should have *known* things were bad—'

'We didn't want you to know,' said Greta, pulling back from him. 'We wanted to get on without you, to show you that we could.'

'Well. Point proven.' He tugged at the end of her braid. 'I've never seen Papa so proud. Mama's stuck your letters to the wall above the fireplace. Kindra finally has a wedding dress, and even Hela has been laughing more than usual.' He cocked a brow. 'In fact, I hear you're the best wrangler Grinstad's ever had.'

Greta laughed, her chest swelling at the pride in her older brother's voice. She had looked up to him her whole life. Now, for the first time, she felt like his equal. 'Come on,' she said, tugging his arm. 'Let me show you the beasts. I bet Baldur and Nel have been missing you.'

'Those two were always my favourites,' he said, eagerly falling into step beside her. With the wolves trotting after them, Tor let her give him the grand tour. She smiled to herself as he followed her deeper into the forest, craning his neck like he had never been here before – as though he hadn't built most of these pens as a teenager with his bare hands.

Tor made sure to greet every beast – reacquainting himself with the ones he had trained and fought alongside in battle, and letting Greta introduce him to those that had been born after he left. They talked at length about the animals, about their care and training routines, and even the battle formations Greta had devised with Captain Vine.

'I could never have imagined you working at Grinstad before today,' said Tor, as they wandered back to the forest path. 'But seeing you with the king's beasts, listening to the way you talk to them and watching how they respond to you . . . well, it makes sense. Your spirit is so alive here, Greta.'

'They trust me. Not just the animals but the soldiers too.' She hesitated. 'And the king.'

Tor inhaled through his teeth.

'Back on Carrig, I've always been known as the youngest Iversen,' she went on. 'The injured one. The weak one. Someone to protect and fuss over. It's been that way since I was a little girl. Sometimes I think Papa still sees me that way.'

Tor frowned but gave no argument. She supposed a part of him saw her that way too.

'But the truth is, I grew up a long time ago, Tor. At Grinstad, I don't feel like that frightened little girl screaming for help in the forest. I feel like a wrangler. Like a warrior.'

'I can see that as plainly as the fallen snow,' he said, turning to sweep some off her shoulders. His smile changed, then, the hum of his anxiety filling the space between them.

'It's your spirit that makes you who you are,' he said, with quiet conviction. 'Not Grinstad. And certainly not the king.'

Her face fell. 'I know that.'

'Then you must also know that there is no real future for you here. Only battles and bloodshed.' He paused, his voice gentling. 'And heartbreak.'

She prickled at his words. 'I don't need a lecture.'

He gave her one anyway. 'The king is marrying Princess Elva in two days' time. Their alliance is crucial to the future of this kingdom. The marriage has been agreed, and it *will* stand. It's out of his hands, Greta.'

She frowned at the sudden tightness in her chest. This was hardly new information – in fact, it was the constant, taunting truth. So why then, did she feel like she had been run through with a sword?

Because you kissed Alarik.

Because Alarik kissed you back.

And a part of you thought that would change everything.

Tor was still talking, pricking a pin in their perfectly pleasant afternoon. 'Alarik is Gevran to the bone. Clear-headed and cold-blooded, just like his father before him.' She couldn't stand the pity in her brother's face, so she turned her gaze on the wolves. But Tor kept going – because he was her older brother and he had to say it. Because she was his little sister and she had to hear it. 'Alarik will never choose his heart over his kingdom. No matter who it beats for.'

She tossed him a withering glare. 'Are you done killing the mood?'

'I'm not saying this to be cruel.'

'I know.' She huffed. 'That makes it all the worse.'

He curled his arm around her. 'Wren and I are leaving for Eana the day after the wedding. Think about what I said, Greta. If you want to work with beasts, to find a life beyond the bounds of Carrig, then come back with us. There's more than enough wrangling work to go around. And honestly, I could use the help.'

His eyes shone with sincerity. His offer was a kindness, yes, but he was telling the truth. There was a place for her in the kingdom of Eana – a new life – if she wanted it. But how could she tell him that Gevra was stamped on her heart? That the wild winds of this country stirred the furthest reaches of her soul? How could she tell him that her love for the king and his kingdom were one and the same? That if she wrenched herself away from it, she didn't know how much of her would remain intact.

It was a big decision, a life-altering choice, and Greta's head was still spinning from the day's events.

'Don't answer me yet,' said Tor. 'Take a few days.'

When she said nothing, only chewed on her lip, he went on. 'Guard your heart, nightingale. Don't let it fall to ruin here.'

They turned back towards the palace, only to freeze at a sudden keening on the wind. Greta's hand went to her chest, clutching at the shock of pain there. Tor doubled over, his breath coming in sharp bursts.

'What *is* that?' he said, stumbling forward, not towards the palace but the snow-capped mountains beyond. The beast that dwelled there was calling out to them. It had been growing restless these past weeks, as though it sensed the new fissure in the mountains and was desperately trying to reach it.

Thunder rumbled through the clear sky.

'That's an avalanche,' he said, straightening up.

'The third in as many days,' said Greta, worriedly. She sensed the creature was trying to punch its way out of the mountains, unsettling the snow and sending new cracks up the rock.

She gave voice to her hunch.

'An ancient dragon,' Tor repeated, in bewilderment. 'Reawakened after all this time . . . I suppose stranger things have happened. I have glimpsed them myself in Eana.' He closed his eyes, and Greta sensed he was tuning his spirit to the thread of its distress. 'How long has the creature been stirring?'

'A few months,' Greta guessed. 'It's buried deep.'

'It feels strange,' he said, uneasily.

'Alarik thinks it's dangerous.'

'Alarik might be right.' Tor's frown deepened. 'What happened last year with Oonagh Starcrest must have affected the rest of the mountains. Who knows how far her dark magic burrowed before she left this land.' He snapped his chin down, his eyes flashing in warning. 'Whatever happens, don't try and free it.'

Greta glowered at her brother. Wasn't he moved by the beast's pain like she was? Didn't it tug at his wrangler's heart? 'You sound just like Alarik.'

'Good. At least he hasn't completely lost his head when it comes to you,' muttered Tor. 'The last time we excavated those mountains, we pulled out an undead witch who started a war that nearly killed us all. Let me talk to Alarik about a plan for the dragon. In the meantime, leave the mountains be. They're trouble.'

Greta swallowed her protests, still thinking about the beast and how she might help it as he stalked ahead, clicking his teeth for Elske to follow. Tollo and Gale trotted after him, too.

Greta jogged to keep up just as Wren Greenrock came sauntering down the path towards them.

She was cradling Dash and Boo in her arms, cooing at them every couple of steps. She stopped before Tor, turning her glittering smile on Greta.

'Hello, at last,' she said warmly. 'I'm Wren. I hear you're the best Iversen.'

Greta dipped her chin in greeting, immediately understanding how her brother had fallen head over heels with the charming witch queen. 'Don't let Hela hear you say that.'

'*Ahem*,' said Tor, pointedly.

Wren held up the cubs, squishing her face between them. 'Look what I found, Tor. Twins!'

'Wren,' he said, on a sigh. 'You promised you wouldn't steal any of the animals.'

'I never said anything about cubs.'

Greta chuckled. 'I'm afraid Saga would be greatly distressed if you took her cubs away.'

'Then we can take her, too.' Wren beamed. 'They can be part of Elske's retinue.'

Tor gently wrestled the cubs from his beloved. 'There's no room in the sled, darling.'

Wren frowned as she relinquished them. 'What if you got out and walked?'

'You'd miss me too much.' He flicked her gently on the nose, and she nipped at his finger.

'You can play with them while you're here,' Greta suggested. 'Have your fill of their cuteness before you head off again.'

Wren leaped to embrace her. 'No wonder Alarik is obsessed with you,' she said, pressing a kiss to her cheek. She pulled back and removed a vintage bottle of frostfizz from the inside of her travelling cloak. 'Why don't we get an impromptu picnic going, and drink ourselves merry?'

The queen's voice was light, but there was a certain shrewdness in her emerald gaze. Greta suspected that Wren had heard about her kiss with the king and was trying to distract her from his impending wedding with good company, loveable beasts and what appeared to be the king's most expensive bottle of frostfizz.

Buoyed by a surge of gratefulness, she reached for the bottle, eager to spend some time with her brother and his love. She would worry about the sting of heartbreak later.

And tomorrow, she would think about the rest of her life.

CHAPTER 37
Alarik

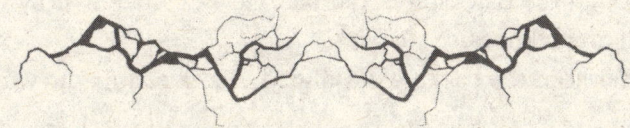

It was dark outside when Alarik finally left his war room. A headache bloomed at the base of his skull. He had been out of sorts all afternoon, having left his conversation with Wren only to run straight into Lief. The steward was like a wolf with a bone, intent on finalizing every inane, last-minute wedding detail he could come up with on the spot.

Alarik had almost taken a cue from Tor and flattened the steward with his fist when an unexpected avalanche pulled him outside. He had stood on the front steps of the palace, frowning up at the new fissures in his mountains.

Somewhere within, the beast was growing impatient. He could hear it more keenly now, feel the ripples of its frustration like a brisk, biting wind. He was going to have to do something about it, before the mountains caved in and fate intervened. It would take careful planning, and more soldiers than he could spare right now. Not while Vask was still breathing down his neck.

Alarik had been standing on the front steps when Elias arrived. The spymaster hopped out of his sled sporting a stark frown that demanded urgent attention.

They had gone at once to the war room, where Elias relayed his scouts' grim tidings from the north. Queen Regna was furious. Having failed to kidnap the Gevran wrangler and losing the Spear in her attempt, she was regrouping, joining her remaining forces with soldiers from Ryberg. In one moon's time, she was going to storm right through the Blackspires and take Gevra while its army was still on its knees.

Without the backing of Halgard, Alarik's kingdom would fall.

If he didn't secure his borders, he would lose everything.

His alliance – and the marriage that begot it – was more important than ever. And yet, no matter how he tried to keep his mind on the advancing tides of war, Alarik couldn't stop thinking about Greta.

He had to talk to her. To tell her he was sorry. Not for the kiss – no. The kiss was the best thing that had happened to him in years – but for what would come next.

After leaving the war room, he bid goodbye to his cousin, before heading down to the lower floors of the palace.

Standing in front of Greta's bedchamber, he nervously fixed his collar, swiped a hand through the unruly strands of his hair and knocked.

A moment later, the door creaked open. His wrangler was dressed for bed, wearing a pair of soft navy pyjamas with her copper hair falling in loose tresses down her back. Her cheeks were flushed, and her eyes were red.

His stomach twisted. 'Have you been crying?'

'What are you doing here?' she said at the same time.

'I wanted to see you,' said Alarik.

'It took you long enough,' she said, a barb in her voice.

He deserved that.

'I was giving you and your brother some bonding time. I didn't want to ruin your reunion by getting murdered by him.'

Her nose scrunched as she considered his excuse.

He said again, 'Have you been crying, Greta?'

She snorted, then turned around, leaving the door ajar. He took that as an invitation to follow her, slipping inside and closing it after him. He looked around, taking in her meagre little chamber. And hated it at once. The bed was too narrow, there was no natural light, and the walls were damp. It was a wonder she hadn't gotten sick.

She quickly tidied up her desk, shuffling her letters into a pile, then moved to perch against it. 'Did you come down here to judge my lodgings or do you want to say something?'

Another barb. His wrangler was all bite tonight.

He sighed as he leaned against the wall. 'If you want me to go, I can—'

'No, don't go,' she said, her bravado faltering. Betraying a glimpse of her true emotions – hurt, and a hint of lingering desire. 'Stay. We can talk.'

He nodded slowly, not quite sure where to begin. 'I'm sorry about today,' he said, completely ineptly.

'Which part?'

Again, he was taken aback at her boldness. Not that he didn't deserve it. She was just different tonight. A little sharper, colder.

'The aftermath,' he said, because even though the kiss had complicated matters, he could not bring himself to regret it, to deny that crucial taste of happiness.

'Not the kiss, then.'

He thought she looked relieved.

'Not the kiss,' he said. 'Not even a little bit.'

'All right.' She huffed a mirthless laugh, then hiccuped. She pressed her lips together, but her body jolted, betraying the next one.

Her eyes rounded in surprise.

Alarik frowned, taking a measured step closer. Moving into the delicious heat of her body, and the heady scent of her hair, her skin. Jasmine and . . . He sniffed.

Frostfizz?

'Greta Iversen,' he said, arching a brow. 'Are you *drunk*?'

'No!' She shook her head violently. '*No.*' Another hiccup wracked her slight frame. 'Maybe.' She groaned into her hands, then peeked at him through her fingers. 'Only a little.'

Alarik laughed. So, she hadn't been crying over him. She had been drinking with her brother and Wren, passing the afternoon with a bottle of frostfizz. The realization loosened the knot in his chest. 'Well, that explains Lief's tantrum earlier. He went blue in the face, swearing someone was stealing from the crate of wedding frostfizz.'

Greta froze.

Alarik cursed himself.

There it was, the ice bear in the room, the unsaid thing they could no longer avoid. His wedding to Princess Elva was hurtling towards them like a mountain sled, and Alarik could do nothing to stop it. He searched for something to say, anything to soften the unintentional blow, but words deserted him.

It was Greta who spoke, dropping her hands from her face and taking a steadying breath. 'You're getting married the day after tomorrow.'

'Yes,' he said, quietly.

She nodded, not quite looking at him. 'Of course.'

That *of course* burned through Alarik's chest. 'I have to.'

'I know.'

'If there was any other way—'

'Please don't,' she said, finally raising her gaze. Her eyes were so blue, like the sky after a blizzard. 'Don't explain. I understand.'

Another twist of his stomach. He hated the strange finality of this moment, how it felt like an ending he wasn't ready for.

She curled her arms around herself. 'It doesn't matter anyway. I'll be leaving in a few days.'

A terrible coldness trickled through him. 'What?'

'Tor and Wren offered me a place at Eana,' she said, with unnerving coolness, as though she was simply giving him today's training report. 'I'll be going back with them after your wedding.'

Panic gripped Alarik by the throat, the words springing from him in a rush. 'You can't leave. We're at war.'

'Your beasts are trained. They will answer to you.'

'No.'

Her brows lifted. '*No?*'

'You're staying here, Iversen.' His tone was clipped. That of a king, commanding his soldier. Not a man begging his lover not to desert him. 'I don't release you.'

She pushed off the desk. He could practically see the beast in her rising to the surface, ready to tear into him. 'You don't have to, *Your Majesty*,' she said, through her teeth. 'I release *myself* from this place. I release myself from this hell.'

'*Hell?*' he reeled. 'Since when has this been hell for you?'

'Since you kissed me back!' she snapped. 'Since you made me feel like I meant something to you!'

'You do mean something to me!' he snapped back. '*Freezing hell*, Greta. You mean *everything*.'

She balled her fists. 'And yet you have the nerve to come to my room at midnight to remind me of your wedding to someone else!'

Alarik recoiled, her words slamming into him. They were harder than her brother's punch, burrowing much deeper. Because they were true. There was nothing he could say to make it better.

His shoulders sagged, the fight leaving him all at once. 'You can't go,' he said, not bothering to hide his desperation.

'Why not?'

'Because the beasts will miss you,' he said, his voice ragged. He was messing this up. He was messing this up and he couldn't seem to stop. 'Because *I* will miss you.'

Her eyes flashed, and he thought for a moment she was going to hit him. Or yell at him. But the fight went out of her, too, and she slumped on to her bed.

He came to his knees, his hands sliding up her legs, like he was afraid she might float away from him. That's what it felt like – this moment – the beginning of goodbye. 'You don't have to go to war again,' he said. 'You don't have to fight.'

'This isn't about war, Alarik.'

'What can I do to make you stay?'

She looked down at him. 'The one thing I would never ask of you. The one thing you could never give me.'

Because he was already giving it to Princess Elva. To

Halgard. And despite everything, she understood that. Greta was too selfless, too good, to expect him to walk away from his promise.

For her, he could be selfless, too. He *had* to be selfless. His love for her demanded it of him. Even as it shredded his heart to ruins.

'If you want to go back with Tor, I won't stop you.' His words were slow and pained, dragged up from the centre of his chest. 'But if you choose to remain here, I'll give you every freedom you desire. Your own hours, your own rules. Anything, Greta. *Anything*.'

There was a long breath of silence.

Her smile turned rueful. 'Let me think about it.'

'All right.' It was better than *no*. Better than *farewell*.

He stood up, and she rose from the bed. They hovered apart from each other, neither one quite sure what to do now.

'I don't want to go to your wedding.'

'Fine,' he said, quickly. He would rather it that way anyway. If he had to see her in the congregation, he might just object to the union himself.

'We can talk after,' she went on. 'When I've made my decision.'

'Fine,' he said again, his throat painfully dry. He was nervous, he realized. He hadn't been this nervous in years. 'Just don't do anything rash.'

'What, like kiss you?' A smile danced across her lips. Alarik didn't know if it was her spirit or the frostfizz that made her say it, but now he couldn't stop thinking about it.

He wanted to do it again.

And again and again and again—

'Stop looking at me like that.'

'Like what?'

'Like you want to devour me.'

'Then I better stop looking at you entirely.'

Her smile dissolved. 'We should stop looking at each other.'

The silence stretched, the heat between them palpable. Alarik's thoughts were rioting, his heart slamming against his ribcage. What if he stayed here with her? What if he gave his crown to Anika, along with the heaving weight of his ailing kingdom, and shirked off his father's legacy for good? What if he got on his knees and asked the fates for the bride he truly wanted? What if—

'Don't lose yourself to *what ifs*.' Greta was suddenly before him, blinking up at him with those knowing blue eyes. There was such sadness in them, he wondered if he had been speaking his thoughts aloud, or if perhaps she had already spiralled through the same questions. 'You'll only torture us both.'

He dipped his chin, their noses almost brushing. She was close enough to kiss. But if he dared, this time he might never stop.

She stepped backwards and held out her hand. 'Friends, then.'

'Friends.' He hated the word, instantly rebelling against the pathetic consolation of it. But he took her hand anyway, her callouses sliding against his own. 'Goodnight, Greta.'

'Goodnight, Alarik.'

He left then, the imprint of her hand still warming his palm, and yet as he replayed her final melancholic *goodnight* in his mind, he couldn't help but think it sounded like goodbye.

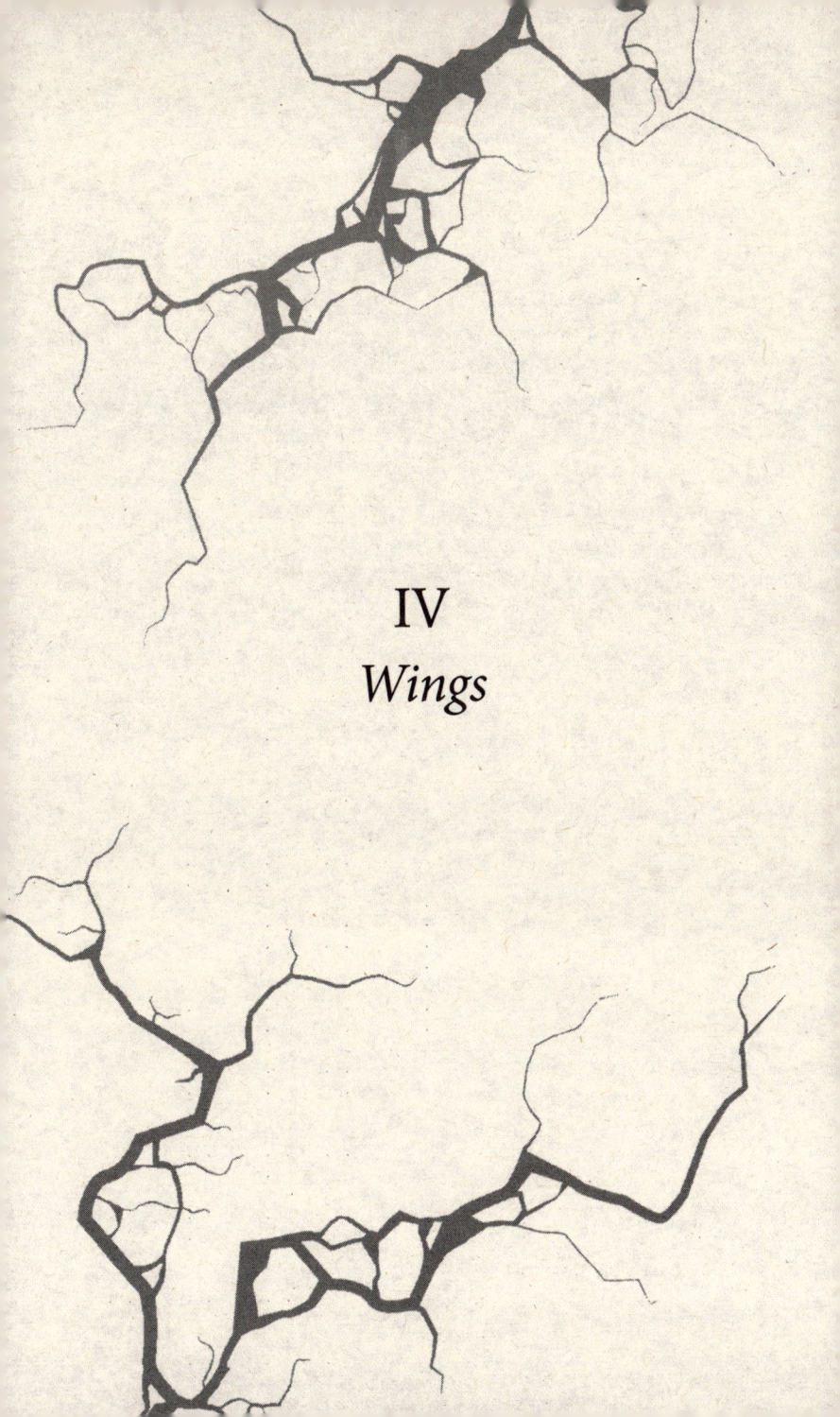

IV
Wings

CHAPTER 38
Greta

It was after midnight in the silent underbelly of Grinstad Palace, and Greta Iversen was tossing and turning in her bed. Beyond the stone walls of her chamber, the north wind howled, demanding that she listen. She frowned in her sleep, her mind splintering from her body before she could stop it.

Cold air curled around her. She could feel herself moving through it, but without awareness of her own body. She was a breeze in the starless night, drifting towards a distant, keening cry.

The sound was rough and desperate, reverberating through her like the pounding of a drum. She followed it through a crack in the rock and felt, rather than saw, the mountain enveloping her, the narrowing walls inching closer, closer . . .

The air here was damp and sad and ancient.

The beast cried again. It was like a noose, tugging her down, down, down, invisible feet flying over loose rock, her eyes straining in the dark. Back at the palace, panic laced her trembling bones. It didn't belong to her – this fear – but it settled like a rock in her chest.

Her wrangler's spirit could ignore it no longer.

The mountains groaned as they cleaved open, rock falling like snow, until it was not a tunnel that Greta found herself in but a tomb. She pushed on, flinging an invisible hand towards the beast, pulling herself by the string that bound them, moving deeper and faster and—

Time stopped, the world freezing around her.

The beast was right there in the darkness. Ancient and unknowable. Impatient.

Its breath cast silver smoke between them.

Greta floated through it.

Two pooling blue eyes peered back at her, so pale and glittering they lit up the cavern. They were a pair of diamonds, each as big as her fist.

That cry came again.

Help me, wrangler, she imagined it saying. *Free me.*

Those wide eyes blinked, and the darkness returned.

Greta fell away from the beast, retreating from the cold, cloying mountain on a ribbon of wind. She floated back to the palace and the bedchamber where her body slumbered, but as her mind and body knitted back together and the dream broke apart, the beast's parting plea echoed deep within her spirit. How much longer could she go on ignoring it?

How much longer would she listen to the rule of her king, when she knew, in her wrangler's heart, that he was wrong?

CHAPTER 39
Alarik

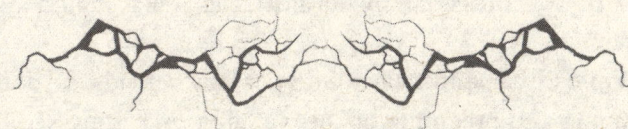

Alarik spent the day before his wedding in a daze. He drifted through the halls of Grinstad like a ghost, trying not to think about Greta Iversen, and failing at every turn. He spent the morning sulking in his art studio, painting the weaver elk in the grazing fields, his fingers itching to add his wrangler there, too, immortalizing the afternoon they had spent laughing and riding together. He refrained, sticking to the landscape and the beasts, smudging brushstrokes of amber and pink across the sky. It was beautiful, and hollow. Devoid of the joy that marked that day in his memory, and yet it would look pretty, he supposed, hanging on a wall.

When Anika came by with coffee and fresh pastries, she suggested he make a wedding gift of it to Elva. He had presented no argument. After all, they were to be married. After all, wasn't that what a good husband did? Gave thoughtful presents to his wife, and not to his wrangler?

Despite his low mood, he was glad of his sister's company, and eager to learn of her adventures overseas, of her lover, Celeste, and their plans for the future now that she had been cured of the terrible sickness that had befallen her some months before. Indeed, it was quite the story, a journey that had taken Celeste's brother, Captain Marino Pegasi, far beyond the known maps of their world to an island that glittered with strange magic and was guarded by fierce mermaids. A dangerous quest made possible by the kind of dauntless family loyalty that Alarik could only admire.

While Elva spent the day with her lady's maids, no doubt primping and preening for the wedding, Alarik passed the rest of the afternoon in his bedroom, pacing a hole in the carpet. It was there he took an early dinner, barely picking at his food, sitting under a portrait of a stern-faced King Soren.

Tomorrow, I will do my duty as king, he silently promised his father.

Tomorrow, I will save our kingdom.

Tomorrow, I will make you proud of me.

It was a strange feeling to do something that made others proud of you, and yet to feel no pride in yourself. Only defeat.

By the time Lief arrived for his final wedding fitting, carrying an armful of doublets and frock coats, the fight had gone out of Alarik entirely. He stood by the window as the steward flitted around him like a chatty butterfly. Alarik stared past him, watching the Fovarr Mountains tremble, imagining the beast that stirred deep within. Every so often, fresh drifts of snow thundered down the slope, the avalanches growing bigger and thicker with each passing day.

The problem would have to keep until after the wedding. Once the war was won, he would deal with the beast. Somehow.

Night fell, cold and starless and far too quiet. Or perhaps Alarik's thoughts were simply too loud. He left his bedchamber to pace the palace halls, hoping the exercise would wear his mind out. It was an effort to keep himself away from the forest to see if she was out there, singing to his beasts, but he had promised himself not to be selfish with Greta.

No matter how badly he wanted to be.

He went instead to the library, where he lit a fire and made a stack of his most treasured books from childhood – the ones his father had read to him, Anika and Ansel, during winter solstices when even the king of Gevra found himself with the day off. Alarik sat in Ansel's favourite chair and lost himself in ancient tales of brave pirates and buried treasure, and mermaids that swam far beyond the edges of the map.

It was here that his mother found him in the middle of the night. Queen Valeska was wearing her velvet dressing gown and fur slippers, her long hair wound into tight curlers ahead of tomorrow's festivities. She lowered herself into the chair opposite him.

'Can't sleep?' he said, setting his novel aside.

'Nanna saw you walking the halls. She was worried about you.'

Nanna should learn to mind her own business.

He swallowed his cruelty. 'I'm fine.'

'Are you nervous about tomorrow?'

He shook his head. Tomorrow wasn't the problem. It was the rest of his life. 'I'm sure Lief has it all in hand.'

'Well, it is his greatest life's work.'

'How sad for him.'

His mother surprised him with a trill of laughter. 'Even despite Lief's most admirable efforts, there is a lingering issue we must address.'

'Oh?' he said, his brows lifting.

'You'll recall the unfortunate issue with Herbert's cello.'

'Vividly.'

'Well, we have lost our string quartet over it. And Princess Elva cannot walk down the aisle in silence.'

Alarik hummed. 'I could have Borvil roar for her?'

Her lips twisted. 'I'm not sure King Nilas would approve.'

'Then have a servant do it,' said Alarik, with a shrug. 'There must be someone around here who can sing.'

She smiled. 'I was thinking we could ask your wrangler?'

Alarik went still.

'I hear she sings to the beasts all the time. Nanna tells me sometimes the soldiers even sneak into the forest to listen to her. Apparently, she's magnificent.'

He drew a slow, steadying breath, trying to quell the sudden fire raging in his chest. It was the worst suggestion he'd ever heard, asking the woman he loved to sing his bride down the aisle. Asking Greta Iversen to bless his union with the perfect spell of her voice. Asking *him* to listen to her sing without running to her.

'Alarik?' His mother pitched forward in her chair, waving her hand in front of his face. 'Did you hear me?'

'I heard you,' he said, in a low voice. 'My answer is no.'

'But you haven't even heard her sing,' she protested. 'We could wake her right now and ask her to—'

'I have heard her sing,' he said, curtly. 'Nanna is right. She is magnificent.'

'Oh.' She beamed. 'Then you can—'

'No,' he interrupted. 'I will not ask her to sing for us.'

Her smile faltered. 'Why not?'

'Because I don't want to,' he snapped.

'Then I'll do it.'

'*No*,' he said, in a half growl. 'I don't want her to sing for me.'

'Don't be so unreasonable, Alarik.'

He stood up. 'Just forget it. All right?'

She stood, too. 'Not until you explain yourself.'

He brushed past her and went to the windows, where the night wind spun silvered snow in great, glittering whorls. He wished he could hurl himself into one.

His mother stalked after him. 'Why are you so angry all of a sudden?'

'Just leave it,' he said, with a huff.

He glimpsed her reflection in the window, her scowling face appearing ghoulish through the glass. 'I'm sure the wrangler would be happy to oblige. We can certainly pay her handsomely for the trouble.'

Alarik's jaw twitched. What part of *no* did his mother not understand? And *why* was she insisting on prodding him about it? 'She's not doing it.'

She threw her hands up. 'For goodness' sake, *why not*?'

He spun around, all that fire bursting from him before he could help it. 'Because I'm in love with her!'

Silence came swiftly, those six words commanding all the space in the room.

His mother stilled, her mouth agape.

'Because I love her too much to humiliate her like that! Because if I ask Greta to stand there and sing for me, I'll never be able to go through with marrying Elva!' He scraped his hands through his hair. 'And that's what you want, isn't it? That's what *everyone* wants.'

His mother barely blinked as she absorbed his words. He slumped on to the windowsill, suddenly feeling the bone-deep exhaustion he had been craving. He wished now he had never bothered to come to the library.

'You're in love with your wrangler?' Her voice was soft as a whisper.

He nodded glumly.

'Since when?'

Since she scolded me over a damned lemon.

He dropped his head, looking at his boots. 'Since she looked past my crown and my reputation and saw someone worth knowing.'

'Is that why you love her?' she said, gently.

'I love her because she's perfect.' Wasn't that obvious to everyone else? It was irritating that he even had to explain it. It was like asking why snow was cold or rain was wet. 'She's fearless and wild and kind and smart and honest.' He grimaced, wishing he could say it better, so his mother would understand. His words sounded paltry and pathetic, a poor tribute to the wonder of Greta Iversen. There was only this – simple and succinct as it was: 'She's everything that's beautiful about Gevra.'

Silence came again, the only sound now the slow shuffle of his mother's footsteps. She took his hands in hers, squeezing tightly until he looked up at her. There were tears in her eyes. 'Then why *on earth* are you marrying Princess Elva?'

Alarik stared at his mother, sure he had misheard her. But her expression was earnest, flickering between sadness and confusion.

'Because that's what my kingdom needs. That's the only way we can survive Regna's war,' he said, the bite returning to his voice. 'This entire wedding was *your* idea.'

She stepped backwards, her hands coming to her face. 'Oh, *Alarik*,' she said, with such devastation he could barely bring himself to look at her. 'That was before.'

'Before what?'

'Before Greta. Before *love*. I didn't think . . . I didn't *know* . . .'

'That I had it in me?' he said, bitterly.

'That you were *open* to it.' She swiped a tear from her cheek. 'I had no idea.'

He gave a rueful laugh. 'Well, now you know. And so do I.'

'Oh, goodness.'

'And what does it matter anyway?' he muttered, convincing himself as much as her. 'Kingdom before heart.' Isn't that what he had always been taught? 'That's what Father would say.'

Her frown deepened. 'I don't know what Soren would say but I do know something about the great kings and queens of this wild, windswept land.' Her voice grew stronger, surer. 'They weren't perfect, Alarik. But they were always honest. True to themselves, and true to their hearts.'

Alarik thought of Greta, and the unbridled honesty that so often got her in trouble, and smiled, despite his sorrow.

'That's what makes our rulers so brutal,' she went on. 'Not hate for other kingdoms but love for this one. Devotion to the beating heart of this land, and all its living creatures. A love so fierce, it has claws.' She laid her hand on her heart. 'Love is the strongest weapon in this kingdom. Love is your greatest ally, Alarik. And if you feel its great, unyielding force pounding in your heart, then you must do what all true Gevran leaders do and follow it.'

Her words gave him pause. 'Even to ruin?'

'Who's to say it will be ruin?'

'If I don't marry Elva, the kingdom will fall.'

'Perhaps,' she said, quietly. 'Or perhaps not.'

Alarik's heart hitched, a part of him grasping at the tiny shred of hope in her words. His head spun, his mind alight with other pathways, other possibilities. 'Are you telling me to cancel the wedding?'

She gave a sad smile. 'I'm not telling you to do anything, son. I'm only saying that no matter what you decide about tomorrow, about the rest of your life, I will support you.' She looked past him then, to the snow-swept sky, her eyes glittering with conviction. 'And wherever your father is, I know in my heart he will support you, too.'

Alarik sat on the windowsill for a long time after his mother left, replaying her words in his head.

Love is your greatest ally, Alarik. And if you feel its great, unyielding force pounding in your heart, then you must do what all true Gevran leaders do and follow it.

As dawn broke across the Fovarr Mountains, and the beasts of Grinstad began to stir, Alarik came to a decision that would change the course of his life – and his kingdom – forever.

He steeled himself as he left the library, thinking not of wars and weddings, but of love. Pure and true and powerful. He was so lost in thought he didn't hear the ferocious roaring on the wind or feel the rattle of the ground beneath his feet.

CHAPTER 40
Greta

Greta woke just before dawn to a sharp knock on her bedroom door. She sat up in bed, rubbing the ache from her chest. That strange dream had invaded her sleep for the second night in a row, dragging her down to the lost mining tunnels of the Fovarr Mountains, where she had found herself staring into a pair of huge, glittering eyes.

She blinked, reminding herself where she was: her bedchamber in Grinstad Palace.

On the day of the king's wedding.

That knock came again, more urgent now.

Outside, the wind was whipping up. Greta hopped out of bed and fetched her robe as the ground began to rattle.

Another avalanche.

A glass of water slid from her desk and shattered at her feet as she swung the door open, hoping, despite everything, that it would be Alarik standing on the other side.

For a moment, her eyes betrayed her. A tall figure stood before her, his blonde hair flickering in the lamplight. She blinked, her heart sinking.

'Elias.' Shock coloured her voice. 'What on earth is

going on?'

The king's spymaster braced himself against the door frame, a look of such urgency on his face, it made her heart gallop. 'It's the beast in the mountain. It's breaking out. It's going to destroy everything. When it makes it to the palace, it will kill the king.'

Panic rose, thick and fast in Greta's chest. Elias was right. Why would a beast in such pain show mercy to the king who had ignored its suffering – its pleas – these past few months? It would destroy their beasts, too. The soldiers and the servants, and all the guests who had already gathered here for the wedding, and were sleeping obliviously in their beds.

The timing couldn't have been worse. It was the king's wedding day. In a few hours, the noblefolk of Halgard would descend on Grinstad, joining the oldest and most important families in Gevra in celebration. The palace would be teeming with royalty.

'Does the king know—'

'There's no time,' Elias cut in. 'He'd only stop us, anyway.'

Greta offered no argument. Elias was right. Alarik would never let her go into that mountain now. Not if the beast was tunnelling its way out. Tor would stop her, too, offering himself in her place.

No, she could not allow it.

'You need to get inside those mountains and wrangle it.' Elias echoed her thoughts. 'Now.'

There was no other way.

'Give me a moment to get dressed. I'll be right out.'

'I'll wait,' he said, stepping back into the hallway. 'I can show you the way.'

She summoned a grim smile, grateful for the spymaster's bravery . . . that she would not have to go into the mountains alone.

Greta moved about her bedchamber in a blur, careful not to nick her feet on the shattered glass. Her thoughts were reeling. Although resolute in her task, doubt nagged at her.

She was about to betray a direct order from her king.

Alarik, the man she loved.

Alarik, who had chosen another.

Alarik, who would never belong to her.

Yesterday had been torture, the hours of indecision feeling slow and endless while she paced the forest, wrestling with the choice before her: to stay and love the king from afar, or to leave and make a new life for herself far beyond the bounds of Gevra. But when Greta thought about it in earnest, she could not stomach the thought of leaving this land or its creatures. She did not need Alarik's love to survive here. She could love his beasts, and dwell in their love in return, devoting herself to the kingdom that had raised her to be kind and fearless, to live and thrive with the song of the wild in her blood.

It was not a perfect life. And it was not the one she truly craved in her heart, but it would be enough for Greta. This place, and these creatures. This king, who had prised her heart open and taught her how to love the man in him, just as fiercely as the beast. She could not hate him for it. She would not leave him for it, even if he couldn't love her back.

And this morning, on the day he would pledge his life to

another, she would do everything in her power to save him.

To save everyone.

Even if it cost her everything.

After pulling on her trousers, she quickly dressed in her warmest frock coat and braided her hair down her back. She donned the breastplate of her armour, grabbed a dagger and some lamb strips, a roll of bandages and a waterskin, and stuffed them into her satchel.

With Elias leading the way, Greta slipped outside into the frigid morning air and hurried around the side of the palace. Candlelight flickered in the lower windows, as the servants rose to prepare for the king's wedding. There was still much to do, and even though a part of Greta was afraid of the task that lay ahead of her, she was glad, at least, that she would not have to hear the violins serenading Princess Elva down the aisle or smell the midnight lilies that filled the halls.

The ground shook, scattering frost across her boots as they hurried across the front lawn. At a stern order from Elias, the palace guards opened the black gates, and they stalked on, towards the mountains, where mounds of fresh snow made a wall across the base of the slopes. They kicked their way through it, Greta's teeth chattering viciously as she raised her oil lamp above her head.

After several minutes, they came to a familiar crevice on the other side of the wall. It was much wider than before. One of several that now sluiced through the vast mountainscape. Elias was right. The rock was splitting open, the peaks groaning as they began to cave in on themselves.

The beast had fallen quiet. It must have sensed they were

drawing nearer.

'How far down is it?' she asked, as they slipped inside the mountain, giving themselves over to the damp, cloying dark.

'That's for you to figure out.' Elias's eyes flickered behind the flame of his lamp, as he stood back, ushering her in front of him. 'Lead the way, wrangler.'

Greta frowned at the new edge in his voice. The fear in it had vanished, replaced by a strange kind of anticipation.

'Move,' he said, bouncing now on the balls of his feet. 'Do your job.'

Unease trickled through Greta. For a moment, she thought about turning back. A part of her urged her to return to Grinstad, to wake Alarik and her brother, and tell them what she was planning, but then a familiar keening sounded from deep within the mountain.

The tunnel trembled.

Elias shifted, blocking the light from outside. 'If you turn back now, you'll damn us all.'

Steeling herself, Greta went into the darkness. Water dripped from the walls and plinked at her feet as she meandered through the tunnel, following the thread in her chest. They journeyed deeper and deeper, until the rest of the world faded away and the only light came from their flickering oil lamps.

When the tunnel narrowed and the ceiling sloped, Greta sensed they were close. She got down on her hands and knees and crawled. Elias followed her lead, his breath hitching in the silence. On and on, inch by inch, they went into the underside of the mountain, and further still, down into the frozen bowels of the earth, where the ground was so cold her fingers went numb.

'Can you hear me, ancient one?' she whispered to the squalid dark.

There came an answering huff from somewhere in the narrowing distance and then a burst of light so sudden and bright, Greta thought she was dreaming. It was followed by an immense blast of heat. It knocked her backwards, her head knocking against Elias's chest.

She quickly righted herself, blinking through the pain to find the light was fading. But the warmth remained, and with it, curling plumes of silver smoke.

Dragon fire.

When she glanced at Elias over her shoulder, a terrible chill went through her.

The spymaster's eyes were dark as midnight, his smile sharp and gleaming. 'Regna was right about you,' he said, with a low, silky chuckle. Gone was the mask of terror he had worn back in the palace, the worry he had feigned for his king. 'You were the answer all along.'

'What do you know of Regna's opinions?' she said, warily.

His smile grew. 'I know she wants her dragon back. And you're going to help me return it.'

Greta curled her fists to keep her hands from shaking. 'And if I refuse?'

'It's not like anyone will find your body down here,' he said, with a shrug. 'Although I'm sure the mystery of your disappearance will haunt my arrogant brute of a cousin for life.' A pause then, his expression turning thoughtful. 'Until I find another way to end it, I suppose.'

Horror suffused Greta. As she sat crouched in the tunnel,

with nowhere to go but into the fire, a startling thought occurred to her: here was another beast she had not counted on.

Elias, the spymaster.

Elias, the turncoat.

Danger faced her from both sides. Dragon and traitor. In that moment, she wasn't sure which one she was more afraid of.

CHAPTER 41
Alarik

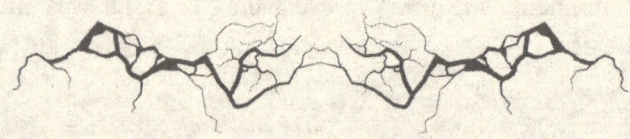

As the sun rose over the spires of Grinstad, Alarik marched towards the guest wing, where he knew Princess Elva would soon be waking up. He had to see her urgently, to steal a quiet moment alone before her lady's maids descended with their trunks of flowers and jewels. He was not looking forward to their conversation – or the ensuing diplomatic fallout of cancelling an entire wedding with barely half a day's notice – but he was resolute in his decision. He was choosing love. He was choosing Greta. He was choosing hope.

He could only pray that Elva would understand. That she wouldn't begrudge him a fool's chance at happiness. And if she wanted to flay him for the timing of it, then he would let her. He deserved it.

As for the pressing matter of Vask, Alarik did not intend to shy away from war. He would rail against Regna's forces until he dethroned the rapacious queen and taught her a brutal lesson in humility. Even if it meant asking the witch queens of Eana for help. Even if he had to get on his knees and beg. A battalion of witches would buy him the precious time he needed to regroup, to build up his own army of soldiers and beasts, and come up with a longterm solution to restore Gevra to its former glory.

He would do it for his kingdom. He would do it for the possibility of a life with Greta. And though the plan was risky and far from certain, for the first time in weeks, Alarik finally felt like he could breathe again.

He steeled himself as he reached the guest wing, ignoring the curious glances from servants who watched him climb the stairwell in his nightshirt. He wanted to tell them to put down their vases of fresh flowers, to set aside the seating cards and centrepieces, and fold away all the last-minute preparations, but he owed the truth of his decision, first and foremost, to Princess Elva.

When he reached the hallway that led to her bedchamber, he slowed, surprised to find the princess of Halgard striding towards him with the same look of fierce determination on her face. She was wearing a green nightgown and a pair of slippers. Her blonde hair was loose and unkempt, and there were dark circles under her eyes.

'Oh good,' she said, with a huff. 'This saves me a much longer walk.'

Alarik shook himself from his momentary stupor. 'What are you doing out here?'

'Looking for you. Somewhat urgently.'

They met halfway along the corridor. Alarik looked her over, trying to make sense of her anxiety. Her hands were bunched into fists and her shoulders were narrow and hunched. 'What's the matter?'

She swallowed thickly. 'I want to call off the wedding.'

Alarik's eyes went wide.

'I can't go through with it,' she said, firmly. 'I don't *want* to go through with it. I'm sorry.'

'Don't be sorry,' he said at once. 'You don't have to be sorry.'

He was so relieved, he could have lifted her from her feet and spun her around until he was too dizzy to stand.

'Ah.' Her lips curled, understanding softening the lines on her brow. 'It seems we are in agreement, then.'

'It seems we are,' he admitted.

'It's one thing to marry a king for an alliance, but it's quite another to marry a man who is hopelessly in love with someone else.'

Alarik tried not to flinch. 'Is it really so obvious?'

'Gevrans are not known for their subtlety.'

'I suppose not,' he murmured. 'I'm sorry, Elva.'

'This is a kindness to us both, Alarik,' she said, gently. 'I don't want this marriage any more than you do.'

'Does your heart lie elsewhere, too?'

'Oh yes.' Her smile broadened to reveal her pearly teeth. 'You see, I am in love with my freedom. I thought coming here would give me more of it, but the truth is, Grinstad is not nearly enough for me. It's too cold. Too isolated. Too wild.' She looked past him towards the snow-dusted forest, the howling wind filling the momentary silence. 'I want to know the warmth of sunlight again. I want to see meadows sprung with flowers and towns filled with people. I want to cross the Southern Sea and explore what lies beyond the boundaries of our maps. I want adventure in all its forms. Coming here has made me realize just how much further I wish to go. I want more than this place. This life.'

'You deserve more,' said Alarik, and he meant it. Elva

was effervescent, a creature destined for more than the snowy tundras of Gevra. She was meant for flowering hills and thrashing waves, for sun-drenched isles and exotic foods. To fly, not to roost. He knew he could not make her happy, even despite his heart's leanings. Because Gevra would never make her happy. 'You deserve freedom.'

'For now, I'll settle for unpredictability,' she said, dreamily.

'That too, then.'

She took his hand. 'Sometimes happiness is a place. And sometimes happiness is a person,' she said, squeezing it. 'You're lucky that yours lives in this palace.'

Alarik smiled. Lucky indeed.

A slant of sunlight slipped through the glass, bathing them in golden warmth. They regarded each other in the upper hallway of the guest wing, their faces softened by relief, their eyes bright with hope.

Elva blew out a breath. 'What now, then?'

'I'll tell Lief the wedding is off,' said Alarik. 'Although it's too late to halt the Halgardian nobility. They should be here by noon.' He quailed at the thought of King Nilas's reaction to their decision. 'I'll have to come up with another way to thank your father for his assistance in the Battle of the Blackspires.'

And to compensate for his many losses there.

Even though Princess Elva was content to dissolve their alliance, he still owed much to the kingdom of Halgard. He would have to offer them something invaluable to prevent another diplomatic disaster. He already had enough war on his hands.

'Gevrans are resourceful. You'll think of something, I'm

sure,' she said, encouragingly. 'And in the meantime, you'll be glad to learn that my father enjoys a tense negotiation every bit as much as a good party. It would be a shame to let all that frostfizz go to waste.'

Alarik embraced Elva. She might not be his bride, but she had become a most treasured friend. Now, and always.

He left her to inform her own lady's maids, taking the stairs two at a time as he went in search of his wrangler. He ran into Johan on his way to the courtyard, grabbing his shoulders and pulling him close.

'I have a job for you, Johan.'

His steward blinked in alarm. 'Your Majesty, you are still in your nightshirt.'

'Never mind that now. Go and tell the servants that the wedding is off. The king and the princess have changed their minds.'

Johan's brows shot up. 'Truly?'

Alarik nodded. 'I'll double your salary if you tell Lief, too.'

Johan winced. 'Oh dear.'

'Now. Where is my wrangler?'

'Yet to surface, I believe.'

It was past sunrise. Greta was never late. Unease coiled in Alarik's gut. It sent him marching back into the palace and down the stairs, where the rest of the soldiers had already risen and dressed for the day. He knocked on Greta's door, then waited.

And waited.

'Greta?'

He opened the door and peered inside. There was no sign of her. The bed was unmade, and the closet was wide open, her clothes spilling out like she had rifled through them in a hurry. The oil lamp on her wall was gone and so was her satchel. There was water and glass all over the floor.

He frowned. Had she left him? Grabbed her things and fled in the night?

No, *no*. She'd never leave without saying goodbye. And where would she go?

His heart climbed into his throat as he stomped from the bedchamber. The ground rattled beneath his steps, the wind roaring through the stone walls. He paid it no mind, his focus solely on his wrangler. She was not in the dining hall or training in the arena. She was not in the forest or by the pens. He arced around the palace, making for the elderberry trees, just as Captain Vine came running across the front lawn.

She stopped Alarik in his tracks, her greeting drowned out by a sudden, thundering crack. The mountains shook as the rock cleaved, the earth thrumming from the force of the quake.

'I've just gotten word from the guards at the gate,' she said, half breathless. 'Greta has gone into the mountains. With Elias.'

Alarik's heart juddered. 'She wouldn't,' he said at once. 'And certainly not with Elias.'

What business did Elias have in his mountains?

With his wrangler?

Dread gripped Alarik, new suspicions suddenly rising to the surface.

Regna's words rang in his head:

Vask has eyes everywhere. *Even in that glittering eyesore of a palace of yours.*

'Elias means to free that damned dragon.'

And he intended to use Greta to do it.

Alarik was running before Vine could respond, spearing his way towards the mountains like a snow leopard on the hunt. They groaned as if to warn him away, but Alarik's whole heart was inside that trembling rock, and he was going to rescue it – rescue *her* – even if it killed him.

CHAPTER 42
Greta

The legend was true. The beast under the mountain was indeed a dragon. It was trapped in a cavern barely wide enough to fit it and it was staring right at Greta as she knelt on the rocky path, its eyes like twin pools of ice-water.

The beast behind her was of another sort entirely. Traitor. Conniver. She could feel Elias breathing down her neck, his sharp fingers prodding her forward, into the cavern.

'Get to it, wrangler,' he hissed. 'Tame that thing so we can get it out of here.'

She glared at him over her shoulder. 'I'm trying to *think*.'

'Regna is a direct descendant of the Vaskan king who bred and gifted this very creature to Gevra. Dragons are the most loyal of beasts. Regna has assured me that this one will answer to her. So, go in there and tell that dragon it's time to finally go home.'

Greta almost snorted. Did Regna really think that was how wrangling worked? That restless, half-starved beasts could be so easily reasoned with? So easily summoned from another kingdom with the simple click of a turncoat's fingers?

'It's not that simple, Elias.'

One wrong move and they could end up as twin piles of ash.

He dismissed her warning. 'Make it simple, before I draw my sword. If you don't wrangle this beast, then I'll make a human sacrifice of you and wrangle it myself.'

He prodded her again.

Greta's thoughts spun, panic lacing her ribcage.

She closed her eyes and tried to breathe. A voice stirred in the back of her mind.

Remember, Greta. You're an Iversen. The song of the wild flows in your veins. A magic as old as the hills of Carrig, a gift beyond compare.

It belonged to her father; those vital words he had said to her before she left for Grinstad came flooding back.

Her heartbeat settled in her chest.

I am Greta Iversen,

And I am not afraid.

When she opened her eyes, her mind had settled, too. She had to be smart about this, think quickly before the dragon struck. The mountain was crumbling. The beast would crash through these walls eventually. That much was certain.

Without direction, it would wreak havoc. And who knew how hungry it must be after all this time? How long it had slept in this icy, endless dark? It could destroy Grinstad, burn the king and all of his guests. But if Greta was careful, and steady, and true to her wrangler's spirit, she could help this ancient beast. They could help each other.

She could save Grinstad and bring Elias down.

To run now would only doom them all.

And anyway, the dragon had seen her.

It was looking right at her.

Silver smoke curled from its nostrils as Greta staggered to her feet and entered the cavern, beholding the dragon in all its wonder. It was impossible, and yet it was before her, a creature so lost to this world, it dwelled now in half-forgotten legends and whispered bedtime stories.

Despite the dragon's hulking size, Greta's terror quickly gave way to awe. Here was the greatest hidden treasure in all of Gevra, a thing so extraordinary she might have thought she was dreaming were it not for the bite of pain in her knees and the hiss of Elias as he came to stand behind her.

'Do something,' he said, impatiently.

'*Shut up* unless you want to get eaten,' she said, without daring to tear her eyes off the beast. 'Let me focus.'

Elias took a step back, flattening himself against the wall.

Greta smiled up at the dragon, careful not to show her teeth. She sensed it was a female by the hum of her spirit. 'You are a beauty,' she murmured. 'A true and utter marvel.'

The dragon's nostrils flared as though it was inhaling the wrangler's praise.

Greta craned her neck, taking in the rest of the creature. She was at least three times the size of her parents' cottage back on Carrig – her large, ridged back covered with thick scales of silvered blue, as though she had been carved from the icy rocks that surrounded them. Wide, pearlescent wings protruded from the middle of her back, spanning out to touch the sides of the cavern as if in mid-flight.

A peculiar pose, given the size of the chamber.

Greta frowned, tracking the slope of a wing to where it was pinned – no, *staked* – to the wall of the cavern. The other was the same.

She reeled backwards in dismay. 'Oh, you poor creature.'

She remembered, then, what Alarik had told her of his father's story.

Cowed by grief and pain, it grew angry and restless, and so the soldiers at Grinstad had no choice but to keep it there. Trapped.

'I am so sorry for what they did to you,' she said, pressing a hand to her heart. 'For adding more pain to your grief.'

The dragon snuffled, and a wave of heat washed over Greta. It blasted the cold from her bones and swiftly returned the feeling to her nose. She sensed it was a kindness. Or perhaps a plea.

'It's all right,' she said, softly. 'I'm going to help you.'

The dragon clawed at the ground, and the sound of rattling chains filled the cavern. Holding out her lantern, Greta sidled around the beast, to see where her left leg was chained to the rocky ground. Somehow, she had managed to shatter the ones that had shackled her right leg, and both forearms.

There was blood everywhere. It stained the ground, mixing with pools of ice-water.

All too aware of Elias's eyes on her back, Greta returned to the dragon's head and raised a gentle hand to her snout. 'You've been so brave, ancient one,' she said, stroking the hard ridges between her nostrils. 'Be still just a little longer.'

For a moment, they stared at each other, the beast's eyes glowing in the darkness. Greta sensed her spirit brushing against her own, sizing her up. She stood perfectly still, bearing her wrangler's soul to this mighty creature, feeling her pride and her pain, her desperate yearning to be free.

She reached into her satchel and removed the lamb strips. It would hardly count as a morsel for a half-starved dragon but she offered them anyway, as a show of friendship.

I won't hurt you.

Please do not eat me.

She half considered offering up Elias, but she could tell by the nearby glint of his blade that he had drawn his sword. She had to tread carefully, play along until the right moment.

The dragon's leathered tongue swept out, gobbling the strips up in a single bite. Greta wiped the saliva from her hand, trying not to quail at the sight of all those sharp silver teeth.

'Right. Time to get to work.' She made for the wall where the dragon's right wing was skewered. She pocketed her dagger, then shucked off her satchel, sizing up the climb.

'You could help me, you know,' she called over her shoulder to Elias. 'You're much taller than I am. And your blade is far longer.'

Elias took one look at the dragon and shook his head. 'Nice try, wrangler. I'm not turning my back to you *or* that dragon.'

'Coward,' she muttered.

'Get on with it,' he snapped.

She used the handle of her oil lamp to slide it up her arm, freeing her hands for the climb. The rock face was slippery and uneven, but she found a narrow foothold. And then another. Slowly and methodically, she hauled herself up towards the dripping ceiling.

There were cracks everywhere, the entire cavern seeming to shake under her. There was a ledge not far from the dragon's wing. Greta's stomach clenched as she pulled herself on to it. Up close, the wing was soaked in blood, the rusty puncture chafing the membranous scales.

She grabbed hold of the iron stake and tugged. It wiggled, causing a spout of fresh blood.

The dragon roared.

The cavern shook. A boulder fell from the ceiling, nearly smashing Greta's skull.

Another nearly flattened Elias.

'What in freezing hell are you doing?' he yelled, ducking from the onslaught of dust and shale. 'You'll kill us all!'

'If you're not going to help, then be quiet!' she yelled back. To the dragon, she said, 'Please, just hold still. I promise I'll be quick.'

The dragon was twitching in pain, its fear as thick as mist between them. If she didn't soothe it into submission, it would bring the whole cavern down. But Greta had never sung to a dragon before. She had never even *seen* one before today. She wracked her brains for the right song – for *any* song – but her mind was blank, her attention spiralling towards that dangerous thrumming in the earth.

She reached for a tune, something soft and low and ancient, and the words came pouring out of her, wrenched from some primal part of her soul.

'Ye dragons were forged in the fires of old,
Hunted for sport by the foolish and bold.
But still, there are those who treasure your kind,
Who worship your strength as they worship your mind.'

The dragon stilled at the lilt of her voice. Greta worked on the stake as she sang, gaining another inch.

'Your fire is fury, your fire is fear,
Your fire protects the soul you hold dear.
Forgive me your pain, my brave ancient one.
Give me your trust and I'll see this undone.'

The dragon slumped to the floor. Flames spouted from its nostrils, turning a nearby puddle to steam. Sweat beaded on Greta's brow as she worked the stake free. At last, it yielded, sliding from the rock and through the wing, spurting blood all over her hands. She was too relieved to care.

The dragon whimpered as its wing flopped down, causing another spill of rubble. Greta tumbled with it, catching herself on a lower ridge. The lamp swung, clanging against her armour, but she barely felt it. She hopped to the ground, then braced herself against the wall to catch her breath.

Elias was closer now, watching her with glittering eyes. 'That was impressive.'

She glared at him. 'Save your praise, turncoat.'

'Maybe you should reconsider your loyalty, Iversen,' he remarked. 'You would do well at Regna's court. You'd certainly be treated better than you are here.'

'What's that supposed to mean?'

'Aren't you tired of being used by Alarik for his own gain and glory?' He curled his lip, revealing the depth of his own resentment. 'Wouldn't you rather sit at a queen's right hand than be a king's plaything?'

Greta's spine stiffened. 'I would rather serve my country and its beasts with devotion than sell out to a grasping, war-mongering queen.'

'I hope it was worth it,' he sneered.

Likewise, she thought, praying her plan would work.

All around them, the mountain creaked, the cavern walls trembling badly now. Water dripped from the ceiling and dampened her hair as she turned her back on Elias and made for the other wing.

She stopped at a wall of ice, drawn to three gold ornaments glittering from within.

Dragon eggs, whispered a voice inside her.

Another wonder. They were frozen so deep, it would take months to free them. Unless the dragon breathed her fire on the ice, but then the entire scaffold would turn to water and the ceiling would cave in, burying them all.

Greta dragged her gaze away from the frozen eggs. The rock on this side was slicker, her feet losing purchase every couple of steps. Twice she slipped and had to start again, her ankle screaming in protest. She refused to give up. Not while the dragon's gaze burned into her back, hope taut as a bowstring between them.

She reached the stake and gave a sharp tug.

The dragon stiffened, sending a blast of fire to the ceiling.

Elias shouted as a hail of rock fell, ducking to narrowly avoid it. Greta hugged the wall, waiting for the onslaught to pass. Growing desperate, she tugged the stake again.

The dragon whipped her head around, huffing smoke at her. A warning.

She burst into song.

'Your fire is yearning, your fire is brave,
I feel it burn for the freedom you crave.
Soon, you will fill the whole sky with your roar,
Together we'll win you the freedom to soar.'

The dragon blinked, then slowly settled.

It was now or never. Greta reached up with both hands, the oil lamp sliding down to her shoulder and smacking her in the chin. She gritted her teeth as she grabbed hold of the stake, stepping off the ledge and hanging her entire weight on the end.

Sweat stung her eyes and moistened her hands. But she held on tight as the stake cut into her palms. It yielded with a rasping screech, freeing the wing and Greta with it. She tumbled to the ground, the stake accidentally dragging at the wound.

The dragon reared up, her spiralling horns slamming into the ceiling.

'NO!' Rubble came like rain, slamming into Greta's arms and back as she covered her head. It pinned her to the ground as a rattling boom reverberated through the mountains.

The dragon beat its wings in panic, causing more rock to cascade from the walls.

'Stop!' cried Greta, trying to dig her way out. 'You're burying us!'

It was too late. The boulders trapping Greta were impossibly heavy, and at least three deep. They made a tomb around her armour, her oil lamp flickering pathetically as it went out.

Elias cursed, his oil lamp flickering nearby. From what Greta could see, he was still on his feet. 'That damned beast is too wild. It's bringing the walls down.'

'Help!' said Greta, desperately struggling for breath. 'The rocks are crushing me.'

Elias backed away. 'This was a mistake,' he muttered.

'You can't save that crazed beast. No one can.'

Rocks had fallen across the mouth of the tunnel, partially blocking the way out. Elias cast his sword aside and started shoving them out of the way. The dragon drew back, smashing its wings against the walls in a panic.

'Come back!' yelled Greta. 'You can't leave me here like this!'

'You had your chance,' he said, without turning around. He was too busy desperately kicking his way through the fallen rocks. 'You failed.' With most of the boulders now dislodged, Elias picked up his oil lamp and made to slip into the tunnel.

Only to meet the point of a glimmering sword.

Greta rasped a breath, hope fluttering desperately in her chest. Were her eyes deceiving her? Was the sudden lack of airflow toying with her mind?

Alarik's voice echoed through the tavern. 'Don't even think about it.'

Elias backed up, his hands rising in defence. 'The mountain is coming down, cousin.'

'Careful with that word, Elias.' Light bloomed at the entrance to the cavern as Alarik stepped inside, keeping his sword raised. 'I can see now family means nothing to you.'

Elias stumbled, falling at the king's feet. 'Not as much as respect.'

'Or coin, I imagine. A title, I'm sure.'

Elias didn't deny it.

Alarik curled his lip. 'You should have come to me.'

'What would you have given me, beyond the scorn of the Felsings?' Elias shot back. 'The family that has shunned me from birth, denied me the riches and title that have always been rightfully mine?'

'I suppose we'll never know now.' Holding his burning torch aloft, Alarik looked down on his cousin in disgust. 'Seeing as you're Regna's spymaster, I'll be killing you either way.'

Elias scrunched his eyes shut as Alarik's blade met the point of his chin.

Through his teeth, the king said, 'Where is my wrangler?'

Greta's vision was fading fast, her lungs choked on ash and dust. She tried to call out to Alarik, but no sound came. He wouldn't spot her here in the fallen rubble, hidden by shadows and rock. Not until it was too late.

A smoky huff made Alarik raise his head.

The dragon crept forward.

With his torch flickering before him, Alarik looked up, into the ancient, glittering eyes of a long-extinct beast, and said, in a strangled voice, 'A dragon, then.' His throat bobbed. 'Good. Great.' Another swallow. 'Forgive the intrusion.'

The beast cocked its mighty head, and with her fading mind, Greta sensed it was taking the measure of him.

Seeming to make its decision, it swung its head in her direction and released a breath of fire. Enough light to make the shadows around Greta fall away.

'*Greta?*' cried Alarik, forgetting all about the traitor at his feet.

He flew to her without a second thought, tossing the torch aside as he came to his knees. Groaning from the effort, he lifted the boulder from her chest and began unburying her from the rocks. She gasped an inhale, coughing the dust from her lungs.

He cupped her face in his hands. 'Are you badly hurt? Can you breathe?'

'Barely,' she huffed. Her chest was badly constricted, and her legs were pinned, but her armour had prevented her ribcage from shattering.

'All right, wildling,' he said, keeping his voice steady as he unburied her, but she could see the panic in his eyes. He was lifting and hurling rocks with the strength of ten men, barely pausing to breathe. 'I'm getting you out. I'm getting you home.'

Alarik was so distracted by freeing her, he didn't notice Elias scrabbling for his fallen sword.

Greta eked a ragged shout. '*Watch out.*'

Alarik turned just in time, narrowly avoiding Elias's strike. He was on his feet in the next heartbeat, running for his own sword. Their blades met in a blinding clash, once and then again.

In the flickering half-light, they looked like ghosts. Alarik was the stronger of the pair, but Elias was quick on his feet and fighting to kill. Greta could feel the dragon's growing impatience, her glittering eyes assessing the men as they fought, as though she was deciding which one to incinerate.

Seized by a growing urgency, Greta set about unburying her legs. Alarik had removed the heaviest rocks, allowing her enough movement to finish the job. When she clambered out of the rubble, they were still fighting. Alarik had drawn blood – a gash in Elias's side and another on his left shoulder, but his cousin was not going down easily.

Greta grabbed her fallen oil lamp.

The dragon began to pace, smoke swirling around her nostrils as she turned on Elias. But the men moved too quickly, circling each other as a great gust of dragon fire swept across the cavern.

Alarik was thrown on to his back. Elias, who had been flattened against a nearby wall, regained his footing quicker. He leaped at the king, just as Greta lunged at him, swinging her oil lamp with reckless abandon.

It slammed into his temple.

He staggered to the side, then collapsed on the ground with a grunt.

His eyes fluttered closed.

They rounded on him as the mountains keened. The dragon roared, but the warning had come too late. The ceiling was falling in.

Alarik grabbed Greta, pushing her back against the wall and covering her body with his own. Rocks pummelled him, swift and merciless, until he sagged against her, groaning into her neck. She tried to hold him up, but he slid to the ground in a heap.

'Alarik!' She rolled him over, but his eyes were closed, his face ashen. He was bleeding badly, his breath coming in laboured wheezes.

She turned her face up to the dragon, tugging desperately on that bond between them.

Help me.

Please.

The beast stretched, making a shield of her wings as more rocks fell, sealing off the tunnel. The mountains were buckling. They had to get out of here. *Now.*

Greta tipped her head back, squinting into the groaning dark. She couldn't climb with Alarik on her back, but maybe they could fly. She grabbed her dagger and crawled to that last shackle, her fingers shaking as she jammed the blade into the lock.

'Hang on!' she yelled, as much to herself as the dragon and the king. 'We're getting out of here!'

The dragon grunted, seemingly urging her to hurry. Greta held her breath, every muscle in her body going taut. Each falling boulder brought them one step closer to death. Even the dragon wouldn't be able to withstand this battering for long.

Breathe, Greta.

Focus.

The lock yielded with a click. She ripped the shackle free, and the dragon roared, not in fear this time, but triumph. The beast stepped on to a mound of rubble, her wings twitching. A warm breeze stirred the cavern.

'Wait!' cried Greta, scrabbling out from under her. She crawled back to Alarik, dragging his lifeless body back to the beast. Tears striped her cheeks and strangled her voice as she looked up into those ancient, frosted eyes. '*Please,*' she begged. 'I can't leave him.'

Greta would sooner cut out her own heart.

The dragon snuffed, her head swooping low to take his collar in her mouth. In one fluid, heart-stopping movement, she yanked Alarik off the ground and tossed him up on to her back.

Greta scrabbled up after him, the thickened scales working like narrow footholds. She threw herself on top of Alarik's lifeless body, pinning him between two large ridges as she grabbed hold of the dragon's spiralling horn. There came a sudden blast of heat, and then a wall of fire so high, it lit up the blackness overhead.

Somewhere beneath them, Elias's body burned and burned.

Greta couldn't bring herself to regret it as she stared up into the yawning dark, praying with every inch of her heart, that somehow, they would find their way through it.

The dragon climbed up the rubble, flexing her wings wider and higher. When she found the space she needed, she flapped once, twice, gathering air beneath her. With a determined huff, she pushed off the mound, Greta's stomach swooping as they dipped to one side. But the beast soon found her rhythm, reclaiming her balance as she rose up, up, up into the unknown.

The mountain narrowed, the stone trembling as it closed in around them. They could only go back down or crash head first into the rock face. Greta squeezed her eyes shut as the wall loomed closer, but the dragon simply ducked her head and loosed an onslaught of flame so powerful it blasted everything before them into smithereens.

Greta pressed her forehead to Alarik's chest, listening to the faint thrum of his heart as the world exploded into rock and fire and smoke and—

Air.

Somehow, there was air.

Crisp and bracing and scattered with snowflakes.

The wind howled as it slammed into Greta. She held on tightly to Alarik as she raised her head, her eyes streaming with relief when she realized they were no longer in the mountain but the wide bowl of the sky.

Not falling. Soaring.

Far below them, the spires of Grinstad glinted in the morning sun. Nobles and servants crowded the front lawn to look up at the sky, screaming at the sight above them – an ancient dragon, rising on pearlescent wings from the crumbling mountains. And on her back, the ferocious king and dauntless wrangler who had dared to free her.

Slowly, seamlessly, their fear turned to wonder.

It was magic, this moment.

A return to the Gevra of old, and the beginning of a new era.

For now came the age of dragons.

CHAPTER 43
Alarik

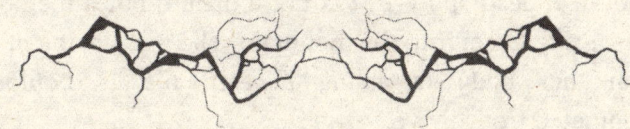

Alarik slept deeply, dreaming of ancient dragons and crumbling mountains, and the woman he loved, soaring alongside him on a slip of wind.

When he woke in his bedchamber, she was there. Standing by the door to his balcony with her arms wrapped around her middle, Greta's gaze flicked from the front lawn to the king's bed. When she noticed him stirring, she rushed to his side.

'You're awake,' she said, perching on the edge of his bed. Concern filled her blue-grey eyes as they swept over his face. 'How do you feel?'

'Confused.' Alarik cleared the cobwebs from his throat, blinking her into focus. Bruises bloomed along her jaw and there was a nasty gash on her forehead. He reached for her, and flinched as pain seared his chest.

'Careful,' she said, laying a gentling hand on his shoulder. 'Your ribs are cracked.'

Alarik frowned, piecing the fragments of his strange dream back together. The more he recalled, the realer it all seemed. And there was certainly nothing imaginary about the shrieking ache in his sides, or the dull throbbing in his head. He felt like he had been pummelled with a thousand rocks.

Wait a second. He *had* been pummelled by rocks. *Mercilessly*.

'There was a dragon,' he murmured.

She nodded encouragingly. 'You remember?'

Alarik's head spun. It was not a dream, but a memory. Elias luring Greta into the mountain. The rock caving in on them, her body trembling beneath his as boulders plummeted from above.

Anger rippled through him at the memory of his cousin's betrayal. 'Elias—'

'Burnt and buried,' said the wrangler, quietly. 'I didn't rescue him.'

'Good,' said Alarik, though the sting of his cousin's betrayal lingered. 'I thought I'd lost you.'

She shook her head. 'You saved me,' she whispered, smiling now.

'You saved *me*, wildling.'

Somehow, they had survived. It was impossible. It was a miracle. He covered her hand with his own, pressing it to his chest to make sure she was real. That he hadn't died in that cave with his arms around her.

'How long have I been out?'

'Hours,' she said, a small dent appearing between her brows. 'The physician examined you. I've been watching over you since he left.' She gestured to the silver wolf curled up at the end of his bed. 'I'm afraid Luna insisted.'

She was teasing him. Returning the excuse he had used when he watched over her after the Battle of the Blackspires.

'Bossy little thing,' he said, threading his fingers

through hers.

She stared at their hands, her voice quieting. 'You missed your wedding.'

'I called off my wedding.'

He wondered if she knew the reason. He desperately wanted to tell her, his heart was thundering so fast, he was sure she could feel it rattling against her palm.

'I went to your room this morning, but you weren't there. I thought you had left me.'

She chewed on her bottom lip, igniting a familiar flare of desire that drove him to momentary distraction. 'I thought about it,' she confessed. 'I wondered if it would be easier that way, to put an ocean between me and you.' She paused, looking away. 'And your new bride.'

Alarik's stomach twisted at the thought.

'But I couldn't do it,' she went on. 'The truth is, I would rather be here with you than anywhere else in the world. If not as your lover, then as your wrangler.' She smiled tentatively. 'As your friend.'

'I have another suggestion,' said Alarik.

Her brows lifted. 'What is it?'

Be my queen.

Easy, Alarik.

One thing at a time. He had just got his wrangler back. He was not about to frighten her off again. 'Give me a few days. I'm working up to it.'

'All right.' She brushed the strands from his forehead, lightly tracing the bruises there. 'You took a thrashing for me today.'

'Light work.'

And he meant it. He would walk into the flaming heart of

the sun to keep Greta Iversen from pain. A little pummelling and a dozen broken ribs was nothing to cry about. Not while she was safe and warm in his bedchamber.

'Hardly.'

'I think we can agree your rescue was far more impressive.'

'Well, that was mostly Fern.'

He cocked his head. *'Fern?'*

'I've decided that's her name.' Her lips curled into a delicious smirk.

Alarik grimaced. This woman and her ludicrous monikers. *'Why?'*

'Because it suits her.' She flashed her teeth. 'It's short for Raging InFERNo of Death.'

Alarik burst into laughter, his ribs screaming in protest.

'See,' she needled. 'You love it.'

'Not as much as I love you, Greta Iversen.'

She went utterly still.

Oops. He hadn't meant for it to come out like that, but the pressure in his chest had suddenly become too much. The words had leaped from him before he could stop them, and anyway, he had been trying to tell her all morning. If not now, when?

His declaration echoed in the silence. It coloured her cheeks, staining them the most alluring shade of pink.

'Oh,' she said, quietly. 'I was not expecting that.'

'I can't imagine why,' he said, throwing the last of his caution to the wind and giving voice to the rest of his adoration before it burned a hole in him. He was in enough discomfort already. 'You are the most incredible woman I've ever known. When I'm with you, I feel like the best version of myself. As a man. As a king. You give me peace, Greta.'

He tugged her into the heat of his body, and she slid her hands up his chest, gently toying with the collar of his nightshirt. Listening, *blushing*, but not quite looking at him. 'All my life, I have never known peace. And now that I have tasted it, I finally understand it. Now that I have it in my arms, I don't want to let it go.' He touched his forehead against hers, their breath mingling. 'Your soul sings to mine, wildling. I want to listen to its song every day of my life.'

She closed her eyes, a soft, ragged noise catching in the back of her throat.

'Let me love you, Greta. Let me earn your love in return.'

She brushed her nose against his. 'Don't you see?' she said, skimming his lips with her own. Heat roared through his bloodstream at the barest touch of her mouth. 'You already have my love. You have my heart and soul.'

He smiled against her. There was no greater gift, no finer treasure in Gevra than his wrangler's heart. He would guard it steadfastly with his own.

And every beast and weapon at his disposal.

She licked her bottom lip, the blush in her cheeks deepening. Her pupils flared, echoing his own desire. This kind of declaration required a kiss, if not a marriage and a lifetime together. 'At the risk of failing as your nurse, are you in too much pain to—'

He kissed her fiercely, his hands sliding into her hair as he claimed her mouth. Her lips parted for him, and his tongue swept in, caressing hers. She wrapped her arms around his neck, pouring herself into him with a languid moan.

The kiss was slow and deep and lingering. Despite their

growling hunger, they were gentle with each other, too bruised and aching to throw themselves into the bonfire of their lust, but every stroke of Alarik's tongue was a promise of more to come, her ragged gasps a fervent, answering vow.

Eons later, they broke apart. Cheeks flushed and eyes bright, neither one of them could keep the smile from their face. With great effort, Greta tore herself away from him and stood up.

'Come to the balcony,' she said, gently tugging him to his feet.

Alarik joined her at the balustrade, where they stood looking out at the Fovarr Mountains, the once unbroken line of peaks now shattered down the middle, as though some great, lumbering beast had trampled through them. Which, of course, it had.

It would take months to properly clear away the rubble and excavate the rest of the caverns, but at least now he could see all the way to the horizon.

Greta pressed a kiss to his cheek, then jerked her chin downwards. 'You'd better say a proper hello.'

Alarik peered over the balustrade to find a dragon sprawled across the frosted lawn. She was lolling on her back, idly picking her teeth with the branch of an elderberry tree.

'Go right ahead, Fern,' said Alarik, waggling his fingers. 'Make yourself at home.'

'This was her home long before it was yours. It looks like she intends to stay.' Greta gestured to the bony carcasses littering the lawn. 'She ate all your wedding food, by the way. Including the ceremonial squid. Lief fainted in horror, and she almost ate him, too.'

Alarik chuckled, swiftly warming to the magnificent beast. 'If she's happy and you're happy, then I'm happy.'

Greta beamed, her smile shooting through him like sunlight. 'So, we'll keep her?'

'Only if you promise to keep me.'

She hummed in delight. 'Then she's yours.'

'No, my love. She's ours.'

But as the dragon stretched, releasing a flaming yawn that set the entire sky alight, Alarik had the sudden unshakeable sense that they belonged to her just as surely as she belonged to them.

He wouldn't have had it any other way.

CHAPTER 44
Greta

Perched on the ridged back of her dragon, Greta looked down on the snow-drenched peaks and sprawling pine forests of Gevra and felt as though her heart might burst with love. It was a jewel, this proud and ancient land, a place so rare and beautiful and wild, it demanded to be treasured.

To be defended.

Greta did not relish the idea of war. She hated the bloodshed and loss and grief that had followed the Battle of the Blackspires, the pain of which still lingered over Grinstad. And yet she understood that at vital times, through the grand and tangled tapestry of history, war was a necessary evil. One that, even despite victory, always exacted a great and far-reaching cost. She reminded herself of that as the familiar black mountains appeared in the distance, their jagged peaks stark against the dawn-kissed sky.

Gruesome memories crowded in on her, making her stiffen in her seat.

'I've got you,' whispered Alarik's voice in her ear. He

tightened his hold on her as he pressed a kiss to her neck. 'We both do.'

Fern was too busy navigating to respond with her usual huff of smoke, but Greta felt the dragon's steadiness in the measured beat of her wings as they descended towards those menacing black peaks.

It had only been a handful of weeks since they'd blasted their way out of the Fovarr Mountains, but that fateful day had forged an unbreakable bond between the three of them. Alarik was overseeing a painstaking excavation of the crumbled mountains, where his soldiers had retrieved three golden dragon eggs from the ice. They were currently thawing in the orangery at Grinstad, though Greta could already sense the spirits inside them slowly yawning to life. It was a thrill to imagine what other extinct beasts might turn up in the thawing ice of those uncapped mountains in the weeks and months ahead. More dragons, she hoped. And griffins and wyverns and mammoths, and perhaps even a unicorn! The possibilities were so enchanting, they often kept her up at night.

Alarik had promised a dragon egg to King Nilas of Halgard, Elva's father graciously accepting the offer and the alliance that came with it. It was more than enough to meet Alarik's debt to the wealthy neighbouring nation, officially freeing him from a marriage that neither he nor Elva had ever truly wanted.

Freeing him to love Greta, wholly and truly, and without compromise.

Greta had loved the king, even in his remote iciness, but dwelling in the unrestrained warmth of his devotion was like being kissed by the sun itself. Every day, she threw herself into that love with wilful abandon, pledging herself not only to the kingdom of Gevra but to the man who ruled it.

'It's beautiful, isn't it?' he murmured now. 'An oil painting at our feet.'

Greta gripped his hand where it rested around her waist. 'Sometimes, the magic of this place feels a dream.'

He hummed his agreement. 'One day soon, it will all be yours.'

'Now is hardly the time to talk about marriage,' she chided, even as a flurry of heat erupted inside her. There was another, graver matter at hand, and it bore a heavy weight. 'We're about to go to war.'

'Hardly,' he said, with a low huff. 'This little skirmish will be over before you can say, *I can't wait to be your queen, Alarik.*'

Fern dipped suddenly.

Greta's stomach swooped as they hurtled towards the Blackspires. Alarik clutched her tightly to him as he directed the dragon over the peaks and into the low-hanging clouds.

They crossed the border into Vask, gliding towards a sea of crimson armour. There must have been at least fifty thousand soldiers, the combined forces of Vask and Ryberg coming to topple Gevra's weakened king.

Or so they believed.

As they dropped from the sky, surrendering their cloud cover, a chorus of shouts rang out. The soldiers slowed, tipping their heads back to reveal the shock on their faces. Some fell to their knees in wonder, while others went still, trying to make sense of the sight before them: a dragon spun from the legends of old. A beast riding with flame in its teeth.

On Alarik's command, Fern circled lower, closer. The soldiers drew back, leaving a lone figure riding out front. Clad in her spiked gold armour, the avaricious Queen Regna chose to make herself known to the mighty winged beast. Whorls of long white hair streamed from her helmet as she leaped from her horse and vaulted forward, her sword raised to the sky, as if to claim the dragon for herself.

It occurred to Greta that the visor of the queen's helmet was too narrow. She must not see them, riding on its back.

'Go on, Fern,' said Alarik. 'Say hello.'

By the time Queen Regna spotted the king of Gevra sitting atop the dragon, it was already too late. Fern reared her head back and released a roar that shook the very foundations of the earth. Then the fire came, an inferno so vast and hot and unforgiving it turned the queen of Vask to ash, until there was nothing left but her helmet and the gleaming blade of her sword. All around her, the earth blackened, smoke curling up and dancing in the morning wind.

Thousands of soldiers froze in wide-eyed terror, silently awaiting their fate. Greta's heart clenched, and for a fleeting moment, she felt their sweeping devastation as if it were her own.

She had known that same guttering fear, once as a girl trying to save her father's life in the forests of Carrig. And again as a wrangler, on her knees in the Blackspires, when death had prowled too close.

Death was here again.

Only now it was theirs to wield.

Alarik lurched forward, readying his next command, but Greta grabbed his hand and pressed it to her heart. She turned into him, her hair brushing the underside of his chin. '*Mercy,*' she whispered. 'There is strength in mercy, too.'

She felt him hesitate, the fate of all those trembling soldiers teetering on the edge of his tongue.

Alarik had already done enough. He had shown the true power of his kingdom in a single, calculated blow, and enacted vengeance on the queen who deserved it. The message was short and sharp, delivered by a ferocious, fire-breathing dragon.

The kingdom of Gevra would never again beg or bow to another.

But it could show mercy. It could know peace.

'All right, wildling,' he murmured, as though he could hear the wish in her heart. 'Here is your peace.'

At a command from her king, the dragon burned a line in the earth, the wall of flames dying out to reveal the king's first and final warning.

A black, smoking boundary.

Stay on your side. Or burn like your queen.

The soldiers drew back from it in their droves, falling over each other in their haste to obey.

Satisfied, the king spoke once more to his dragon, and with predatorial ease, she reared up and away. Fern banked to the right, soaring until the clouds swallowed them, and the distant screams faded into the wind.

Greta laid her head back against Alarik's shoulder, pride simmering in her chest. 'I could get used to this.'

'What, flying?'

'Loving you.'

He chuckled. 'Could you do it forever, wildling?'

'I'm certainly up for the challenge.'

'There's my wrangler,' he said, pressing a kiss to the crown of her head. 'My queen.'

Yes, thought Greta. She could be a queen of this land. A queen of folk and beasts, and all wild things that thrived here, including its fierce-hearted king.

She smiled as the clouds parted in a sea of silver mist, the frozen tundra unfurling towards the horizon, where the towers of Grinstad glittered, calling them home.

Acknowledgements

As Alarik's story draws to a close and I step away from the world of Twin Crowns, I find myself overwhelmed with gratitude for everyone who has invested their time, passion and support into this series.

Eternal thanks, first and foremost, to my co-author and sister-in-law, Katherine Webber. Getting to craft this world with you has been the greatest adventure. Thank you for all the fun, giggles, schemes and glamour along the way!

Claire Wilson, here we are again at the end of another book, where I have to come up with increasingly inventive ways to embarrass you. Simply put, you are an extraordinary agent, the most compassionate friend, and certainly one of the best things that has ever happened to me! After all, I owe my career, my husband, and now my son to you. The trifecta!

Many thanks, too, to Safae El-Ouahabi and Sam Coates at RCW.

To my editors, Lindsey Heaven and Sarah Levison, thank you for making this series soar, and for ensuring that our beloved surly king gets his own happy ending. Lins, thank you for opening your heart to Wren and Rose all those years ago, and for making each one of these books the most incredible publishing experience. From boozy lunches and glittering balls to thoughtful edit letters and gushing book chats, every step of this journey with you has been an utter pleasure.

Sarah Levison, I'm afraid I'm mildly obsessed with you. Thank you for helping me give Alarik a royally perfect send-off. I'll sorely miss your keen eye for edits, brilliant sense of humour, entertaining catch-up emails, and the true sense of joy and kindness that pervades all of our interactions.

Thank you to the brilliant team at Electric Monkey: Lucy Courtenay, Sarah Sleath, Emily Sommerfeld, Josephine Knipmeijer, Ingrid Gilmore, Ellie Andre, Charlotte Cooper, Dan Downham and Francesca Lucci. Thanks, too, to Susila Baybars and Nicki Marshall for expert copy-editing and proofreading.

Thank you to the King of Design, Ryan Hammond, for once again knocking this cover out of the park, and thank you to Grace Zhu for your stunning cover art. Alarik has never looked so good!

Endless thanks to the booksellers and librarians who have supported the Twin Crowns series and its spin-offs. It's been such a pleasure getting to meet so many of you, both in real life and online.

To the readers, thank you for coming on this journey with us, and for sticking around for Alarik's story. I'm so grateful for all the love and excitement you have shown him (and me!) online. It's the greatest privilege to get to share these books, and this special world, with you all.

Special thanks to Abi, Alice, Angelina, Diana, Divya, Elle, Emily, Emma, Gemma, Gigi, Greta, Hannah, Joanna, Katrina, Kellie, LJ, Menna, Rosa, Sam, Saz, Sarah B, Siobhán, Stacey, Steph, Victoria, and Zhi Ling. And wonderful Emelie from Germany, whose enthusiastic support for Alarik's story in particular, has made me smile more times than I can count.

Thanks, as ever, to my wonderful friends and family.

And lastly, to my own kingdom:

Jack, my love.

Cali, my stalwart companion.

And Jonah, my little prince.

*Read on for an
exclusive extract from*

CAPTAIN
OF
FATES

CHAPTER 1
Marino

Captain Marino Pegasi could not remember the last time he had spent so much time on land.

He was at his fourth ball in as many weeks and had been introduced to countless 'eligible young ladies', who had all started to look the same after a while.

It was not that Marino didn't love to dance. He enjoyed a party as much as anyone, maybe even more than most, but where some might become seasick after weeks bobbing above the waves, he found himself becoming waltz-sick after weeks bobbing around the dance floor.

The constant spinning round and round and round, the faces changing but the conversation ever the same. He stayed courteous, bowing to each partner at the end of the dance, even as he heard the whispers from the nobles and royals of Eana, wondering who, if anyone, Captain Marino Pegasi would dance with a second time.

He knew he made a striking figure in the ballroom, standing taller than almost all the guests in his perfectly tailored burgundy frock coat and fitted black trousers, with an embroidered waistcoat over his starched ruffled collar and rakishly tied cravat. And of course, he wore his earrings, three simple gold studs on one earlobe, and two small pearls on the other. At these events, Marino had his tightly coiled black curls tied into a knot at the nape of his neck, but a few always managed to spring free, brushing against his cheekbones as he danced.

And dance he did, with partner after partner. Until the evening came to an end, and he could collapse in a luxurious bed in his guest room at Anadawn Palace, wishing that he was in his own bed on his ship instead.

But he knew that would be rude not only to Queen Rose and King Shen, who were graciously hosting him at Anadawn until his next voyage, but also to his sister, Celeste, who expected to see him at breakfast where they could regale each other with tales of the evening before.

Marino feared he was becoming more proud by the day, increasingly unimpressed with the ladies paraded in front of him.

He would never admit as much to his sister or to Rose, who was almost a sister to him. He knew they were trying to help him. And he had learned long ago that when they teamed up they were a force to be reckoned with. They were certain that this time spent on land, away from his ship, was the perfect opportunity for him to find his match, someone to keep his bunk warm. Someone to care for him, they claimed. So, he kept smiling and laughing and made sure they only ever saw the charming Marino they knew and loved.

How could he tell them that for him love was complicated? Marino had his sights set on a life of adventure, and that meant he was always going to be at sea, looking to the horizon. He was far too much of a gentleman to make any false promises of settling down to the ladies presented to him.

In his heart, Marino dreamed of a romance greater than any he could find in a ballroom. It wasn't that he didn't want love, the opposite of it, he wanted the kind of love that inspired grand gestures and epic adventures. The kind of love those closest to him had found.

It felt like everyone around Marino was starry-eyed and love-drunk. Everyone but him.

Queen Rose and King Shen had wed several months ago, but Rose was still the blushing bride. She could not stop looking at Shen. And when he looked back at her, well, the heat in his gaze was enough to raise the temperature of the entire room. It made Marino feel oddly . . . lonely, in a way he never felt when he was on his own in the middle of the sea.

And nothing had surprised Marino as much as Celeste finding, and keeping, love herself. Celeste had always sworn off true commitment, saying there were too many fish in the sea for her to ever choose only one, and yet here she was, canoodling with Princess Anika of Gevra. Celeste shunned propriety and only danced with Anika at the balls, and the two were a liability on the dance floor – twirling and prancing around with no regard to what song was playing, only dancing to the tune in both of their hearts.

At least Rose's sister, Queen Wren, and her beau, Tor, were away, spending the summer in Ortha, where Wren had been raised. As much as Marino liked both Wren and Tor, he was relieved not to be *entirely* surrounded by loved-up couples.

Finally, it was the last ball of the summer.

It was nearly autumn, but the night air was still warm and inviting enough for the ball to be held outside in the grand Anadawn courtyard. Queen Rose had enchanted the candles to float in the air and garlands of flowers were strung overhead. The musicians played the favourite songs of the season, songs Marino had heard so often, he knew he would never forget them even if he tried.

His back was straight as he twirled Lady Sophie, a petite blonde noblewoman visiting from the northern coastal town of Norbrook. Next to them, Celeste and Anika twirled and laughed, and Marino wished he could dance with someone with as much abandon. Celeste caught his eye and nodded her head towards Lady Sophie, eyes wide with a silent question. Marino shook his head slightly. No, Lady Sophie was not destined to be the great love of his life. Celeste rolled her eyes in response and then focused her attention back to Anika.

'Are you enjoying the evening, Captain?' Lady Sophie asked, and Marino felt a quick pang of guilt for not trying harder to get to know her. It was so easy to keep things at surface level, to smile and charm and never truly let his guard down. Perhaps he should at least make a small effort. It was the last ball, after all.

He rewarded her with a warm smile. 'I am,' he said. He saw how she blushed in response to his smile, which he had to admit was pleasing, even if he had no romantic interest in her. He knew that dancing at a ball, being seen as the catch of the season, was no true hardship. He simply missed the sea, and that wasn't Lady Sophie's fault. 'It is a beautiful night. Queen Rose is, as ever, an exceptional host.'

'This is my first Anadawn ball,' Lady Sophie said, sounding a bit breathless with excitement about it all. 'I've never seen magic before, not until tonight. It's spectacular.'

The land of Eana was ruled by witches gifted with a unique magic. For all of Marino's childhood, witches had been banished and abhorred, and they had only come back into their rightful power when the twin witch queens, Rose and Wren, had been reunited just before their eighteenth birthday.

Rose had been raised in the palace, with no knowledge of her true heritage nor the existence of her twin. Meanwhile Wren had spent her whole life living with a hidden sect of witches far on the western coast of Eana, preparing for the moment when she would take Rose's place and usher in the reign of the witches. Back to their rightful place, ruling the land that had been created by, and named for, Eana the first witch. And while things had not gone exactly to plan for either twin, the result had been something even better – two queens working together for the good of their people. And with the return of the witches to power, and the strengthening of the land itself, many Eanans had discovered their own latent magic. Including Marino.

Marino hadn't known he was a witch until Rose and Wren welcomed magic back into the kingdom. He had been surprised, and then pleased, to know he had the gift. It had once been believed that witches were only able to access one of five distinct strands of magic. Enchanters could do small magic and minor spells of enchantment or manipulation. Healers were gifted with the ability to cure those who were ill or injured. Tempests could control the weather, calling down storms or shifting the wind. Warrior witches had tremendous strength and agility and were unparalleled on the battlefield. Seers could glimpse the future, usually by reading the movements of flocks of beautiful starcrest birds that were unique to Eana.

When Marino had first discovered his witch heritage, he realised he was a natural tempest. It was a joy to sail on the sea and practise his gift – catching a strand of wind in his hands and then sending it to fill his sails so his ship practically flew over the waves.

Now, since Rose and Wren had freed all five strands of magic, Marino could access *all* his gifts. Every witch still had a dominant power, but with practice, they could master all five strands. Marino's power was growing stronger all the time.

Hearing Lady Sophie's awe made Marino feel a twinge of guilt for being so immune to it all. 'There is nothing quite like an Anadawn ball,' he said, and he meant it. Then he turned his attention back to Lady Sophie. 'And what do you like to do in Norbrook?' She was a beautiful dancer, but he felt no draw towards her, nothing made her stand out from any of the many others he had danced with all summer, but he should give her a chance.

Lady Sophie held her head high. 'I am quite an accomplished pianist. And I paint as well.' She sounded unbearably smug, and Marino had a sneaking suspicion that she was exaggerating her talents.

He nodded, trying to muster more interest. 'What do you like to paint?'

'Horses, mostly. We have quite the impressive equine collection, you know. And the occasional self-portrait, of course.' She fluttered her lashes coyly, as if even she was immune to her own charms.

Marino cleared his throat. 'And do you like the sea?' Perhaps she painted seascapes. 'I've not been to Norbrook, but I've sailed past it before. The coast is quite dramatic.'

She scrunched her nose up. 'The sea! Goodness no. The salty air ruins my hair, not to mention my jewellery!' Her laugh was high and sharp. 'And the smell of fish! No, it is not for me. I prefer to stay in town. Or go riding.'

'But!' she went on, clearly seeing Marino's disappointment and seemingly remembering what he did. 'I do love to watch the sun set from my father's house. The light *is* very pretty when it dances across the waves.'

'So it is,' said Marino, with a deep sigh. Saying she liked sunsets did not endear her to him, not because he disagreed, but because he had yet to meet someone who didn't enjoy a sunset. It was akin to saying that she enjoyed breathing.

They finished the dance in silence, and Marino bowed politely before turning away and striding to the edge of the dance floor.

'Marino!' Rose swept towards him with a warm smile. 'Come, let us dance.' Rose looked radiant. She was wearing a flowing pale green gown embroidered with golden thread and her long chestnut hair was loose and hung to her waist. On her head was a delicate gold crown inlaid with emeralds, and matching jewels winked on her wrist and fingers. She beamed at Marino, green eyes sparkling, and Marino couldn't help but smile back at her.

'How did you find Lady Sophie?'

'A very fine dancer,' said Marino diplomatically.

'And? Do you want me to invite her to tea tomorrow? I've not spent much time with her, but I am happy to get to know her better if you enjoyed her company.' Rose's eyes were wide and hopeful.

Marino raised his brows. 'I do not think she is the one for me. But I appreciate the effort.'

Rose sighed. 'Marino! It is the last ball of the season. And none of the ladies in Eana have caught your eye. No noblewoman *or* any of the witches! How will we ever find you a love match?'

'Rose, with Wren away, surely you have more important things to do, like running a kingdom? Playing matchmaker for me should be at the very bottom of your to-do list.'

Rose wound her arm through his and guided them towards the drinks table, the very place he had been heading before she caught him on the dance floor. 'Marino, finding you a love match is not on my to-do list. It gives me much joy!'

'At least one of us is enjoying it.'

Rose rolled her eyes. 'Oh, Marino! You are impossible. But you know I am not one to back away from a challenge.'

'I know that all too well,' said Marino, with an affectionate grin. 'We grew up together, remember?'

'Rose, my love, my forever queen, are you badgering poor Marino again?' Shen had appeared next to them, looking debonair as always in his red and gold royal regalia. Through his marriage to Rose he was now a rightful king of Eana, but he still ruled his own land, the desert-based Sunkissed Kingdom.

The Sunkissed Kingdom had been lost in the sands long ago, hidden from the rest of Eana, but Shen and Rose had rediscovered it. When they did, they found not only an entire kingdom, but Shen's history and heritage, as well as his right to the throne. Now the pair of them ruled both lands together, allowing the Sunkissed Kingdom and Eana to prosper alongside each other.

Rose pouted. 'Shen! I'm not badgering him. I'm helping him!'

Shen raised his brows. 'Marino?'

Marino cleared his throat. 'Ah, well, she did take me to the drinks table when I sorely needed a drink. So, yes, she has been helping.'

Rose preened. 'See?' Then she swatted Marino on the arm. 'Marino! I am helping more than that!'

Shen laughed as he handed Marino a glass of wine. 'I'm sure you are missing your ship. And the freedom that comes with it. Perhaps I can join you on a voyage one day.'

'You will do no such thing,' said Rose. 'Leave me to run both of our kingdoms while you go off gallivanting with Marino? I think not!'

Marino clinked his glass to Shen's. 'Ah, as we both know, the king answers to no one but his queen.'

'Too true,' Rose said smugly. But then she leaned up to press a kiss to Shen's cheek. 'I suppose if you really wanted to join Marino on a voyage you could. But wouldn't it be more fun if I came along too? And Celeste and Anika! Why don't we plan it for when Wren and Tor are back?' She turned to Marino. 'You know, I've never been to the southern continent. And I've always wanted to go to Demarre. Is it nice in the autumn?' She clapped her hands together with glee. 'Oh! It could be an official royal visit. What a wonderful idea, Shen!'

Shen shook his head in bewilderment. 'Ah, yes. That was my *exact* idea.' But he was smiling at Rose, taking delight in her clear joy.

'Marino, what do you think? You've been missing your ship all summer, and this way you can be back at sea and we can all still be together!' Rose beamed at him.

Marino took a small step back, suddenly dizzy from more than the wine. He felt overwhelmed by all of Rose's plans. It was one thing for her and Celeste to decide what he was doing while he was in the palace, and entirely another thing to imagine them all on his ship for weeks on end. 'Autumn is a wonderful time to visit Demarre.'

'Oh, there will be so much to plan!' said Rose, sounding delighted by the prospect. 'And Marino, who knows? Perhaps you'll find someone to your liking in Demarre.'

'Perhaps,' he said with a smile. 'Perhaps. Now, if you'll both excuse me, I think I must retire for the evening. It has been, as ever, a delight.'

'Won't you stay for the fireworks?' asked Rose. 'Please? This is the last ball of the season, after all.'

Marino didn't want to disappoint Rose, so he slung an arm around her and Shen and grinned at them both. 'I wouldn't miss it for anything.'

Photo credit: Julia Dunin

CATHERINE DOYLE is the award-winning and internationally bestselling author of the Twin Crowns series, The City of Fantome series, The Storm Keepers trilogy, *The Miracle on Ebenezer Street*, and *The Lost Girl King*. Catherine grew up in the West of Ireland, and her books have been published in over twenty-five languages. She holds a BA in psychology and an MA in publishing.